A DAUGHTER'S HEARTBREAK

Kay Brellend

PIATKUS

PIATKUS

First published in Great Britain in 2023 by Piatkus

1 3 5 7 9 10 8 6 4 2

Copyright © 2023 by Kay Brellend

The moral right of the author has been asserted.

A CIP catalogue record for this book
is available from the British Library.

ISBN: 978-0-349-43552-7

Typeset in Palatino by M Rules

Printed and bound in Great Britain by
Clays Ltd, Elcograf S.p.A.

Papers used by Piatkus are from well-managed forests
and other responsible sources.

MIX
Supporting
responsible forestry
FSC® C104740

Piatkus
An imprint of
Little, Brown Book Group
Carmelite House
50 Victoria Embankment
London EC4Y 0DZ

achette UK Company
vw.hachette.co.uk

w.littlebrown.co.uk

Kay Brellend is the bestselling author of *The Campbell Road* series, *The Bittersweet Legacy* trilogy, and *The Workhouse to War* trilogy. Kay never imagined she would become a writer, certainly not a writer of novels inspired by her own family. *'Writing has been an absorbing journey for me. I have learned much about my ancestors and their toughness and resilience and I feel pride in my roots in the worst street in north London.'*

Please visit her website http://www.kaybrellend.com for news, upcoming titles and more.

By Kay Brellend

The Bittersweet Legacy series

A Sister's Bond
A Lonely Heart
The Way Home

The Workhouse to War series

A Workhouse Christmas
Stray Angel
The Workhouse Sisters

For all those who lost their lives making munitions during the World Wars.

Prologue

April 1899, Silvertown, East End of London

'Take a little sip . . . you'll like it.'

The girl wasn't sure she would like it but she wanted him to think her grown up. And drinking and smoking cigarettes was what adults did. She'd gazed through enough pub windows at a misty scene of laughing people with glasses in hands. Sometimes she'd see her mum and dad in there; but not very often as they weren't big drinkers. They were respectable East End folk who spent what little money they had wisely. And that's why she was hesitating. If she was found out, she'd be for it. Her mum, especially, was strict.

'Come on . . .' he urged in a throaty voice. 'Don't try it, won't know if you like it.' He put the bottle on the ground between them.

She looked at him from beneath her lashes; she wanted to please him. She'd liked him for a long while, since she'd been at school; her friends liked him too but none of them believed he'd actually ask one of them to go out with him. He'd asked her. He was eighteen and handsome, with a

1

dangerous smile that made butterflies dance in her belly whenever it was turned on her. She picked up the beer and upended it, pulling a face as she swallowed a mouthful of bitter froth.

'You're a sweet kid, Iris Hall.' He chuckled softly, and held out a hand for the bottle. 'And the prettiest girl around.'

He was a little bit too far away for her to reach his outstretched fingers. She put the bottle back in its midway spot. 'I'm not a kid. I'm sixteen in six months. Been out at work for ages.'

'So you have; in the drapery. That Randall kid still sniffing around you, is he?'

Iris felt herself blushing though the twilight shaded her colour. 'Bruce is all right,' she said defensively.

'Is he?' He sounded sardonic. 'Well, he's a lucky sod, I'll give him that. Son of a businessman.' He blew out an envious laugh. 'He'll have that shop one day. Whoever he marries will have a cosy life. Thought of that, have you?' He settled back onto the grass sprinkled with fallen cherry blossom from the branches overhead. The muscles in his arms strained his shirtsleeves as he pillowed his head on his hands.

'That's not why I like him,' she said sharply. He was implying she was only friends with her boss's son for his inheritance. It wasn't true. Throughout their schooling she and Bruce Randall had been pals.

'Come here . . . come on I won't bite . . .' He shifted a hand from beneath his dark hair and beckoned her with a lazy finger. She stayed where she was and after a moment he sat up and rested his elbows on his knees. He pulled cigarettes from his pocket and lit one, aiming clever smoke rings at the canopy of pale flowers above.

She watched him, mesmerised by his open mouth and his fingers, twirling the cigarette, and wished he'd kiss her again. He had before they'd sat down; it had been a long lingering kiss that had buckled her knees, making it easy for him to guide her onto the grass. Bruce didn't kiss her like that; he was often clumsy, and rushed as though he believed his mother might burst in and tell him off.

'You wanted to try a smoke as well, didn't you?' He turned the cigarette to present it to her. 'Just suck on it ... gently ...' He smiled. 'Start you off slowly till you get used to it.'

There was something in his tone that Iris didn't understand and didn't like. His eyes glittered in the deepening dusk and made him look even more roguish. She'd felt excited and elated when he'd asked her to meet him this evening. Sidney Cooper had lots of girls to choose from. He'd singled her out to speak to in the High Street, making some of her friends jealous. Then one evening he'd waited for her after work and told her he thought she was pretty. Such compliments were nothing new; her old classmates envied her wavy auburn hair and rounded figure because most of them still looked like skinny kids. When they found out she'd been for a walk with Sidney Cooper after dark, and let him kiss her, they'd turn really green.

The thrill of being alone with him was fluttering in the pit of her stomach, but she felt a little on edge too. She was afraid her brother would get into trouble for not stopping her going out while her parents were visiting their friends. She'd waited until he was reading in his bedroom before slipping quietly out of the back door.

'It's getting late ... I'd better go now. My parents will be home soon ... and if I'm not there ...'

He curled his fingers about her wrist as she made to get up. 'Hey ... not leaving me yet, are you? Don't worry, I'll get you home in time. A liking for booze 'n' fags isn't all I've got to teach you, sweetheart.' He jerked her forward and found her mouth with his.

The kiss wasn't so nice this time and Iris yanked back. He wouldn't let go of her though and suddenly there seemed to be no space between them. 'Me dad'll be out looking for me,' she said, breathing hard. 'I have to go home. He'll go mad at you as well as me.' The threat didn't work and she pushed him as his weight on her shifted to her shoulders. She was forced backwards and pinned to the ground by her wrists, his knee wedging between hers. Her frantic movements were releasing the delicate scent of blossom as she tried to squirm away. He stilled her face with fingers that gripped her jaw.

'I'm not scared of your ol' man, and girls shouldn't tease boys,' he whispered in her ear. 'That's something else you need to learn, Iris Cooper.'

Chapter One

October 1916

'You better had go home, or you'll be for it.'

'I'll be for it either way,' Clover Cooper told her younger brother. 'It'll be the second time this week I've put me coat back on after I've only had it off half an hour. I'll get the sack then we'll be short on rent. Tell Mum I'll be back to see her dinnertime.'

'She says you have to go home right away, Clo.' Johnny snatched a peek at the woman behind the shop counter trying to eavesdrop. 'I ain't going back there. I'm already late. Me pals went on without me.' He felt irritated to have missed out on larking about. Being penned behind a desk until the midday bell let him out into the playground was a grim prospect for a ten year old who hated school.

'For heaven's sake ...' Clover muttered in exasperation. 'What's happened then since I left for work?' She'd gone from the house in a rush as she'd nipped in to see her grandmother first. Thinking back, Clover wasn't sure she'd got a reply after calling out a goodbye to her mum who'd still been in her bedroom. At seven in the morning her

5

mother was usually busy with kettle and teapot. Clover hadn't dwelled on it at the time when going out of the door, munching on her breakfast toast. Somebody else had been on her mind and she'd hoped he was thinking about her.

Romance was forgotten for now, though. Aware her brother was sidling towards the exit she grabbed his arm. 'Are the girls playing up, or have you been up to mischief again?' She knew her brother could be a tyke.

'No, I ain't,' he huffily said. 'And the kids seem no worse'n normal.' He reported on their eighteen-month-old twin sisters. 'Mum looks queer and she's acting queer 'n' all. Shouted at me through the bedroom door to come and get you.'

'Queer?'

'Not herself. I had to do me own breakfast,' he indignantly announced.

'She's got a headache, d'you think?'

Johnny wrinkled his nose, searching for a better description of his mother's demeanour. 'Dunno really . . . but when I went to tell her I was off to school, her door was locked and I could hear her crying in there.'

'Perhaps she's been drinking.' As soon as she'd said it, Clover realised it was too early in the day. Iris Cooper was an evening tippler who said a drink helped her sleep. It was rare for her to suffer for it in the morning. Not unheard of, though.

Johnny gave a sulky shrug and edged away again. He'd done his bit and wanted to get going in case his big sister suggested he play truant to nursemaid the rest of the family. He might not like lessons but being stuck at home with a grumpy mother and two demanding toddlers was worse than school in his book.

'Go and fetch Nan. She'll know what to do.'

'Mum said I mustn't. She only wants you.'

'Miss Cooper! Serve, please. Customers are waiting.'

'I'll have to go,' Clover whispered. 'Tell Mum I'll come back and see her on me break . . .'

'No fear. I'll miss the register and get the blackboard rubber in the neck.' The bell on the shop door was set a-clatter as Johnny made his getaway.

Clover couldn't concentrate on what she was doing with the dragon breathing down her neck; she measured two yards of calico four times to make sure she would cut it straight. Allowing an inch over what was paid for would land her in it. As would wrongly pricing it. Two lots of six-pence and three farthings had seemed simple to calculate yesterday and she felt annoyed with herself when the sum failed to come immediately.

'One 'n' one pence ha'penny please,' she burst out and breathed a sigh of relief when neither Mrs Randall nor the customer objected to her mental arithmetic.

Mr Randall was the boss; his wife was usually to be found taking it easy out the back, reading journals or knit-ting garments to display in the drapery window. But every so often Bruce Randall went to the wholesaler's to put in an order, leaving his wife in charge.

'What was that all about, Miss Cooper?'

'Mum needs me to pop home for a short while, Mrs Randall.' Clover had expected to be interrogated the moment the customer had gone. 'My brother says she's unwell.'

'Oh, I see . . . overdone it again, has she . . .'

'I'd like to go now it's quiet.' Mrs Randall's heavy hint that her mother was hungover annoyed Clover. Iris Cooper bought gin and that didn't go unnoticed when everybody used the same shops. Some neighbours understood why

Sidney Cooper's wife would need a drink, married to him. Silvertown wasn't renowned for housing paragons of virtue, yet Clover knew her father was worse than most of the men. A woman like Martha Randall wasn't sympathetic to those less fortunate. Her mild-mannered husband had probably never raised his fist to his wife or child. This wasn't her first snide comment about Clover's mum, and when it came to family, Clover was loyal. 'Dock me pay, if you like,' she announced, tilting her chin. 'I'll miss a dinner break later as well. But I'm going now cos me mum needs me.'

Martha planted her hand on the polished wooden counter, barring Clover's way. 'This is the second time this week you've sneaked off.'

'The little 'uns needed some medicine. They've had bronchitis. Mum didn't want to take them out in the cold to get it herself. Anyway I was only gone half an hour.' Clover was disappointed that Mr Randall had blabbed on her. He'd not seemed put out at the time and had handed her a florin advance on her wages to get the jollop.

Iris Cooper was too proud to approach neighbours to ask for tick on her behalf. Neither did she allow her own mother to lend a hand, yet Elsie Hall lived just round the corner. There had always been a rift and that puzzled and saddened Clover. She and Johnny liked their nan and often visited her. Their mother rarely did, so once a week Clover took her little sisters round in the pram to see their grandmother. She was a blunt and forthright woman, but then so was Iris. Something had gone on to sour the relationship between mother and daughter, years ago. Neither spoke about it, so Clover had drawn her own conclusion that it was to do with her dad. Sidney Cooper needled most folk and it was unlikely his mother-in-law was an exception.

'Would you let me pass, please?' Clover gave up waiting for Mrs Randall to stop imprisoning her. For a moment she thought she might get her face smacked so furiously red had the woman turned. That was it … she'd get the sack now for insolence.

'You'll go back home on your break and not before.'

'I have to go now.' Clover pushed past, already removing the scissors dangling at her waist on a sturdy piece of string. Her mother wouldn't summon her for a trivial reason and instinct was urging her to hurry up.

'You rude girl. You can look for another job. My husband will tell you the same so don't go crying to him.' Martha marched off to tidy wool skeins crammed in cubbyholes on the wall.

Clover hastened towards the back room to retrieve her coat then headed for the door, aware of Mrs Randall's mutterings.

Outside, the High Street was crowded with people and distant calls of the merchants hawking their wares on the market could be heard. A group of local women were by the shop having a chinwag; and she gave them a polite nod and set off. She spotted Henrietta Randall coming towards her on the other side of the road. They were friends despite Henrietta, or Nettie, as she was called, having been instructed to avoid her socially. Nettie had told her mother she wasn't a kid anymore and she'd pick her own friends, thank you very much. She'd settled on her own job too, and was studying to be a secretary rather than be pinned beneath her mother's thumb in the family business.

'Got a day off college this morning, Nettie?' asked Clover, having jogged over the road for a quick word in passing.

'No such luck. I had to come back for my Pitman

textbook. I'd forgotten there's a shorthand typing test this afternoon.' She had slowed down and caught Clover's arm as she tried to speed past up the road. 'Where are you off to in such a hurry?'

'Mum sent Johnny to get me. Think I've upset your mother, taking time off again, but I have to go. Must be something urgent.'

'Oh, sorry . . . quick, off you go then.' Nettie gave her arm a little push. 'Best of luck. And don't worry about Mum, I'll speak to her.'

Clover thought her friend's reaction a bit odd. 'Have you heard something on the grapevine?'

'Not about your family. A girl at college got called home this morning. Her dad bought it at Ypres.' Nettie shook her head. 'The poor girl was sobbing her heart out and all the others were saying they were worried about their fathers. Apart from me, of course, and our teacher. My dad's not up to it with his dicky chest, and the teacher's dad's too old to go to war. Anyway, the bad news girl was in a dreadful state. I'm sure it's nothing as drastic for you . . .' she called out as Clover broke into a run without saying goodbye.

Why didn't I think of that? The phrase circled Clover's head as she dashed along. She had jumped to the conclusion the drama at home concerned her mum, not her dad. The postman might have brought a notification from the war office. Her father hadn't written in months, so she had no idea if he'd been in the thick of it over there; but it wasn't unusual not to hear from him. He wasn't a letter writer. Neither was their mother. Clover and Johnny wrote to their rifleman father and asked him how he was. Unless he wanted some treats sent over to France they rarely got much response. Their mother would penny-pinch to afford the biscuits and cigarettes he wanted, despite being grateful the war had put distance between them. If Sidney Cooper was gone for good, his wife might feel differently though.

By the time Clover turned into her street, she'd convinced herself she'd never see her father again and her chest was tight and her face wet with tears. Her mother wouldn't have told Johnny about this. Or anybody else. Her eldest daughter was the person Iris Cooper turned to in a crisis, and she'd been doing so since before the girl left school. At sixteen years old Clover often felt burdened ... unable to properly cope with it.

The terraced house in which they lived had long ago lost its front door and been subdivided. Her fingers were shaking so much she had trouble turning the key in the lock of their lodgings. The Cooper family rented the ground-floor accommodation and upstairs was vacant because the roof leaked. The landlord said he'd fix it but he never did; he resorted to emptying buckets.

'Mum!' She dodged furniture to speed through the empty room into the rear lobby and burst into the bedroom her mother shared with the twins.

Iris Cooper was lying in bed, her complexion comparable in colour to the pillow supporting her head. The toddlers were topped and tailed in the pram and their mother had some fingers clamped to the handle, jigging it in an attempt to keep them quiet.

With the curtains still closed the room was shadowy and Clover took hold of the edge of one to yank it back.

'Leave that; don't want no prying eyes on me.' Iris was conscious the communal privy at the rear of the yard overlooked this room. 'You must take care of your sisters for me, Clover, I don't feel up to it today,' she croaked.

'Oh, what's happened, Mum?' Clover dropped to her knees by the bed. 'Did a letter come about Dad?'

Iris struggled up onto her elbows. Her hair, usually neatly wound into a bun, hung in long auburn tangles about her shoulders. 'A letter? Postman's not been, 's'far as I know. Why d'you ask about your father?' She clamped some fingers on her daughter's wrist. 'Is he coming home? What've you heard?'

'Oh, thank heavens ...' Clover let out a pent-up breath. 'I bumped into Nettie Randall and she told me her friend's had bad news from France. I thought you'd got a letter too, about Dad, and that's why you'd sent for me ...' She broke off, staring at her mother's gripping hand that showed blood beneath the fingernails. A sharp peer at her mother's hollow-cheeked, pallid face followed. 'What's wrong, Mum?' She pressed on the mattress to assist her to her feet. The covers had been disturbed and she'd glimpsed a stain on the bottom sheet and on the hem of her mother's chemise. Apart from that scrap of cotton, Iris had nothing else on.

'Just a monthly. Worse than normal, that's all it is.' Iris sounded evasive. 'Take the girls out of the room.' Her hand dropped away from the pram handle. 'You'll have to look after them for me until I've sorted myself out. Go on ... hurry up and see to them.' Iris moved to get out of bed and exposed a heap of linen on her other side. She flopped back down with a moan of pain and her hands began to knead her abdomen.

Her mother hadn't seemed to be intentionally hiding the bundle of towels yet Clover instinctively knew she'd not been meant to see it. She moved round the bed and cautiously picked it up. Having felt something solid within, she peeled back layers of cotton.

'Put that down, I'll deal with it.' Iris had opened her eyes to see her daughter gawping at the premature baby. 'Was a boy; came too early.'

Even before she'd fully digested her mother's meaning Clover's eyes began smarting with tears.

'If you'd done as you were told you'd not have seen would you?' Iris sounded gruff and frustrated. 'I said put it down. Nothing can be done for the mite. Take care of Rosie and Annie for me. I'll be all right soon.'

Clover almost dropped the doll-like child as shock receded and she realised this was real. She altered her grip, cradling him against her body and touched his fluff of fair hair with a trembling finger. He felt warm, not cold as expected; a sob expanded her chest and her tears dribbled from her chin onto his still cheek. She felt unbearably sad but hastily put down her dead brother on hearing her mother groan. 'There aren't more babies to come out, are there?' she fearfully asked. Two had been produced last time. Clover remembered that day when the noise from this bedroom seemed to go on and on and she'd been constantly on the move fetching hot water and rags at the midwife's bidding.

'Don't think so. Some mess is still in there … taking it's time coming out,' Iris explained between pants. 'Put the kettle on and bring me some hot water and a flannel. I want to wash. Go on! Do as you're told, Clover. You've got to help me until I'm back on me feet.'

'Why didn't you say you were expecting a baby?' Clover turned away, trying to control her emotions. She'd not anticipated any of this. Previous calamities had been half expected. Her father's violence and drunkenness, her brother's misbehaviour leading to her mother's fight with

13

a neighbour up the road. Clover had received fair warning of being dragged into all of that before the worst of the trouble erupted.

Not an inkling of this tragedy though had she foreseen. She wanted to pick up her tiny brother and love him, but what good would that do? Nothing to be done about the mite, she'd been told. She felt furious with her mum and with herself. Her nan was wise; she would know how to cope with this. She'd not stand in a daze, feeling useless and jittery as Clover was. Her anger was overcome by anxiety as Iris jerked up her chin with a grimace of pain stretching her mouth.

'Don't worry, Mum. You'll be all right.' Back to the bedside Clover sped and sank down to grip her mother's hand. 'Nan'll be able to help you better than me. I'll get her.'

'You won't!' Iris wriggled her fingers free and reared up again. 'Don't mention this to her or anybody, you hear?' she panted. 'Just me and you know what happened this morning and that's how it's gonna stay.'

'Mrs Waverley came and helped when you had the twins,' Clover argued. 'I'll fetch her instead then.'

Rosie and Annie had been born when her dad was at war, not that he would have been much help if he'd been around. He spent most of his time in the pub with his pals. 'You're not listening to me.' Iris thumped a weary fist on the mattress. 'Don't need nobody. We'll deal with this by ourselves.' Iris nodded at the gin bottle on the floor by the bed. 'Hand me that. It helps with the pain.'

Quickly, Clover did as she was told and watched her mother swig from the bottle. 'I'll write and tell Dad then; he might get leave and come home till you're feeling better.'

'You don't write and tell your father anything.' Iris

shouted to be heard over the toddlers. Their mother's stressful voice had started them grizzling.

'But ...' Clover began.

'But ... nothing.' Iris kept firm hold of the gin as she levered herself up, grimacing with the effort, and propped her shoulders against the iron bedhead. Her anguished frown softened as she gazed at her daughter. At sixteen, Clover was a lovely-looking girl. Her thick auburn hair and green eyes reminded Iris of herself at that age. She was thirty-two now and the rigours and disappointments of a bad marriage had aged her beyond her years. She still received compliments though.

The boys sniffed around Clover. But her girl wasn't stupid or naive. She was smarter than her mother had been at that age. Clover had liked school. She'd learned her sums and had an enquiring mind. A child to be proud of ... who would cotton on quickly to why this morning's drama needed to be kept from Sidney Cooper, and everybody else. Iris would rather have that conversation here and now than suffer her eldest child's damning looks in the days to come.

'I know it won't be long before you work it out for yourself, so I'll come straight out with it.' She paused to find the courage to admit to something shameful. 'The baby wasn't your father's child, Clover.' Iris took another swig, handed Clover the gin, then sagged back onto the pillows as a contraction undulated her distended belly, making her wince.

'What? But ...' Clover put the bottle on the floorboards.

'Never mind.' Iris stared at the ceiling. 'There's nothing else you need to know,' she added firmly. 'But you understand, don't you, why this has to be kept secret.' She swung her head to gaze at her daughter's shocked expression. Then she closed her eyes. 'Your father hasn't been back home in

15

nearly a year. They can all count round here.' She paused as though she might say more about it but changed the subject. 'The girls have had some bread and jam so no need to feed them. Sit them on the potty then get them dressed and take them out for a good while so I can have some peace and quiet.' She rested a hand over her eyes as though to shut out the morning light striping between the curtains.

'I told Mrs Randall I'd only be half an hour,' Clover blurted, unable to pick a question to spit out from the countless number cramming her head. Was her mother going off with another man? Was she leaving her father? Was she leaving all of them?'

'You won't be going back to Randall's today,' said Iris. 'And don't worry about that old cow. I'll sort her out.'

Chapter Two

'Oh ... no ... just my luck,' Clover groaned beneath her breath as she bumped the pram down the front step and took a quick look about. A hawker had turned up and was selling second-hand clothes from a barrow stationed in the middle of the lane. Neighbours were milling about the cart, bartering for better prices, and calling their 'mornings' to one another. There was nothing for it but to keep going now she'd been spotted. Turning tail would arouse suspicion and she didn't want that.

She returned greetings while briskly pushing the pram along the pavement. Appearing purposeful might make them leave her alone, she hoped. Everybody round here used her shop to buy their sewing things. If ambushed she'd be asked why she wasn't behind the counter at this time of the morning. People could sniff out gossip and a change of routine would provide the scent. Chins would never stop wagging if it came to light why Iris Cooper's eldest girl had missed work to look after the twins. Her mother had a chill ... that was the safest thing to say if trapped into conversation; she speeded up nonetheless.

Mrs Waverley was holding up a dress by the shoulders,

to inspect it, but she dropped it to the barrow and waved. Clover put her head down and straightened the pram blanket while crossing the road, feigning ignorance of the woman approaching her. Once she'd turned the corner, she slowed her pace but her heart continued racing.

She trudged on with no destination in mind, gazing at the bonneted heads of the twins. She stroked the cheek of the tot closest to her. They were almost too big to fit in the pram together and sat facing one another with a cover draped over their tangled legs. Rosie took up most room; she was a larger, happier child than Annie, who'd entered the world three hours after her sister. She was still cutting the teeth her twin had got a month ago, and was struggling to catch up Rosie in other ways, too. Clover came to a halt to search for the dummy, lost in the blankets. She gave it to Annie, and a comforting peck on her hot cheek before setting off again, vigorously rocking the pram. It was a game Annie liked and she stopped whimpering and clapped her hands.

Clover wanted to take a breather. Her legs had plenty of life left in them, but to quieten the chaos in her head she'd need to sit still to concentrate. She halted by a low brick wall and perched on it. The girls were playing pat-a-cake. Clover had taught them that as soon as they were both able to sit up. She softly sang the song to them while staring back the way she'd come.

She didn't like the idea of nobody being with her mum. Iris might attempt to get out of bed, and faint, crashing into something and hurting herself. Clover had followed orders rather than upset her mother by being disobedient. The coward in her would sooner stay away and avoid seeing the blood again. She longed to find things had returned to normal when she got back, with her mum her usual clean and tidy self, pegging out washing while moaning about the neighbour's cat digging up the garden. She knew she was wishing in vain, and anxiety curdled her stomach.

She closed her eyes to calm herself but her infant brother's white face floated behind her eyelids so she stared at the weeds sprouting from the pavement instead.

That tiny baby wasn't her father's child.

Her mother didn't have a boyfriend ... did she? Well, of course, she must have, Clover ridiculed herself. It was a long time since she'd believed in tales of gooseberry bushes. How had her mother found the time to meet a man, though? She was at home most of the time; she took in washing to earn a wage even though Clover's grandmother had offered to help with childminding so her daughter could get a better paid job. Iris was always run off her feet, but particular about her appearance. She set high standards for her children, too. Johnny's hands and neck were given the once-over before he was allowed out. The twins were dressed in pretty clothes that Iris would knit in the evenings; today she'd been in no mood to bother about being particular. Neither had Clover; she'd grabbed the first things that had come to hand to put the girls in before leaving the house although they were usually in matching outfits.

Clover had noticed some silvery strands lightening her mother's auburn hair, and a few lines around her eyes and mouth. For all that, Iris Cooper was the most attractive woman in their street, in Clover's opinion. So who was the man that also thought her beautiful?

They rarely had social calls. The tallyman who collected insurance and Christmas club money, and the rent collector turned up on the dot every week. She'd never seen those men enter their lodging. Her mother wouldn't risk messing around with a fellow known to all the neighbours. The coal merchant needed to come inside to do his job though. He marched straight through the parlour with a sack on his shoulder and out into the backyard to shoot the coal into the bunker. The day he was due her mother would spread old newspaper on the floor to prevent his oily boots dirtying the boards. Iris Cooper bought stock in the summer before the colder weather put up prices. He'd delivered in June but had said he'd be back because he owed them another sack and some kindling. Perhaps he had been back while she'd been at work and Johnny had been at school ...

Clover thought about him some more. He was a handsome, fair-haired man beneath the soot. She had spotted him in the local park, looking spruce. He'd been with this wife and family and she'd been with her friends. He had recognised her and given her a wink. He was about her mother's age, Clover guessed. Perhaps Iris also found him charming. Her father wasn't charming; he was a bully who drank too much. Clover wished he was different, and that her parents were happy together, but she knew they weren't and that saddened her ...

'How d'you manage to skive off, eh?'

Clover rubbed tears from her eyes and jumped to her feet at the sound of that familiar voice. Her grandmother, shopping bag swinging, was on her way towards her. Elsie Hall was a tallish woman in her early fifties who was always well turned out even when taking a trip to the corner shop. Her felt hat and beaver coat would have led a person to believe her to be middle class rather than a munitions worker, capable of swearing like a trooper and scrapping in the street. Even before her grandmother reached her, Clover could detect a scent of lavender water.

Elsie fussed over her youngest grandchildren in the pram then straightened up and studied her eldest. She cocked her head. 'What's up then? You look as though you've lost a shilling and found an 'a'penny.'

Clover tried to smile but couldn't quite manage to. She pressed together her lips to stop them wobbling.

'Oh, what's up, love?' Elsie put a comforting arm around the girl's shoulders. Clover hadn't stopped for a cup of tea when she'd dropped off that drapery order. She'd handed over the wrapped parcel of wool then got going, in case she made herself late for work. The girl was conscientious, so something untoward had happened for her to return home. 'You've not upset Mrs Randall and got the boot, have you?'

Keeping secrets from her nan was horrible. Clover wanted to confide in her, not deceive her. 'I've taken an early dinner break.' It was only a white lie, but a lie none-theless. Not a very convincing one, either, at mid-morning. 'I'd better get going now these two have stopped grizzling.'

'I wasn't born yesterday, y'know,' said Elsie with an old-fashioned look. 'You've been crying. You weren't late for work after bringing me that stuff, were you? If I've got you into trouble I'll speak to Martha Randall . . .'

'It's not that, Nan . . .'

'What is it then?' Elsie waited briefly for a reply before clucking her tongue and taking another guess. 'That Fletcher lad's upset you, I suppose. He's not worth losing your job over, dear.'

Her grandmother's soft and sympathetic tone was Clover's undoing. 'It's nothing like that; I'm worried about

Mum . . .' Mitigating her betrayal with a shrug was awkward with her arms crossed over her chest, suppressing a sob.

'What's up with her?' Elsie Hall adjusted the bag looped on her arm.

'She's in bed, resting.' Clover was economical with the truth.

'Had one too many, has she?' Elsie was aware her daughter would drink when things got on top of her.

'Don't think so, Nan . . .'

'I'll pop in on her while you take the little 'uns to the park.' Elsie held out a hand. 'Give me your key.'

'I can't,' Clover said. 'Mum told me not to say anything. I wanted to come and get you or Mrs Waverley cos I was in a panic, but . . .' Clover dropped her chin, feeling guilty and disloyal. Yet seeking help from an older woman seemed the only right thing to do. 'I don't know how to make her feel better, Nan.'

'Well, I do. Give me the key, Clover,' ordered a grim-faced Elsie. Mrs Waverley was a handywoman, required to deliver a baby or lay out a body. When a labour went wrong, one job often followed the other. Living in the same street, Doris Waverley would see Iris most days, but she wouldn't suspect a thing. Not when Mrs Cooper's husband had been away fighting in France all those months. Elsie knew her daughter though and had noticed her belly protruding beneath a loose pinafore intended to conceal it. She had kept her suspicions to herself, not wanting to worsen a long-standing family rift. Back then, when it started, she'd had a right to interfere in her teenage daughter's life. Iris was a married woman now, off her mother's hands and old enough to fight her own battles. If she was in trouble though, Elsie wouldn't stand by and watch her sink.

'You've done the right thing.' Elsie patted her grand-daughter's shoulder and slipped the key she'd been given into her pocket. 'I won't ask you no more, that way you can keep your promise to your mum. Off you go to the park.' Elsie gave the toddlers a farewell peck on their cheeks, then set off with a determined expression.

'What're you doing here? Did Clover go and get you when I told her not to? The deceitful little ...'

'Quieten yerself down, Iris,' Elsie cut across her daughter's complaint. 'Don't go blaming the girl when she's done nothing wrong. Ain't her fault I bumped into her in the street. She tried to avoid me but I wasn't having it. I could see she was in a right state.'

Elsie was already taking off her coat. From the moment she'd entered the gloomy, malodorous room the staleness of blood and sweat had put her on edge. The fur was dropped onto the chair under the window, her hat was unpinned and followed. Elsie drew back the curtains a fraction to let in some light. 'Clover's not in as much of a state as you though, is she?' Having taken a good look at her daughter, she was battling to remain composed. Iris's face was haggard with strain and shockingly white. 'Are you in labour? Well, are you?' Elsie hurried a reply while rolling up her sleeves. She marched closer and spotted the almost empty gin bottle by the skirting board. Elsie tugged the cover from her daughter's grip to stare at the gore in which she lay. 'Gawd's sake. What's happened, Iris? Have you had an abortion ... or brought this on yourself?'

'No ... done nothing,' Iris moaned. 'I wanted this baby. I started to miscarry this morning and it's taking ages to

23

finish. Just need to catch me breath to clean meself up.' She turned her head away on the pillow to avoid the mix of pity and disgust widening her mother's eyes. 'You can get off home now you know you're not needed.'

Elsie ignored that. 'You wanted this baby, did you? And how the bleedin' hell did you think you'd get away with that? He might be a pig but he's not a fool.'

'Don't care. I'm leaving him.'

'Does he know about any of this?'

Iris moved her head side to side on the pillow. 'I've not written to Sid in ages.'

'Damn good job you have kept this to yourself, my gel. If you've a shred of sense you'll keep it that way and think of the children you have got.' Elsie rallied herself and stomped away to the washstand where earlier Clover had left an enamel bowl half filled with warm water. It was cold now, but she wrung out the floating flannel and returned to the bed, wiping her daughter's thighs, rinsing and repeating until the water turned scarlet. As fast as she removed the blood more appeared, making her frown.

Iris didn't protest at her mother's ministrations; she closed her eyes and tears seeped from between her lids. Finally, Elsie said, 'Who you sleep with is your business. But Sidney's the children's father and your family deserve better than this.'

'I deserve better than this,' said Iris on a sob. 'You made me marry him even though you knew what he was like.'

'If you'd kept your knees together at fifteen, like I'd warned you to, you could've waited until the other one got free of his mother's apron strings ... if he ever did.' Elsie started to roll the sheet from its bottom edge, easing her daughter to one side so she could yank the soiled linen from under her and strip it from the bed. She folded it up carefully to prevent the mass of slime and clots escaping, then dropped the bundle by the door. 'I'll dispose of the afterbirth and boil the sheet.' As she straightened, she noticed what was in the cot Rosie and Annie shared. The urge to see her grandchild was overwhelming. Disturbing the swaddling cloth she gazed at a small face and gulped in a shuddering breath. 'Girl or boy?' she croaked.

'Boy . . .'

'Older than I thought it'd be. About seven months, I'd say. Looks like him. Fair.' Elsie quickly covered the boy.

'You're not surprised then.'

'Not about him. But I'm ruddy astonished that you let him knock you up.' Elsie had conquered her emotions and was back to business. 'Does he know?'

'Oh, yeah . . .' sighed Iris. 'Told me to get rid of it. Gave me money.'

'That was nice of him,' said Elsie sourly.

'Not seen him now in months . . . not since I gave him his money back.'

'I'd've kept it.' Elsie approached the bed with the baby her daughter was beckoning for. 'Did Clover see this poor little mite?'

'Didn't want her to, but she did,' said Iris. 'She knows it's not her father's. She'd've worked it out for herself, anyhow.'

'Yes, she would. It's best she knows about these things,' said a philosophical Elsie. 'She's a good-looking girl and old enough to be attracting this sort of trouble.'

'You know Archie Fletcher's keen on her, don't you?' accused Iris.

'I know she likes him.'

'Well, I don't. He's no good and I don't want him sniffing around.'

'Now you know how me 'n' yer father felt about you sneaking out to meet Sidney Cooper. Can't say you wasn't warned ...' Elsie gestured hopelessness. It was far too late to be scoring points in that old battle. 'Clover's got her head screwed on,' said Elsie. 'Handsome is as handsome does is how she'll see it.' Elsie had lost her daughter's attention. Iris was crooning to the baby, its little body bobbing violently against her heaving chest as she wept. 'Oh, love ... you didn't really think he'd leave his wife and take you on if you had his kid, did you?' Elsie sorrowfully shook her head and began rummaging in a drawer to hide her watering eyes. Right now, Iris was in need of practical help more than consolation. Having found a clean nightdress, Elsie urged her daughter on to her feet.

'It's your fault I didn't get the husband I wanted.' Iris pushed her arms into the clean cotton gown.

'He and his lot didn't want you, did they? Not good enough ... and that was before they knew your belly was full of another man's child,' said Elsie. 'It was trouble enough getting the man responsible to do his duty.' Despite her legitimate defence, guilt rolled around in her guts. She'd done what she'd believed to be right. Her late husband had been more lenient, talking of adoptions and orphanages so their daughter's disgrace could be hushed up. Elsie had stuck to her guns and said their first grandchild must be brought home from the convent where Iris had given birth. That was something she'd never regret. Her stubborn streak had protected the little innocent in the rotten business. 'Sit on the chair while I change the bed. You're still bleeding and need to rest.' She bent down to tear a clean edge off the soiled sheet, folding it up into a pad for her daughter to use. 'You'll need some antiseptic or you'll end up with an infection. I've got some Eusol at home.'

Iris wasn't listening; she was stuffing the rag between her thighs and brooding on the past. 'Dad didn't want me to marry Sid. He would've sorted things out, if you'd let him. Nobody would've known.'

'How can you say that now?' Elsie's voice was suffocated by anger. Her early years had been spent in an institution and she knew what such soulless places were like for children. 'You would've left Clover with the Sisters of Mercy, would you, so you could act innocent and hook Bruce Randall? He meant more to you than your own daughter, eh?'

'Yes!' cried Iris.

'You're not so wicked as to abandon your own newborn in a nunnery.' Elsie moved her head in disbelief. 'And you went behind his back with Sidney Cooper. That's not real love. That's gin talking.'

'Sid's got a persuasive way about him.' For the first time in a long while Iris made another attempt to explain to her mother why she'd been infatuated with the local hound. What she'd never told anyone was that Sidney Cooper had wanted more than the kisses she was prepared to give, and had forced her to lay with him behind the mission hall. 'Never a day goes by I don't wish I could turn back time,' she said bitterly.

'Yeah . . . we all wish we had that clock. Be a rich woman if I knew where to find the damn thing,' said Elsie drily and pushed the drawer in the chest shut.

Clover hadn't intended to eavesdrop. She'd come back because Annie had messed herself and needed changing. Raised voices had been coming from the bedroom so she'd decided not to interrupt and make matters worse. She'd hovered outside ... and made matters worse. What she'd overheard had made her tremble and hold her breath while her heart raced faster and faster and she couldn't stand it. She made a clumsy dash to get away before she was discovered listening, but collided with the scuttle dumped in the passageway.

Elsie glared a warning at her daughter then hurried out of the room. She found Clover halfway along the corridor, on her hands and knees, picking up coal. 'Why've you come back, dear? Where's the twins?'

'Left them on the path in the sun,' Clover blurted. 'I forgot to take a clean nappy with me. Came in to get one and knocked this over. I'll change Annie outside then go to the park.'

Elsie noticed her granddaughter couldn't meet her eyes. 'Did you hear what we was talking about?'

Clover shook her bent head, throwing a fistful of lumps into the scuttle. 'How's Mum? Is she feeling better?'

'She's weak. After a rest she'll need to have a bath. I've got some antiseptic at home. You could fetch it while I take care of her.'

'Glad you'll stay with her ...' was all Clover said.

'Don't reckon I need to repeat what your mum's said about keeping this private, but I will cos it's important. What's happened has to be our secret, Clover. No speaking to friends about it.'

Clover certainly didn't need that drummed into her. She'd not allowed herself to be waylaid even when a good friend had wanted to chat. She'd sped past with Annie wailing, giving credibility to her shout that she was in a tearing rush to get home. Now she wished she had stopped to talk

28

to Jeannie Swift and had arrived too late to eavesdrop. Her mother's horrible declaration would echo in her head forever. She couldn't turn back the clock any more than her mum could.

'And I reckon you know you mustn't ever speak of this to your father, either.'

'I do know . . .' murmured Clover.

'I don't like you being caught in the middle of this,' sighed Elsie. 'But you are, and you have to be grown up about it all. Your dad's not had leave in a long while. He could turn up at any minute, so we need to be prepared to protect your mum. If he ever found out the truth . . .' Elsie didn't finish her warning. Clover was aware her father would beat the living daylights out of his wife for this betrayal.

Clover darted a glance at the door as though anticipating the chaos. She'd seen him hit her mother for nagging him for being drunk. She always tried to intervene but got pushed aside, and was often hurt from crashing into the furniture. She licked her lips and nodded vigorously in agreement.

'We'll stick to a story about your mum being laid up with belly ache,' said Elsie. 'Neighbours might bother you with questions about where she is, so be prepared. Johnny can be told the same when he gets back from school. There is a bug going about. I've had bad guts meself.'

Clover got up, rubbing her dirty palms together. 'I know what to do, Nan,' she said.

'Knew I could rely on you. Perhaps me 'n' Iris might be on better terms from now on then at least something good will come out of it.'

'Hope so . . .' said Clover gruffly.

'You're the best granddaughter any person could hope

for. And that's why I'm not afraid to ask you to be as brave about this as a proper adult.'

'Who you talking to?' Iris called. 'Has Clover come back?'

'She's getting a clean nappy for Annie,' Elsie shouted back then said to Clover, 'You ready to show how brave and grown up you can be, to help your mum?'

'Yes ...' Clover didn't doubt herself though she'd been pitched headlong into womanhood whether she liked it or not. Her life had changed; her relationship with her mother would never be the same. She felt battered and confused. She didn't want to know more secrets than she should. She'd been her mother's first port of call in a crisis for years and had resented the responsibility but cherished her mother's faith in her. Now she saw it differently: perhaps Iris hadn't been demonstrating her trust but demanding something back for the sacrifice she'd made sixteen years ago.

'Your mum's in a bad way at the moment, and she's tipsy. So if she's short tempered and says things she shouldn't, then you just put it down to her not being herself.' Elsie tilted up her granddaughter's chin. 'You understand, don't you?'

Clover nodded. Her grandmother knew she'd overheard something not meant for her ears.

'Right ... well, there's a good deal to sort out yet,' sighed Elsie. 'But first things first. Bring the pram inside, love.'

Elsie watched the girl, head bowed, approaching the door. She felt disgusted with Iris for having said what she'd said, even if it had been a drunken outburst made in the belief it would remain private. Elsie was pretty sure it hadn't, and no excuse ... no sorry ... would be clever enough to fool Clover, or make her feel better.

Archie Fletcher was the first boy her granddaughter had

shown an interest in; Elsie doubted she'd even had more than a few kisses. Yet already Clover knew there was a dark and cruel side to desire that could blight lives. The girl was an adult now, all right.

Chapter Three

Elsie Hall was no stranger to dealing with a crisis and believed herself adequate to the task of coping with the bust-ups that were part and parcel of being a wife and mother. But after she'd brought up the possibility of Sidney Cooper's long overdue leave she'd begun to feel on edge. Her granddaughter's preoccupied look and frequent glances at the door, indicated that she also feared fate playing a nasty trick on them.

Clover did indeed have her father on her mind, in particular the last time she'd seen him all those months ago. He had arrived without warning last Christmas, looking roguish in his khaki uniform with his cap pushed back on his head and a cigarette dangling from his lips. Clover had dashed to welcome him with a hug and received a customary playful fist beneath her chin. Being his favourite, Johnny had received more of his time, and a Christmas present in the shape of a deutschmark banknote. A prisoner of war had swapped it for a cigarette, he'd said. His wife's rolling eyes had displayed her scepticism. Clover had also suspected he'd stolen it and had given it to Johnny as the landlord of the Rose and Crown had refused the souvenir in payment. The twins had barely received a glance from their father.

Then, before the kitbag was off his shoulder, he'd raided the household kitty so he could go to the pub. His wife hadn't made much of a protest, preferring him out of the way. Sidney Cooper had been drunk for most of the Christmas holiday. Even Johnny had been glad to see the back of him when he left for France a week later. Then the missing rent had to be found and the money Clover had saved to celebrate New Year with her friends went into the jar to make up the shortfall.

'If you'd rather not do this, I'll not blame you.' Elsie picked up Rosie, who was attempting to climb into the pram to be taken out for a ride with her twin.

'I want to do it, Nan,' Clover said firmly, and carried on fixing Annie's harness to the sides of the carriage.

'If your mum was feeling better I'd go out myself.' Elsie jogged the lively toddler, squirming to get down. 'I can't leave her though while she's like this.'

'People would think it odd, you pushing the pram.' An apparent healing of their notorious family rift would attract inquisitiveness.

'That's a thought, love.' Elsie's frown gave way to a weary smile. 'Doris Waverley would chase me up the street, wanting some answers, then I'd end up putting her nose out of joint.'

Clover chuckled though neither of them were in a laughing mood. 'I'll be back soon as I can,' she said.

Elsie gripped her granddaughter's shoulder in praise and affection then shut the parlour door behind Clover.

For the second time that morning Clover took scouting looks up and down the road before easing the pram over the threshold into autumn sunshine. She'd felt nervous the first time but was doubly so now, despite the barrow boy and his crowd of customers being long gone.

The lane was quiet apart from the repeated thud of a football hitting the flank wall of the terrace of houses. Bobby and Charlie took no notice of her and continued taking turns aiming shots at crumbling brickwork. Winnie Pincher's sons rarely attended school and were too rough and ragged for Johnny to associate with, so said his mother. To Clover, those Pincher lads no longer seemed so rough or ragged. Who would associate with Johnny Cooper ... or any of his family, for that matter ... if their secrets leaked out?

The pram wheels began collecting debris overflowing from the central gutter, but she stayed walking on the road, unwilling to risk being hijacked on the pavement by a neighbour emerging from a doorway. Her guts felt watery and ice prickled her cheeks though the air was mellow. Leaning into the handle for support, she made for the corner on her wobbly legs.

She loved her mum and was praying she'd soon be well, but was glad to put some distance between them. Her nan's reassurance that Iris hadn't meant what she'd said was of comfort but hadn't completely persuaded her she wasn't an unwanted child.

Rosie had been left behind to make room in the pram. The stillborn had taken her place and was concealed beneath the colourful knitted blanket, close to Annie's socked feet. Clover knew not to stare at the bump in case she drew attention to it. The idea of the dead baby being discovered caused her knuckle bones to almost burst through the skin as they tightened on the pram handle. How would she ever talk herself out of it?

Sunlight was winking on the windows of the houses, making it hard to spot any faces. She prayed the neighbours were all too busy to bother spying on her and she'd manage to quickly carry out her instructions to put her brother beneath the eiderdown on her grandmother's bed. Elsie had said she would deal with his burial.

Clover stopped herself dwelling on pitfalls that might never occur and instead occupied her mind calculating how many turnings she'd yet to take. Uncurling some stiff fingers from the pram handle she plunged them into her pocket to reassure herself she'd got her grandmother's house key. She felt metal and her tense shoulders dropped an inch. The antiseptic was under the sink and she mustn't forget it. On she hurried, glancing about. If she spotted any acquaintance she'd make a diversion. Only another few minutes and she'd be there and could relax . . .

'Miss Cooper . . .'

She tottered around in alarm, jigging Annie up and down rather too violently and making her cry. The blanket covering the infant had folded back on itself revealing a glimpse of a tiny face. Clover clumsily threw the blanket into place and kept going. The vehicle accelerated then slowed down in front of her this time. She'd paid scant attention to passing traffic, and that had been a mistake, as had been leaving the back streets and venturing onto the main road for quickness. She recognised the saloon car and the tall, fair-haired fellow who'd got out of it.

'Why aren't you at work?' asked her boss, frowning at her.

Clover moistened her lips; this pitfall certainly hadn't crossed her mind and she fought back the urge to wail hysterically.

'Aren't you well, dear?' Mr Randall asked though it

seemed she was. He'd watched her pushing the pram along at quite a pace.

'I ... I took time off, Mr Randall,' she blurted. She couldn't look at him or the pram. Instead, she stared at the cartons of goods piled on the back seat of the car. He was on his way back from the wholesaler's with stock for the shop.

'Is something wrong?' He came closer and noticed her face was chalk white and her large green eyes unblinking, making her appear to be in a trance.

'I've an errand to run.' She stooped over the pram to fondle her grizzling sister's cheek and block his view of the hillock beneath the blanket. His son was within his reach if he stretched out his left hand. He'd wanted him dead, anyway. Had paid her mother money to make it so. 'Sorry, in a rush ... have to go ...' Although he was still talking to her, she set off up the road and didn't stop even when he sharply called her name. She turned the corner and broke into a run, panting, while Annie stopped crying and giggled in delight at the lovely ride. Clover came to an alley and darted along the narrow space between the high sides of houses. She flattened her back against the wall and watched out for the car. It passed by at a normal speed; he'd crawl along if he was looking for her, she reassured herself. She stayed where she was, anyway, waiting for her ribs to stop rocking.

She'd get the sack for definite. She didn't care; she couldn't carry on working at the drapery after finding out her mother loved Bruce Randall more than her husband ... more than her eldest daughter ... and maybe more than her other children, as well. Silent in the pram was the baby Iris had wanted but couldn't have. Clover bit her quivering lower lip. She wished the little boy had lived too. She patted the covers around him, found Annie's dummy and gave it to her, then emerged from the alley.

'You took your time. I've been run off my feet trying to deal with everything by myself.'

'There was a jam of carts by Spitalfields. Didn't Clover turn in for work this morning? I saw her along the road.' Bruce Randall had pre-empted receiving a barrage of complaints about their assistant by bringing up her absence himself. He'd driven back to the shop turning over in his mind possible causes for the girl's peculiar behaviour. He knew it could only be something to do with her family.

'She arrived at the usual time but wasn't here five minutes. Her brother came to fetch her.' Martha folded her arms over her bosom. 'She blatantly defied me and manhandled me out of the way when I tried to stop her leaving. The girl's lazy and insolent. She's had enough chances and won't get any more. I'm sacking her.'

'There's no need to be hasty . . .' Bruce began stacking the boxes of stock inside the back door.

'I say there is.' Martha pulled a tablecloth out of a carton to examine it. 'I never wanted to give her a job in the first place. I know why you took the girl on behind my back, and paid her more than she's worth. And it wasn't because she's your daughter's friend, so don't bother coming out with that. You employed her because her mother's your friend . . . that's the truth, isn't it? You're late back because you've been with Iris Cooper. Does Clover know about you two?'

'Don't talk rot . . . you're being ridiculous.' Bruce cut across his wife's rising voice and whipped back outside to continue unloading the car.

'Ridiculous am I?' She'd followed him into the backyard

37

where he'd parked, and her accusations kept coming. 'I think you've been seeing Iris Cooper since her husband's been at war . . .'

'Keep your voice down,' he snarled in an uncharacteristic show of authority. He raised his hat to a woman passing by outside the gate. 'You'll show us up in front of our customers,' he hissed.

'If people knew more about what you get up to we wouldn't have any customers,' said Martha. She watched him loosen his collar with a finger and knew her suspicions were valid. He still had feelings for Iris Cooper. What she couldn't be sure of was whether those feelings were returned and they'd committed adultery. She guessed they had. 'What you see in a slut like her is beyond me.' She angrily shoved him away as he made a conciliatory move towards her. 'Once her thug of a husband finds out what you've been up to, you'll both be sorry . . .'

'A customer's waiting to be served and we can't afford to lose a sale.' A faint clatter of a bell was heard coming from inside the building. 'We'll speak about Clover's job later.'

Martha's money mindedness had given him a reprieve. His wife's sniping was nothing new and normally washed over his head. Not today though; she'd thrown in his face something she'd every right to be het up about because it was true.

His obsession with Iris had withered after they both got married to other people all those years ago; just a quiet and private friendship had continued. Then the war had come and taken Sidney Cooper away, presenting them with an opportunity to revive dormant feelings. If one or other of them had a happy marriage it wouldn't have happened. He wished it hadn't. Iris getting pregnant and deciding to keep the baby had been a disaster. She'd told him not to worry when returning the money he'd given her for an abortion: her husband wasn't too bright about women's matters and would assume the baby to be his, she'd said. Bruce wasn't convinced about her being able to pull that off and had ended things between them. They weren't even friends any more.

He drove his fingers through his fair hair while dwelling on more recent events. Why hadn't Clover wanted to talk to him? The girl wasn't usually standoffish or nervous but she'd been both. Thankfully, Sidney Cooper was still on the Western Front. He was a brute and already bore a grudge from knowing he wasn't the husband his wife had wanted. He'd relish taking his revenge if he worked out that Iris had fallen pregnant with her first love's child.

At least only he and Iris knew for certain that anything had gone on between them. The baby wasn't due for months; there was still time to sort things out, and if an adoption was needed to keep the secret hidden, then he'd arrange it.

Elsie Hall had a compact lodging; it comprised of a parlour containing a cooking stove and a back slip room where she slept. She'd lived at this property since before her husband died. Clover barely recalled her granddad. She'd been four when he passed away and the family rift had made meetings few and far between back then. Years later she'd been told he'd been sick with pneumonia. A warm feeling usually accompanied his memory so Clover knew she'd liked him. But he would have arranged for her to be adopted so her parents weren't forced into a bad marriage. Only her nan hadn't wanted her to be left behind for strangers to raise.

Clover's chest swelled with gratitude, strengthening a connection that those early years apart couldn't destroy. When old enough to walk to and from school with her friends, she used to sneak off to visit her grandmother once a week. Her mother had found out what made her late home on Fridays, but hadn't banned the get-togethers. Once Johnny was in junior school he came along too and they'd be treated to sandwiches and custard creams for tea in this little place. And Mr Lewis who was her nan's friend and neighbour would come in sometimes and teach them how to play cards. Not once had Elsie Hall said a bad word about their mother. She'd avoided speaking about their father; so did a lot of other people stay quiet rather than criticise Sidney Cooper to his children.

Relief hadn't yet loosened the knot in Clover's guts though she'd done everything she'd been told to do. The antiseptic had been wrapped in a cloth and stowed carefully in the pram so as not to disturb Annie. The child had settled down to doze now she had the pram to herself.

Clover began to prowl around the parlour, seeking comfort in familiar things. She picked up the wooden-framed photograph of Iris as a girl of about twelve. Abundant dark ringlets sat on the pale collar of her sailor suit and she was smiling confidently at the camera. She looked beautifully serene, as though she believed life would always be kind. There was an identical frame, holding the picture of a stern-faced young man of about eighteen. Iris's older brother had moved to America and Clover knew little about him or her cousins.

She dropped into her grandmother's armchair, sagging back into the cushions. She'd like to stay forever in this cosy home that smelled of Sunlight soap. Annie was softly snoring, blissfully ignorant of the catastrophe that prevented her big sister even closing her tearful eyes for more than a few seconds.

Too restless to relax, she got up and went into the bedroom. Sitting down on the mattress, she folded back the eiderdown and looked at the baby. It seemed wrong to leave him here all alone. She hadn't covered his face again after his swaddling cloth had been bounced off in the pram. When she'd first seen him at home she'd been too shocked to take much in. Now she studied him properly, thinking him perfectly beautiful with his white as snow, powdery skin. He had fair lashes and eyebrows. She began choosing names that might have suited him. She settled on Gabriel because of his angelic looks and because if there was a heaven, he surely deserved to be there.

She leaned forward, intending to kiss his forehead but jerked back. She stared at him, straining for another sound while wondering if Annie was murmuring in her sleep. Clover's finger hesitantly touched his forehead. He felt warmer than before but surely he would after being muffled in layers of wool. She watched him fixedly and detected a tiny movement behind his eyelids. She lowered her head, unable to believe the proof of her own eyes, but there it was again. She gasped and her hands covered her mouth as she jumped to her feet and scuttled backwards.

For a whole minute she stood still then began to pace by the side of the bed, her fingers gripping her scalp in shock. The tiny scrap was alive and there was nobody to ask what to do to help him. If she raced back and told her nan to come and have a look for herself it might be too late: he might never move or squeak again. Better to take him back with her for quickness. Then her mum could see him as well. The baby she had wanted. Her grandmother had been adamant though that he must be spirited away immediately in case somebody barged in and discovered what had gone on.

Her grandmother hadn't seen and heard what she just had, though. What should she do? She rushed to the bedside to peer at the infant; his tiny lips seemed puckered and she was sure they hadn't been like that before.

She gingerly wrapped him up then lifted him as though he were made of glass, trying not to press on his tiny bones. She willed him to stay exactly as he was with that expression on his face until she could show them at home. They'd decide what to do. She couldn't.

'Sorry about earlier,' Clover gasped out. 'I'm still in a tearing rush, though. I'll pop round later ...' Clover knew that promise was unlikely to be fulfilled. She couldn't believe what awful bad luck this was, bumping into her friend again when she'd only one more turning to take to reach home.

'Crikey, you are up to your eyes in it today, Clo.' Jeannie Swift caught hold of the pram handle as Clover would have whizzed past her. 'Don't envy you, looking after the kids; it'd drive me crackers being saddled with them all the time.' She glanced in the pram at Annie, wide awake now and chewing fretfully on her dummy. 'Didn't know you had the day off. I'm on nights at Gudgeon's. Some more men left to enlist so us women are getting offered their jobs. Overtime's there too if I want it, cos we're upping production.' She tickled Annie's cheek. 'Once you've taken this little 'un home, we can have a bun and a cuppa in the caff this afternoon. I don't start work till seven so plenty of time for a natter ... cos actually, I've got things to tell you—'

'Can't,' Clover interrupted. 'Got to help Mum with the twins today.' She wheeled the pram forward but her friend didn't take the hint to remove her hand from it. 'Mum's caught that stomach bug going round. Nan's with her, but she's got to go to work later.'

Her voice had become shrill the moment she'd noticed Jeannie looking at the bump beneath the cover as though wondering how big Annie's feet could be. Clover prayed that the baby would stay still and quiet. While dashing along, she had watched and listened constantly for a sign of life from her brother but the hum on the street and the ruts negotiated had prevented her attributing any sound or movement to him. She was terrified by the thought of him dying while in her care. Her grandmother would regret putting faith in her to do this important job. Her distraught mum would have her hopes raised only for them to be dashed. Hysteria had made her imagine seeing and hearing things, that's what they'd think, and would blame them-selves for having treated her like an adult. Clover forcefully moved the pram forward, almost jerking her friend off balance in her desperation to get home.

'Oh, go on then.' Jeannie snatched her hand away from the handle. 'I thought I'd do you a favour, and treat you to a bite to eat. But I won't bother, if you want to be like that.'

'I'm sorry, Jeannie, it's just Mum's waiting ...' Clover frowned an apology and hurried away. She hadn't covered more than a few yards when she spotted two uniformed soldiers emerging from the Rose and Crown to lean on the wall outside in the sunshine. One of them she recognised and she slowed down. 'Your dad's home, Jeannie,' she blurted over a shoulder.

'I was just gonna say he's back on leave,' Jeannie said

huffily. 'And you'll have a nice surprise 'n' all.' She wasn't absolutely sure her next revelation would be well received. Mr Cooper was always charming to her and attractive for an older fellow, in her opinion, but everybody knew he could be a swine to his family. 'Your dad's inside.' She jerked her thumb at the pub. 'They sailed on the same troop ship. If you knock on the window he might come out and say hello.' She turned away with a sniff. 'Anyhow, can't hang about. Mum's doing bangers 'n' mash. It's me dad's favourite and I said I'd go to the butchers for sausages.' She marched off up the road.

For a second Clover stayed immobilised by shock, slap bang outside the pub where her father was. If he glanced out of the window he'd come out ... right now ... might even fiddle in the pram to lift out his youngest daughter. His eldest swung the pram around and tangled her feet beneath the wheels in her panic. A second later, Clover was hurrying back up the road.

'I know you're hungry, love,' Clover muttered. Her little sister had had enough of being outdoors, rattled around in the pram. 'I'll find you a biscuit when we get home, for being a good girl.' She leaned forward and found the dummy and offered it up. Annie wasn't interested in that now she'd been promised a biscuit, and pushed it away with her tongue.

Clover had headed back to the alley where she'd hidden before, to catch her breath and have an inner debate over what on earth she should do next. In trembling haste, she uncovered her brother while her sister continued to whimper and hold out her arms to be picked up.

The little boy's lips were parted and she held her breath,

wondering if he might start to cry. Only a whisper of sound reached her ears but it was enough. She leaned back against the brick wall, overwhelmed with joyous relief that he was still breathing. If she took him to her grandmother's house and left him there, as she'd been supposed to do, she could head homewards. But her father might by now be indoors. It wouldn't be easy getting her grandmother on her own to garble out a potted version of what had happened. Elsie Hall was a cool character but even she would be thrown by such astonishing news. Clover knew it was vital her father's suspicions weren't aroused; he had to swallow the reasons given for his wife's illness.

Yet, the baby needed immediate care. He was so tiny it was hard to believe he was alive at all. She could take him straight to hospital ... but the nurses would question her about who she was and where she lived. A doctor might bring the baby back and her dad and everybody else in the street would know what had gone on. Then all hell would break loose.

She'd heard of people finding abandoned babies on doorsteps but she couldn't leave her little brother like that with no idea when he might be discovered. Besides, her mother would read about it in the paper and go mad when Clover owned up. She continued to gaze at him with a mixture of pity and affection. He was a marvel but so still now. She bent her head to listen for a heartbeat. Annie grabbed her hair and tugged, making Clover yelp. She freed herself from those small fingers, but the toddler had given her a needed jolt.

She had to stop dithering like a soppy fool and do something, for little Gabriel's sake. He might look like a pretty doll, but he was real flesh and blood and needed food. In

45

the short time she'd known him, she'd grown to love him, and couldn't bear it if he died now. He deserved to have a life . . . whatever that life might turn out to be.

The broad oaken door remained closed; she wasn't leaving until she knew he was safe. She'd given two hefty pulls on the bell then dashed back to hide behind a hedge of tangled privet and ivy. A path from the road wound through apple trees and shrubbery up to the convent building. She'd not wanted to announce her arrival by crunching up to the entrance on the shingle. Instead, she had laboriously bumped the pram over rough grass, littered with windfalls, while chanting pat-a-cake. When that failed to keep Annie amused, she'd swooped on an apple, polished it on her skirt, then gnawed off a piece of tart juicy flesh for her sister to suck and nibble.

Her arms were banded over her chest but that hadn't done much to slow her heartbeat and her head continued thumping. She parted some foliage and peered through the sticks. Still nobody had opened the door. She didn't fancy emerging from her hiding place to yank on the bell again in case she was caught red-handed. She'd left the baby on the step, wrapped up in his swaddling and the pram blanket. In the shade of the orchard trees the autumn air was chilly. She took off her coat and was draping it over Annie's legs when the unmistakable sound of creaking hinges reached her. Peeping around the greenery, she saw a white-veiled nun in the process of crouching down to examine the bundle on the flags. Without rising, the young woman gave a shout, summoning those inside.

Clover had recently discovered that her own life had started at this place. Luckily, she had been taken home from the Sisters of Mercy. Once her mum was well again, and her father had gone back to war, then Gabriel, as she now thought of him, might be claimed and brought home to his family. She knew such a happy ending was unlikely, unless her mother meant what she'd said about leaving Sidney Cooper. It was doubtful Mr Randall would break up his family for a baby he'd not wanted, and go off with Iris. Yet Clover wished that would happen so her baby brother got the same chance she'd been given. Perhaps a better chance would be his, with parents who loved one another.

Two more nuns clad in dark veils had joined the novice on the step. Clover quickly bit off another piece of apple and gave it to Annie as she impatiently jigged. It was time to go. After their shock at discovering a foundling wore off, those nuns would turn their thoughts to who was responsible for the deed. They might begin to search the grounds.

Stealthily, she backed away, rousing angry insects as she pulled the pram over smashed fruit. Her eyes were trained forward to spot pursuers but she darted glances over a shoulder at intervals to locate obstacles. She stayed in the orchard's shadow, taking a twisting route over the cider-scented ground towards the exit. Once at a safe distance, she turned, racing towards the open gates with the pram bouncing before her, then bolted straight across the road and around the first corner encountered, before allowing herself to slow down. She leaned against the wall and tried to listen for trouble through the thump of blood in her head. Several quiet seconds passed and she peeked around an edge of brickwork. Nobody had followed. 'Bye, Gabriel . . .' she whispered. 'For now.'

Chapter Four

'Well . . . what can I do for you?'

'I'm here to speak to Clover Cooper.' Martha Randall subdued her surprise at being confronted by this person to bridle at the tone of voice used. 'If she's not home, her mother will do instead.'

'Will she now?' purred Elsie Hall, and her tongue found the inside of her cheek.

Martha was aware this woman had a reputation for being belligerent, but she wasn't scared of her or her daughter, even if they had made up and joined forces. She wordlessly demanded entry by stomping onto the top step, but stopped short of barging past.

Elsie Hall had an impressive height and build for somebody of her age and breeding. It wasn't until the woman opened her mouth that she showed herself up as common. Neither could she hide what she did for a living, should she want to. She had the jaundiced complexion of somebody regularly handling toxic chemicals. Canary Girls, as the female bomb workers were known, were a common sight in an area that housed many munitions factories, and more springing up all the time to satisfy an increasing demand for weaponry to win the war.

For all that detracting from her looks, Elsie Hall was still attractive and well dressed. Martha considered herself effortlessly middle class and found it distasteful when inferiors appeared better than they were. 'I'll speak privately to Mrs Cooper. Is she in?' She jerked a nod towards the interior.

'In or out, 'fraid you're out of luck on seeing either of them, Mrs Randall. Me daughter and me granddaughter's unavailable right now.' Elsie remained determinedly blocking the entrance, thinking no more highly of the visitor than she was thought of. Martha was no beauty, that was for sure. The boxy shape of her mud-coloured coat made her figure appear shapeless, and her old-fashioned bun didn't do her mousy hair any favours either. 'Clover's already told you her mum's poorly so I'll ask you not to bother us.'

Henrietta had said that servicemen's families were receiving bad news from France, to excuse Clover's insubordination. After hearing that from her daughter, Martha had been even more determined to warn Iris off. A widow with small children to rear would want a new husband and Martha could guess where Iris might look to steal one.

Bruce would be horrified if he ever found out she'd confronted Iris. He might rush over to apologise. The very idea made her grind her teeth. Her aim was to drive them apart, not push them together. Now she was here though, she might as well see things through rather than squander the effort it had taken to gee herself up for a showdown.

'Mrs Cooper might not appreciate me broadcasting a complaint about her daughter on the doorstep.' Martha slung a significant glance sideways.

Elsie craned her neck to stare boldly at a group of women being entertained by the unusual activity at the Coopers' house. They shuffled along the lane a bit, allowing Elsie to return her attention to the visitor.

This stuck-up woman got on her nerves and she didn't envy Bruce Randall, being married to her. She'd always felt more exasperation than dislike for him. It was a shame he hadn't possessed the gumption to defy his parents and stand by Iris after Sidney Cooper seduced her. Elsie believed he had wanted to but forfeiting his inheritance for love had been a stretch too far. Perhaps he was still spineless, and had sent his wife to do his dirty work and sack Clover. After he heard what Elsie had to say about this morning's drama, he'd change his tune.

Until Iris was fit enough to handle wet sheets again to earn a wage, Clover's pay was crucial, and the girl deserved to go to work without fear of being picked on. Martha didn't seem to have conquered her jealousy, any more than Sidney Cooper had got over being an also-ran in his wife's affections. Elsie wondered if Martha knew her husband had rekindled his first love affair.

'I know you've been put out, Mrs Randall.' She stood aside and found a smile of sorts for the sour-faced biddy, stepping over the threshold. To give the woman her due, she deserved some sympathy, married to an adulterer. 'I'm here now, taking charge of everything. So when me grand-daughter gets back from running an errand I'll send her straight into work.'

'My husband and I have been badly let down by her. She's unreliable and impudent with it.' Martha fiddled with the buttons on her coat. 'Where is her mother? I need to speak to Mrs Cooper.'

Iris had heard the hum of conversation in the corridor and opened the parlour door, thinking Clover had returned. She was still in her nightdress, holding her toddler daughter by the hand. 'Oh ... it's you.' She sounded startled on recognising the face peering over Elsie's shoulder.

'Get yourself back to bed,' Elsie hissed, half turning around. 'I can deal with this.'

Martha attempted to dodge past but was butted backwards by one of Elsie's sturdy hips and ended up outside on the step again.

'I've things to say to you ...' shouted Martha, leaning at an angle to see past the sentry.

Elsie rolled her eyes in exasperation and one of her arms shot out, ushering Martha back inside. The door was shut before the neighbours could investigate.

Martha started a brisk march along the hallway but slowed down when she got a better look at Iris. Gone was the aggravatingly attractive woman with abundant auburn tresses. Iris's hair was usually neatly styled, but today hung in rats' tails, and her eyes were sunken into putty-coloured hollows. She looked like a tramp, not a Jezebel. A twinge of shame came over Martha, but it wasn't due to Clover having told the truth after all. Neither had pity for a sick woman prompted it. She'd accused her husband of being late home because he'd had a liaison with a woman who looked fit to collapse, not fornicate. She owed Bruce an apology and eating humble pie with him didn't come easily.

'You'd better shove off, Mrs Randall. My daughter should be resting in bed.' Elsie had soon positioned herself in the space between the two women eyeing one another like cats trapped in an alley. 'You've seen for yourself that Clover's not swinging the lead. Her mum's got enteritis and believe me you don't want to catch a dose of it.'

Rosie was clinging to her mother's legs, and Elsie scooped

the child into her arms. She jerked her head to indicate that Iris should return to her bedroom, then addressed their unwelcome visitor. 'Clover'll be back serving your customers soon, Mrs Randall. That's a promise.'

'She won't.' Martha had begun to back away. 'She's not wanted. She'll get what pay's due after I've made sure there aren't any threads or needles unaccounted for. Tell her she's sacked. Good day.'

'Just you 'ang on a minute,' bellowed Elsie at the woman hurrying off. 'What are you implying ... *unaccounted for ...*'

Before Martha could escape, the door was opened and a man appeared framed in the opening. His arrival caused his wife to groan beneath her breath and his mother-in-law to curse beneath hers.

Martha was too het up to be surprised to see Sidney Cooper, large as life and oozing rough masculinity. She glared at him to step aside. He did with an exaggerated sweep of his arm, allowing her passage into the street. Then he tilted the army cap back on his springy dark hair and turned his attention to his family.

'What's she after?' He sounded suspicious and his startlingly blue eyes gathered more creases at their edges.

Neither Iris nor Elsie had sufficiently recovered from this extra blow to find a reply.

'Some homecoming this is.' He flung his kitbag to the floor. 'What's put faces on boots? Something must've happened for that snooty cow to come calling.'

'Clover's got sacked from her job at the drapery ...'

'Iris ain't feeling at all well ...'

The two women spoke over one another in their haste to satisfy his curiosity.

Depending on his mood, Sidney Cooper might become

sentimental or aggressive after drinking. They could both detect the yeasty aroma of beer about him and knew he'd stopped off at the pub before heading home for a family reunion. Mother and daughter gave silent thanks for that small mercy.

'What's up, love?' He held out his arms invitingly but they were returned to his side when he was close enough to see Iris looked a mess.

'She's suffering with sickness and diarrhoea,' stated Elsie firmly. 'Ain't surprising, considering the state of that privy out the back. Sanitary Board needs to get onto the landlord or everybody'll go down with it.'

Sid grimaced in disgust. He'd had a belly full of filthy latrines and guts' ache over in France.

'Go and say hello to Daddy.' Elsie sent the little girl towards her father. Rosie was a friendly child and didn't hesitate although this man was virtually a stranger to her.

He swung up high the smiling toddler he'd last held when she was a babe in arms. He couldn't tell the twins apart having seen little of them, and not taking much interest in the girls when he was around. He pecked her cheek and Rosie wrinkled her nose as his unshaven jaw tickled her face.

'D'you feel up to getting dressed, Iris?' Elsie quietly asked while Sid was distracted with putting his cap on Rosie's head. 'Be best if you did.' They both knew that a soldier back on leave would have more than boozing on his mind after a long absence from his wife.

Iris nodded. 'I'll tidy myself up and put on some clothes.'

'I'll keep him occupied . . . make him some tea.'

'Thanks, Mum.'

Elsie gave a wry smile. 'Long time since you said that to me, love.'

*

53

Iris was watching her husband playing clap hands with Rosie. He sensed her eyes on him and gave her a wink. His insincere charm had been her undoing years ago. She knew it for what it was now. There was no point wishing that he could be different. She'd been married to him for too many years to believe he could change. Before he sailed back to France his selfishness would see him ignoring the children and causing arguments about having money to squander.

She'd come to accept his violence and it no longer churned her insides in the way it once might have. The thought of the kids going hungry, or getting on the wrong side of him, were different matters though. She was thankful to have her mother's support, and regretted that bitterness had kept them apart for so long.

'Wish you'd let us know you had leave, Sid,' said Iris, determined to start off on the right foot. 'I'd've put on a spread for you this afternoon ... made some buns and sausage rolls.'

'State of you, gel, you don't look like you got makin' a pot o' tea in yer.'

Iris's lips twitched sourly at his sniping tone; his mask was slipping sooner than expected.

'That's why I'm here,' said Elsie smoothly. 'I'll get the kettle on, then when Clover gets back she can go to the corner shop for a few things and I'll make you a sandwich.'

'Where is Clover? Why's she got the sack? What's the reason for it?' He reeled off his questions, broodingly watching his wife slipping out of the room.

'Iris needs a bath to kill off the germs so Clover's gone for disinfectant. Mrs Randall didn't like her taking time off to help out.' Elsie gave concise answers.

'Well, that ain't right. I'll sort the Randalls out while I'm back,' he said with a curling top lip. Sidney Cooper had been itching for an excuse to confront Bruce Randall.

'Let's talk about that later,' soothed Elsie. 'For now, you take the weight off, Sid.' She picked up the kettle and was relieved to find it full. The standpipe was outside in the yard and fetching water would leave Iris unprotected. Her son-in-law was a volatile character; it was hard to judge what he might do or say next, and his wife wasn't up to an inquisition, or any amorous attention. 'Wasn't expecting to see you, out o' the blue, like this,' said Elsie.

'Wasn't expecting to see you either, Mrs H.' He put Rosie down on the settee and began unbuttoning his khaki jacket. He slumped down next to his little daughter and spread his arms along the threadbare chintz of the chair back. His boots began a restless tap dance on the cracked lino. 'Very strange . . . you being here. Things are all patched up between you 'n' Iris then?'

'Times like this, I'll rally round me family,' said Elsie. 'I've heard of folk entering the infirmary with enteritis, and only coming out again in a pine box. I'd not live with me conscience if I didn't offer to help when I could've.' Elsie carried on setting cups and saucers. 'Ain't disappointed, are you, Sid, that we've let bygones be bygones?'

'Nothing to me, either way. If I'd had a bit more in me pocket, I'd've got a pie in the pub and saved you going to trouble on my account.'

Elsie knew he was angling for a handout. If she'd had money to spare, she would have given him some, simply to get rid of him. It was a shame he'd run through his cash or they wouldn't have seen anything of him until closing time.

'So, has me wife gone against me and got herself a factory job while I've been away?'

'She's still taking in washing, though why you'd object to her earning a decent wage in a factory is beyond me.'

'Ain't your business though, is it, Mrs H?'

'Got long at home, have you, Sid?'

'Only a week. When I was in the Rose and Crown just now I spotted Clover out the window, pushing the pram. She's taken the other twin with her then.'

'Little 'un was grizzling. Annie likes a ride in the fresh air ...'

The stilted conversation was brought to an abrupt halt by the sound of Clover's return. Luckily, she'd heard her father's voice and knew he'd arrived home before her. She'd been preparing for this meeting, but gulped in a huge steadying breath before wheeling the pram into the room with a grin stretched across her face.

'Hello, Dad,' she burst out. 'I knew you were back. Just saw Jeannie Swift and she told me.'

'I saw Jeannie 'n' all,' he said, getting up to pat Clover's arm in welcome. 'Your friend's getting a good-looking gel. Not a patch on you, though, eh?' He grazed his fist playfully over her chin, as he always did, looking her up and down. She seemed to have turned from girl to woman in the time he'd been away and his compliment wasn't flattery. 'You're as pretty as yer mum was at your age, y'know. And she was a cracker.'

Clover knew her grandmother was watching her; she could feel the air thick with tension as Elsie waited on tenterhooks to see how she would deal with this meeting. 'Glad you're back, Dad. Missed you, y'know,' she carried on with some conversation, rehearsed all the way home from the convent. 'I bet it's rotten over there in France. How've you been? You look well on army rations.' She'd not studied him properly; she'd been busying herself unfixing Annie's reins to avoid meeting his eyes for more than a second at a time. It had registered though that he appeared muscular and handsome and in need of a shave.

'Been giving them Germans what for, love. That's what I've been up to.' He jerked a nod in emphasis.

'Bet you were at Ypres, weren't you?' She recalled the name of the battle Nettie Randall had mentioned earlier; she'd talk about anything to avoid her thoughts straying back to Gabriel, alone with strangers. At this moment nearly all the rest of her family was around her. Only Johnny was absent. But, one wrong word and it would all fall apart.

'Ypres ... Somme ... been everywhere. But don't intend to talk about none o' that going on over there.' Her father shook his head, sucking on his teeth. 'Want to forget it for a while.' He ruffled the fine dark hair of the child, whimpering in the pram, and sagged at the knees to peck Annie's cheek. His attention started her howling, making him mutter beneath his breath.

'Annie's not so outgoing as Rosie,' said Elsie. 'She'll soon get used to you, though, Sid. Johnny'll be back from school soon and pleased as punch to see you.' She hoped mentioning the boy would take the frown off his face, but something else occupied him as he dwelled on his eldest acting the little mother to his twins.

'Have boys been pestering you, Clover?' He wagged a finger. 'You tell me names, and I'll see 'em off while I'm back.'

'No ... not got boys after me, Dad,' Clover quickly said.

'Sit down, Sid, tea's almost brewed,' Elsie butted in, before the name of the youth Clover liked cropped up. There were more than enough problems to contend with as it was. 'You

57

fetched the Eusol, did you, Clover? Hope you lot don't all get the diarrhoea and sickness, like Iris.'

Clover knew her grandmother was spelling it out so she was aware of what her father had been told so far. She pulled the bottle out of the pram and offered it in a hand that shook. Her father didn't notice her nervousness but her grandmother did and their eyes met and held for a long moment.

'Don't want no tea. I'll go now and have it out with Randall.' Sid sprung up. He was bored already and the noise the twins were making was grating on him.

'You don't need do that right now, Sid; it might all blow over. Anyway, it'll be better if I go. Me and Mrs Randall's already had words about this, see.' Elsie explained for Clover's benefit, 'She came here earlier, looking for you.'

'It's up to me to protect me kids.' Sid sounded shirty.

'Don't want either of you to go,' Clover butted in, rocking the pram vigorously. 'If I've lost me job, I'm glad cos I was gonna hand in me notice anyhow. Jeannie just said they're taking on at the munitions factory, and working nights at Gudgeon's you can earn good pay.' She'd spoken on the spur of the moment and not very truthfully, but realised applying to be a munitionette wasn't a bad idea. And a mention of more money had seemed to appease her father. He drew a packet of Woodbines from his pocket and took one out. Her grandmother looked relieved to see him settling down and turned her attention back to the teapot.

'I never agreed with you working for the Randalls anyhow,' said her father, justifying his outburst. 'Was done behind me back while I was in France.' He struck a match and put it to the cigarette clamped in his mouth.

58

'Dad!' Johnny charged in, beaming, the sole member of Sidney Cooper's family genuinely pleased to see him.

The boy didn't get a hug; Sidney put up his fists and engaged in a mock fight, parrying and dodging and mimicking boxers' grunts while ash from the sucked on cigarette sprinkled the front of his uniform. Pretending himself defeated, he ruffled Johnny's dark hair and gazed at his favourite child with genuine pride and affection.

'You've shot up, son,' he said.

Johnny grinned from ear to ear. 'Mum never said you was coming home today. Gonna take me over the marshes to play football while you're back, Dad?'

"Course . . . bring yer pals along . . . make a match of it at the weekend if you like.' It was a promise frequently made and rarely kept.

'I'll tell 'em now.' Johnny backed away then sped from the room.

Sidney slumped back into the settee and slung the fretful toddlers a pained glance through a haze of smoke. 'Might as well have stayed in the pub.' He took another long drag on the cigarette.

'Annie's hungry . . .' Clover fumbled with the biscuit tin lid. She'd been so intent on not putting a foot wrong that she'd neglected to get Annie something to eat. There was hardly anything left so she broke a digestive in half and gave the twins a piece each.

Quiet descended, interspersed with Annie's hiccoughs. Clover glanced quickly at her grandmother. The noise the girls had been making had been a distraction at least. She anticipated troublesome questions from her father filling the void.

"Fraid I'll have to send you on another errand, Clover.'

59

Elsie found something to say. 'We'll need a loaf for sand-wiches and your dad might like a few Garibaldis. Seem to remember those was your favourite biscuit, Sid ...'

'I'd sooner get meself a pie in the Rose 'n' Crown ...' He glanced meaningfully at his mother-in-law.

Clover was used to him scrounging for money so under-stood what he was getting at. She went into her bedroom and brought back her savings tin. Tipping out the coins onto the table she took back just a shilling from the copper and silver to keep. 'Been saving up for us to have our treat when you got home, Dad. Mum's too poorly for an outing though, so I want you to have it for a welcome home drink.'

On some Saturday afternoons before the war they would walk along the river, then find a place to sit and eat chips from newspaper, and share a few sweets. Their father had ants in his pants, her mother would say, when getting them ready to go out, and couldn't abide sitting indoors cooped up for long. Even when quite young, Clover had realised it suited her mother to be out of the house as well. It was within the four walls that Sidney Cooper vented his temper. Outside, with a brood of pretty, occupied children drawing admiring glances, and a brown ale in his hand, he felt so much better about family life.

How her mother had managed to put something by from the housekeeping money to pay for those safety days was a miracle to Clover. Yet she'd just bought him off too ... and she'd wanted new shoes.

'That's decent of you, love.' Sidney was already scooping up the cash. 'I'll pay you back, o' course ...'

Clover knew that was pie in the sky. He never paid any-thing back.

'I'll just go and tell your mum I'm popping out then.' A

chirpy Sidney shrugged into his jacket then found his comb and started sprucing up his hair.

Elsie strode off with a cup and saucer rattling in one hand. 'I'll take Iris her cup of tea before it's stewed.' The bloodstained sheet and empty gin bottle had been bundled into her shopping bag by the time Sidney strolled in with his cap under his arm.

'Ah, you look more yourself now, love,' he crooned to Iris. She was clothed in her good dress, sitting on the edge of the bed, brushing the knots from her hair.

'I'm off to catch up with a few pals. Give you a chance to have that bath then we'll have a cosy time later, shall we?' He nuzzled her cheek before leaving the room, whistling.

Mother and daughter looked at one another in stark relief, though they knew it was a reprieve not a victory. 'Get back into bed and rest,' said Elsie the moment she heard the parlour door being banged shut. 'I'll heat some water and bring in the bath.'

Elsie found her eldest granddaughter sitting on the settee, cupping her face in her hands. 'Well done.' She patted Clover's shoulder then with a groan sank down beside her. 'What bloody awful luck to have, and all on the same day.'

'Got something to tell you, Nan . . .' Clover sprang up and glanced agitatedly towards the bedroom where her mother was. 'I don't want Mum to know about this.' She screwed up her eyes but tears leaked out. 'When Jeannie said Dad was back, I had to do something for the baby and didn't know where else to go.'

Elsie levered herself up with a puzzled look on her face. 'Calm down, Clover, and spit it out slowly.' She waited, but her granddaughter seemed to have trouble composing herself. 'You did do what I asked you to?' Elsie prompted.

'Couldn't ...' Clover shook her head, then in bursts of trembling whispers she told Elsie what had happened. When finished, she said, 'I didn't imagine it, Nan.'

Elsie licked her parched lips. 'I believe you, though it's a miracle considering the tiny size of him. Perhaps the bumping about in the pram was what the poor mite needed.'

Clover watched her nan's wondrous expression fading away into a frown. 'Should I have brought him back here even though Dad was home?'

Elsie cradled her granddaughter's wet cheeks between her palms. 'Thank goodness you didn't,' she said. 'You did the right thing ... the only thing there was to do. I'm so proud of you,' she fiercely whispered. 'Now you must put it from your mind or it'll drive you mad. Once your dad's gone back to France and your mum's feeling better, I'll deal with it. You just leave this to me now and try to get back to normal.'

'We'll get him back, though, won't we?' Clover's eyes were wide and bright with pleading.

'Have to wait and see about that, Clover ...' Elsie was unable to be completely honest. With her clever granddaughter's help she'd seen off the worst of the trouble for now. With luck, it would stay away. Elsie wasn't about to go looking for it to bring it back.

Chapter Five

'Ah, I guessed you might still be in here with him. Come away, my dear, you'll upset yourself.'

The Mother Superior had opened the door of the nursery and found the youngest of her colleagues cuddling the abandoned waif. She took the infant from the novice's arms and the feel of his sparrow-like bones beneath the swaddling made her sigh sorrowfully. 'I know you want to save him, Sister Louise, but the poor mite is barely alive.' She put the boy back in his cot and turned to the young woman who was wiping away her tears on her veil. 'Unfortunately, we cannot always have the happy outcome we want.'

'He's so tiny ... so beautiful.' The novice had moved to the cot to gaze down through splintery vision at his ethereally perfect face. She placed a fingertip to his white cheek. 'So cold, aren't you, you little love.'

'The very premature ones struggle to keep warm.' Mother Superior placed a hand on the younger woman's arm. 'Listen to me; we will do our best; that is all we can do.' She tucked the blanket more firmly about the baby's fragile body. 'The poor chap has a mountain to climb and most of it he must do on his own.' She found the water bottle beneath the blanket. 'I will refill this with hot. We will keep him comfortable and not let him suffer.' She paused. 'Now go downstairs and have your tea. Food is still set upon the table but will be cleared away soon.'

'I'm not hungry. He might be hungry, though,' said Sister Louise. She prowled around the cot, unable to leave, or to take her eyes from the infant. 'The wet nurse went home. She said he wouldn't suckle.' She picked up the feeding bottle, left on the nightstand. 'I told her she must use the breast pump. She has left some expressed milk in here for him.' Sister Louise had tried to feed him with it but though she managed to gently insert the teat between his lips they didn't move against it. She thought the teat was too big for him to manage.

'I fear he's too weak to suckle or swallow. Don't force it on him or it might make him choke, doing more harm than good. You are young and new to these tragedies, Sister Louise.' Mother Superior smiled wryly. 'I, on the other hand, have seen far more of this sort of thing than I've wanted to. These barely alive scraps sometimes survive for a short while but most are prone to maladies, and rarely reach a first birthday.' She gazed at the silent cot. 'And if he does attain that milestone he will be a weak boy in a harsh world. A workhouse or an orphanage isn't a nice place for a bullied child to be.' She sighed. 'Don't cry, my dear,' she said. 'As the years turn and your experiences grow, you will come to accept, as I have, that sometimes it is a kindness not to intervene but to let the Lord decide.'

'His mother wants him to live,' said Sister Louise fiercely. 'If she didn't love him and want that, she wouldn't have brought him here. She trusts us to save him.'

'We might be His disciples but we're not miracle workers,

Sister Louise,' said the Mother Superior with mild irony. She turned at the door with the water bottle. 'Would you have him endure being tormented for his frailty with nobody to love him and make it better? The world is a wicked place. Indeed wickedness is what has brought him into being. I would say he is a war baby, the illegitimate son of a wanton, or a woman ashamed of what she has done while her husband is fighting overseas. These foundlings suffer for the sins of their mothers. All we can do is pray for them all.'

When the Mother Superior had gone out Sister Louise picked up the boy again. He felt just as cold. She felt a strong instinct to hold him beneath her clothes to warm him and fiddled with her habit so she could snuggle him close to her breast. She felt his leg brush against her as though he liked her body warmth. Quickly she stood and went to the stand for the bottle of milk. Keeping him swaddled in her clothing, she inserted the teat delicately between his lips. 'Please, just take a little,' she whispered to him, stroking his face. A small amount of milk dribbled down his chin and she knew he'd not swallowed a drop. She put him into the cot and quickly ripped a piece of white cotton from the hem of her veil. Dipping it into the milk she inserted the small rag into his mouth and squeezed drips from it. She saw his tongue stir to taste it. She repeated what she'd done, keeping her fingertip between his lips to provide the opening for the sodden cloth. She waited, caressing his face and whispering to him to encourage him to swallow it. He seemed to have done so as none came out. Painstakingly, she carried on until a quarter of the milk in the bottle had gone. He didn't open his eyes or make much of a sound other than a little snuffle that she took to be contentment when his tongue remained still against the milky rag.

She smiled, feeling a surge of triumph as she lay him back into his cot. She piled the blankets on top of him and touched his face again. He seemed warmer, whether from her body heat or from producing energy to feed, she couldn't be sure.

She did know that she wouldn't ever give up on him. Mother Superior was a good woman, made weary and cynical by years of dealing with people hardened by deprivation.

Sister Louise believed life was life and it was her wish and her duty to do her utmost to give the boy a chance to forge his own destiny. That was the task the Lord had set her.

'Where's your mother? Your family?' she bent to whisper and planted her lips to his forehead. 'You're too beautiful to go to waste. You'll make it. I know you will. You'll make your mother proud.'

Chapter Six

'Oh, sorry to bother you. I only popped round to have a quick word with Jeannie. I'll come back tomorrow though as it's late ...'

'Don't be daft ... it's nice to see you, dear. Come in. Not a nice night, is it?' A wiry little fellow in his dressing gown stood in the open doorway of his home. 'You're not late; I'm early for this get-up,' chuckled Jeannie's father, beckoning Clover inside. 'I'm not turning in yet, just it's heaven to be out of that scratchy old uniform and resting me bones in something clean 'n' comfy. Army boots are lumps of lead in comparison.' Smiling blissfully, he wobbled a slippered foot at her. "Spect your dad's complaints about a Tommy's life are enough for you, so won't bore you with no more o' mine ...'

'Stop rabbiting and let the girl get inside, Jim,' said his wife, fondly budging him out of the way to close the front door. 'You're right on time for a drink of Ovaltine, Clover. Reckon you need one on a foggy night like this.'

'Thanks anyway, Mrs Swift, but I only wanted a quick word with Jeannie then have to get back.' Clover felt awkward intruding on this cosy scene, complete with glowing gas mantles, and an aroma of mouth-watering fried sausages and onions.

'Jeannie told me you've got a lot on your plates.' Mary Swift clucked her tongue in sympathy. 'What rotten luck, your mum being poorly just as your dad's back on leave. Can't be easy at home for you. Though your grandmother's rallying round, so I hear.'

Elsie had also commented on their awful luck but Clover believed it hadn't all been bad. Fate had been wonderfully good to baby Gabriel. It was a miracle that couldn't be spoken of though. Neither could she put him from her thoughts. His small, sweet face occupied a corner of her mind and even her hankering to follow her grandmother's advice to get back to normal couldn't fade it.

'Thought I recognised your voice,' said Jeannie, stopping halfway down the staircase and peering over the banister. 'Better come up then.'

The invitation sounded half-hearted, but Clover didn't hesitate in accepting it. She nipped past the middle-aged couple before more questions about life at home came her way.

It was obvious Jeannie was still smarting so Clover attempted a reconciliation as soon as the bedroom door was shut. 'Sorry I was abrupt with you. I wasn't being off. I really wanted to go to the caff, y'know, but there was absolute chaos at home.' She rolled her eyes, and flopped down on a narrow bunk bed pushed against the wall. Jeannie took the one facing her that her elder sister, now married, had once used. The Swifts occupied a whole house rather than half, as the Coopers did; when in civvies Mr Swift had a better paid job on the docks than Clover's dad. Sidney unloaded ships; Jeannie's father worked as a clerk in the Customs

House. A sound of laughter drifted along the landing from the bedroom Jeannie's three younger brothers shared.

"S'all right . . . sorry I got in a huff.' Jeannie shrugged her understanding. 'Just I did have things to say to you. Is your mum feeling better?'

Clover nodded, relieved Jeannie wanted to make up. She got on well with her although Jeannie was nearly two years older.

With the air cleared, Clover allowed herself to wilt in tiredness and suppressed a yawn. Twelve hours had flashed past since she'd risen that morning. She couldn't have been more wrong anticipating another mundane day at the drapery awaited while getting dressed. She still felt woozy with shock from having things she'd taken for granted wrenched from her. Even her job and her little pot of savings had gone.

'Bought this today . . . not sure if the colour suits me though.' Jeannie had been experimenting with make-up before Clover turned up; she took the hand mirror discarded on the eiderdown and began to finish doing her eyes.

Clover found her friend's slow considered movements soothing to observe and it took her a moment to break out of her trance to give her verdict. 'Too dark . . .' she said, having watched two blonde eyebrows being transformed into black slugs.

'Want to try?' Jeannie offered the mirror and pencil. 'You won't need much as your eyebrows are already quite dark.'

Clover shook her head. 'Johnny calls me ginger.' Her brother had dark hair, similar to his father's, and the twins also showed promise of their fine locks turning a deep brown. Clover and her mother were the redheads, and took after Elsie Hall.

'Here ... I got this as well in Gamages.' Jeannie held out a pot of rouge. 'Try it; you can rub it off before you go home.'

'Best not ... Dad doesn't miss a trick and can't risk starting him off when he's been boozing.'

Jeannie knew things must be fraught at the Coopers': Clover rarely made a direct complaint about her father. She put aside the mirror and cosmetics and wiped make-up off her face.

Clover would have liked to linger over this visit but her grandmother was waiting for her to return. Elsie had said she'd not outstay her welcome. Sidney would be suspicious if he rolled in from the pub and found his mother-in-law still there. Iris seemed perkier and adamant that she and her eldest daughter could cope between them now she was on the mend. Before heading back home, Clover had something to ask Jeannie. 'D'you reckon I'd get taken on at your factory?' She stopped lounging against the wall and sat up straight to say, 'I got the sack today.'

'Mr Randall sacked you? Just like that?' Jeannie sounded indignant. 'The bloody mean so-and-so.'

'Mrs Randall did, cos I had to take time off again.' Clover grimaced. 'Don't care. I want another job anyway.'

Jeannie looked thoughtful. 'You're younger than me; could be the most you'll get at Gudgeon's is a tea gel job until you train up on a machine.'

'I'll say I'm seventeen then.'

Jeannie winked and pointed to the make-up. 'Use a bit of that and chances are you'll get away with it, too. Our boss likes a pretty face ... not that any of us gels look very fetching in the get-up we have to wear. Ugly uniform, and rotten ol' cap to plonk on your hair. We're lucky though at Gudgeon's: we fabricate copper and tin and all that sort of thing.' She paused. 'Up the road at Brunner Mond they're handling TNT, poor sods.' Jeannie couldn't but notice that Clover's grandmother, in common with all bomb girls, had jaundiced skin, and paler hair in places where strands would escape from caps while filling shells. Jeannie was thankful not to be a Canary girl, ruining her looks to earn a pay packet. 'Be smashing if you do get a job and we can work together,' she said. 'You can join us lady footballers. It's a right lark.'

'Lady footballers?' Clover choked a disbelieving laugh.

'There's little men's football any more now they're closing up the clubs. So some of us girls at Gudgeon's are forming a team. We're not the only place to do it; other factories have ladies' teams as well. Mr Ryan – he's our boss – watched a ladies fixture up north. He said they didn't take the game very seriously and it ended up being silly. The players were clowning about in fancy dress but it was arranged to raise money for a war charity, so I suppose that's all right.'

Clover approved of that sentiment.

'I've persuaded Freddie Ryan that we could do the same and raise some money for the servicemen. We're filling men's places at the factory benches and doing a proper job; don't see why we can't fill their football boots 'n' all. Most important of all, the spectators might donate more to see a proper game of football with no larking about.'

'Hear, hear . . .' said Clover.

'The northern gels have donated money towards a servicemen's convalescence home.'

'Sounds like a brilliant idea.'

'Mr Ryan played regularly as a professional when he was younger, then semi-professional,' said Jeannie proudly. 'Since the rotten Football Association have closed the grounds until after the war he's keeping his hand in by knocking us lot into shape in his spare time.'

'Johnny's been moaning about no fixtures. Seems mean putting sportsmen out of work to make them enlist,' said Clover.

'Mr Ryan picked me first for the team. He said I looked the type who could kick a ball.' Jeannie giggled. 'He saw me mucking about with some of the lads on me dinner break. One of them fancies me, bless him. He's only sixteen and challenged me to kick a ball up to the top of the fire escape. I agreed to go out with him if he won.' She shrugged. 'Neither of us managed it in the end but I let him take me to the caff for a cup of tea.' She sprang up and started demonstrating some training moves while explaining, 'Me and a few other girls go over the park and practice what Freddie showed us: star jumps and dodging about obstacles.' Jeannie sank back onto the mattress. 'We've enough volunteers now to have a five-a-side match. Our side lost against the day shift, and I haven't let the gel who booted me in the shin forget that I owe her one.'

'I'll come 'n' cheer you on if you play another game.'

'No good sitting on the sidelines, Clover Cooper. If you get a job at Gudgeon's, we need you in the team,' said Jeannie. 'I know you can run fast cos I've seen you chase Johnny up the road.' As an afterthought she added, 'You should mention during your interview that you're nippy on your pins and play football. If Freddie thinks you'll be an asset to the team, it'll give you an advantage.'

'All I need's a good wage for now,' said Clover, rather wistfully. She'd like time to herself but even when in good health her mother relied on her to help out with the twins. 'This Freddie Ryan ... he's a friendly sort is he then?' Clover had noticed her friend spoke of her boss in a familiar way.

Jeannie nodded and sat beside Clover to share the eiderdown with her. She draped it around them both as a blast of icy air infiltrated the window, rattling the sash and billowing the curtain at them. 'Gets chilly up here in the evening . . . be Christmas before we know it.'

'Better get used to the cold if you're intending to charge around in your bloomers on a football pitch,' ribbed Clover, sending them both into fits of giggles.

'Knickers, is the accepted term for kit, I'll have you know,' said Jeannie, starting them off howling again.

It felt good to release the tension of a horrible day and Clover laughed until she was wiping tears away on the back of her hand.

'Now what's so funny? Or perhaps it's best I don't know.' Mrs Swift backed into the room, bearing a tray. 'I've brought you both a cup of Ovaltine. I know you're in a rush, Clover, but won't take two ticks to get this down you. You'll need a warm-up before your walk home. That fog's really coming down.' She put the tray onto the bedside stand then peered at her daughter as Jeannie wiped mirthful tears from her eyes, smearing her complexion with a residue of black make-up. 'That doesn't suit you, Jeannie. Only trollops paint their faces.'

'Marie Lloyd will be pleased . . .' said Jeannie.

'No need to be sarcastic, dear. She's on the stage. A clear complexion is all a nice girl needs . . .' She broke off at the sound of bangs and thumps coming from the adjacent bedroom, accompanied by some whooping. 'The boys are jumping off the beds again. One of these days they'll go straight through the ceiling.'

'Bloody little tykes,' said Jeannie after her mother had gone out. 'Oh, for a place of me own and some peace and quiet.' She shrugged off the cover to hand Clover her drink.

This was peace and quiet to Clover, however noisy it got. She envied her friend her happy parents and her sausage and mash dinners and her Ovaltine at bedtime. The house was filled with warmth, no matter how draughty the room. She picked up her cup and sipped the hot drink.

A different noise drew their attention. The tap came again, making Clover frown. She was sure a pebble had hit the window. Jeannie recognised the sound too. She looked cagey when she twitched the curtain aside to peer down.

'Won't be a tick,' she said, putting down her Ovaltine. 'A bloody nuisance has turned up.'

'Who is it?' Clover was about to take a look but Jeannie made a point of closing the curtain.

'It's only factory business. I know what she wants and will soon send her packing.'

After Jeannie had gone, curiosity got the better of Clover. She moved the curtain and peeked down. The fog made it difficult to see much but she could make out the crown of a woman's hat and a finger being pointed aggressively at Jeannie. Clover could also hear slightly raised voices, but their conversation was indistinct. Jeannie glanced up at the window and Clover quickly withdrew, not wanting to be seen spying.

A few minutes later, Jeannie was back, rubbing her cold palms together. She pounced on her warm drink and guzzled it all down.

'Everything all right, is it?' enquired Clover. She could tell Jeannie was still brooding on whatever had been said.

'Yeah ... soon got rid of her, the troublemaker.'

'Is she the one who plays dirty and kicked you in the shin?' asked Clover, feeling indignant on her friend's behalf.

'Two can play dirty,' muttered Jeannie. 'Now about this job at Gudgeon's . . .' She changed the subject. 'I know you need a regular pay packet but factory work can be quite a shock at first to somebody used to a nice quiet job. It's dirty and the noise can send you mad. Might be best if you had a go at getting your old job back first, Clo.'

'Don't think I stand a chance of that; anyway, if you can do it, so can I.'

Jeannie hadn't meant to sound patronising. She'd known Clover Cooper since they were at school and had seen the younger girl take no nonsense from any playground bullies. But they weren't kids now; she'd seen women cut tips of fingers off on clattering machines. She only had her friend's best interest at heart. 'Does Nettie know you got the sack today?'

Clover shrugged and sipped Ovaltine. 'They might have told her when she got back from college, I suppose.'

'She should put in a word for you with her parents. You are supposed to be pals, after all . . .' Jeannie fell quiet.

'Why did you say it like that?'

Jeannie placed her empty cup on the tray then leaned forward and took Clover's hand. 'You two might have a falling-out soon.' She paused. 'Wasn't sure whether to tell you this, but, here goes, cos friends shouldn't do the dirty on one another.'

'Got an answer for me then, have you, Clover Cooper?'

Archie Fletcher emerged from the fog and spoke to her as she turned into her road. He'd been on her mind long before materialising at her side and startling a gasp from her. Knowing he'd been hanging around close to her home increased the thumping of her heart. If her father discovered she'd told a lie about boys being after her, she'd be for it, and so would Archie.

'You've not knocked at me door, have you?'

He shook his head. 'I heard on the grapevine your old man was back on leave. Don't worry, I'll steer clear while he's home.'

'If you didn't knock, how d'you know I'd gone out then?' Clover didn't think that Archie prowling about in her road was steering clear, and she wasn't convinced that trouble wasn't brewing.

'Old girl was sweeping her path ...' He jerked a nod to Mrs Waverley's house. 'She said she'd seen you go off about an hour ago. In and out all day with the little 'uns she said you was. Not been at work then?'

'No, Mum's ill. You'd better shove off. Dad's gone to the Rose and Crown and might already be on his way back.'

'I was in there meself earlier and saw him half-cut, propping up the bar. He ain't on his way back yet ... he's well occupied.'

Clover was aware of a sneer in Archie's chuckle. Loyally she stood up for her father despite the depressing news that he'd be reeling in later. 'All the Tommies back on leave deserve a welcome home drink after what they've been through.'

'Yeah ... s'pose they do ...' Archie sounded apologetic and took her wrist to draw her into the misty shadows with him. 'What's up?' He sounded puzzled when she pulled away.

'You asked me for an answer and I've got it for you. I don't want to go to the pictures with you on Saturday. And

I don't want to see you any more either.' She tried to pass him but he stretched out an arm, leaning on brickwork to block her in.

'Why's that?'

'You've been seen up an alley, kissing Nettie Randall. You're not two-timing me with her, Archie Fletcher.'

'Who told you that load o' rubbish?'

'Doesn't matter. It's true, isn't it?'

There followed a pause and she knew he was considering whether to lie and say it wasn't.

'Ain't my fault she likes me, Clover. I was trying to tell her I'm not interested cos I'm with you.' He stroked her cheek but Clover jerked away from his fingers.

'Didn't try very hard, did you, if you were kissing her?'

'I was only thinking of you, you know ... being nice to her. I was worried you'd lose your job at the drapery if I upset her. She's the sort could turn jealous and get you sacked.'

'She wouldn't do that. But I reckon you'd encourage girls to chase after you. So you're not my sort, Archie Fletcher.'

'That's nice thanks for trying to help you keep your job.'

Clover snorted a sour laugh. 'Too late for that. I've already lost it. And actually it's a blessing in disguise cos I'm applying for a better job at Gudgeon's munitions factory.'

'So it's Jeannie Swift stirring up trouble, is it?' He nodded his head. 'Might've known. She was always at it when we was at school together.'

Clover knew they had been classmates. Jeannie had said even at fourteen Archie Fletcher had been popular with the girls. His good looks and easy charm had attracted Clover too and at eighteen he seemed more sophisticated than boys her age. He always had a pocket full of cash and splashed out on treats when he took her out. She'd felt special. But the gloss had gone off his generosity, and his fair hair and blue eyes.

Jeannie had tried to warn her about his roving eye before. Clover hadn't listened, believing what he said about her being the girl for him. Jeannie didn't make up stories or make mistakes, though. She had looked sorry for bringing this into the open. Clover had felt wounded and foolish until her pride had come to her rescue. Now she felt angry as well. The man she'd daydreamed of marrying one day had admitted kissing her friend. Worse still, he'd come out with a pathetic excuse, killing her feeble hope for a plausible explanation.

Nettie Randall, she realised, was more important to her than Archie Fletcher. She wasn't going to fall out with her, especially not now their relationship had altered. Only Clover knew why that was though.

They shared a little brother, and whether the baby survived or not, in Clover's eyes that made them almost sisters. And she'd never fight over a boy with her sister.

'If Nettie wants you she can have you, but I reckon she'll see through you 'n' all.'

Archie stepped up to her and kissed her hard on the lips. Clover pushed him off and let fly with a slap for good measure. 'And don't come back here looking for me cos cheats make me sick.' She rushed past him and started down the road.

'That's why your mother's ill, is it, Miss Prim?' he jeered, rubbing his stinging cheek.

Clover hurried on with her face burning and tears blurring her vision. She fought an urge to dash back and ask him what he thought he meant by that. She feared she knew. Somehow it had already got out that her mother was unfaithful. The idea of the miscarriage being gossiped over as well made her groan.

She stopped and found her handkerchief to scrub at her eyes before glancing over a shoulder. There was no sign or sound of Archie. His speedy disappearance was bitter sweet. It told her more about him than Jeannie had. If he'd sincerely felt something for her he'd have tried harder to woo her back.

But he had told her something useful: her father wasn't home yet. If he had some money left Sidney Cooper would stay in the pub until he was chucked out at closing time. She had a few spare minutes to compose herself. Her mother might not notice she was upset but her grandmother was sure to.

Clover crossed the road and carried on towards the park. The gates were locked at this time of night and she wouldn't go in there anyway after dark. Tramps did . . . they pushed through the gaps in the railings to sleep on the benches. Her mother had warned her and Johnny to go round the other way when coming home during the early dusks of the winter months.

Clover walked on, struggling to convince herself that Archie's spite was meaningless, and the calamity at home too new to already be doing the rounds.

The street appeared empty and she couldn't hear the footsteps of anybody about to emerge from the mist. The whispering was in her head, she told herself. A gruff chuckle reached her ears, and she no longer believed her mind was playing tricks on her. She stopped to peer through the window of the greengrocer's shop she was passing. There was no sign of life nor a light in its murky interior. Feeling unsettled, she started to head back home.

Another rumble of low, secretive voices pulled her up. Clover hurried back to peer into the greengrocer's yard through the closed iron gate. She could see an outline of a two-wheeled cart, handles angled upwards. Beyond was a tower of pallets that didn't quite go high enough to conceal two people. Clover kept squinting into the gloom until the shifting mist again revealed the couple by the wall. All she could see of them were their heads and shoulders, their bodies were behind the boxes. But her father's bushy dark hair was silhouetted by the gas lamp bracketed on brickwork. The greengrocer's wife was about the same age and size as Clover's grandmother. So it wasn't her he was with.

This woman was short enough to need to stretch up to place her arms about his neck. Their faces became level and Clover realised he'd lifted her up, then the fog hid them once more. But their grunts remained audible.

Clover stumbled backwards then turned and dashed towards home.

Chapter Seven

The remaining clothes peg gripped in Elsie's teeth was all that prevented them chattering from the cold. She quickly removed it and jammed it onto the loose edge of the wet sheet. She'd been unaware she was being watched until she heard a disembodied voice.

'Are you taking in washing to pull in a bit extra?'

'No, I ain't. Just got behind with some chores, if you must know.' She'd not needed to turn around to locate the fellow in the hazy darkness; she knew he'd be standing on his side of the fence, arms crossed. A smile had crept across her face and she'd warmed up simply from hearing his familiar wry tone.

'That's a shame, love. Thought you must be on overtime rates or summat, slogging away at this time o' night. If you was, I'd give you a hand for a small consideration. You dunk 'n' I'll mangle.' Bill Lewis planted a hand on the frost-rimed fence, and chuckled. 'I could do with a little earner. Dratted coal bill's doubled in price and needs settling.'

'You daft sod.' Elsie chafed her perished fingers against her pinafore to get the blood flowing. He was teasing her, but if she asked him to mangle a sheet he would. Bill

Lewis didn't take the view that helping out with house-work made him less of a man. Her husband had been the same sort of character, willing to pitch in. Her son-in-law on the other hand was a lazy parasite at home. He'd chosen to join his younger pals going to the recruiting office despite men with families not being expected to serve. Sidney Cooper had always preferred their company to that of his wife and kids and liked burnishing his Jack the Lad image. Before he shipped out in the autumn of 1914 he'd strutted around in khaki, inviting pats on the back. In Elsie's opinion, he wasn't looking so full of him-self after being in the trenches. He seemed glad to be back on home soil.

'So why ain't you at work?' Bill's bristly chin remained hunched into his turned-up coat collar as he spoke. 'Thought you was on nights at the factory, this week. But then ain't seen so much of you lately . . .' His tone invited a comment.

'Been busy. Didn't get back in time to clock on at the fac-tory. Me daughter's been under the weather and in need of another pair of hands.' Elsie picked up the empty laundry basket and wedged it under her arm. She stepped closer so they could properly see one another over the fence. Bill Lewis was one of the few people she didn't mind knowing her business. Skeletons might sneak out of their respective cupboards when they sat reminiscing, drink in hand, but they'd kept confidences. Opening up about the illegiti-mate baby, even to a trusted friend, would be a step too far, though.

'Glad to hear you're back on better terms with Iris.' He patted her cold hand, then held it in his. 'You've had a good day, Elsie, all things considered.'

'P'raps yer right,' said Elsie. 'Her husband's come back on leave, so I'll be on the sidelines until he's gone.' She didn't need to say more; Bill knew the character of the man from working with Sidney Cooper on the docks. Elsie stamped her numb feet on the path and reluctantly withdrew her fingers from their warm nest. 'Right, I'm off inside before I catch me death.'

'Fancy a nightcap to warm you up? I've got half a bottle of port staring me out.'

'Can't have that then,' said Elsie. 'I'll come over ... help you get rid of it.'

'You do know that sheet's gonna be just as wet and stiff as a board in the morning, don't yer.'

'Yeah ... just the damn thing was staring me out. Glad to get it out of me way,' she said. 'I'll finish up here then be over in a little while fer that drink.'

Inside Elsie's back door there was a communal sink and a tin bowl. The water she'd washed the bloodied sheet in glittered black beneath the mean flicker of an oil lamp standing on the draining board. She opened the door again and threw the contents of the bowl onto the garden then, picking up the lamp, she let herself into her lodging. She sank down onto the chair that, unbeknown to her, her granddaughter had settled into hours earlier when troubled by thoughts of family.

Elsie was pondering on the future though, not the here and now. Iris and the infant boy, with luck, should quickly get stronger and live their lives in ignorance of one another. There was no other way if a disaster were to be averted. Clover ... poor kid ... was burdened with what she knew but in time today's upset would fade. She'd get a husband and children and new worries to blur the old. Maybe a daughter would go against her mother's teaching and choose a boyfriend unwisely, and the wheel would turn.

Elsie pushed herself upright with a sigh. She didn't feel like socialising but Bill Lewis was her best pal. He had lived next door almost as long as she'd been in her lodging, and had lost his wife to cancer two years after she lost her husband to pneumonia. They had all got on; Elsie was particular about friends but had liked his wife, Sarah, and lent her knitting needles and cups of sugar or milk when needed. The girl had scrupulously returned everything, with thanks and something on top. Elsie's late husband and Bill would go to the football at the weekend and stop off for a pint on the way home. Despite the age difference they'd had common interests and had been lucky in being neighbours during those years.

'There's something I've been wanting to speak to you about, Elsie.' Bill put down his drink on the hearth by a smouldering coal fire. He came over to perch on the arm of her chair and rested a warm hand on her shoulder.

'Well, thank Gawd you're not down on one knee.' Elsie had a feeling she knew where this was going and would rather dodge him light-heartedly. Over a few months she had noticed that his glances had become twinkly and his casual touches more frequent.

'I'm still gonna say it cos I can take whatever you throw back at me. We rub along nicely, and have done for years, can't deny it. How about we move in together? Don't have to stick around here if you'd rather not give 'em all a reason to chinwag. We could up sticks and find a new place . . . leave them lovable ghosts of ours here in peace.' He glanced around, smiling at the memory of his wife. Sarah would sit in the chair Elsie was occupying and crochet while he told her how his day on the docks had gone. 'Plus sharing bills would save us a few bob,' he ended on a pragmatic note.

Elsie raised her hand to squeeze his fingers, splayed on her shoulder. 'Best to stop you there, love,' she said. 'I appreciate us being friends, and would hate to spoil what we've already got.'

'We could have more, living as man and wife. Don't have to sign on the dotted line if you don't want to.' Bill sank down to sit on the floor by her chair with his knees drawn up and his elbows resting on them. He picked up his port and took a sip then rotated the glass between his palms.

Elsie studied him in profile; he was a rugged, well-built fellow. The rolled-up sleeves of his shirt revealed muscular forearms and his greying hair and strong jawline was burnt orange by the coals. A lot of widows would be very happy to have him propose to them. And she was woman enough to feel flattered that he wanted her.

'I'm older than you, Bill.'

'So what. Ain't by that much . . .' He turned to face her.

'Ten years . . .'

'Ain't a lot.' He snorted.

'It is for a man who's not yet got any kids. You could pick up with a younger woman, able to give you a family. I won't do that.' She paused. 'I'm fifty-two next birthday and done with childrearing. I've got me grandkids now and trouble enough as it is.'

'Sarah was a few years older 'n' me. When a baby didn't come along straight away it wasn't a problem. Neither of us had a big hankering for a family.'

'You didn't have much chance to find out if you'd change yer mind, though, married just four years,' Elsie gently pointed out. 'Once you'd got your home straight, you might've turned your thoughts to sons and daughters to mess things up and make yer life a misery.' She patted his shoulder in a mocking way.

'Sarah was me real big love but I wasn't bothered then and can't see me fretting about it now she's gone.'

'Don't say that; you're a good-looking fellow, in your prime still. You should settle down again with a young wife. You'd make a smashing father.' She rubbed his cheek with the back of her finger. 'Your Sarah used to tell me she'd had three proposals . . . not one of 'em from you. She chose you though so asked you outright to marry her. She was a good strong gel and it's a crying shame you lost her too soon.'

He nodded his bowed head in agreement. 'It is; but I'm still here and she ain't, so got to live me life without her.' He smiled nostalgically. 'True, that is, she did propose.'

'There you are then. Your turn to do the deed second time round. And not with me,' she spluttered, as a glint appeared in his eye. She knew she had to either step up or let him go. She'd had a good marriage for almost twenty-one years, but now had her independence and a well-paid job as a munitionette. Elsie had got used to coming and going as she pleased. She did love Bill in her own way, but the mundanity and proximity of married life could stifle that, leaving them both with regrets.

'I'd make you a good husband, Elsie,' he said.

'Know you would. But I'd not make you a good wife. And I'd sooner we carried on as we are, having a nice meal and a drink from time to time.' She paused. ''Course, I'd understand if that comes to an end once you find a proper girlfriend who wants you to herself. Ain't so ancient that I don't recall there's more to keeping company with a fellow than sharing his port.' She pushed his shoulder, making him smile. 'You've been a long time grieving over Sarah, and we've bored each other silly talking about good times had with our other halves. Could be it's time to move on . . . make new memories . . .' She got up and put the empty glass on the parlour table. 'Now I'm ready for some shut-eye. Promised to meet me granddaughter tomorrow and take the little 'uns to the park. Get them out of Sid's way for a while. He's not got the patience for having toddlers around.'

'I reckon our other halves would approve of you 'n' me filling the gaps they left.' Bill levered himself upright and took her hands in his. He leaned forward and placed his lips on hers. Not a proper kiss but enough to let her know there was more on his mind where she was concerned than practicalities. 'Reckon I've fallen for you, Elsie. So, think about it, will you?'

'No, love . . . I'm gonna forget it now 'cos it's the right thing to do. For both of us.'

When Clover returned from visiting Jeannie Swift last night, Elsie had arranged for them to meet up in the lane bright and early this morning. She'd done what she could for Iris for now, and intended to avoid Sidney Cooper. He could start an argument in an empty room and Elsie wasn't skilled at keeping the peace at any cost. Then Iris and the kids would suffer for her temper. Elsie could still help out by occupying the toddlers for some of the day. Clover was between jobs and could also pitch in while her mother gained her strength.

'How's things at home this morning?' Elsie took over pushing the pram containing the toddlers as they proceeded towards the park.

'Mum was up early to make breakfast.' Clover had tried to make eye contact with her mother but Iris hadn't seemed to want to. Not that it would have been the right moment to bring up that overheard conversation about her own start in life. Her mother had looked utterly sad and defeated. Clover guessed Iris was yearning for her little boy. Knowledge of his existence burned Clover's insides but she'd have to bear it. It had to remain a secret, perhaps forever.

'What time did your father roll in from the pub?'

'Only a little while after you went off home, Nan. He just flaked out on the settee and stayed there all night. He's still there. I got the girls dressed and after they had some breakfast, brought them out before they woke him up. Johnny's gone to school. So it's just Mum 'n' Dad at home.'

'Mmmm ...' rumbled a thoughtful Elsie. She raised a hand to Mrs Waverley, darting out to collect her milk off the step. 'Knew she'd put herself in our way. She's itching to find out what's gone on so might as well give her our version or she'll make up her own.'

'I'll carry on to the park.' Clover wasn't going through the farce over and over again. She found it depressing, and wasn't sure she was a convincing liar anyway.

Elsie strolled towards the neighbour while Clover took over pushing the pram, and dwelling on a person who was a convincing liar. Archie Fletcher had fooled her. She'd let him kiss and caress her in the belief he meant what he said about them settling down together when she was older.

Perhaps she was being naive about love and marriage. Her mother and father were both unfaithful; Mr Randall cheated on his wife. Perhaps a lot of couples were stranded with the wrong people after mistaking infatuation for love.

Then they just had to put up with the misery of it. Not her. She'd sooner stay a spinster. She'd work hard and get herself a nice home and live alone or with an unmarried friend, rather than endure a cold sham of a marriage.

At first she'd felt sorry for her father. She'd believed he was the wronged party, and entitled to be bitter from knowing his wife didn't want him. The theory had given her a better understanding of why he seemed angry all the time. Until she saw him with that woman.

The night through she'd been turning things over in her mind while the noise of Johnny's snoring rattled in her head. She'd realised what Archie meant when he shouted out that final insult before disappearing. He'd known her father was with a woman, and that was making her mother feel sick. And if Archie Fletcher knew Sidney Cooper had a fancy woman, he probably wasn't the only one.

'Could jaw the hind leg of a donkey, that one,' said Elsie. She'd marched up behind Clover, who'd entered the park and started perambulating over crisp fallen leaves. Elsie indicated the bench they were approaching, and stopped by it. She used a gloved hand to sweep the russet-coloured foliage off the seat before plonking down her bag and sitting next to it. 'Better day than I thought it'd be after last night's fog.'

'There was a bad frost when I got up,' said Clover, settling beside her nan. 'The inside of the bedroom window was covered in ice so I got dressed in bed.' She'd wriggled beneath the covers, rolling on her stockings and pulling on her skirt and blouse while her breath puffed clouds into the air.

'Can't grumble at nice sunny days like this when it's

nearly November. It'll draw in early though ...' The quiet lengthened and Elsie slanted a look at her granddaughter's profile.

Clover's dropped chin almost touched her chest and she'd kept a hand on the pram, rocking it to keep her sisters quiet. The little girls looked adorably pretty, dressed in lemon matching sets of knitted bonnets and jackets. But they were starting to get restless and have a tug of war over their rag doll.

'I left the baby wrapped in the pram blanket on the convent step. Mum'll ask where it is.'

'Well, you left it at mine, didn't you?' soothed Elsie. 'You can leave all of those little details to me to explain.' She'd been anticipating her granddaughter returning to this. The girl was going to be like a dog with a bone about her half-brother. Elsie wouldn't ever forget about him either; but she had accepted that nothing could be done. There'd be no fairy-tale ending to this story.

'I could just go and ask the sisters how he is—' Clover started.

'You can't,' Elsie immediately interrupted. 'If you show your face they'll tell the coppers the foundling's mother's turned up. Nobody wants their sort sniffing around Silvertown, asking after a girl with your description.'

It certainly hadn't occurred to Clover that she might be deemed to have given birth to him. But she knew girls of her age – and younger – got knocked up, as Jeannie called it. A classmate had grown a belly at thirteen and been taken out of school.

'I'll wait till Dad's gone back then think of a story before I go and speak to the nuns.' Clover was desperate to have her nan's support in this, despite the pitfalls.

'You won't. Listen to me, Clover, the poor little mite isn't strong and might not make it. Raising your mum's hopes could be the cruellest thing of all. She's still not right. She's had a bad time of it, up here, too ...' Elsie tapped her head. 'When she seems more herself, I'll tell her what's gone on and then it's her decision to make, not yours.'

'I know ...' Clover whispered, feeling put in her place.

'Now buck up.' Elsie nudged her granddaughter. 'You've got a job to find, young lady. Have you any ideas where to start?'

'Me 'n' Jeannie spoke about factory work yesterday.'

'Well ... factory work's not always pleasant, certainly not as nice as the shop work you've been used to. But it can be better paid and something different could be what you need. Biscuit factory and jam factory are taking on. But make sure you pick up your wages from the Randalls. They owe you a reference as well. If you don't want to face them and ask for it, I will. Sooner it's done, the better. I could go this afternoon ...'

'It's all right ... I'll see to it. I'm going to apply at Jeannie's factory. We spoke about it last night and she reckons I've got a chance if I say I like playing football.'

'One of me friends at the Women's Institute was talking about factories starting up ladies' teams. Jeannie's given you shrewd advice.' Elsie chuckled. 'I like Jeannie Swift; got her head screwed on, that one.'

'The football coach is her boss, and we might arrange a charity match to raise funds for the injured servicemen.'

'Our committee will find a home for donations. The Red Cross people are always coming by, rattling a tin for the Voluntary Aid Detachment.'

'I will tell him that if I get me job.' Clover smiled. Her nan was never backward in coming forward. They sat quietly for a while then she said, 'If I don't get taken on there, would your factory offer me a job, d'you think? I'm a hard worker, Nan.'

'Know you are, love. I wouldn't want you working there, though.' Elsie pursed her lips. 'I've been a factory hand at Brunner Mond since just after your granddad died. Back then it was different. We was all about making caustic soda not bombs. When we started purifying TNT for munitions the work got nasty.' She tapped her sallow-skinned cheek. 'You're too young and pretty to end up looking like this. I could do with a change myself but I'd feel bad about packing it in when every day we're told we need more production, not less. We've all got to do our bit to get this war won.' Elsie chucked her under the chin. 'Let's brighten up. You stick to Jeannie's idea and play a bit of football. I'll come 'n' watch . . . bring me whistle.' Elsie dropped a wink. 'Blow it to give your lot an advantage.'

'You can't do that, Nan,' Clover burst out laughing. 'You'll get us chucked off the pitch.'

'Stick out me leg on the sly then and trip 'em up when they run down the line.' Elsie blinked up at the blue sky with an expression of wide-eyed innocence while shooting out a booted foot.

Clover guffawed and the children clapped hands and joined in giggling and bouncing in the pram.

'Good to see you looking cheerier, love,' said Elsie and leaned in to peck Clover's rosy cheek. 'Come on . . .' She got up. 'Let's go and find a caff. I'll treat you to a cup of tea and a currant bun. Yeah . . . you little monkeys heard, didn't you?' Double handed she ruffled the twins' soft locks as their excited bouncing increased. 'Only half a bun each though or you'll be sick.'

They set off at a slow pace for the park gates. 'Make sure you wear shin pads,' said Elsie, turning the pram into the street. 'Don't want no broken legs to top it all.'

Chapter Eight

'Where you off to, love?'

'Nowhere. Going up the shops. Nothing in the house for tea.' Startled, Iris babbled a reply. Seconds later, she was evading her husband who'd padded up behind her in his pants and vest, and was trying to catch hold of her.

After the kids had gone out she'd washed up the breakfast things then intended to make herself scarce, fearing this might happen. She'd checked Sidney was still curled up towards the back of the settee, before stealthily picking up her coat and bag. He'd been keeping a sly eye on her all along, though, while pretending to be asleep. He'd slipped out of his shirt and trousers and she'd not been aware of him doing that either while her back was turned.

'Get the groceries later, eh?' His forearm encircled her waist, drawing her away from the door and against his sinewy body. 'Kids are off our hands for a while so let's get cosy. Not even had a kiss off me wife in months ...'

She could feel his unshaven chin on her neck and his morning erection poking into her hip. The smell of stale alcohol seeping from his pores was mixed with that of a woman. She reckoned she knew who he'd been with last night. 'Can't do it with you, Sid. Sorry, but me guts are still aching.' She pulled herself free. 'Perhaps in a few days I'll be up to it ...'

She wasn't bothered about him playing around ... it'd be a bit rich if she was, all things considered. She was relieved that he'd met up with Lucy Dare and left her alone. Not that Iris had got much rest. With a twin daughter sleeping either side of her she'd nevertheless remained vigilant in case he sobered up on the settee and tried to squeeze into their bed. The girls' presence wouldn't put him off; she'd tried the ploy before when dog-tired and desperate for sleep. He'd put the twins in their cot, careless of their whimpers at being disturbed.

'Wrong time of the month for me, Sid.' He'd grabbed her again, his beery breath clouding her face and making her recoil. 'Don't want to make a mess in the bed.'

'Never mind about that. I'll help you change the sheet afterwards,' he said, squeezing her buttocks.

'Clover'll be back any moment with the twins,' insisted Iris, clinging to the hope it was so. She was bleeding sporadically from the miscarriage and her womb was unbearably tender. 'They've been gone ages and only went for some air ...'

'Better not waste time then, eh?' He chuckled low in his throat.

She shoved him, and caught off guard, he staggered back several paces. The backs of his calves bashed the settee and he collapsed with a grunt onto a deflated cushion. She gazed at him, sitting there in his underclothes, unshaven and unwashed, and felt pity as well as disgust for the man she'd married.

He'd hit her more times than she could remember, and

95

taken her rent money, leaving them hiding from the land-lord on a Monday. Yet somewhere in that crumpled man was the youth who'd fleetingly overwhelmed her reason. She knew he regretted that uncontrolled passion too. He could have had a happier life just as she could've. But for one mistake – one time when they'd thought they wanted one another – they'd have settled down with the people who suited them.

Lucy Dare was made for him; at the age of seventeen she'd had lots of admirers and was rumoured to be a good-time girl. She certainly was on the game now and didn't give a damn who knew it. She'd never married, or had children as far as Iris was aware. But she knew her husband had never outgrown Lucy.

'Going out shopping, eh?' Sidney sounded sarcastic. 'Randall's drapery on the list of places to go, is it? You've been seeing him, haven't yer?' He sprang up and lunged at her, dragging her by the arm. 'You think I don't know why his missus come here yesterday in a paddy? She was here to warn you off, not fire Clover.'

'Clover has been fired.' Iris wrenched herself out of his grip. 'She wants a factory job. Better pay. She told you about it.'

He snatched his trousers from the back of the settee and shook them in readiness to pull them on. 'I'll sort this out with Randall; should've done it yesterday.'

'No ... don't. You'll make everything worse for Clover.' Iris spread her hands in supplication. 'Don't take it out on her. Your daughter won't get a reference, Sid, if you go round there shouting the odds.'

He dropped the trousers with a curse. 'You're right. Shopping can wait, and so can Randall ... fer now.' He yanked Iris's coat off her shoulders and tossed it to land on the floor next to his trousers. 'Get in the bedroom. I'm yer husband, and got rights, whether you like it or not.'

Elsie had left her granddaughters in the café to go and apologise for not clocking on at the factory yesterday. Before setting off for the bus stop, she'd left a sixpence on the table next to the filled teapot, and told Clover to put the coin in her pocket. She reluctantly did, with thanks. Another pot of tea and a tanner was little enough compensation for what the girl had gone through. The money might provide an outing with a friend for some light relief. Not Archie Fletcher, though, she hoped; Iris could be on to something saying she didn't want him hanging around. When on her way home last night Elsie had seen him strutting along, smoking, as though he was cock of the walk. Another fellow was on her mind too and soon put paid to thoughts of Archie.

For weeks she'd sensed something was different between her and Bill Lewis. At first she'd brushed it off as her imagination. She'd racked her brains for a memory of having unwittingly encouraged him to think she was after more than friendship and had avoided him. She'd missed him though, so had agreed to that drink. After the day she'd had yesterday, his had been the shoulder she'd wanted to cry on . . . but she hadn't. Her troubles were too raw and too shocking to be spoken of even to her best friend.

She'd told him she'd not give the matter of them becoming a couple any more thought, yet here she was doing just that. She felt like an excited teenager, not a widow with grey in her hair and a pocket handkerchief, snotty from wiping her grandchildren's noses.

Girls like Clover had a right to thrills and fancies and thoughts of boyfriends. She didn't. Not at her age. Not when she sincerely believed Bill needed a young wife to grow old with and sons and daughters to cherish. A decade from now she might be burdened with his regrets, and he might be burdened with her decline.

She'd certainly felt her age when she'd got home from Iris's yesterday. Though exhausted she'd not slept well even with Bill's port lulling her. And from the look of Clover this morning her granddaughter hadn't got any rest either.

Elsie got on the bus and found a seat. Banning every bloody man from entering her head, she concentrated on concocting some sweet talk for her supervisor to ensure she kept her well paid night shifts at Brunner Mond.

Clover was thinking of Archie, specifically about whether he would apologise and try to win her back. After his churlish parting shot she guessed he'd simply drift away as though their budding romance had never been. Having seen him in his true colours, it would be for the best. Nonetheless, she felt humiliated that she couldn't keep her first boyfriend interested for longer than a few weeks.

The twins were still seated in the pram, contentedly chewing on crusts of currant bun. She poured herself fresh tea then settled back, closing her eyes against mellow autumn sun streaming through the windowpane and warming her face. A rat-a-tat on the glass jerked her to attention and she saw Jeannie grinning at her. Clover beckoned, indicating there was a drink going begging by pointing at the pot.

'Blimey, you seemed out for the count,' said Jeannie, flopping into the chair. 'Catching flies, you was.'

'Didn't get much sleep,' said Clover, bashful at being caught snoozing unawares.

'Ain't surprised, what with everything going on,' said Jeannie darkly. 'Are you going to have it out with Nettie or with Archie?' She poured tea into Elsie's used cup and added sugar, rattling the spoon to and fro against china. 'I'd have something choice to say to the pair of them.'

'Don't go interfering; I can fight me own battles, Jeannie.'

'Know you can ... just sayin' ...' Jeannie didn't take offence at the slap down and drank her tea.

Clover wanted to give her meeting with Archie more thought before telling Jeannie about it. She didn't want him back, she told herself, but she didn't want him to have the last word either. And she was curious about the identity of the woman she'd seen with her father. She suspected Archie might know her.

'Stuck with the terrors again, eh?' Jeannie rolled her eyes at the noisy toddlers. Annie had finished her piece of bun and was trying to snatch Rosie's, resulting in fisticuffs.

'They were being good a moment ago; reckon they're showing off for your benefit.' Clover gave Annie a sip of her tea to pacify her.

'Can't stop long,' said Jeannie, draining her cup. 'Me sister's coming over with her baby. Dad's been away fighting for so long he's not seen his first grandkid yet.' Jeannie gave the table a little drum roll to get her friend's attention. 'But the best news is that this morning I went to the factory to see how the land lies on vacancies. The outcome was that me good friend, who's a natural at playing football, has got an interview with my Mr Ryan.' Jeannie pulled a folded paper from her pocket and with a flourish pushed it towards Clover. 'That's the application form to fill in and

99

there's a date and time on it for you take it back with your reference.' Jeannie sniffed. 'One thing though ... he said he'd like you to have a run out over the park. I'll come as well. Don't mind hanging around one bit.'

Clover didn't know whether to whoop or groan at the news she'd have to pass a trial. She did know Jeannie had done her a huge favour and she felt guilty for snapping just now. 'Thanks ever so much.' She leaned across the table to squeeze her friend's hands. 'Just not sure about a run out ...'

'We've got time to train in the park,' said Jeannie, reading her friend's panic. 'Bring Johnny along, if you like, and his pals. We'll get some practice tackling.' She broke off to wave through the caff window at a soldier. He winked and touched a finger to his cap brim, giving Clover a lengthy stare as he passed by. 'Didn't know he was back on leave.'

'Who is he?' Clover glanced over her shoulder at him, meeting his eyes again as he was looking back. She blushed and turned away but not before she'd seen him smile.

'Freddie Ryan's kid brother. Neil's a handsome rogue; Freddie's good looking too. They're not that alike, though, and Neil's too young for my taste.' She sighed. 'But at least he's fancy free.'

Clover thought Neil Ryan was strikingly handsome: tall with hazel eyes and black hair, he was the opposite in looks to Archie Fletcher. The stripe she'd seen on Neil's khaki sleeve she believed made him a lance corporal. 'Is your Mr Ryan married?' She had an uneasy feeling that Jeannie felt more than just admiration for Freddie Ryan's footballing skills. Mooning over a married man was daft; Clover wasn't sure whether to tackle Jeannie over it or keep quiet in case she was barking up the wrong tree.

'He is . . .' Jeannie put an elbow on the table and cupped her cheek in a hand. She seemed about to explain how she felt but instead straightened in her chair. 'Oh . . . look who it is . . .' She struck a finger to her lips. 'Don't forget to button it. Get your reference to take to your interview before telling Nettie Randall what you think of her.'

Clover had also spotted her thunder-faced friend; having spied them seated at the window table Nettie started marching in their direction.

'Dunno what's eating her. She's the one deserves a mouthful.' Jeannie stood up, anticipating trouble.

'I was just on my way round to have it out with you.' Nettie began to speak before the caff door was properly closed behind her. 'Why didn't you come over yourself for your back pay?' She plonked herself down on the chair Jeannie had vacated and pointed an aggressive finger at Clover. 'I didn't agree with you getting the sack, but you've got no right to cause that sort of trouble for us.'

'Get out me chair . . .' Jeannie yanked on Nettie's arm to move her but was shaken off.

'Never thought you'd hide behind family, Clover Cooper, but seems I was mistaken.' Nettie tossed her mousy-coloured curls off a shoulder and jutted her chin.

'My nan's been round, has she?' Clover stood up, buttoning her coat, and let the brake off the pram. She was annoyed and disappointed that Elsie had poked her nose in when she'd agreed not to.

'Your nan?' Nettie barked. 'It's your bloody father causing trouble, as usual. He punched my dad in front of customers in the shop.' She glared at Jeannie, who'd snorted in amusement. 'It's not bloody funny! Mum's gone mad and is threatening to report Sidney Cooper for assault. And

Mrs Waverley was in the shop, so now everybody'll know about it.'

Clover felt she might bring up the bun she'd just eaten. She shook her head to indicate this was all news to her and began backing out of the door with the pram.

Jeannie dropped into Clover's chair and pushed her face close to Nettie's across the table. 'Not her fault what her old man does so leave her alone. Anyhow, you owe Clover an apology after dropping yer drawers for Archie Fletcher when you knew he was already seeing her.'

Nettie gasped and started to speak.

'Don't bother denying it; I saw the two of you in Brewer's Yard. So you'd better make sure that Clover gets her reference, or I'll tell everybody about it, including your mum 'n' dad.' With that, Jeannie swept out and made sure to give Nettie a pointed stare through the window as she passed by on the outside. It was a wasted effort as the girl had turned her back, refusing to meet her eyes. Jeannie could see her red face though and knew she was feeling ashamed of herself. Which was really the most Jeannie could achieve. Nettie couldn't make her parents write a good reference for Clover if they didn't want to. And grassing Nettie up for stealing somebody else's man would make Jeannie a rotten hypocrite. But at least Nettie Randall had been given something to chew on.

Jeannie caught up with Clover along the street and they walked in silence for a while before Jeannie said, 'You'll need a reference to take to the interview or you won't get a job.'

'Got more chance of getting me old job back, than getting a reference now,' said Clover sarcastically, blinking back angry tears. She'd been pinning her hopes on the factory job. It'd seemed the one bright spot in the gloom. She took the application form from her pocket and held it out. 'Won't be needing this. But thanks anyway.'

'Keep it; I'll say you can't make that appointment but would like an interview another time.' Jeannie put a comforting arm about her. 'See how things go, eh? Once your dad ships out things might calm down with the Randalls.'

Clover arrived home to find the place deserted. Her mum's bedroom was as dark and sour smelling as it had been yesterday. The clean sheet had been stripped off, leaving the stained flat mattress on display. She opened the curtain and noticed the washhouse door stood ajar. The twins didn't complain when put in their cot; they snuggled up together, thumbs in mouths. Clover went outside and found her mother stooping to light the copper.

'Got backache, Mum?' Clover had noticed Iris's grimace of pain as she straightened up.

'Mmm ... not feeling properly meself yet.' The blood-stained sheet in the washing basket was gathered up and Iris dumped it into the copper, holding it under the water with the dolly.

'I'll do this. Go inside and rest.' Clover took the detergent-bleached wood from her mother.

'Thanks, love.'

'Where's Dad?' Clover had expected her father to be at home as the pubs weren't yet open.

'Gawd knows.' Iris had left the washhouse and muttered a reply over her shoulder, 'He's out ... so that's good enough.'

'Mum ...' One ominous-sounding word drew Iris back into the shed. Clover hated the idea of worrying her mother about the rumpus, but forewarned was forearmed. 'Nettie just told me Dad started a fight with Mr Randall. They might report him to the police for assault.'

'He just couldn't leave well enough alone, could he?' Iris sighed. 'We won't see your wages if he's got them.' Her aching body and overwhelming problems didn't distract her from practicalities.

Clover felt her temper bubbling in her chest. If her father had been home she would have had it out with him and risked taking the clout it would have earned her. She'd worked long hours for her pay and wanted it. More importantly, Iris was obviously unwell, and he'd not seen his children in ages, yet none of it mattered much to Sidney Cooper. 'I'm going to find him and get my wages.' Clover drove the dolly down on top of the floating cotton, hating her father for his selfishness.

'Just leave him be … please, love … for me. Don't want him coming back in a paddy.'

Clover started to whip up the suds again, cuffing her perspiring brow as the heating water wafted soap-scented steam at her face. She was aware her mother had remained behind her and glanced over her shoulder, sensing they both knew more needed to be said. 'Don't think Dad would've picked a fight over me getting the sack. Or even about me back pay.' Her mother had taken the news of the fight as though it wasn't wholly unexpected. And that had started Clover thinking. 'Has he found out you had a baby with Mr Randall?' she burst out.

Iris yanked shut the washhouse door to keep any beady eyes or flapping ears at bay. 'What's your grandmother said to you?' she hissed.

'Don't blame Nan. I overheard you two talking yesterday about things that went on a long time ago. Things that happened when I was born.'

Iris dropped her chin and remained quiet while her mind picked over that bitter conversation with her mother. 'Well, you've learned no good ever comes of eavesdropping then.'

'Oh, I have . . .'

'Hearing half a story won't do.' Iris tilted up her daughter's chin. 'First thing to say is that I love you, Clover. Your father does too; but finds it hard to show it. We're not perfect, either of us, just two square pegs trying to fit into the round holes life's given us. But we'll carry on muddling through best we can.' They'd always lived hand to mouth yet considered themselves better off than some families. No charity for them, no Salvation Army handouts or queuing at the soup kitchen. But since Sidney quit his employment on the docks to take the king's shilling Iris had felt their security becoming shaky.

'You won't leave him then?' Clover felt emboldened to ask. Her heart wanted her family to stay as it was, but her new-found maturity accepted her parents had already broken some of their shackles.

'Time for fresh starts has passed,' said Iris flatly. 'Perhaps if things had turned out differently yesterday, I'd be braver and chase dreams . . .' She took Clover's face between her palms, rubbing her thumbs on petal-soft skin scattered with pale freckles. 'You make sure you chase yours down and don't let them get away.' She placed a kiss on her daughter's forehead. 'You've grown up while I wasn't looking. And I should've been. I've taken you for granted and that wasn't right either, not when you're so important to me.'

Clover covered her mother's rough-skinned hands with her own and felt a rush of fierce love for her. 'You wanted that little baby, didn't you?' There'd never be a better time to get this off her chest and confess about taking her brother to the nunnery.

'What're you two doing hiding away in here? The nippers are bawling fit to bust. The cot's soaked where one of 'em's had an accident . . .'

Mother and daughter had been deaf and blind to Sidney approaching until the planked door was creaked open, startling them into skittering apart.

'Can see what I'm doing, can't you? I'm washing the sheet you said you'd help me with.' Iris recovered sufficiently to go on the attack and was rewarded with his discomfited look. He didn't like being reminded of forcing himself on her.

'Make us some tea, love.' Sidney gave his daughter's chin a larky bop with his curled fingers. 'Look, brought in some buns for elevenses.' He swung the paper bag he held, and a hint of cinnamon mingled with the smell of Sunlight soap.

His sudden appearance had started Clover's heart thudding, but she wasn't intimidated and she wasn't impressed by his generosity. The buns had probably been bought with her money. He wouldn't have known he'd butted in at completely the wrong time but that didn't stop her feeling even angrier with him. Frustratingly, she'd lost a perfect opportunity to learn more about her start in life and to tell her mother about Gabriel.

Being aware of his existence was a joy and a torture to Clover. She imagined her mother might be equally torn in two by knowing he was alive. Sidney Cooper would never allow another man's child into his family so Iris must be brave and chase her dreams to reclaim him. The baby was safe with people who would care for him. If Iris knew that, it might at least ease her grief and be the tonic she needed to get better.

Clover pushed the washing dolly onto her father, surprising him into taking it. Then, relieving him of the paper bag bulging with warm fragrant buns, she went back to the house to put the kettle on.

Chapter Nine

After trouncing his rival – Randall had gone down with one punch – Sidney believed he was on a roll. Instead of heading straight home, he had gone to the bookies with his daughter's pay in his pocket. Triumphs kept coming: he'd bet on an outsider that romped home, resulting in a profit that was again staked at good odds. That win brought him a small stack of banknotes and many envious looks following him from the betting shop. So had a local tramp; the elderly fellow regularly loitered outside the place in the hope of benefitting from winners' generosity. He was wasting his time hoping for a farthing from Sidney Cooper.

He had presented his daughter with her wages, his elation allowing him to overlook the fact her thanks weren't as fulsome as he would've liked. Sidney had other concerns: like flashing his cash in the pub until last orders, then hogging Lucy Dare's company until the early hours of the morning.

His quest to run through his winnings before returning to France kept him out of his wife's way. In those final days, he'd treated his family to a genial side of himself, and his son to a new football. He never did play a match with Johnny, though. After drinking and fornicating to his heart's content, Sidney would come home to a dark, quiet house and kip on the couch. So Iris got the bed to herself on the nights that were left to them. She also got a week's rent money tipped into the kitty jar and a new apron. She barely glanced at it, but she knew the peace offering wouldn't have come from Randall's drapery. Neither had any complaints, nor a visit from the police, following the rumpus.

Iris hadn't expected any trouble, anyway; Bruce Randall wouldn't want officials unearthing a crime of passion, any more than she would. Wounded pride rather than jealousy had made Sidney Cooper seize an opportunity to attack his wife's heartthrob. She hadn't forgiven him for starting the fight; she'd simply accepted he had a right to be angry, and thanked her lucky stars he didn't know exactly why that was. She'd remained calm, guarded her tongue, and counted off the hours until his leave was over. Finally it was.

'Ready then?' she asked Sidney who was rummaging under the bed. 'You'll miss your train if you don't watch it.'

'Seen my other boot?'

'The twins were trying them on; it's probably in the parlour.' The toddlers had taken a boot each, giggling as they slid the heavy leather an inch before toppling forward.

'Me shaving kit?' he demanded, hobbling back half shod and fiddling with the knotted laces on the other boot.

'I already packed it in the kitbag for you,' said Iris, lifting Annie into the pram.

'Done me summat to eat on the journey, have yer?'

'Got you a meat 'n' potato pie and a custard tart fresh from the bakery when they opened this morning. Packed 'em right on top so they don't get squashed.'

He looked pleasantly surprised to have been treated to more than jam sandwiches. He found something else to carp about. 'Suppose Clover won't be back to see me off.'

'Don't know; the misery probably won't let her have time off,' said Iris. 'So not her fault, is it?'

The tobacconist on the High Street had sacked his book-keeper for incompetence. When Elsie had been buying her cigarettes the fellow had moaned about not having the time to do the accounts himself so the figures tallied to his satisfaction. Elsie had pounced, persuading him to give her granddaughter a week's trial serving behind the counter so he could concentrate on his books. He went for it, and said if the girl proved to be a good worker and provided him with the reference he'd been told she was waiting for, he'd consider making the position permanent.

Iris was grateful her mother had stayed away while Sidney was home. But she owed Elsie her thanks for push-ing a note through the door about Clover's job opportunity. Iris intended to make sure her daughter got her reference and her full-time job.

'What're you doing back home?' Iris grabbed her son's shoulder as he tried to slink past. Johnny had gone off to school at the usual time, but reappeared.

'Me teacher's all right with me taking an hour off to say ta-ta to Dad.'

'Is that so?' Iris's tone and raised eyebrows let him know she wasn't swallowing it. 'Well, now you're here, take charge of your sisters for me while I help your father get the rest of his stuff together.'

Johnny jumped to it, making himself scarce; he'd expected to be sent straight back to school with a flea in his ear for fibbing. He wheeled the pram outside onto the path and ignored Charlie and Bobby Pincher, down the lane, who stopped bouncing a football to jeer at him acting soppy.

No school today for them. The School Board Man hadn't turned up in months to find the absentees. When he did show his face their mother would tell him to sling his hook. But after he'd gone they would be shouted at for bunking off and causing trouble for her. A few weeks of slouching into class would follow, then it would all be forgotten. Out would come the football again, and to keep on her right side, they'd run errands for ha'pennies for those neighbours who would associate with Winnie Pincher's sons.

Johnny carried on rocking the pram and stuck up two fingers as the taunts became louder. He glanced over a shoulder in case his parents had seen him earn himself a clipped ear.

A few minutes later, the little party was on its way up the lane, past the Pincher boys who slung glances at the family but kept quiet. The Coopers were respectable, whereas they knew they weren't. Their eyes remained on the jaunty soldier. They envied Johnny his father. They hadn't seen theirs in ages . . . just a procession of 'uncles' who came and went.

"Bye Sidney; look after yourself,' called Mrs Waverley over a shoulder. The woman was scrubbing her front step. Other housewives were also on their knees in front of open doorways, carrying out the morning ritual, but chose to turn a blind eye. Sidney Cooper wasn't well liked at the best of times; after picking on Bruce Randall – who most folk agreed seemed a nice chap – Sidney had plummeted further in the popularity stakes.

Doris Waverley pulled herself upright with the help of the door frame then shook her hanky at him. 'Glad to see things are all better for you lot then . . .'

Sidney doffed his cap; he wouldn't allow her insinuations to rile him. Neither would Iris. She tilted her chin and slipped a hand through her husband's arm in a show of solidarity.

When they were close to the top of the lane, Clover appeared. She waited for them to reach her, holding a stitch in her side. 'Mr Bailey let me have half an hour off to come with you,' she gasped out. She'd run from the High Street, hoping she'd not missed them. That morning her mother had looked unwell again but had brushed off her daughter's concern, blaming the rushed preparations for Sidney's departure for making her sweat. Clover could see a sheen of moisture still on Iris's complexion despite the cold air.

'So, that's all of us, then.' Sidney grazed his knuckles on Clover's jaw, pleased to have his good-looking wife and kids all around him.

Iris was struggling to keep up with her husband's swaggering pace and let go of his arm to lag behind. She linked arms with her daughter and they continued to walk more slowly behind the menfolk and the pram. Sidney's whistling was interspersed with him singing snatches of risqué songs. He seemed happy enough, but he wasn't. Only Johnny and the twins – who had got used to their father now – were content on this sharp November morning. Clover was shivery, not from cold, but from an inexplicable sense of something sinister lurking.

Sidney Cooper shifted the heavy kitbag on his shoulder and cursed beneath his breath at the prospect of returning to war; he regretted volunteering in the first place. At the start, it had seemed an enjoyable adventure to go overseas with pals, but the reality was lice and dirt and sickness. Or you could be killed, and not nicely. He didn't want to leave

112

Lucy Dare, either. She needed to earn her living and he knew how she'd do it. Nothing new there; she'd been street-walking most of her adult life. But she'd told him that he was special, not like the other men who were unnecessary evils. She was special to him; he didn't take his business elsewhere. French brothels didn't count in his opinion. But much as he liked Lucy he hadn't wanted to see her again this soon.

She'd said she would see him off but he'd believed that to be a tipsy joke on parting last night. He felt annoyed she'd done this when he was maintaining his role as a respectable family man. He didn't acknowledge her, neither did she expect it, and continued pretending to browse the window display of dustpans and brooms.

Iris had noticed the blonde by the hardware store. Lucy Dare had turned out early in the morning, in her glad rags, to watch Sidney Cooper's reflection pass by. It was all she could do for decency's sake.

Oddly, Iris felt sorry for her; she would gladly give up her place in this charade to Lucy. She envied them what they had. Her hopes of love had died but she was planning to corner Bruce Randall. No billet-doux, like before, to arrange a tryst. She'd catch him unawares so he'd be unable to avoid her. A final meeting was needed to draw a line under everything. Bruce didn't like loose ends either. It would suit him to know that their child hadn't survived.

The run-up to Christmas was a busy time for any shop-keeper but especially for one hoping to sell tablecloths to folk who normally ate off upturned crates. The respectable working class scrimped all year to save into a Christmas club to treat themselves on the big day. Extended family would congregate around a begged, stolen or borrowed decorator's trestle table, or something similar, and enjoy a modest feast, decently presented. The damask cloth would then be pawned on Boxing Day.

Bruce Randall gave up trying to wedge extra cartons of linens onto the rear seat of his vehicle and beetled backwards, having become aware of a shadow blocking the light.

'What ... what are you doing here?' he stuttered and blushed, having emerged into the open and discovered he wasn't alone. He glanced about in agitation then recalled he was on relatively safe ground. Martha wasn't about to pounce on him. She was in Silvertown and he was parked outside the wholesaler's in Cheapside.

'Don't worry ... it's not a demand for money,' said Iris, thrusting a letter at him. 'I don't want anything from you for myself.' She'd known she'd catch him here, aware of his Tuesday routine; it had been the only day of the week he'd manage to slip away to see her.

Their illicit trysts could be counted on one hand. Two had taken place in her bedroom while Clover was at work and Johnny at school. The twins had been in the pram in the parlour. Those winter afternoons had been dark enough for Bruce to slip in and out, so to speak, without the neighbours being aware of him. She had conceived their son when he booked them into a boarding house in Marylebone, on a Sunday afternoon. A chance meeting with an old school friend had led to an invitation to have tea in town, the older kids had been told. Clover had encouraged the outing, offering to care for the younger ones while Iris enjoyed herself for a few hours.

It had seemed worth it at the time, to keep Bruce's love for her alive. When she contemplated her deceit now, Iris would burn with shame. There had been truth in the ruse though: they had been classmates. She, the mischief maker, and he the teacher's pet. That mischievous streak should have been left behind in the playground but had clung to her nature and led her astray when young and vivacious.

Justifying her guilt was no longer important. The love affair that had begun when she was fourteen, and slunk along for almost two decades, was over.

Finally, having regarded the envelope for some moments, Bruce took it by an edge as though it contained a bomb. A moment later, he yanked open the passenger door, and whispered for her to get in. 'How have you been? What's happened?' he garbled, slipping in beside her. Having stared at her belly and reassured himself it was nice and flat he relaxed back into the seat.

He'd feared her irate husband had worked out whose baby she was carrying. But money had been the only thing on Cooper's mind when he burst into the shop weeks ago. Bruce had intended to pay Clover her wages, anyway, but her father wasn't interested in a conversation, he'd wanted a fight.

Iris could have hated him for looking relieved they'd no baby to share and cherish; but remnants of her love for him poured balm on the churning pit of her stomach. He had the mild appearance of her father: fair hair, fair complexion – presently bearing a yellowing reminder of Sidney's fist on the cheekbone. Her father had been the opposite to her mother in looks and temperament. Elsie, with her storm brown hair, had been the robust disciplinarian. William had been a slow, gentle man, nothing like the edgy womaniser Iris had married. But she wasn't about to apologise to Bruce for her husband's behaviour, neither would she mention his wife's vile hint that Clover had been pinching things from their shop. They'd have to shoulder some of the blame for their bitter spouses acting the way they did.

'Why did you come looking for me? What's happened?' he prompted her when she sat contemplating her entwined fingers.

'I wrote it all down ... didn't know if you'd stop and talk, y'see.' She nodded at the letter scrunched in his hand, prompting him to stuff it out of sight in a pocket rather than open it. 'I'll say this now, though: Clover came home that day because of an emergency you had a hand in. I lost our baby and had a bad time of it. So, all things considered, the least you can do for us is help her get a new job. It's what I expect, and if you don't deliver, I'll come and find out why.' Iris opened the car door and got out as fast and daintily as she could. The effort made her gasp and steady herself against the car roof as her head swam.

He got out too and hurried round the vehicle to grip her arm. 'What? You mean you've only just got rid of it?' His mind had hurtled back and forth over events and dates and worked out that they collided. 'Martha saw your husband arrive home that day. She said you weren't dressed and looked ... ill ...' 'An unkempt slut' was how Martha had actually termed it.

'Bet she said more than that.' Iris wasn't fooled.

'You were right then: Sidney just assumed it was his.' Bruce patted her hand in praise for pulling it off.

'He never knew about the baby.' Iris withdrew her fingers. 'And I didn't get rid of it on purpose,' she said hoarsely and blinked back tears she didn't want him to see. 'I miscarried and it was all done before Sidney turned up. All he knows is that I was poorly when he got back.' Iris wiped beads of sweat off her face with her cuff.

116

Bruce shuffled to and fro, a hangdog expression on his face as he battled with guilt that sprang from an overwhelming feeling of relief he knew he'd little right to. They had both been let off what could have been a dangerously sharp hook. 'I'm so very sorry about what happened, Iris. Thank heavens it's over and done with now.' He heard her snort, somewhere between a sour laugh and a sigh. 'I'm not making light of it, dear; I know it must have been a dreadful ordeal for you. I'd no idea Martha would come over and sack Clover either.'

'Wasn't your wife got to me. I can handle her. The baby's taken it out of me.'

'Your health wouldn't have suffered so badly, if you'd done as I said and got rid of it straight away,' he said defensively, stung by her thinly veiled accusation.

'*It* ... was a boy ... our son ... if you're interested in knowing.' She pulled away from him and in doing so lost her anchor on the car. She stumbled to support herself against an iron gate bearing the wholesaler's nameplate. Elegantly, Iris drew her coat around herself and straightened her hat in readiness to set off. She knew she must look drunk ... she felt drunk, but she'd not tasted a drop of gin in days.

'Iris, you look dreadful, darling.' He strode up and fixed both hands on her, fearing she might collapse. She was very pale and beneath his fingers he could feel her shivering. 'You're cold. I'll take you home. I'll stop round the corner, make sure we're not seen together.'

'No, thank you. I can make my own way.'

'Don't go yet. Tell me a bit about the little one. It's not that I don't care.' A gesture and sigh expressed how hopeless he felt. 'I wish things could be different between us. I should've defied my parents all those years ago and married you.' He clasped her wan face between his hands then seemed to remember they were in public and shoved them in his pockets.

'You didn't though, did you, Bruce?' said Iris. 'You chose the family business and a wife who'd plough some money into it for you.' She smiled acridly. 'There wasn't a hope in hell of me, Iris Hall, up the duff and piss poor to boot, competing with any of that.'

She read his faint distaste at her way with words. He'd never liked that aspect of her character – the vulgar part, inherited from her mother.

'There's no point in going over spilled milk …' He sounded distant.

'Quite agree,' she said briskly. 'So let's hear no more of it.' She felt her throat closing over the lie. Even now, without the baby she'd wanted, she'd pack up herself and the kids and go with him in a heartbeat. He'd never give up what he had, and would pass on to his legitimate son when the boy was old enough. She indicated the letter in his pocket, a triangle of white sticking up against his dark jacket. 'After you've read it, I'd burn it if I were you. The nosy cow you married is bound to find it otherwise. Bet she goes through your pockets.' Iris couldn't help but spit out a cheap shot about Martha even though she herself went through her husband's pockets. It was only sensible to be aware of what Sidney was up to in case his whoring, gambling and drinking impoverished the lot of them.

It was while looking in his wallet for IOUs that she discovered a brunette in France had given Sidney her photo. Iris hadn't a clue what the French writing on the back meant; the only word she recognised was *'cheri'*. It

118

was an affectionate term, so she imagined Lucy Dare was out of sight out of mind when Sidney Cooper was on the Western Front.

'I won't see you again. Just send Clover her reference, soon as you can.'

'Iris . . . please . . . wait . . .'

She heard his suffocated voice hissing at her to stop; he was still ashamed of her, desperate not to draw attention to them as a couple. Yet nobody in Cheapside knew them. Here, they could have been for a short while, people in love.

She didn't reply or turn around. She kept walking in careful wobbling steps towards the bus stop.

Chapter Ten

Lucy Dare had never envied her sister although Beatrice had a comfortable house, a handsome husband and a couple of nice kids. Not that she was allowed to see her nieces; she was a shameful disgrace, unwelcome to visit any of her family. Well, so be it; at thirty-three she'd spent half her life off the rails and regrets were no use.

At school Lucy had noticed that the boys were more important than the girls; even the dunces in trousers were instructed in earning a living. Girls like her were steered towards domestic service, to ground them in following in their mothers' footsteps as skivvies: find a man, produce a brood of kids and be grateful for your lot, they might as well have said. The majority of girls had played along, her elder sister included; but not for Lucy Dare the grind of married bliss, thank you very much. She'd watched her mother doing her best and having the beauty knocked out of her, not by her husband's fists but by his ruthless selfishness.

Before long, her sister might have her self-satisfied smile wiped off her face. The other day Lucy had spotted her brother-in-law looking cosy with another woman. She'd felt furious on Beatrice's behalf, but she wouldn't spill the beans; she'd not be believed and would probably be accused of being a jealous troublemaker instead of an ally. She'd leave it to the rumour mill to bring bad news to Beatrice.

There was someone Lucy had long believed she did envy. Iris Cooper operated at the other end of the clock to her, so Sidney's wife and mistress rarely bumped into one another. A respectable woman would be turning in for the night when Lucy's working day started. Having dragged herself out of bed at what seemed like the crack of dawn to see him go, she'd ended up watching his wife instead. The shop window had revealed a staggering deterioration in Iris as her reflection passed by. Lucy's eyes had followed her rather than the sprightly scoundrel out in front.

Sidney Cooper had been Lucy's incurable weakness since childhood. He'd wanted to marry her, but she'd hesitated . . . a peculiar caution for a wildly besotted sixteen year old, afraid to tell her mum she was pregnant. Sidney hadn't liked the rejection and Lucy had let her elder sister take her to an abortionist before her belly grew and their parents kicked her out. She had briefly regretted it on discovering she'd had first claim on the man forced into a shotgun wedding only months later. She was still fond of him despite knowing he was as rotten as her late father had been.

The shock of seeing his wife had been the best treatment for Lucy's addiction to Sidney Cooper. Iris was a similar age to her and had been gloriously pretty in her youth with her abundance of russet-coloured hair and a pair of sparkling green eyes. Now she looked fit for the knacker's yard.

Lucy smiled encouragingly at the fellow seated opposite her at a table in the Rose and Crown public house. He'd been talking to her. She couldn't have told you about what, though, and she didn't know his name. It didn't matter

121

anyway. She never took much notice of what punters had to say after they'd agreed on how much. This one was balding but acceptably lower middle class; possibly a clerk, smartly dressed and clean hands. She had no truck with navvies with dirty fingernails, her childhood sweetheart excepted, of course. She also liked men to buy her a drink first. She didn't need Dutch courage; she needed a pretence that in half an hour, something sordid would be less so. Lucy considered herself to be a high-class working girl, and maintained her standards.

In the pub this evening was somebody fanciable who, like Sidney, was charismatic enough to make her overlook her prejudice against working-class men. She'd been keeping him under observation while reflecting on her life. He was seated at another table with Iris's mother. Aware they were neighbours, Lucy hadn't thought much of it when she'd spotted them together on other occasions. But recently Sidney had made a snide comment about his ganger liking his women long in the tooth. Lucy had started wondering and watching for a sign they could be more than friends. Astonishingly, she'd just glimpsed it in Bill Lewis's smile. A good-looking widower, unencumbered by kids, could pick and choose, yet seemed to have settled for dried-up Elsie Hall.

Lucy had always found Bill attractive, and quite a challenge, being a dock worker who didn't eye her up. He seemed decent and that impressed her. Like her, he seemed destined for better things. Together, they might make them happen.

She'd noticed a grey hair the other day and her widening hips straining her stays. For Bill Lewis she'd give up the profession and Sidney Cooper, too; she'd been flogging a dead horse there for years. Since seeing his haggard wife, she no longer wanted him to move in with her, anyway. She sipped her port and eyed her quarry over the rim of her glass, noting he dressed well outside of work. His shirt and waistcoat fitted his muscular chest snugly, whereas her beanpole clerk's gaping collar exposed a scrawny red neck. Bill also had a quiet, yet authoritative way about him. Sidney Cooper resented anybody telling him what to do but Bill kept him in line on the docks. Any moaning by Sidney was done behind his ganger's back rather than to his face. Lucy's lips curved in a private smile; turning respectable before her face and body went downhill would be a sensible move.

'You've got an admirer, Bill,' said Elsie.

'Well, thanks, love,' he said wryly. 'Been waiting a long time to hear you say so . . .' He raised her hand and pecked the back of it.

'I think you know who I mean,' said Elsie, jerking her fingers free. She wasn't as amused as she was making out and when he got up, chuckling, to refill their glasses, she gave Lucy Dare a pointed stare. Just a shot across the bows.

Lucy lifted her drink in mocking salute before downing the dregs and nudging her companion. It was time to go. She'd staked her claim and now it would be a waiting game to see who won. Elsie was a handsome woman for her age, even with a sallow complexion, and Lucy could see men might find her attractive. But she wasn't bothered; she was a blonde with a twenty-year age advantage, and a firmer face and body. She reckoned there was no contest.

On his way back with the fresh drinks, Bill glanced at the empty table. Elsie noticed that look. 'She's gone. Go after her if you like.'

'Threesomes ain't my thing. Anyway, rather stay here with you.' She was jealous, which was a good sign that it wasn't as cut and dried as she made out. But Bill wasn't a player of these sorts of games; he was an honest, straight-forward man. 'Are you going to move in with me, Elsie?' he asked quietly.

'You've had me answer on that.' Elsie sipped her drink ... while her guts writhed. She had told him to find somebody younger and Lucy Dare was that all right. No denying the girl was pretty, if spoiled goods. But then Bill Lewis wasn't interested in virginal maids; if he had been, he wouldn't be sitting here now. The idea of him getting together with that particular woman, though, stuck in Elsie's craw. 'You know she's me son-in-law's fancy piece, don't you?' The feather trembled on her hat as she jerked her head at the door swinging shut.

'Yeah, I know ...' Bill took a swig of beer. 'Used to live in the same street as the Dare family before I up 'n' joined the merchant navy.'

'Your Sarah told me you quit that lark to marry her.'

'She didn't want a man who was never there.'

'Can't blame the girl,' said Elsie. 'If kids had come along they'd never have seen their dad.' She paused. 'Didn't know you was acquainted ...' A sniff and another jerk of her head stood in for naming Lucy.

'I hardly know her. She and her sister were just school-kids when I lived with me mum 'n' dad. When I was back on shore leave I'd visit me folks and see Sidney Cooper hanging around by the Dares' house. He couldn't have been more than twelve or thirteen back then. She was probably a bit younger.'

'Never was a pair deserved one another more than those

two,' said Elsie sourly. 'Shame they never got hitched and saved my Iris a lot of heartache.' Elsie had seen a slight improvement in her daughter's health at first but she'd declined again. After grilling Iris about why that was she'd discovered that Sidney had forced himself on his wife. If Elsie had known about it before he went back to France she would have ripped his head off his shoulders.

'How's Iris doing?' Family problems were always on Elsie's mind, and Bill was glad of a change of subject. They'd been enjoying a quiet drink and he'd been building up to a proper proposal, but the atmosphere had cooled and it no longer seemed the right time.

'Not as well as she should be,' said Elsie grimly, and left it at that. She was soon brooding again on the defiant look Lucy Dare had given her. It had nothing to do with getting one over on her daughter where a man was concerned; the cow was intending to get one over on her. Elsie was surprised but not upset to know people had started to see her and Bill as a couple. She knew she looked good for her age but nevertheless was flattered. It wasn't the first time Bill had drawn female eyes when with her. The other women weren't as brazen as Lucy though in showing their appreciation. 'She's still unwed, could be she's got you in her sights, Bill.' His opinion of the blonde was what she wanted.

'More likely she was staring at you, Elsie. Probably scared you might set about her for causing trouble in the family.' It was a valid point but Bill had received come-hither looks on other occasions from Lucy Dare. He wasn't blind and he wasn't a monk so noticed good-looking women who stared at him.

Elsie was the woman he wanted, in his life and in his bed. So he'd give her more time to come around to the idea of them being housemates and lovers. But he couldn't wait forever.

'What can I do for you, sir?'

'Nothing thanks, love.'

'Sure about that? Must be something . . .'

Bill folded his newspaper, tucked it under his arm then gave Lucy Dare his attention. 'What you hoping to do for me?'

'Take your order.' She winked. 'Rock salmon? Haddock? Ha'porth of chips? Anything you like . . .'

It seemed that the proprietor of the fish shop was expecting his customers' quizzical looks this evening. Wally Watson gestured impatiently and nodded through the steamy window, wordlessly confirming that she was acting on his instruction.

Bill had been waiting in the cold and dark outside Wally's place to buy his evening meal. He'd glanced up from reading the depressing news reported from the Western Front and spotted Lucy Dare inside. She'd come out clutching a notepad and pencil rather than her supper. Bypassing the others hunched into their coats at the front of the queue, she'd headed straight to him.

'I'm collecting the orders so we know what to start frying. Wally's me uncle . . .' She jerked her head at the elderly fellow, clattering whisks in pans of gloopy batter, and banging burnt crisps off wire baskets.

The idea of working in her uncle's shop had come to her after she spotted Bill Lewis queuing up outside last week. Her hunch that he would be a regular had paid off. She'd started on Tuesday and lo and behold by Friday had struck gold. 'I've told me uncle it's a waste to cook up stuff that might not be needed, so this is how we do it now.'

126

'Bet Wally never knew he needed you,' said Bill sardonically, blowing into his cold palms.

'He wouldn't be the first man to come to that conclusion. Or the last . . .' She gave him a lingering smile.

'Haddock 'n' chips then . . . ta,' said Bill trying not to laugh as he felt her fingers brush his thigh. Subtle, she wasn't.

'Lucy's my name,' she prompted.

'Yeah, I know who you are.' Bill opened the newspaper again, another rueful smile tugging at one corner of his mouth.

'I've not forgotten you either, y'know, Bill Lewis,' said Lucy, pleased he'd remembered her. 'You lived up the road from us, with your mum 'n' dad and your big brother.'

Bill tuned out and raised the paper to shield himself from hard-eyed looks being slanted at him over shoulders.

'Any chance o' those wot's been waiting longest gettin' served?' snapped a thin-faced woman at the front of the queue. She looked Lucy up and down then turned her back with a tsk of disgust.

'What's so special about him?' demanded another complainer.

'He's a man, ain't he?' Sneered a woman gripping a small child by the hand. 'And they're the only ones she's interested in, the little . . .' The punchline was muttered inaudibly.

'Gawd, you're an impatient lot.' Lucy bit her tongue against retaliating. She was a reformed woman, doing respectable work . . . as far as this lot knew. 'Don't bite me head off; only got one pair of hands, y'know,' she said cheerfully, moving along the line and scribbling down orders. Most of the women knew of her reputation and turned up their noses when barking their preferences. The few men waiting liked this new personal attention from a good-looking blonde though. Wally's wife was an old dragon in comparison. Nobody walked off in a huff; the boss was good at frying fish and filling bellies on the cheap, and that was what mattered.

'Get yer pinny on, gel,' said Wally as his niece put the order pad on the tiled counter and he peered at it. 'Friday nights is always busy. Start tearin' up newspaper 'n' give them chips a good shake ... get 'em crisp right round.'

Wally Watson was a real uncle and was genuinely fond of his wayward niece. From a young age she'd stood up for her downtrodden mother, who'd been his elder sister. In his turn, Wally defended the girl, which hadn't always been easy considering what she got up to. Lucy was as larky as a kid, but the truth was, she was no spring chicken any more, and he was glad to see her choosing regular work. She'd also benefit from regular cares and worries that a husband and kids would bring, in his opinion. Family life would soon knock the sense into her. For now, it suited him to have a nippy assistant. His takings were up since Lucy arrived. His wife's gout had put her on a stick and recently she'd been a liability, slipping and slid-ing on the greasy floor.

'Put you in extra chips ... and salt 'n' vinegar's already on 'em, 'case you fancy a little nibble on the way home.' Lucy winked on handing over Bill's newspaper-wrapped parcel.

Wally had one gimlet eye on the bubbling fish and one on the rugged fellow handing over his payment in coppers. If she thought she was picking up punters on his premises, she had another think coming.

'See you soon then,' Lucy called, as Bill shouldered a path through waiting customers to get outside. He acknowl-edged her by raising a half-hearted hand and she was disappointed that he didn't turn around. She kept on shovelling up chips and wrapping fish, her fingers flying from vinegar bottle to salt pot, to newspaper, while constantly thinking of Bill. Since talking to him, she liked him even more and her ambition to nab him was exciting her into feeling restless. She wanted it done … achieved, but knew he wouldn't consider her a serious girlfriend until she was decent. Only her uncle would take her on, a fallen woman. Wally didn't pay much, and smothering the stink of chip fat that clung to her clothes with perfume didn't come cheap. For now she had to keep her regular West End clients, but it shouldn't cause problems as they were a discreet distance from her own doorstep. She'd headed to Covent Garden after the shop shut on two evenings this week. Until she was confident she had Bill Lewis twisted about her finger, a backup plan was vital.

Bill headed towards home, unwrapping the fish supper as the vinegary aroma tickled his taste buds. He started on the chips, chuckling between chews. Maybe a year ago he might have welcomed Lucy's attention. But somehow, Elsie Hall had got beneath his skin and he felt more irritated than flattered by the younger woman's persistence.

'Oi, hold up … forgot yer change …' Lucy charged up behind him, still wearing her fat-spattered pinafore.

Bill turned around, with a chip held halfway to his mouth. 'Didn't need any change. Give you the right money.' He chewed and waited. It would be best to get this over with now in case she came banging on his door.

'Oh …' Lucy sensed his aloofness. 'Well, might as well take what's on offer, now I've put meself out.' She held out some coins in a fist and gave him a sweetly crafty smile.

Bill leaned back against the wall and cocked his head at her while eating chips. He offered her one and she took it and settled beside him. 'Wasting your time with me, love. I'm getting married.'

'Elsie Hall?' She dropped his make-believe change into her pocket with a sigh.

'Yep.'

'Bit old fer you, ain't she?'

'Nope.'

'Well, what a waste ...' She turned to face him with a sulky expression. 'If she dies in the meanwhile ...'

'Watch it.' He pointed a warning finger. 'Just so much of you I'll take ...'

She smirked. 'I can take all of you – want me to show you?' She cupped his groin. Good old-fashioned fornication was all she had left in her armoury.

'Chrissake ...' Bill, snorting an embarrassed laugh, shoved her aside. 'How d'you get into this, anyway? Your sister turned out all right.'

'Did she now? Well, could be that sort of *all right* ain't for me.' She felt indignant to be roundly rebuffed, and was glad of the wintry darkness hiding her fiery face. She'd heard something akin to pity in his voice and that was the last thing she was after from Bill Lewis. 'Could say a rich rogue seduced and abandoned me,' she said lazily. 'Be a lie, though.'

'Yeah ... be a lie, all right. Sidney Cooper never did have a pot to piss in.'

'Elsie told you about us, did she? Me 'n' Sidney being a thorn in her side?'

'Nah ... she didn't tell me. Nobody had to tell me. You're common knowledge.' He folded the newspaper over his supper and started to walk on. 'Clear off now. Be lucky if you don't get sacked, messing around like this.'

He started to jog across the road, hoping to reach home before his food was stone cold. He cursed, aware of his groin feeling uncomfortably full from her teasing.

Chapter Eleven

'How are you doing then, Clover Cooper?'

'I'm all right, thanks . . .' Her reply would have been less polite but for her boss being in earshot. From behind the stockroom's half-closed door he'd be listening and probably watching too to see how she dealt with customers. 'What can I get you?' To hide the colour bursting in her cheeks, she rearranged cigarette packets on the back shelves.

'Half an ounce of Virginia shag, please, love.' Archie Fletcher propped an arm on the polished wooden counter and winked a bright blue eye when she glanced over her shoulder. By peering at an angle he could glimpse the proprietor hunched over a desk with a burning oil lamp at his elbow. 'I only come in to speak to you. I've been thinking about you all the time, Clover.' He kept his voice low. 'I thought you was having me on when you said Randall had sacked you.'

'Shut up . . .' she hissed. 'Mr Bailey'll hear you.' She selected a small brass weight then shot tobacco onto the scales from a wooden box. In her agitation she'd tipped out too much so picked off pungent brown strands, dropping them back whence they came. Her boss didn't know she'd been sacked, but there was more to make her heart skip than that: Archie looked suave in his railway togs with a badged cap tilted on his fair hair. Her father suited a uniform too, although in civvies he wore a docker's get-up of donkey jacket and drill trousers.

'Heard your old man floored Randall over you losing your job.' Archie leaned closer until their faces were almost touching across the counter.

A quick peek at his sultry expression confirmed her suspicions that he'd more on his mind than keeping their conversation quiet. She moved away, realising he'd been close to kissing her.

'You found out all of this from Nettie, I suppose.' Nettie had taken to avoiding her if they spotted one another in the street. In a while things should blow over then Clover would tell her friend she'd no hard feelings about their dads, or about Archie Fletcher. Where he was concerned, her pride had suffered the most. She'd seen another side to him and was no longer swayed by his roguish smile.

'Got your old man's ways, ain't yer, Clover.' He rubbed his jaw, reminding her she'd already punished him. 'Maybe it was your mum taught you how to dish out right-handers. Poor cow must've had practice married to Romeo Cooper.'

Prodding her into defending her father to mock her, wouldn't work. Her father's adultery wasn't news to her, but his girlfriend's identity would be. She was itching to have a name but wouldn't give Archie the satisfaction of hearing her ask for it. 'If you've got something to say, better find the guts to spit it out.'

'What I know about your dad ain't fit talk for his daughter's ears.'

'I know all about his *friend* . . . so nothing you could tell me there.' That wiped the smirk off his chops; he stopped lounging on the counter and jerked himself upright. Clumsily, she bagged the tobacco, collecting escaped dregs and dropping them in before thrusting the bag at him. 'There you are. Now clear off, and mind your own business about my family.' She turned her back on him.

'On the house then, is it? Thanks very much,' he said innocently.

'Half an ounce of Virginia shag, I believe you said.' Mr Bailey had fully opened the stockroom door. 'The gentleman owes you seven pence, Miss Cooper.' He fixed a suspicious eye on the two of them. He recognised Archie Fletcher, not only as a customer, but from a local pub they both frequented. Bailey knew the younger man was popular with the girls, unsurprisingly as he was a tall, good-looking individual, if cocky. 'Did the gentleman have any Rizla papers or matches?' His narrowed eyes searched the counter for something half hidden, ready to be slipped across, buckshee, after his back was turned.

Girls were like putty in the hands of these charmers; youths made worse employees though. The last one he'd apprenticed had filched cigarettes for himself and his brothers then announced he'd enlisted to be a fusilier. He was fifteen but wanted to be a war hero so had lied about his age to the recruiting sergeant. Mr Bailey felt grateful not to have sons, although at one time being childless had been an unbearable sorrow, especially for his late wife.

'I only gave him tobacco ...' Clover found her voice, her cheeks fizzing in embarrassment though it had been a genuine mistake. 'Seven pence, please.'

Archie counted out some coppers then tipped them onto her outstretched palm. 'There we are, Miss Cooper ... and good day to you.' He doffed his cap to the proprietor and gave Clover an exaggerated wink that renewed her blush with angry colour.

'Rather too full of himself, that one,' said Mr Bailey after the bell clattered on Archie's departure. 'Not the sort of admirer for a respectable girl.' The comment was accompanied by a significant nod for Clover to take note.

Mr Bailey understood the Flash Harry had flustered his new assistant and was ready to overlook her mishap. In fact, he'd taken to Miss Cooper. She had a wholesome prettiness and a straightforward, pleasant manner he appreciated. Nevertheless, he believed in maintaining a distance between himself and his employees. 'Tidy those pipes while it's quiet,' he said. 'I'm off to the bank before it closes. I'll look in Smith's window ... see if they've upped their prices. This war is making things short, and when things are short, unscrupulous sorts take advantage.' He went into the stockroom then poked his grey head around the door. 'I'll go out the back way.'

He always did, but nevertheless felt obliged to tell her he was being cautious. It was sensible for him to be so; he was a weedy fellow, in his late sixties, who looked as though a strong wind might take him over. If anybody was intending to rob him of the takings they'd loiter out the front, was his thinking. Clover reckoned carrying a bag of cash down a dark back alley was daft. She began rearranging clay and wooden pipes on their racks though they looked tidy enough already to her. But she willingly did it, relieved not to have got told off in front of Archie.

Soon bored with that, she went to the window and peered past the display of fat cigars and fancy lighters into the gloom. It would soon be closing time; she was eager to go home and see how her mother was. Iris had collected a client's washing yesterday evening, dragging along her moaning son as she'd felt too weak to carry the load back herself. Her mother said she was ready to start earning again, but Clover didn't think she looked fit enough to work. Airing her view had earned her a reminder that they couldn't live off fresh air, and that Christmas was coming. Most of her father's army pay went into the kitty, and so did Clover's wages. She had earned well at the drapery, managing to save for treats, but now received considerably less. Her good job at Randall's had come courtesy of her friendship with Nettie, she'd once thought. She'd wised up now. Her mother had got her – and lost her – that job by having a love affair with Bruce Randall.

A white mist beyond the bow window drifted across her vision, drawing her mind to the here and now. She held onto the display shelf and, by leaning and staring side-ways, could make out a man's dark-clad figure. The bow's mullioned glass made it difficult to identify the profile beneath a hat brim, but she knew it was Archie, smoking and lounging against the wall. She quickly withdrew in case he spotted her. So he was intending to ambush her when she finished work, was he? She was tempted to con-front him first, before Mr Bailey got back. Her boss would leave the back way with the loaded money bag, but return empty-handed through the front door. She didn't want him to jump to the conclusion that she and her 'admirer' had been up to mischief in his absence. He'd be gone longer than usual as he was diverting to check on his rival's prices. That fellow Smith had a cheek opening his tobacconist shop so close to Bailey's, which had been established far longer, so Clover had heard her fuming boss say, more than once.

The smoke outside had dispersed and she approached the window again to investigate, hoping Archie had grown bored of waiting. At that moment he shifted to look in, and they ended up staring at one another. He jerked his head, beckoning her. She took a deep breath and marched outside.

'Why're you hanging around when I told you to clear off? You trying to get me into trouble?'

'Slow down . . .' he said, taking her arm to draw her closer. 'Won't cause no trouble, just want to tell you I'm not seeing Nettie no more.'

'Well, you've wasted your time dawdling then, cos I'm not interested in hearing about it.' She turned to go back inside but he kept hold of her arm.

'Look, you've had a sulk and . . . all right I'll say I'm sorry I went out with Nettie.' He rolled his eyes as though she was making a fuss over nothing. 'Was only a couple of times, anyhow . . .'

'I'm not interested in listening. You listen instead, Archie Fletcher. Nettie's welcome to you, if she wants you, that is. More important though, Mr Bailey'll be back in a minute and go bonkers when he catches you making a nuisance of yourself.' She tried to squirm free but he swooped to kiss her, right there in the street. She gave his chest a double-handed thump and jerked back her head to gasp, 'Let go of me!'

'Don't you tease me, you little cow.' Archie forced another kiss on her, prompting Clover to start kicking his shin until he roared in pain.

'Everything all right, is it?'

'What's it to you, pal?' Archie had spun around to confront a soldier sporting a single stripe on his sleeve. He'd stopped with his hand on the door as though about to enter the shop.

'You're annoying the young lady,' said the lance corporal, and started towards them.

'I'll annoy you instead, if you like, for sticking yer nose in where it ain't needed.' Archie sauntered to meet him, chest puffed.

It was a prime target that received a powerful one-handed shove which sent Archie tottering then stumbling off the kerb.

Clover regained her senses at the same moment Archie found his footing and charged at his opponent. She whipped between the two men before a fight started. 'It's all right . . . it was just a tiff and he was leaving anyway. Do you want serving in the shop?' She'd recognised the soldier; Jeannie had pointed him out as her boss's brother when he walked past the café weeks ago.

Archie wasn't backing down that easily after being shown up in front of the girl he aimed to win back. He liked Clover more than the others he dallied with. Most were only after a husband to get them out of two rooms crammed with their parents and a brood of younger kids. The pushovers were soon forgotten. She was quite a challenge. And Archie liked a challenge. He swung a crafty right hook that glanced off a shoulder as the soldier managed to react in time and sway sideways. The next thing Archie knew, he was sprawled on the ground, but not for long; he was hauled up by his sleeve.

'Get off me clothes,' he snarled, red-faced from humiliation and a well-aimed jab. After wrenching himself free, he furiously brushed down his navy blue jacket. He was proud of his job as a railway guard and made sure to look after his uniform.

'You're all right . . .' said the soldier. 'Anyhow, a man who likes a fight would suit khaki better. Thought about doing it for king 'n' country, have you, mate?'

Archie stopped tidying himself up. He was sensitive on this subject: a mad-eyed woman, dressed in black, had stuffed a white feather in his face yesterday, just as he'd been about to signal the all-clear for the train to pull out of the station. She'd bawled at him that he should go and fight like her son had. She wouldn't go away, delaying the train by over three minutes. The disruption to the timetable had been as galling to Archie as being shown up in public. He wasn't taking it again. He took an aggressive step forward, fists curling at his sides. 'I'm a railway worker.' He poked his uniformed chest with a finger. 'Reserved occupation. You sayin' I'm yeller?'

'If the cap fits, mate . . .' The soldier swooped on Archie's cap, knocked to the pavement. Following a cursory dust off, he plonked it atop a thatch of messed up blond hair. 'After all, this one's too small for a head as big as yours.'

A hysterical giggle scraped its way out of Clover's throat, but she found the sense to grab Archie's arm. She was roughly pushed off and he threw another punch that again missed its target. His fist went straight through a square of mullioned glass in the shop's Victorian bow window, making him yelp and curse just as Mr Bailey hove into view on his way back to the shop.

A crowd of spectators was pulling together to watch the entertainment. A small woman was on tiptoe trying to see what was going on over others' shoulders. Archie began flapping, then wrapping his handkerchief around his bleeding fingers. He'd spotted her and so had his opponent. In fact, the soldier's regard made the blonde shrink back behind heads.

Clover only had eyes for her boss, who was hobbling along on his spindly legs as fast as he could to investigate the commotion outside his premises. She turned on the two men who'd landed her in bad trouble. 'Hope you're both bloody well pleased with yourselves. You've probably lost me me job.'

Archie grabbed her shoulder, preventing her going inside. 'Bet you'd like a word with your old man's tart, wouldn't yer? There she is ... with the blonde hair.' He nodded and, realising she was being picked out as worthy of attention, the woman ducked down. 'Lucy Dare's her name. Take a look.'

Clover did, but the petite woman sporting a large feather in her hat had already started to hurry away and she only got a glimpse at her pretty face.

Lucy knew all of Sidney Cooper's kids by sight, but they didn't know her and she didn't want them to. Especially Clover, who was the absolute spitting image of her mother as a young woman. Clover had already looked distressed without Archie Fletcher stirring things up on the family front. Lucy knew that was what he'd been doing, the troublemaker. Something else was clear about him as well: he had a yen for Sidney Cooper's daughter. And, maybe, Neil Ryan did too. They'd appeared to be fighting over her.

'Your dad ain't any different to me,' sneered Archie. 'Though I can do better than hooking up with the likes of her. Takes all comers does Lucy Dare. She's a working gel; and you're just a kid who ain't got a clue. When you grow up, come 'n' find me ... can't promise I'll still be interested though.'

'Find you?' stormed Clover. 'I never want to clap eyes on you again.' She pointed a finger at the soldier who was using a booted foot to sweep broken glass off the pavement into the gutter. 'Or you. Go on, clear off, the pair of you.'

She wrenched herself free of Archie's hand and marched back inside to await what she knew would be another sacking.

Chapter Twelve

'We'll start off with a few exercises, to warm up,' said Jeannie, who had shrugged off her long gabardine coat to reveal she had on her football kit underneath.

'You kept that quiet,' spluttered Clover, looking down in dismay at her drill skirt and trim ankle boots.

Jeannie, in all her glory of dark-blue knickerbockers, red jersey and long heavy ribbed stockings that reached almost to her knees, seesawed a striped cap over her pinned up blonde hair until it snugly encased her skull. She then pivoted around, arms spread, to invite her friend's opinion of her appearance.

'You look ready for business, all right, Jeannie,' giggled Clover. There was nothing alluring about the get-up, that was for sure. Those who sniffed that women shamelessly showed themselves off playing football were wide of the mark. Clover admired her friend's brash, no-nonsense attitude, and her fine-fettle figure. Jeannie might be dressed like a man, and be larking about posing this way and that with flexed biceps, but there was no disguising her femininity.

Jeannie had arranged for them to meet up on the corner

of her road and they'd walked together to the park for their first kick about, as Jeannie termed it. She'd been carrying a bulging canvas bag, which contained the ball, and a few bits and pieces to keep them free of bruises were also in there, Clover had been told. She watched her friend unpacking the Aladdin's cave. Shin pads, socks, two pairs of studded boots and then a jersey and a pair of knickerbockers, similar to the ones Jeannie was wearing herself, were produced. Finally, out came the ball.

'Well, you gonna take it seriously, or not, Clover Cooper?' Jeannie held up the knickerbockers and top. 'This is our team strip.'

Clover's cheerful smile drooped and she said, aghast, 'You're not expecting me to put those on?'

'I am.'

The dark blue knickerbockers were swayed in front of her. Clover whipped a glance to and fro, searching for onlookers.

'You can change under your coat,' said Jeannie. 'Hardly anybody about.'

'It's coming on to snow, that's why everybody's gone home,' grumbled Clover, crossing her arms to keep herself warm.

'You won't feel cold in a little while, promise you that,' hooted Jeannie, putting on some football boots. She placed the other pair by Clover. 'Come on, hurry up, Cooper, knees up . . .' Jeannie barked, jumping to her feet to start running on the spot.

'Oh, let's have them then,' said Clover, casting a scouting look about. She took the kit and started fiddling with her skirt hooks beneath her coat. She placed her clothes beside Jeannie's gabardine mac on the park bench then yanked on the team uniform. Jeannie was right though: on a December afternoon, coming onto dusk, families were heading out of the park. Nobody had taken much notice of the two young women loitering by a park bench.

Clover felt oddly liberated when standing in her lightweight get-up, and rolled her shoulders, her self-consciousness sliding away with every movement. She started copying Jeannie, who was now doing jumping jacks. Quite soon Clover was panting while Jeannie carried on instructing her in a normal voice, her breathing unaffected by the exertion. Sideways runs over rock-solid grass came next and Clover nearly tripped herself up, unaccustomed to the clumsy boots weighting her feet. Still her friend had energy to spare and Clover forgot about feeling inadequate to the task and found her competitive spirit. At school she'd been able to sprint and jump hurdles. She was younger than Jeannie too and wouldn't let herself down by falling too far behind. It soon became clear that running yourself ragged, serving behind shop counters and seeing to little kids and the housework wasn't the right sort of exercise. She glumly realised she wasn't as fit as she'd believed herself to be.

'Not cold now, are you, Cooper?' Jeannie stopped jumping and walked over to pat Clover on the arm. 'That's put colour in your cheeks.'

Their laughing breaths became ghosts in the fading light.

'Right, let's tackle the ball then before it gets too dark to see the blinkin' thing,' said Jeannie, holding out some shin pads. 'Here, put these on.'

'You're not going to kick me, are you?' said Clover, but she tied them onto her calves.

'Won't if you score a goal.' Jeannie winked then marked out a goal with another pair of shin pads. 'Only joking ...

144

you're doing well so far,' she praised. 'There's gels in the reserves don't look as good as you doing jumping jacks. But being fit don't necessarily mean playing football will come naturally. And if it don't . . .' Jeannie shrugged philosophically. 'Do your best. And remember, pay packets are resting on this.' She struck an innocent pose, palms placed together and eyelashes a-flutter. 'Oh, Freddie Rayan . . . you should watch me friend dribble a ball. And what passin' 'n' defendin' skills that gel's got. Freddie Rayan . . . honestly . . . you must see her for yourself . . .'

'Oh, give over,' Clover guffawed and gave Jeannie a push. But joking aside, she knew Jeannie was being serious when she said that showing an aptitude for playing football might get her the job she wanted.

'Off we go then', said Jeannie and dropped the ball to her feet. She'd run towards the spaced shin pads and scored a goal before Clover was off the mark.

'Now, you try to stop me doing that when I next make a break for it.' Jeannie came back dribbling the ball from foot to foot. 'Let's see if you favour the right or left foot,' she said.

Clover made a crafty lunge for the ball and gave a triumphant shout on successfully taking her pal by surprise. She charged towards the goal, telling herself a bit of guile was no bad thing in this game. She was forcing her tired legs to keep pumping and lift the heavy boots. Each bound onto solid ground jarred her bones up to her hips. It wasn't long before she heard Jeannie pounding close behind. Clover panicked, kicked wildly and missed her target . . . but not by much.

'Reckon you're set for the reserves on that show alone,' said Jeannie, who was panting now after the chase.

'Really?' Clover held her aching ribs but felt elated by her friend's praise. She started back towards the bench, keeping the ball controlled at her right foot. The studded boots felt less burdensome and she dodged her friend's tackle and booted the ball forward with a powerful kick. There was a rhythm to it she realised . . . and a balance that came from tightening and loosening of muscles. Slowing for breath was important too, she was thinking when it felt as though her lungs might explode. Jeannie pulled level with her and swept the ball away in a clean tackle before turning and heading back to score another goal. Clover collapsed onto the bench on top of her clothes. She threw back her head and an abundance of dishevelled russet-coloured curls escaped their pins and cascaded to her shoulders. The winter sky had lost its light and the frost in the air was chilling the sweat on her face but in her throat rasped a taste like sparkling wine.

'Oi, giss that back,' roared Johnny. Spluttering and coughing, he gave chase but his laughing sister swerved neatly past him.

Clover had been heading homewards in the bitter twilight when a stray football rolled in her direction. With some nifty footwork, and her skirts held high, she'd dribbled it past the trio, unbeknown to her, sharing a crafty cigarette. Bobby Pincher was a year older than the other two and the fastest on his feet. Having commandeered the roll-up and jammed it in his mouth, he was soon catching her up, but she whacked the ball between the spaced jumpers on the ground and punched a fist in a victory salute.

'Yer sister's got a better right foot on her than you have, Cooper.' Bobby spat out the cigarette stub to hoot his appreciation.

Clover scooped up Johnny's new leather football and bounced it on the cobbles. The race up the road had left her giggling, but it wasn't her intention to embarrass her brother in front of his pals. She was still exhilarated after spending the afternoon with Jeannie. It had come as a surprise that she'd enjoy playing football. It had also come as a surprise when Jeannie hadn't said 'I told you so' after hearing about Archie Fletcher causing serious trouble. She'd simply given Clover a hug and called him an unrepeatable name as they walked towards home in the twilight.

'You lot should have come football training with me,' she said as Johnny bowled up to reclaim his ball.

He gave his sister a disgusted scowl at the very idea. 'Gels don't know nuthin' about playing football.' He pressed his thumbs against the firm leather panels. 'Needs pumping up now you've messed about with it,' he said darkly.

'Football's a man's game,' added Charlie, who affected to look the part by posing nonchalantly against the wall. The brothers not only envied Johnny his father but his pretty sister too. They always got a smile rather than a turned-up nose from Clover Cooper when she passed by. Charlie was an inch taller than his elder brother, but both of them were shorter than Johnny, who took after his dark-haired, strapping father. Despite being malnourished, mousy kids, the Pincher boys had vim and swagger to rival their peers.

'You can't play football in a skirt, anyhow,' Johnny mocked.

'Tucked it in me bloomers,' said Clover. She succeeded in amusing him and he guffawed along with his pals.

More often than not, Johnny seemed to be in a mood lately. He could appear as though life's trials didn't affect him; in fact, he fretted about his father, risking his life in a foreign land, and about his mother, struggling to make ends meet while plagued with ill health. Ignorant of those circumstances, he blamed his big sister for losing her employment and burdening Iris with extra anxiety.

'I hope I'm as good a player as Jeannie one day.' Clover continued chatting about football as they walked towards home. 'She's in the ladies' team at her factory and I couldn't get the ball past her just now.'

'I'd like a go at tackling her.' Bobby's half-broken voice creaked like a rusty hinge, and a shadow of a moustache edged his top lip. At almost fourteen, he already had an eye for the girls.

'She'll run rings round you all. That'll shut you lot up about girls can't play football—' Clover broke off to wrinkle her nose, and sniff her brother's jumper. 'Have you been smoking?' His sudden, cagey expression was answer enough. It didn't come as much of a surprise; she'd hardly done a day's work at the tobacconist's before he'd begun to wheedle for her to snaffle him some Woodbines. She'd bitten his head off and he'd blamed his pals for prodding him into it.

The Pincher boys were tagging along behind, but they stopped smirking and started moseying towards their own home, dismantling the goal by swiping two holey jumpers off the ground on passing.

'If Mum finds out you've been smoking you won't 'arf be for it, Johnny. Can't you behave yourself when you know she's still not well? Anyhow, why aren't you indoors? It's Sunday and you've got school in the morning.' Clover was surprised their mother hadn't called him in by now. Iris didn't like him playing in the street after dark – especially not with the notorious Pincher boys who were often still to be seen aimlessly roaming late into the evening.

'She don't mind . . .' said Johnny evasively. 'Anyway, I'm not a kid. I'm twelve and had enough of school. Bobby's finished fer good; he's got a start down Poplar market. Charlie reckons he's gonna get taken on as a barrer boy as well. And he's a month younger than me. And their mother don't mind.'

'Well, yours does. She's already said you can't leave school until you're fourteen.'

Johnny had bunked off lessons last week to look for work that would pay more than coppers. Running errands and helping the milkman at the weekend was kids' stuff now he'd found out what the Pinchers could earn. 'I'll bring home ten bob from the market, plus buckshee fruit 'n' veg,' he boasted. 'Get tips 'n' all as it's close to Christmas. Loads of deliveries to do, see. Ain't as though Mum don't need the money now she's not up to doing much, and what with you always getting fired, I reckon I should go to work.'

Clover didn't have an answer for that even though it hadn't been her fault she'd got the sack on either occasion. She'd betray her mother or herself by trying to explain, so simply shrugged in an apologetic way.

'A bloke was looking for you earlier.' Johnny bounced his ball. He could see he'd wounded his sister and felt bad about it. 'I was by the gate and told him you'd be back about teatime.'

'Did he give his name?' If Archie Fletcher had been hanging around again she'd have plenty to say to him; she'd sooner he just kept his distance now though.

Johnny shook his head. 'Didn't recognise him; he was dressed in uniform. '

'Railwayman was he?'

'Nah . . .' He broke off and peered into the gloom. 'Here he is, coming back now. You got an army boyfriend, then, Clo?'

'Don't be daft.' It was a relief to know Archie wasn't prowling about. She recognised the man approaching and wasn't absolutely sure she had anything polite to say to him either. A moment later, she was marching down the road, stopping only to send Johnny home when he started following to be nosy.

'I know you're going to tell me to clear off. And I will.' The soldier raised his hands in surrender. 'First, would you let me say I'm sorry ... please?' He had come to a halt by a lamp post, hands stuffed into his pockets and his shoulders hunched up to his ears. He was without his cap and the misty gaslight lent a silver sheen to his bowed dark head.

'So you should be sorry,' Clover grumbled though his humble stance had disarmed her. 'Look, I know it wasn't really your fault, but you shouldn't have interfered.'

'I thought he was a chancer trying it on with you. Perhaps I got it wrong and Fletcher's your boyfriend. Is he?'

'Not any more.' Clover avoided his eyes but could feel the weight of his gaze on her. She was ashamed to admit, even to herself, that once she'd very much liked the idea of being Archie Fletcher's girl.

'Glad about that cos he certainly don't deserve you.'

'How d'you know him?' she asked.

'Don't really – he's an acquaintance of me brother's in a roundabout way.' He paused. 'Before I go any further, be best if I introduced myself.'

'I know who you are. Jeannie told me after you walked past the caff that day.'

'I noticed you too,' he admitted wryly. 'Made it me business to find out your name. I'd still like to do it properly, if that's all right.'

'Go on then.'

'Neil Ryan ...' He extended a hand and gave her fingers a firm shake. 'Pleased to meet you, Clover Cooper. My brother made some enquiries about you for me. Seems Jeannie's our go-between.' His smile soon vanished. 'Heard on the same grapevine you got the sack.' He propped a hand on the lamp post and shook his head. 'Really sorry about that. I could go and have a word with your boss – explain it wasn't your fault ...'

'No ... thanks all the same. Mr Bailey gave me notice. I finish on Friday.'

'Did he go mad at you?'

'Well, he was understandably upset.' Recalling his distress made her guts wriggle in shame. He'd shaken his head and repeatedly said he was disappointed in her while his bony old fingers picked broken glass out of the window display. Her help had been rebuffed so she had stood humbly by, fearing he might burst into tears at any minute.

'I would've offered to board it up, but didn't know if I'd make matters worse by coming inside.'

'Mr Bailey used an old box. He was frightened things could get pinched through the hole overnight.' She paused. 'Most of all he was bothered about people gossiping and going elsewhere. He's always moaning about losing customers to Smith's, down the road. They're his worst enemy.'

Neil gave his jaw a self-conscious rub. 'I've added insult to injury then. I went there for cigarettes. I needed a smoke after all the excitement.'

Clover rolled her eyes. 'Bloody hell. I won't tell him that, or he will have a bad turn.'

They exchanged rueful smiles that transformed into chuckles.

'Shouldn't laugh ... I do feel sorry about it,' said Clover, dropping her chin.

151

'Are you in trouble with your folks, as well?'

'Mum was all right about it, actually. She was more annoyed with Mr Bailey than with me; she reckoned I deserved a bonus not the sack for trying to stop a fight outside his shop.' Iris had also said a reference from the drapery was on its way so she might as well send in her application for a factory job. Iris wouldn't say any more about the Randalls but nothing had been posted through the door yet.

'What?' Clover had noticed Neil Ryan giving her an old-fashioned look.

'Was a bit more to it than that, as I recall ...'

'I shan't get my mum in a lather over Archie Fletcher. She never liked him.'

'Sensible woman, your mother ...' said Neil drily.

Clover sensed there was a dig at her in that comment. 'Well, you've said sorry, so you can get going now.'

He didn't move, other than to make himself more comfortable, with his back against the lamp post and his face tilted up towards shimmying gaslight. 'Don't suppose he's been back to pay for breaking the glass. I noticed he scarpered pretty sharpish.'

Clover sighed an affirmative. This fellow had hung around afterwards though; he'd caught her eye through the window and with an eloquent shrug enquired if he could do anything. Still irate, she'd turned her back on him then. He had just irked her again, yet strangely she was content to stay here with him. 'I hope Mr Bailey won't make me pay for the damage out of me wages.' Being short on rent was a concern she'd only just given proper thought to.

'I'll pay for the glass; least I can do after having a hand in losing you your job.'

She almost declined the offer but then thought, why be proud about it? His fist hadn't caused the breakage, but as he'd rightly said, he'd had a hand in it. 'Thanks,' she said briskly. 'We can't afford something like this. My mum's poorly . . .'

'Very sorry to hear that, and hope she's better soon,' he said.

Clover didn't elaborate. She suddenly swung around on hearing her brother bawl out her name. He was waving frantically at her from their doorway. A moment later, he was bounding in their direction.

'Gotta come home, Clo,' he gasped out. 'Mum's lyin' on the floor and won't wake up. I tried to get her on the settee.' He shook his head in violent distress. 'Can't move her on me own . . . but she's not dead . . . she sort of moaned at me . . .'

Clover's heart had leapt to her throat, a throbbing and burning sensation, muscling to choke her. She came to her senses and without a word, raced towards home, Johnny puffing in her wake.

Chapter Thirteen

Iris Cooper was lying on the parlour floor, half beneath the table. She appeared to have collapsed while pressing her lady's bedsheets. The iron had scorched a black-edged hole straight through the cotton into the pine table and a smell of charred wood hung in the air.

Clover's trembling hands clattered the iron safely onto the hob grate then she crouched down. The meagre lamplight in the room didn't disguise her mother's ghastly colour, or a mark on her forehead where she'd banged herself when falling. Clover gently touched it and felt cold clammy skin beneath her fingertips.

'Oh, Mum,' she whimpered. 'Please wake up.' She put her ear then her hand to her mother's chest and eventually felt a faint pulse. She closed her eyes in relief.

Johnny fell to his knees just behind. 'What's up with her?' His breath was hurtling against her neck and he shook his sister's shoulder in a wordless plea for reassurance.

'Could be her bad bellyache's come back and made her faint.' It was a poor explanation but it would have to do. Clover knew her mother hadn't properly recovered after having baby Gabriel. She slipped an arm beneath Iris's shoulders and tried to ease her up. 'Get her legs ... she needs to be in bed,' she instructed her brother. He did as he was told and they managed to shift their mother out from beneath the table. They couldn't lift her though and soon gave up pulling on her limbs for fear of hurting her.

'D'you want me to do it?'

Clover swivelled around on her knees to find Neil Ryan standing in the open doorway. She scrambled up, nodding vigorously. 'Would you bring her in here?' She rushed to the bedroom door.

He quickly strode to help, scooping Iris into his arms and standing up with her.

'Go and see if Nan's home.' As soon as her mother was on the bed, she faced Johnny. 'Tell her we need her urgently.'

The boy stood in a daze but jumped out of it when his sister shouted at him, shooing him away with two hands.

Clover covered her mother with the eiderdown then bent to place a tender kiss on a sunken cheek. She gently shook a limp arm, calling to her mother and stroking a strand of hair off her damp forehead. She got no response although tiny breaths were lifting her mother's chest. Clover became aware of her little sisters in their cot. The twins were standing up behind bars, their fingers curled on the top rail; two little dark-haired angels quietly watching as though they knew something serious was unfolding. Having gained attention, Annie wanted to be picked up and held her arms out to the closest adult. Neil brushed her cheek with the back of his finger but left her there.

'Where's your father?'

'Serving in France.'

'You've got a lot on your plate, haven't you, Clover Cooper?' Neil said huskily.

155

It was a common enough condolence yet hit its mark. She bit her quivery lower lip and tears dripped from her eyes.

He stepped closer and put his arms round her, rubbing her back in comfort. 'Could be she's only tripped and given herself a bit of a bump on the head. A good sleep might do the trick.'

Clover shook her head and he didn't try again to fool her.

'Shall I fetch a doctor?'

She scrubbed her eyes with a hanky as the tears flowed faster. 'Mum doesn't believe much in doctors ... says folk like us get sent to the workhouse infirmary and once you're in those places you don't come out.'

Annie started to cry, not her usual howl – a drone that prompted Neil to lift her from the cot to quieten the eerie lament.

'Is she wet?' Clover asked, having seen him examine his arm supporting the child.

'Yeah ... don't matter ...' He gave the toddler to Clover and then approached the bed to stare at the invalid. In the army he acted as a stretcher bearer, among other things, so got to hang around hospitals quite a lot. He knew a seriously sick person when he saw one. 'I'll go and find a doctor,' he said.

'What's all the noise about, son?'

'Is me nan at work, Mr Lewis?' Johnny burst out, having recognised Elsie's next-door neighbour calling to him. 'We need her to come right away ... it's me mum ... she's ...' Johnny choked and sniffed, unable to speak his worst fears.

Bill had been almost home from his Sunday afternoon ritual of a trip to Poplar baths when he spotted the boy hammering on Elsie's door and speeded up towards him. 'Better slow down, lad, and start at the beginning.' A minute later, with a garbled account of the emergency at the Coopers' going round in his head, he said, 'Go home and help your sister, son. I'll fetch your grandmother. She's probably at the factory, but don't worry, I'll find her for you. Won't be long. Go on, off you go . . .'

Bill watched the boy hare away then with a weary sigh dumped his belongings inside his front door. He took the opposite direction to Johnny, jogging across the road, towards the High Street.

There was nothing to do but think at a time like this. And Elsie was already on his mind. He'd not seen much of her since the incident with Lucy Dare in the pub. They'd finished the evening harmoniously with him kissing her cheek, as usual. It was an ironic ritual that made them part with a smile. Though for Bill the joke was wearing thin.

He'd not bumped into Lucy again. He'd taken to avoiding Wally's place and bought his suppers elsewhere, which was a nuisance as Wally was cheapest and best. But he'd keep his distance from Lucy. She had a saucy, tempting way about her that could easily turn a man's head. Then everybody, himself included, would be shocked to know he'd got too friendly with Lucy Dare.

A young wife and a family was naturally what most single men of his age would want for the future. But Elsie Hall was a soulmate. During the aftermath of Sarah's death, Elsie had been the only one who understood him. His grief had turned him surly and lost him friends. She neither shunned, nor cosseted him, but gave as good as she got, yanking him up by his bootstraps whether he liked it or not. She was a true companion who just happened to be a looker, too. Even before his wife died Bill had thought

Elsie's husband a lucky bloke to have her. His admiration had deepened into love, and it was a crying shame that Elsie's reluctance to spoil his life was now spoiling his life. Her selflessness only made him love her more. He knew she loved him back but didn't want them to slide into blame and regrets after the honeymoon was over. To him, not having his own children honestly didn't matter, but her daughter and her grandchildren were so important to her that she found his attitude incomprehensible, and therefore liable to change.

Family was the light of her life, especially since she'd regained a good relationship with her daughter after many wasted years. Elsie would always put the Coopers first.

Bill hoped he was on a fool's errand and Iris Cooper would already be back on her feet and scold her mother for turning up and making a fuss. He hardly knew Elsie's daughter but imagined them to be similar characters who disliked the spotlight even if deserving of it.

That's what he hoped ... but his rolling guts weren't of the same mind. He put on a spurt, taking the short cut along the towpath, then into Fort Street to bring the factory into sight.

Chapter Fourteen

'I could arrange to have your mother moved to the infirmary but I don't think it would be worth disturbing her . . .' The elderly doctor paused then added gently, 'That is to say, it wouldn't be helpful and might distress her unnecessarily.'

'But she'll get better, won't she?'

'Your mother's gravely ill, Miss Cooper.'

'Then you must give her some medicine,' shouted Clover, and repeatedly pushed his arm to turn him back towards the bed to attend to Iris.

The old fellow took no offence at being jostled; he plucked her quivering hand off his sleeve and began to pat it in comfort. 'She isn't in great pain, I assure you.'

'If you can't help her she must go to a proper hospital not the workhouse infirmary. My nan'll be here soon,' threatened Clover, pulling herself free. 'She'll make you listen and take Mum to Poplar hospital.' Her rudeness was out of character but all she had left to keep at bay her terror. A scream was clawing at her throat for release and she was controlling an urge to shake him into action. She didn't want him to be kind and tactful. She wanted him to make her mother well. Somebody had to because life without her was unthinkable.

'Not going to no hospital,' croaked a voice. 'I'll stop here.'

Unbeknown to the two people in the room, Iris had come round and was attempting to struggle up on the mattress. The effort was beyond her and she sank back as Clover rushed to drop to her knees by the bedside.

'Don't need a doctor. Tell him to go away, Clover.'

'Go to hospital, Mum, please. You'll get medicine to make you better.'

'Get rid of him, don't need no quack ... I was giddy and fell over, that's all.' Agitation lent Iris strength but she again failed to elbow herself fully upright. Collapsing back, her shaking hand touched the throbbing bump on her head.

'I've done what I can for your mother.' The doctor gave the distraught girl's shoulder a sympathetic squeeze as she rose to her feet. He wished he had some encouragement to give but he was an honest fellow and didn't deal in false hope. A brief examination of the patient had confirmed his suspicions. He saw cases like this far more often than he wanted to. Miss Cooper had confirmed that the twin toddlers being cared for in the parlour were the youngest children. She had admitted that her mother had recently been pregnant though. Her tiny nod and wary look had given the game away when he questioned her. Something untoward had gone on but he wasn't here to moralise or interrogate about an illegal abortion. A natural stillbirth could be to blame for the abscess poisoning Iris Cooper's blood. And it was that, rather than mild concussion from fainting, that would prove fatal. He judged the damage was done many weeks ago, and help had been sought far too late.

'Clover? Has he gone?' Iris called weakly, staring blankly at the ceiling.

'I'll write a letter to the authorities requesting your father's immediate return home.' The doctor's reassurance came in a low fast voice. He wanted to remove himself and avoid distressing the sick woman with his presence. He'd learned Mr Cooper was an infantryman in France. This family was luckier than some. The war was filling Flanders graveyards with fathers, and British homes with orphans. In a case like this, if no elder sibling was present to care for motherless younger ones, the unfortunate children ended up in an institution. This girl seemed old enough and capable enough to somehow hold the family together if the worst came to pass. And she'd mentioned a grandmother who would doubtless pitch in to save them from the workhouse. 'Shall I fetch your brother in now?'

'No ... not yet, sir ...' Clover wasn't ready to cope with Johnny's grief on top of her own.

'I'll wait outside then until you're ready to talk some more.'

Clover, shivering in shock, returned to the bedside. Sinking down onto the floor, she gripped her mother's cold hand.

'Don't cry ... you're a brave girl,' Iris whispered. 'I know you'll take care of the twins for me. Johnny's a big boy now and can help you.'

'You'll soon be well again, Mum,' said Clover, bowing her forehead against her mother's hand to hide her lying eyes. 'Dad'll come back and you'll get better and everything will be fine for all of us.'

Iris drew their entwined fingers closer and pressed her icy lips to her daughter's knuckles. 'Don't be frightened. I'm not. Until your dad gets home, you've got your nan to help you.'

'She'll be here soon. Mr Lewis is fetching her from work. Shall I let Johnny come in and see you now you're awake? And the girls?'

'In a minute. Want to speak to you first.' An almost indiscernible smile pulled at Iris's lips, as bloodless as her complexion. 'Who brought the doctor? Not seen that soldier before.'

Clover hadn't realised her mother been awake then. 'He's Neil Ryan, a friend of Jeannie's. He offered to look after the twins till Nan gets here. Johnny's too upset to cope with them.'

'Mr Ryan's nice then,' said Iris. 'That's good ... I think you like him ... a kind man is the right sort.' Another smile softened her pinched features but it soon faded. 'I feel so hot, take the cover off me.' Her fingers slipped off the sweat on her brow to fall back to the pillow.

'You're cold, Mum.' Clover felt her mother's tears trailing over her fingers as she touched her clammy cheek. 'I'm sorry, Mum, it's my fault ...' She hung her head and quietly sobbed. 'If I hadn't gone out and left you it wouldn't have happened. I was only playing football ... I could've stayed home and done the ironing ...' Her clenched fist thumped her thigh in punishment. When it got too dark to carry on in the park, Jeannie had nagged her to have a drink in the café before they headed home. They'd both felt parched and hungry after running around and had tucked into a plate of biscuits with their teas. Those few extra minutes of enjoyment seemed unbearably selfish now.

'Hush ... I wanted you to go out and enjoy yourself. You'll be picked for the football team when you get your factory job. Did the second post bring your letter from the drapery?'

Clover gazed at a glimmer of hope brightening her

mother's ashen countenance. No envelopes had been lying on the mat when she got back but she'd say or do anything to nurture that peaceful expression. She nodded and rubbed her cheek against her mother's hand in thanks.

'I knew he'd do it for us.' Iris sighed in contentment though her tears continued sliding down to wet the pillow. After a few quiet seconds, she burst out, 'I wanted his baby, I've been punished and so's the poor innocent mite. Wait for me in heaven . . .' she croaked a plea to her lost boy.

Clover hadn't forgotten about Gabriel; her half-brother was always at the back of her mind. She'd seen wisdom in her nan's advice, though, to concentrate on life's necessities. The baby was being cared for . . . Johnny could look after himself, but her sisters had to be clothed and fed. Rent had to be paid, and chasing dreams had to be saved for a magical day over the horizon when such indulgence was possible. The realisation that her baby brother might now never come back where he belonged rammed a painful tightness beneath her ribs. Her nan had been right about that too. She'd reminded Clover the other day not to distress her mother with any careless talk about the baby's whereabouts. Iris believed her stillborn boy to be laid to rest in her mother's garden and nobody had corrected her assumption.

But that was then and this was now. Clover couldn't let her mother torment herself with thoughts of a precious child suffering because of her transgressions.

'You haven't been punished, Mum, neither has Gabriel. I called him that cos he needed a name.' Unable to bear to watch her mother rocking in grief, the truth had tumbled out. The moment Iris quietened and turned her head to stare at her, Clover wondered what she'd done. She shrank into herself, but it was too late to take back the secret.

With surprising strength, Iris kept hold of the fingers slipping from hers. 'What happened that day?'

Quickly and quietly, while glancing at the door, fearful of interruption, Clover poured everything out. By the time she'd finished the guilt had gone; she felt as though a burden had been lifted and her mother's serene expression was the solace she'd longed for.

'Is that true?' demanded Iris. 'You're not just saying it to soothe me?'

'It's true ... swear it. I couldn't bring him back. Dad was here.'

'Oh, thank you, Clover ...' Iris relaxed her hold on her daughter and closed her eyes. 'I know you'll watch over him, if you can. So will I ... if I can. I'll watch over every one of you.'

'You were ill before, Mum, and got over it. You will again. Please try ... for us ... and for Gabriel.'

The quiet protracted and Clover thought her mother had drifted into a doze. She made to rise but Iris spoke to her. 'You deserved a better mother. I know you heard me say a bad thing. I didn't mean it ... swear that's true. I love you, Clover ... you've been the best daughter to me ...' Her voice faded into a sob of contentment.

Clover kissed her mother's cheek. After a few minutes, Iris appeared to have sunk into another slumber that intermittently rumbled her breath in her chest; thankful she seemed settled, Clover tiptoed outside to see if her grandmother had arrived.

Elsie was on the parlour threshold, tearing open the buttons on her coat then yanking it off, while demanding answers from the doctor. The moment she noticed her granddaughter emerging from the bedroom she flung aside her fur and hurried over, white with anxiety. 'How is she?'

'She's fast asleep . . . snoring.' Clover had never witnessed her grandmother in a real panic before. She hoped her news would be reassuring, but it didn't bring comfort to Elsie.

'I'll go and attend to her.' The doctor exchanged a glance with the middle-aged woman, battling to control her emotions in front of her grandchildren. Being older, with experience of nursing gravely ill people, they knew what the rattle signified. 'I'll let you know when it's time to come in,' he solemnly said.

Elsie pulled off her hat and dropped it on the crumpled heap of beaver skin. She'd no intention of waiting to be invited; she was going to her daughter immediately.

'This is Neil Ryan . . .' Clover whispered an introduction to her grandmother but Elsie was already distracted by Johnny, sitting on the floor with his arms about his drawn-up knees, weeping.

'I want to see Mum,' he hiccoughed. 'What's wrong with her?'

Elsie held out a hand to the boy. He scrambled up and rushed into his grandmother's embrace and they disappeared into the bedroom.

'Sorry you got drawn into all our troubles,' said Clover, somehow remembering her manners. Neil Ryan was standing by the settee, keeping an eye on the little girls seated on it. He was doing his best to amuse them by flicking coins then conjuring them up from behind his back.

'No need to be sorry. Glad to help.' He gave her a smile but didn't overdo the sympathy. He'd heard the doctor give his diagnosis just now and knew this family was in the throes of a tragedy. He knew how it felt to lose a beloved parent. He'd lost one and never known the other and had never found comfort in other people's well-meant sentiment. 'This little 'un's tired. Keeps yawning.' He chucked Annie beneath the chin.

'I'll put her to bed ...'

Clover lifted Annie up but hadn't taken more than a step when the doctor came out of her mother's bedroom to beckon her.

'You should come in now, my dear. Bring the children if you want to let them say goodbye as well.'

Clover looked blankly at him until she heard her brother keening and snapped out of it. 'No ... not yet ... can't be yet ...' She swung a wildly beseeching look at Neil.

"S'pect the girls might like to see their mum,' he gently encouraged and briefly, lightly cuddled her. 'Best of luck to you all; if you need any more help with anything ... anything at all ... just ask Jeannie to pass a message on to Freddie. I'll come.' He took a backward step then another then turned and bowed his head as he left.

Chapter Fifteen

A branched gas mantle on the wall behind the shop counter shed enough light onto a stool below to allow Martha Randall to sew. She would often do needlework in the quiet hour before supper, usually seated more comfortably at the kitchen table. She'd watch the boiling dinner pots and her husband would stay below and serve any stragglers then lock up. But Bruce was about as much use as a toy soldier these days. One spiteful word from somebody and he was liable to go AWOL. Better that he peeled the potatoes, and she held the fort against all-comers.

Martha's brooding was interrupted by a rattle of crockery. She glanced up from her work to see her daughter entering the shop through the stockroom. Nettie had a cup and saucer, complete with stowed biscuit, wobbling in each of her hands. One set was placed on the shop counter for her mother. Martha frowned over the top of her work spectacles, but the girl ignored the wordless reprimand and dunked her digestive in tea that looked stewed. Normally, Martha was a stickler for food being consumed upstairs. Crumbs and tea stains spoiled the stock, and slipping standards didn't go unnoticed by customers.

Since nobody came in any more she didn't bother making an issue of it.

Not so long ago they'd been the ones treated to sympathy after Sidney Cooper ran amok in the shop. His wife's sudden death had changed all that. People had switched sides and spoke of Clover being unfairly sacked, provoking her father into standing up for her. The Randalls were now the villains, accused behind their backs of burdening a sick woman with the final straw that broke the camel's back. 'Heartless money grubbers', Martha had overheard somebody say, on passing a circle of neighbours' cold shoulders. Once they had been respected as pillars of Silvertown society but Martha wasn't about to let the likes of factory workers and dockers' wives defeat her. Her husband was troubled though, and not only about gossip. She'd told him to buck himself up and be grateful nobody knew the real cause of friction between the Coopers and the Randalls. He hadn't answered her, or even looked at her. Ever since the news broke of Iris Cooper's passing, he'd inhabited his own miserable world.

'I heard Dad crying upstairs.' Nettie burst out with the reason she'd treated her mother to some tea: an advance peace offering might ease the way for awkward questions had been her thinking.

For the second time this week she'd heard gruff sobs coming from her parents' bedroom. On the first occasion she'd been too embarrassed to bring it up. Her parents argued a lot and her father was a sensitive soul, but she'd never known him to end up in tears. As for her mother, it would take a German bomb dropping on the till to make her reach for her hanky.

Nettie had long known her parents weren't happily

married, but they shared a love of earning money and through it had provided their family with a comfortable home. Her younger brother was privately educated and would inherit the business. Her mother visualised a chain of shops once her studious blue-eyed boy took over the reins. Nettie knew she, being a girl, hadn't been deemed worthy of the same opportunities, but her mother had agreed to pay for her secretarial college course. It had been the day after Nettie turned sixteen and declared she wasn't working in the drapery any more. She'd threatened to get a factory job, then walked off leaving her mother choking on her after-dinner sherry.

Nettie felt confused and a little anxious that the status quo could be under threat. Shop takings were down, but she knew that wasn't solely responsible for this bad atmosphere. 'Why's Dad so upset?' She shook her mother's arm to get her attention.

'Oh, I don't know,' Martha replied, having finished attaching a trio of shimmering mother of pearl orbs onto blue satin. 'Your brother's bothering his mind, I expect. You know when Paul was home for the holiday he complained about his boarding school.' Martha snipped the thread with scissors then used a hand to shovel loose buttons towards the edge of the counter where they cascaded into a cedar wood box. 'I don't think he should attend the local grammar school instead, but your father made an enquiry for next term.' Martha fitted the box into its cubbyhole in the dresser. 'We've had words about him mollycoddling the boy.'

Nettie knew all this was true, but she wasn't falling for it making her father cry. Her mother was being evasive, giving weight to her own theory that something odd had been going on. Her cup and saucer was plonked down, slopping tea onto her half-eaten digestive and the polished countertop. 'I thought Dad might be upset about Mrs Cooper,' she blurted.

Martha began blotting the spillage with a remnant of calico grabbed from under the counter. 'I've told you before no drinks at the counter; and what makes you say that?' she snapped.

Mother and daughter avoided one another's eyes. They both had their own reasons for their consciences pricking them over that family. Martha never permitted the feeling to linger, though.

'I saw Dad going into the cemetery with some flowers.'

'He didn't go to her funeral on Christmas Eve,' retorted Martha with something akin to triumph in her voice. On the busiest day of any year, customers had stayed away and their till remained silent. The place was like a morgue, she'd said to Bruce, without thinking. Her gaffe hadn't even registered with him. He'd been immersed in thoughts of Iris Cooper being laid to rest by her family. Family he'd regretted not being a part of.

They'd made an effort to enjoy Christmas Day for their son's sake. He was a bright boy but at thirteen years old needed to toughen up. She'd told him so and he'd returned to Norfolk in the New Year, promising to stand up to the school bullies. She doubted Sidney Cooper's son was lily-livered. That man would know how to stiffen a boy's backbone for his own good.

'I saw Dad going into the cemetery only last week; perhaps he was visiting another grave.' Nettie offered an escape route. Her mother's jealousy was showing, giving weight to an alarming possibility for her father's distress. He'd had a crush on Clover's mum!

'He probably felt obliged to pay respects to the woman.' Martha buffed furiously, unfolding the rag to find a dry part before starting again. 'Clover was our employee for a long time and we do things properly whatever our views on people. I sent a card to the family ... no acknowledgement ... wasn't surprised.' Martha turned to her daughter. 'You've not seen Clover for a while, have you? No bad thing, of course – the girls at college are more suitable friends.'

'I thought it'd be best to stay away for now,' replied Nettie, going on the defensive herself. 'I expect she's got her hands full with the twins.' It was quite true, but not the whole story. She was ashamed of the way she'd behaved where Clover was concerned.

'I hope she thanked you for delivering the reference your father troubled himself to write.' Martha hadn't agreed with that either, but like the grammar school business, Bruce had done it anyway. Her daughter's awkward shrug drew a snort from her. 'Typical. No manners and incapable of keeping a job. Fancy causing men to fight over you like that. The girl resembles her mother in more than looks it seems.'

'You never liked Mrs Cooper, did you?' Nettie could understand why her father had liked Clover's mum; she had too.

Mrs Cooper would welcome her visits, clearing away a stack of nappies – mostly clean – so a seat emerged on a sagging sofa. Cups of tea were always offered ... and turned down. Nettie was used to better than weak brews made with yesterday's leaves and milk. She'd down a gallon of dishwater now to make things better for that family. College girlfriends weren't a patch on Clover Cooper. If a girl or boy tried picking on posh Henrietta Randall in primary school, they'd answered to her best friend. And she had repaid Clover's years of loyalty by being horribly mean to her.

'I wasn't friends with the woman, if that's what you mean,' replied Martha, giving a final stroke to the shiny wood. 'Hardly surprising as we had nothing in common.' She pursed her lips. 'I'll always speak as I find. But I don't speak ill of the dead so . . .' She dropped the rag, gesturing that a distasteful subject was closed. Before her daughter could reopen it, she swung from behind the counter to attend to sliding home the bolts on the door. 'Closing up early,' she announced. 'There's a committee meeting at the Friends of the Red Cross this evening.' Those middle-class allies were her sort of people.

Nettie collected the cups and went through to the storeroom then up the stairs to the apartment that spanned the top floor. She passed her parents' bedroom but no noise was issuing from it and she wondered if her father had gone out. The parlour was a long narrow room. One flank wall was studded with a pair of large casements that overlooked the street. The space was home to heavy mahogany furniture and a large Eastern rug adorned the floorboards. Martha Randall favoured country house style and saw no reason not to stuff an East End flat with wormy reproduction Chippendale. The kitchenette was at the back with an aspect over the yard. It was a square room with a small modern cooker and a china sink with a brass tap. Nettie clattered the cups and saucers into the sink, pouring away the cold tea.

'Oh, for pity's sake,' sighed Martha, coming up behind her. 'He hasn't put the dinner on.' With much crashing of the larder door she upended a bag of potatoes and started to peel some.

172

Nettie found a saucepan and a knife and pitched in. 'I did bump into Johnny Cooper this morning. He was on his way to school.' The chance meeting had put the family at the forefront of her mind and stopped her brooding on Archie Fletcher for a while. 'I asked Johnny how they all were. He said all right but he seemed very sad.'

'Is Mr Cooper home yet?'

'He said his father arrived at the beginning of the week. Johnny wasn't his usual cheeky self; he didn't want to talk for long.' Despite her mother's prejudice against the family, Nettie thought Johnny was a polite lad. After a short, stilted conversation he'd thanked her for her good wishes for them all.

'Every cloud has a silver lining. I expect that's how Mr Cooper will see it,' said Martha acidly. 'At least the war in France is over for him.'

Chapter Sixteen

Sidney Cooper wasn't glad to be home; he'd come to the conclusion he'd sooner slog through muddy trenches than piles of soiled nappies. He wasn't used to being assaulted by howling toddlers clinging to his knees, whining at him to pick them up. Clover did most of the nursing and house-work but she was looking for work during the day which kept her out for too long. Sidney had quickly come to the conclusion that she had to stay home while he escaped to the docks. Going cap in hand to his ganger for work didn't appeal though; he and Bill Lewis had never got on. But if the grating boredom of family life had been bearable, Sidney Cooper wouldn't have joined up in the first place. Back then, before the war, he had only two children, and they'd been past the annoying baby stage. The twins had been born while he was in France and he'd only had to put up with them for a week at a time when on leave. Besides, Iris had always taken charge of them. The shock and grief of losing his wife was peeling away, exposing a raw prickle of resentment that she had gone and done this to him.

'You took yer time, gel.' Sidney stood fists on hips, puffing furiously on a cigarette. 'You look worn out. No luck then,

I take it.' His dishevelled-looking daughter seemed to be making a meal of unbuttoning her coat.

'I've got a start in the laundry if I want it; they gave me a trial, that's why I'm late.' It was why she looked a state, too. Her knuckles were stiff and swollen from dunking washing and her thick auburn hair, usually neatly coiled at her nape, hung in lank skeins around her weary face. The overworked muscles in her shoulders protested as she reached to peg her coat behind the door. A soapy smell wafted from wool saturated with steam . . . it reminded her of her mother. 'It's not much of a pay packet. But, Jeannie's going to speak to her boss at the munitions factory, so fingers crossed cos that's better wages.' She'd forced some brightness into her tone and held up two hands forming lucky symbols, but wasn't feeling as optimistic as she sounded.

The local *Gazette* had printed a paragraph about the fight at the tobacconist's before Christmas. It was New Year now and still the war dragged on, giving people tragedies to chew over. She encouraged herself to think her story was old news and her father wouldn't hear about it. But . . . if he did, he'd demand the details and go looking for Archie. That would be her lot then. There'd be another bust-up and local employers would view Clover Cooper as definitely more trouble than she was worth.

'Well, never mind about that,' said Sidney, dropping his cigarette butt on the floor and grinding a toe on it. 'Can't wait no longer for you to turn up trumps. I've decided I'm getting me old job back.' He'd raised his voice to drown out the noise of his youngest children. He'd dumped the twins in their cot to get them out of his way, but they'd heard their sister's voice and were calling out to be released from their prison. 'See to those two before I dish out a hiding.' Sidney

175

wore a pained expression as he jerked his head towards the bedroom door. 'Not stopped all day, the little bleeders.'

By the time Clover led the girls by the hand into the parlour, her father was flipping on his cap, on his way out of the door. A moment later she realised why he'd sent her out of the room then made a swift exit. The kitty jar had been emptied of most of the rent money. Her eyes burned with angry tears. She was bewildered too. Her father had returned from France distraught over losing his wife yet seemed to quickly recover, making Clover wonder if he was horrible enough to already be seeing Lucy Dare. The name glided easily into her mind, yet she'd not thought much about her father's lover since finding out her identity. There'd been too many other things to think about. And now her beloved mum was safe from being hurt, Lucy Dare seemed unimportant . . . no threat whatsoever.

Clover took off her sisters' wet nappies, sat them on their potties, then put on her pinafore and set about making sandwiches for their tea. Rosie started whimpering; she was turning as grumpy as her twin now their impatient father was storming around in their daily lives. Clover always did her best to pacify them, but talk of heaven and angels were of little comfort to two confused little girls, missing their mum. A bang on the door halted Clover chanting 'Humpty Dumpty', in the hope of keeping them sitting still while she worked. She stopped cutting the loaf, put down the knife, and went to open up. Her grandmother wasn't paying a call, as she'd imagined. Neil Ryan gave her a hesitant smile that pulled his mouth aslant.

She'd not seen him since the night her mother died, but had often thought of him. After the funeral, when feeling calmer, she'd told Jeannie about his help and that she'd like to thank him properly for what he'd done. Jeannie hadn't seen him either, though, and in her opinion he'd probably returned overseas.

She'd been staring at him in a daze and blushed. She was tempted to whip off her stained pinafore; instead she used it to rub crumbs off her hands.

'Just came to see how you're doing, and if you need anything.' He propped a hand on the wall.

'Thanks, but Dad's home now,' she blurted, and hoped to high heaven that he didn't come back and discover her with a soldier. It was the first opportunity she'd had to get a proper look at Neil Ryan. At other meetings, darkness or disasters had deprived her of the time or inclination to appreciate his appearance.

Now she assessed him as being an inch or two shorter than Archie but broader. Archie was lean from top to toe but this man had an athletic body, quite like her father's: broad shoulders and narrow waist. Soldiers' physiques were improved by the rigours of army service, she imagined. He was wearing khaki, with his cap in his hand, and highly polished boots gleaming beneath the weak light spilling from the doorway. She'd not had time to neaten herself since returning from the laundry and next to him, she felt slovenly.

He was equally taken up in looking at her and for a full minute nothing was said. Eventually, her embarrassment penetrated his mind and he stopped staring and started to explain his visit. Clover began to speak at the same time.

'I'm a bit busy at the moment,' she said.

'I hope things are getting better . . .' He smiled and gestured for her to carry on. 'Ladies first . . .'

'I'm in the middle of getting the girls' teas ready.'

'I won't stop then. I would've come back sooner but didn't want to get in the way. As I am doing now ...' He sounded rueful.

'I wanted to speak to you too, actually,' she said, feeling more relaxed. 'To say thanks for what you did.'

'Glad to help.'

Her jumpy heart was reminding her of possible reper-cussions to this meeting, nevertheless losing his company seemed worse than being caught out by her father.

Neil Ryan had been a friend to her and she'd seen few of those lately. When Jeannie Swift turned up the other day, her father had embarrassed Clover by ogling her blonde friend one minute then making it clear the next she was outstaying her welcome. He'd treated his mother-in-law to the same churlishness. Elsie wasn't so easily deterred though and hadn't said goodbye to her grandchildren until she was good and ready.

'Right ... well, won't keep you as it's a bad time ...' Neil had noticed her glance over a shoulder as the twins began making a noise.

'I've just put the kettle on for tea.' She grabbed his sleeve to stop him turning away. 'Dad's not home, so come in for a few minutes, if you like. The girls might remember you.'

They did remember the man who'd shown them magic tricks; Annie jumped up and overset her potty in her haste to get to him.

'Could've been worse,' said Neil ruefully. He'd bent to say hello to the child and noticed only a puddle of urine on the lino.

Clover rolled her eyes and searched for a cloth to clean up.

Rosie got off her potty without mishap. She squat-ted to investigate something soggy on the wet floor.

'Fag,' she chirped then stamped a bare foot on the cigarette stub.

Clover's cheeks burned; she was thankful her little sister hadn't imitated another of her father's bad habits. He swore when they irritated him; Clover knew this because she'd heard obscenities coming from the twins' innocent mouths. She swung Rosie up to stop her splashing in wee, and plonked her on the settee, out of the way.

'You make us a nice cuppa char and I'll see to this.' Neil took the rag from her. 'Was my fault anyhow, surprising them like that.' He crouched down and gave her a grin. 'Better'n being on latrine duty over there, I can tell you.'

She watched him wipe up the cigarette butt off lino littered with fresh burn marks. Usually she swept up after her father but hadn't been quick enough this time. They might be poor, and live in a run-down house, but she kept things as clean as she could. She was furious that her father had made them look squalid. He'd had time to settle back into home life and to stop treating the place like an army dugout.

While Neil mopped, she finished making the sandwiches then settled the girls at the table to tuck into their teas. Once the cleaning up was done and hands had been sluiced in the enamel bowl, she took off her pinafore. She gave Neil his cup of tea then perched on the arm of the sofa. He took the other end and a harmonious quiet descended, broken only by the sound of clinking china and the twins enjoying their food.

'My dad never gets more than a week or so at home,' she said, inviting an explanation for his long stay in England.

'I'm back for a few months, training new recruits at a ground in Enfield.' He put his empty cup on the table. 'Did you find a job after Bailey sacked you?'

She shook her head. 'After Mum ... well, wasn't up to job seeking straight away,' she said huskily. 'Can have a laundry job if I want ...' She didn't want; she'd watched her beloved mother knock herself out struggling to manoeuvre yards of sopping cotton with red raw hands. Walking into that laundry earlier, the reek of soiled linen had brought with it a stark image of her mother toiling in the washhouse, back bowed. She'd blinked back tears at the sight of those women staring into boiling tubs. The supervisor had given her a sharp look, so she'd rubbed her eyes pretending steam had got into them.

'My nan's been wonderful, helping out with rent and bills until Dad was home. He's hoping to get work on the docks again.' Sidney would continue to scrounge from his mother-in-law, if he could, job or no job. Clover intended to pay something back as soon as she found work.

'Saw your brother down the road, playing football with his pals,' said Neil. 'Stopped and had a quick word with him. He told me you and Jeannie play football in the park sometimes.'

Clover's smile faded and she turned away.

'Did I say something wrong?'

She shook her head. 'It's just ... I'd been playing football the afternoon Mum came over poorly.' The memory of that day, enjoying herself, while her dying mother lay collapsed on the floor would always haunt her.

He hunkered down at her side, then reached to take her hands to hold in comfort. 'You feel guilty about it, do you?'

She nodded, swallowing a noisy sob.

'I feel guilty about my mum too,' he said, lowering his face. 'You're luckier than me; you knew your mum. I wish I'd known mine. Biggest wish I've ever had and can't make it come true.' He let go of her hands and raised one of his fingers to tap his temple. 'She's in here, though. 'S'pect you keep a little corner free for your mum as well, don't you.'

'Always.' She sensed he was about to get up so grabbed his fingers to keep him with her. She was keen to know more about his family. Hearing other people's lives were holed with heartache saddened her, but also helped her feel less alone. Her father, Johnny, her little sisters, they weren't hollowed out with grief and guilt as she was. 'Is your mum dead?' She watched him nod and grimace an affirmative. 'What about your dad? Where is he?'

'He's gone as well. But I remember him. I was six when he passed away. My dad was a fine gentleman but he got involved with bad people. Ireland's troubles make it a tricky place to be for some folk. So my gran and grandpa brought me and my half-brother to England when we were just kids, to get us away from the dangers back home. It'll be safer for the wee lads,' he mimicked in a faultless Irish accent. He chuckled sourly. 'Now Freddie's making munitions in Silvertown and I'm firing 'em in France.'

Clover digested all that. She had noticed a slight lilt to his accent and now he'd explained his background she understood its source. 'Will you go back to your homeland?'

'Never go back. The bad people killed my dad and the nuns killed my mum.' He slipped his fingers from hers and stood up, with a speed that told her he'd said all he wanted to.

The mention of nuns had propelled thoughts of Gabriel into Clover's mind. 'The nuns?' she whispered, horrified. 'What did they do?'

'Enough about it. You've trouble of your own to be getting on with. Didn't mean to be a misery like that.' Neil shoved his hands into his pockets. 'Anyway, I should go now . . . let you get on with the little ones.' He smiled at Annie, rubbing her eyes. 'Sleepy heads are ready for bed.'

'You don't want to tell me much about your family. Yet you know lots about mine.' It wasn't a complaint, more of a stated fact. 'I know you didn't have a choice in the matter. Our troubles landed on you whether you liked it or not.'

He chuckled ruefully at her persistence. 'So you want to know more . . . all right then. My mum was a wild colleen by all accounts. I know she was pretty, I've seen a picture of her. She fell for a rough sort, but he wasn't the fellow who loved her. Donald Ryan asked her to be his wife. She'd said yes, but then chose to go to a mission to have me, rather than marry him. She trusted the boy who'd sired me would rescue her and claim us both . . . make the fairy tale real.' He remained quiet for a moment. 'She died there and the man she'd betrayed brought me home to be with my brother and grandparents. Donald Ryan was a widower with a kid of his own but he adopted me and always treated us equally, as his sons.'

Clover digested all of that. 'The tricky people in Ireland who killed your stepdad . . . one of them was your real father?' she said.

'That's it. A fight over a woman . . . a dead woman; love . . . honour . . . religion. All those worthy things that end up bloody.' He turned to her. 'Enough of such talk in front of the children.' He smiled. 'Tell me about your football. I'm more of a rugby boy; Freddie's the footballer, and pretty good at it too.'

Clover was keen to know more about his story but didn't want to seem prying so let him change the subject. She suspected he knew about the ladies' football team at

Gudgeon's as his brother was the coach. She was pleased he was prolonging his stay with conversation. 'Only went for a kick about the once. Jeannie's talented and did her best to show me some tactics.' A nostalgic smile curved her mouth at memories of that wintry afternoon which seemed half a lifetime ago. 'I hoped I might get a job there with her, you see. Being good at football, like her, would impress Mr Ryan, she said.'

'Ah, that's what he sees in her, is it?' said Neil sardonically. 'D'you still want a job there?'

'Haven't got a reference and Jeannie says I need one.' She paused. 'Munitions factories should have strict rules, or dodgy sorts could sneak in there and sabotage the bombs.'

'Nobody would take you for a German spy.' He came close enough to skim a teasing finger on her cheek. 'Anyhow, I know you're not a dodgy sort, so I'll vouch for you. Least I can do after getting your name in the paper.'

She groaned. 'So, you saw it as well, did you?'

'Yeah.' He hung his head then gave her a serious look. 'I'd do it again though ... stop him manhandling you.'

'I'm glad we met, even that way, cos otherwise you wouldn't have been here when ...' She shrugged and let it go. They'd spoken enough about the night her mother died.

'I'll have a word with Freddie about vacancies. He owes me, and I owe you for losing you your job in the first place.' He paused. 'Have you seen anything of Fletcher?'

She shook her head. 'Don't want to either.' She had actually glimpsed him, a few days ago. He had been arm in arm with Nettie. She'd not felt jealous, but had been sad to think Nettie would inevitably drift further away from her. At school they'd been close yet her friend hadn't come to pay condolences or even just to see how she was. Her brother had told her about bumping into Nettie and that she'd asked after them all. If Archie was off the scene a reconciliation was possible. First, Nettie had to discover for herself, in the way Clover had, that beneath his smarm and good looks was a rather nasty character. Tricky, Neil might describe him.

Clover guessed Neil's guilt over his mother stemmed from her having died in childbirth. Clover had taken her baby brother to a convent believing it to be a safe place for him. She'd never felt comfortable leaving him with strangers though. After hearing Neil's story, her disquiet was growing.

She caught a glimpse of his hand approaching before it closed on her wrist and he drew her to her feet. Excitement fluttered in her belly as she saw a sultry gleam in his honey-coloured eyes.

'Would you like to go for a walk or have a bite to eat one evening? Won't outstay my welcome now, but I would like to see you again before I leave for France.'

Clover wanted to see him again, but she couldn't wait that long to ask him about the nuns. The question died on the tip of her tongue. The door burst open, making her skitter back, but thankfully a smaller version of her father motored in.

'What's for tea?' Johnny was breathless and red-faced from playing football and carried the fresh scent of January frost on his clothes.

'Umm ... fish paste sandwiches. Cut yourself some bread.' She sounded abrupt. It wasn't his fault he'd scared her half to death, but she was jangling with nerves, unable to even feel relief to see him rather than her father. Had it been a tipsy and belligerent Sidney Cooper barging in on the cosy scene, he would have picked a fight in front of his children.

Johnny started sawing at the loaf while grinning at them. 'You two lovebirds then, are yer?' He yelped as he cut his finger while not watching what he was doing.

'For goodness' sake, Johnny,' Clover scolded, while helping Rosie get down from the table. The twins had finished eating and were again restless. 'Think you should go now, Mr Ryan.' She was pink-cheeked and apologetic.

'Yeah, reckon I should,' he said, chuckling at the family chaos.

She watched him over a shoulder as he walked to the door then raised his hand in farewell.

'Has it stopped bleeding?' she asked Johnny, who was winding his handkerchief about the small cut.

'Dunno . . .' He peeled away an edge of cloth to frown at his stained skin.

'Looks all right to me,' she said. Having cut two slices of bread, she put down the knife. 'There, spread it yourself, I'll be back in a minute.'

She raced out into the corridor and caught up with Neil as he was by the entrance to the street. 'Thanks for coming.' She halted a few paces away.

He drew her slightly to one side, denying any prying eyes a view of them. 'I won't forget to speak to my brother. You'll get a job . . . might make the football team, too. You any good?'

'Not really.' She pulled a face then on impulse hugged him, a mingling of gratitude and natural affection for a man she felt she knew and could trust although they had only met a handful of times. Feeling rather awkward, she stepped back before his arms were fully about her.

'Will you write to me when I go back over there?' he asked. 'I'd like to . . .'

'How old are you, Clover Cooper?'

For a moment, Clover had to stop and think. She'd been about to say sixteen, but recalled that her birthday had passed by, unnoticed and uncelebrated, at the beginning of the month. 'Seventeen. How old are you?'

'Twenty-one ... feel a lot older sometimes.'

'Well, you don't look it. I thought you were younger. About nineteen like Archie.'

'Forget about him, shall we?' He dipped his head, touched together their lips and threaded his fingers through her thick auburn hair. 'You've the look of an Irish colleen, you know,' he teased and kissed her again.

Clover was just melting into the kiss, more leisurely and honeyed than Archie's rushed assaults, when she heard a man whistling. It was always the same tune. Sometimes her father would sing 'Mademoiselle from Armentières'. Her mother would tell him off for it. The last time she'd heard the saucy words they had been entering the railway station to see him off to war. Her mother had been warm flesh beside her ... but ill ... very ill. Clover hadn't realised on that day that Iris Cooper had already started to slide towards her death.

'My dad's coming,' she hissed. 'You'd better get going now, but would you meet me at the top of the road tomorrow ... about six o'clock?' She couldn't wait for him to release her and pushed him away. 'I want you to tell me about what happened to your mum at the mission because ...' She couldn't explain now. She needed a better time than this if she were to recount Gabriel's story. The whistling was getting louder and so was the sound of her father's boots.

A brief nod was her answer, and she gave him a swift peck on the cheek then hurried away.

*

186

'Evenin', said the younger man, and touched the brim of his army cap. He stepped off the kerb to avoid being bumped into. He received a mumbled response from Sidney Cooper who wasn't so tipsy that he'd miss a fellow Tommy. He was in civvies but liked to think soldiers could sniff out one of their own. If the docks didn't suit him he'd go back and fight alongside those comrades, he promised himself with an emotional sniff. A couple of pints and a whisky chaser had helped him forget that not so long ago desertion had seemed the only way out of the perils he faced day in, day out.

Since his wife had died he had a choice of two paths. Family or France. Bill Lewis was almost part of the family now he'd got cosy with Elsie. She wouldn't see her grand-kids go hungry so would be useful in helping him get his old job back ... and a pay rise.

Sidney chuckled to himself. That could wait for now. Lucy Dare was first on his list of things to do. Since he'd been back he'd been trying to bump into her but no luck. He imagined she was keeping her head down, feeling guilty over Iris.

He had a proposition for Lucy that would repay his late wife in some small part for their betrayal. Iris's kids had been her life. She would want her motherless chil-dren looked after, and he needed someone to keep house while he was away working or fighting, whichever he chose to do.

It had been over two decades since he'd joined in the game of kiss chase in the playground. He'd caught the blonde girl all the boys liked and he'd got his reward. He'd considered Lucy Dare to be his future wife from then on. A few years later, with school days behind them, she'd still been on the right side of respectable, but had turned him down. Things were different now though; she was older, still good looking, but not the head-turner she'd once been.

She'd have to give up the game; he'd never live down being married to a prostitute. He'd sooner marry someone homely ... someone mature ... someone like his mother-in-law ... the idea popped into his head, making him snort in amusement. Seriously though, he told himself, if a suitable widow crossed his path he'd hook up with her and carry on seeing Lucy on the side. All that courting malarkey took time and effort, though, he mocked himself, and he couldn't be bothered with any of it.

He knew Lucy inside out, and she was on the spot. She'd be the second Mrs Sidney Cooper, and they'd be married as soon as a decent period of mourning allowed. She'd have to shape herself up into a good wife and mother, or he'd do it for her.

Sidney had halted outside his house, about to go in, but now he had Lucy on his mind he decided there was no time like the present to track her down and tell her the good news.

Chapter Seventeen

When walking past the pie and mash shop earlier in the week, Lucy Dare had spotted Bill Lewis through the window, sitting at one of the tables. She knew he hadn't gone off fish and chips. It was her he was avoiding. Well, she wasn't giving up the chase that easily; in fact she'd taken it as a positive sign that he wasn't indifferent to her. If he had been, he'd still be queuing up outside Wally's place on a Friday night, ignoring her hints and winks. She was a temptation to him, that's how she saw it, and if anybody knew how men ticked, she did.

'Buck yer ideas up,' snapped Wally, nudging his star-gazing niece in the ribs. 'That's the second time you've wrapped 'addock 'stead of rock. Woss up with yer, gel?'

'Nuthin'... sorry, Wal.' Lucy righted her mistake and then used her pinny to wipe her greasy fingers as the customer went out, leaving the shop empty. She rested her back against the tiled wall. 'Gaspin' fer a cuppa, y'know. Go 'n' make us a brew, shall I, Uncle Wal?' If she could get out from under his nose, she'd have time to slip out the back way and go and see if Bill was at the pie shop. She was like a schoolgirl with a crush, and had considered going round and knocking on his door on some pre-text or other.

Her uncle didn't rise to the bait as she started sidling towards the back room. She might be family but no liberties were taken on Wally Watson's time. She'd get her tea break at the end of her shift and not before.

'Gissa song then, Canary.' Wally had turned his attention to the two factory girls who'd come in for their regular Friday night order of chips.

'Will if you gissa double helpin', Tubs,' the brashest of the two said. She leaned her elbow on the high counter, propped her yellow chin on her hand and began to warble a tuneless version of 'The Lambeth Walk'.

'If I was you, Uncle Wal,' said her friend. 'I'd give her double helpin' to put a sock in it.'

'Gawd, yer right about that.' Wally was screwing his face up into a pained expression. 'There yer go then ... two double 'elpin's fer me favourite gels. I've put in a pickled onion each ... vinegar's good fer the froat me wife says.' He smirked. 'An' don't come back no more or you'll put me out o' business.'

'Cheeky sod! See you next week then, Uncle Wal.' They slapped down their coppers and went off chattering about their dance hall trip planned for the weekend. Wally gave them a wave through the window.

The river and factory workers had all been in to collect their suppers on their way home from their day shifts. Those two Canary Girls were usually the last of the Brunner Mond lot to rush in, giggling, then rush out, filling their sallow faces with vinegary chips. No offence was taken on either side for the ribbing; he called them 'Canaries' and they called him 'Tubs' or 'Uncle Wal' now they'd heard Lucy do it. Those munitionettes were doing dangerous work for the sake of their Tommy fathers and brothers and sweet-hearts and were heroines in Wally's eyes.

The next big rush would be due after the pubs turned out. Wally was ready for a breather. His short legs were home to a roadmap of varicose veins that throbbed like billy-o if he didn't get off his feet during a lull. He'd joked with his gouty wife that they didn't have a decent set of pins between them. He came out from behind the counter and eased his bulk down into a metal chair positioned at the solitary small table. Wedging an elbow in between the condiments and ashtrays on the dented top, he propped a jowl on his knuckles. His free hand ferreted in his pocket for a packet of Player's. Wally lit a cigarette, took a drag then stabbed the burning tip at his sulking niece. 'You've got Sidney Cooper on yer mind, I reckon.'

'I ain't,' harrumphed Lucy, coming to slump down oppo-site him at the table. 'Gissa fag, Uncle Wal,' she cajoled, drumming her fingers restlessly. She was smiling at him but still brooding on Bill Lewis.

Wally pushed the Player's and a box of matches across the table and settled back, his batter-spattered apron straining over his pot belly. 'We all thought you 'n' Sidney would get hitched, y'know, back when you was at school together.' He gave a nostalgic sigh. 'Your aunt reckons him an 'andsome fellow. And your old mum liked him, y'know.'

'If she could spot a wrong 'un,' muttered Lucy beneath her breath, 'she wouldn't have married me father.'

'Wossat?' Wally cupped his ear for her to repeat herself.

'Nuthin ... just sayin', I miss me mum.' That was true, she did, she thought, blowing smoke up at the ceiling. A vision of her mother in her mind's eye was being replaced by a rugged masculine face. She wondered if she should call round Bill's and make out she'd heard he wasn't well. She could take him a portion of haddock 'n' chips ... say she was worried he wasn't eating properly.

'Terrible shame Sid's wife dyin' young,' said Wally, shaking his head. 'Poor kids.'

'Need the privy.' Lucy jumped up, clutching her belly. If he wasn't letting her go and make the tea, she'd resort to having a sudden guts' ache to escape. If she was quick she might be able to intercept Bill on his route home if he was at the pie 'n' mash shop.

Wally watched her rush out of the door. He sucked his teeth, and stubbed out his cigarette. He'd overdone it dropping those heavy hints about her and Sidney. He'd not intended to upset the girl, rather the reverse. She was bound to be sensitive over it all and he'd acted like a bull in a china shop. As far as he could see, though, her boyfriend would soon be looking for a wife, and she was already front of the queue. She needed to make sure she stayed there as there were lots of recent war widows needing a man to replace a dead husband. With Lucy's reputation dragging her back, there wouldn't be many such chances coming her way.

Wally pushed himself to his feet as a youth entered the shop wanting a ha'porth of chips. Still preoccupied, Wally dished up a rare mountain of them into newspaper, making the happy customer drop his copper, grab his parcel and scoot before the mistake was rectified.

Wally had known for ages about Sidney Cooper and Lucy carrying on behind his wife's back. Everybody knew. It'd be a crying shame if his niece let her conscience get in the way of making things legal with the man she'd stuck by, but could never before call her own.

Sidney Cooper's reflections more or less mirrored Wally Watson's. He knew Lucy could be hard as nails but she had a softer side too. He guessed she was feeling awkward about seeing him too soon, with his wife barely cold in her grave. Well, nothing could be done to wipe out their affair or to bring Iris back, so there was no point fretting over it, in Sidney's view.

He'd turned into a street of ugly terraces facing one another across a narrow lane. He stopped by a door with barely a strip of paint left on it and gave it a polite rat-a-tat.

'Lucy in, is she?'

'No, she ain't, and if you see her you can tell her from me if she don't stump up her share o' the rent she won't be coming back here. She's a bleedin' ponce, you can tell her that 'n' all. Now piss off.'

Sidney had the door slammed in his face by the surly brunette who shared a bedsitting room with Lucy. It rather upset him, being spoken to like this when he'd been feeling mellow after passing the nice young Tommy in the street. He hammered on the door with his fist. 'Mind yer manners, you old bag,' he shouted.

She didn't open up to have another go so with a final whack to the splintery wood, he started off up the road. If nothing else, the altercation had sobered him up and he had quite a spring in his step and a direction in which to head.

Somebody in the pub had told him Lucy had been spotted working in her uncle's shop. Sidney had guffawed so hard he'd had to wipe tears from his eyes. Lucy Dare was more likely to be found shovelling coal than frying fish. But he knew where Wally's chippie was, and feeling a bit peckish, decided there'd be no harm going that way and killing two birds with one stone. He could buy a fish supper and have a word with Wally about these rumours he was hearing.

He didn't need to go as far as Wally's place. He'd spotted Lucy standing beneath the railway arch by the pie and mash shop and with her was the other person he had on his list of people to see.

They'd heard him approach and turned in unison to look his way. Bill Lewis crossed the road and was soon heading in the opposite direction without a glance back. Sidney watched Lucy, watching the man turning the corner. She appeared on the brink of going after him. A seed of suspicion was planted and wasn't unearthed when she hurried towards him. He'd detected caginess beneath her smile. The seed started to sprout.

'Been looking for you fer days, gel.'

'Been busy ... working ...'

'He's work, is he?' He jabbed a nod up the road.

'Him? Don't be daft. He's your mother-in-law's feller.'

'Yeah, he is. So what would you have to say to him if he ain't a punter?'

'Just ... passing condolences onto Elsie ... about ... well, you know what about.'

'Ain't passed condolences on to me, have yer? Why's that? You been avoiding me?'

'Said, ain't I, I've been working.' Lucy sounded shirty. She might have been sleeping with him for years, but she slept with lots of men. He'd always known what she was ... what she did ... and he'd no right to act as though he now owned her because his wife was off the scene. She intended to carry on seeing who she liked and doing what she wanted. She'd been wavering over whether to pack him in for good; she wasn't now. Bill Lewis or no Bill Lewis by her side, she was done with Sidney Cooper. 'I've got to get back. Me uncle Wally's waiting for me.'

In blocking her path he'd brought himself close enough to distinguish a smell of cooking lard. 'Bleedin' hell!' he exclaimed, and sniffed her hair. 'You have been frying fish, ain't yer. What a pong.'

'What's so funny about that?' she snapped as he hooted in derision. 'Nothing wrong with getting an honest job, is there?'

'Calm down . . . just havin' a joke.' He started to schmooze her, nuzzling her cheek, and snaking an arm round her to fondle her buttocks. 'I'll walk back with you. Heard you was working in Wally's – surprised me it did, I have to say.' He linked their arms, too possessively for Lucy's liking, and started to urge her towards the fish shop.

Lucy pulled away from his control. 'This ain't right, Sid, after, you know . . . what happened to Iris. It's too soon . . . disrespectful . . .' She began taking small backward steps. 'I'll catch up with you another time.'

'You think I was born yesterday, doncha?' he snarled through gritted teeth. 'You're after Bill Lewis.'

'So what if I am,' she shouted impetuously, knocking away his grabbing hand. 'Ain't none of your business. I ain't yer wife. And bleedin' glad about that 'n' all after what happened to the poor cow.'

Sidney's open palm cracked against her cheek, sending her to her knees on the cobbles. It wasn't the first time he'd hit her. He'd hit most of the women in his life, including his mother. It was the only way to shut them up when he'd heard enough from them.

'Was gonna ask you to marry me, you bitch.'

'Well, 'case you do, here's me answer in advance,' Lucy panted out, in between sobbing and nursing her stinging cheek. 'Don't want to marry you. Never did. Turned you down, remember.'

'Dunno what I was thinking anyhow, inviting a whore into me home.' He contemptuously pushed her down with the toe of his boot as she struggled to get up off the ground. 'Got kids to think of – me teenage daughter needs somebody respectable around her. And that ain't you.'

Lucy scrambled up to point a finger in his face. 'Your precious Clover's no angel,' she scoffed. 'She's knocking around with Archie Fletcher and not only him either. I've seen two of 'em fighting over her. Got sacked from the tobacconist's, she did, for acting like a little tart with customers. Ask anybody.' Lucy was maddened by his insults but retained enough sense to keep back Neil Ryan's name. She'd enough trouble with family as it was without making matters worse. She didn't give a toss about Archie Fletcher. He was overdue a hiding. He'd tried to get her to do it with him and had got nasty when she refused.

Sidney was dazed by what he'd heard, and Lucy saw a chance to escape. She ran up the road, casting glances over a shoulder, fearful of pursuit.

He sniffed in disgust and spat onto the pavement after her. Then with grim determination etched on his face, he set off in the opposite direction, following Bill Lewis. He'd be first, then after that he'd sort out his eldest daughter. And Archie Fletcher.

When she realised he wasn't coming after her Lucy stopped and leaned back against the wall with her chest heaving. She felt bad dropping Clover in it, but she'd been unable to control her tongue or her temper with him treating her like dirt. Lucy gnawed at her thumbnail wondering if she should try to pacify Sidney. More likely she'd enrage him further and earn herself another black eye. She could feel the throb in her cheekbone and knew she'd be sporting a shiner in the morning. They'd argued before but never as badly as this. She needed to collect her wages and wouldn't get them if she didn't finish her shift. She had rent to pay or her roommate would kick her out. The mean cow had threatened to do so before and this time Lucy reckoned she meant it.

Wincing in pain, she mopped her tear-stained face with a sleeve then straightened her dishevelled clothes. Her stocking had got torn when he'd knocked her down and blood was trickling from her grazed knee. She pulled the wool to cover the wound then tilted her chin and marched on towards the fish shop.

She needed a plausible excuse for her long absence. Telling Wally her guts' ache had necessitated a search for bog paper for the privy was the best she could come up with. As was telling him she'd tripped up and bashed her face on the kerb in her rush to get back and finish her shift.

Chapter Eighteen

Elsie had spent a good fifteen minutes loitering behind her net curtain, watching for her neighbour to return home. The moment she identified his big body approaching through the gaslit gloom she'd sped to open her door and catch him before he disappeared inside.

'Have you got a tick, Bill?'

'Always got time for you, love.' Bill tipped his head at his front door. 'Coming in with me then?'

'Oh, no rush. Have your tea then come over when you're ready. Don't nod off though and leave me in the lurch,' she said ruefully. 'I'll be waiting for you.'

'That sounds like an offer I can't refuse . . .' He chuckled; the dusk might be concealing her colour but he knew brash Elsie Hall was blushing. 'I've had me tea; stopped off for a pie on the way home, so I'll come over now.' He withdrew his key from the lock and made his way down his path and up hers. 'No time like the present, eh, Elsie?'

She smiled although his innocent remark had jolted her daughter back to the forefront of her mind.

For her and Iris the present and future had vanished and the past had been squandered through bitterness. The birthdays and Christmases that should have been spent together had been lost. Elsie had never experienced joyful times welcoming a new life into the family; grandchildren that could be celebrated, not denied like the poor mite her daughter had given birth to only months ago. What a wicked trick fate had played on Iris just as bridges were being built back. A route to her baby son might eventually have revealed itself and some happy memories been forged to blot out the wasted years.

'Not on shift this evening?' asked Bill, now standing beside her.

'Got a couple of days off. Back to work Monday.'

'Hope you've got the kettle on, love. Could murder a brew.'

'Can do better than that.' Elsie had snapped out of her melancholy and given him a wink. A few minutes to herself, to take off her apron and pull a brush through her hair, had been her plan. She'd acted on the spur of the moment, and overlooked the fact that Bill might too.

She led the way into the back parlour. The scene had been prepared with a bottle of port and two glasses set on a table lit with a solitary candle. A small mound of coal was burning in the grate, assisting in illuminating the room and dancing shadows on the walls.

'This is a nice surprise,' he said, as he took in the cosy atmosphere. 'I should go home and freshen up.' He grimaced down at his rough attire and hobnail boots.

'You're good enough for me.' She clasped his hand and gave it a firm affectionate shake. 'Now you're here you'd better stay or I might chicken out.' She started untying her apron strings, frowning with the effort of putting her rehearsed conversation in the right order. 'You've been a big help over the past weeks, Bill, and I can't let it pass unremarked. You've always been a shoulder to lean on but this time – with Iris – it's been different. I fell to bits and I honestly don't know what I would've done without you . . .'

'Hey, you don't have to thank me, love. I might not have kids of me own but that don't mean I can't imagine the hell of losing one.'

Elsie nodded her appreciation for his empathy, then dropped her chin as tears began to slide down her cheeks.

'If we're doing speeches then I should thank you, for letting me share in your family over the years.' He took up the conversation, allowing her time to compose herself. 'When your grandkids used to pop in after school, I'd look forward to that, y'know. I got to tuck into jelly 'n' cake for a start.' His teasing was rewarded with a croaky chuckle. 'I used to wish I'd had a nan like you when I was a kid. Most me 'n' me brother got off our nan was a kick up the backside if we forgot to fetch along some snuff swiped out me father's tin.' He shook his head at the memory. 'Cor, she was a bruiser, that woman, God rest her. Me old granddad was scared of her.' He cocked his head at Elsie and glimpsed another smile breaking through. 'Honest truth, that is.' He shrugged. 'I looked forward to having a game of cards with your Johnny . . . till he started beating me. Little sod could earn himself a living as a sharp.'

'You was the one taught him how to palm cards, as I recall,' said Elsie, back to normal and sounding sardonic.

'That's true.' Bill rolled his eyes. 'Anyway when those two stopped coming over so often I missed 'em.'

'Clover grew up and started work, and Johnny . . . well the boy prefers his pals to his old nan's company now.' She'd fond memories of those visits too and smiled nostalgically.

'As for Iris,' said Bill, 'never really knew the gel, but I felt I did cos you told me so much about her. Did me heart good when you two made up.'

'And mine . . . never been so happy.' Elsie dabbed away a few more tears. But the worst of her grief was spent, for now at least. 'Any old how, I've not forgotten that you helped pay for me daughter's funeral.' She was business-like again and stuffed her wet hanky up her sleeve. 'I'll pay it back soon as I can. Could wait forever and a day for me son-in-law to offer to settle up with you, or even to thank you for giving his wife a decent burial.'

'Let's not talk about him.' Bill drew her closer. 'What's really on your mind, Elsie? I know it's not money.'

'No . . . not money . . . though it is a consideration, and shouldn't be overlooked.' Elsie turned her attention to the port and poured two measures. She handed him his glass then gulped from hers. 'I want to marry you, Bill, if you'll still have me, that is.' She finished the port in another swallow, feeling as nervous as a virgin on her wedding night. 'I'd very much like to marry you, actually.'

'That's the best news I've had in a long while.' He put down his drink and cupped her strong handsome face before kissing her lips.

'You should know why I've had a change of heart.' She rubbed her hands over his, the factory damage on her palms butting against the horny ridges on his fingers.

'I know why, Elsie,' he said. 'You've got four grandkids that need looking after because their father's a useless parasite.' His tone was mild but there was a gravity in his expression. 'It's a lot for you to take on, on your own.'

'At my age, you mean?' She cocked her head, demanding his honesty.

'At any age, love,' he said wryly. 'I'm ready fer the challenge, if you are.'

She freed the hanky from her sleeve as her eyes began prickling again. Bittersweet feelings had set her off this time, not grief. Bill had no children of his own, but for her he'd care for another man's brood because Sidney Cooper was too rotten to do it himself. 'There's something else to tell you, Bill. I've not spoken of this before cos it was too personal and painful . . .' She paused. 'If I start at the beginning, you'll understand why I've kept it quiet.'

'I don't want you to upset yourself again.'

'I have to . . . it's important,' she said simply. 'Everything should be straight between us if we're to be husband and wife. I'd sooner know now if you still want to go ahead after hearing all my reasons for wanting us to be married.'

'I'm listening then.'

'I've got five grandchildren, not four. And there's one final thing I have to do for Iris. I owe it to her, you see, to bring her little illegitimate baby back home, if I can.'

Some several minutes later, and even before she had finished recounting the tale to him, she could see he was shocked. And Bill Lewis didn't shock easily. He got up and refilled their glasses to the brim then handed one to her.

'Your granddaughter Clover must be made of strong stuff to have coped with all this.'

'She is . . . she's the loveliest girl, bright as a button and not a cowardly bone in her body,' said Elsie proudly.

'Thing is, how on earth are you gonna square this with Sidney Cooper? He knows how many kids he's got.'

Elsie swayed her head, wordlessly conveying that she'd not the foggiest idea. She watched for his reaction as she said, 'Might seem a bit far-fetched, but it is possible the boy could be ours. My body's still doing what it needs to, if you get my drift. And I could find an excuse for why we decided to keep it all hidden until after we got married.' His response was to throw back what remained of his port and noisily swallow it. 'I'll understand, if you want to have second thoughts, Bill. Wouldn't blame you at all . . .'

He came to sit down by the side of her chair. 'I love you, Elsie, but ain't gonna lie any more than you are. So can't say I'm overjoyed to hear things are more complicated than I thought, when they was already complicated enough. What about the baby's father? If you start wheeling a pram about, Randall might guess the truth. Will he claim his boy?'

'Bruce Randall's too weak to do anything like that,' said Elsie with a hint of contempt. 'He gave Iris money for an abortion; he didn't want the child. I reckon he'll keep schtum and let us carry on cleaning up his mess so he can pretend he's a virtuous bloke.'

Bill rested his elbows on his knees and gazed at the coals changing colour. Eventually, he said, 'If you think that line might work, I'll go along with the baby being ours. Only thinking though it would be easier getting things off the ground if Sidney wasn't around.'

'Could be he won't be for much longer,' said Elsie. 'I saw Mrs Waverley earlier . . . gossip who lives down Sid's road,' she explained. 'Doris knows everything about everyone before they know it themselves. She told me something I didn't know: Sid's been saying he's sorting things out at home so he can go back and fight.' She pursed her lips. 'Clover's in line for a factory job that'll put some cash in her pocket and give her a chance to play football with her friends. I'll not see Sidney Cooper take that away from her and turn her into a drudge.' Elsie paused. 'As for that trollop he knocks about with, I won't see her near my grandkids. And that's final.'

Bill was aware of a recent development in that set-up; when Lucy Dare had accosted him outside the pie and mash shop she'd said she was packing in Sidney Cooper. Bill hoped he'd made it clear it was of no interest to him what she did. But it wasn't the right time to bring Elsie up to date with Lucy's infatuation with him.

'The worst thing is . . .' Elsie gave the saddest of sighs '. . . Iris should still be taking care of her kids herself. She was on the mend until he turned up on leave. It's his fault she died.' Elsie dug her elbows into her knees, covered her face with her hands and sobbed.

Bill wasn't sure how Sid could be blamed, but kneeled in front of Elsie's chair and enclosed her heaving shoulders in an embrace. When she quietened, they sat in silence for a while, picking through their own thoughts on how the foundling could be reclaimed and legitimised. Bill gave up first on finding a fail-safe solution. He took her hand and held it cradled in his. 'How about we forget all of it for a little while, Elsie, and make our plans. I think we should get married straight away.'

'I do too. At the town hall. Just us. I'll tell Clover and Johnny afterwards, when it's done.'

He leaned in and gave her a kiss. 'Let's toast our engage-ment then, eh?' He stood up, and held out a hand to draw her to her feet.

For the first time, she put her arms around his neck to kiss him leisurely and passionately, savouring the taste of his liquor-coated lips. 'I'll toast us, Bill, but not here . . .' She let go of him to pick up the bottle and the glasses. 'We could get com-fortable in there . . . if you like.' She nodded at her bedroom door.

'Thought you'd never ask.'

'Hope I've not forgotten how to make a baby.' She was only half joking. There had been many barren years without a man in bed beside her.

'Don't worry, love,' he said, swinging her up in his arms as though her buxom body was feather-light. 'I haven't ...'

The noise had woken Elsie up, though she didn't realise it as she surfaced from a lovely sleep. The sensation of warm masculine skin beneath her cheek was unfamiliar ... quite startling ... then she remembered. A smile crinkled her cheeks and she stretched, barely wincing as long dormant bones and muscles protested at their recent exercise. Bill hadn't been asleep; he'd been cradling his naked fiancée in one arm while the other pillowed his head. While gazing up at the ceiling, he'd been marvelling at the siren masquerading as Elsie Hall. He'd love her whatever, but discovering they were as well matched in bed as out of it was undoubtedly a delightful bonus for them both. The less pleasant excitement entering his life had barely got a look in as he'd lain appreciating his good luck and watching the moon stripe silver across the ceiling. Pretty good omens, he'd been thinking. And then the banging had started. He'd vainly hoped Elsie would sleep through it. There'd been a lull in the noise and Bill was praying the bastard had gone away ... but that would have been too easy.

The racket began again, closer and louder, and accompanied by Elsie's name being bellowed this time, instead of his.

'Gawdsake.' Elsie struggled to sit up, still in a daze. 'Somebody's hammering on me door, Bill.' She scrambled towards the edge of the bed.

'Just ignore him and he'll go away.' Bill knew who it was

and it wouldn't take Elsie long to liven up and identify her son-in-law's coarse voice either. If Lucy Dare had made good on her promise to jilt Sidney Cooper this evening he would have put two and two together and come up with the wrong answer after seeing them talking.

Elsie was belting her dressing gown with a grim expression on her face. 'It's bloody Sid. I hope the children are all right,' was her first concern. 'He's probably after another handout,' she reassured herself. 'Well, he can have a few home truths instead.'

Realising she intended to open up, Bill swung his legs over the edge of the bed and started pulling on his trousers. 'I'll see to him. He's probably after me, love ...' He wasn't quick enough to prevent Elsie marching out of the room, yelling at Sidney to tone it down.

The moment the door was opened, Sidney barged into the passageway, knocking Elsie back a few paces. He gave her and her nightclothes the once-over. Then his attention was grabbed by the man emerging bare-chested from the bedroom. 'Well, ain't this cosy,' said Sidney with lewd sarcasm.

'Keep yer comments to yerself.' Elsie wasn't taking any moralising from him. 'What is it you want, I'm busy.'

'Can see that, love.' Sidney growled a dirty laugh. It didn't come as a surprise to him that they were lovers but what he heard next knocked him for six.

'We're getting married tomorrow. So if you've fetched up here to cause trouble, Cooper, you can clear off. Don't need it and ain't putting up with it.' Bill had moved to position himself in front of Elsie. The men were almost chest to chest, Bill slightly shorter but broader than Sidney, who seemed too shocked to recharge his belligerence. He stopped lounging against the wall and straightened up with his jaw sagging.

'Married?' Sidney strangled the word, swinging a glance between them.

Elsie imagined she'd need to get used to that sort of reaction in others. She wasn't about to let him know that he'd wounded her though. 'If nothing important's brought you here, sling yer 'ook,' she snapped.

'I reckon you're about to have them rose-tinted specs knocked off yer bonce, Elsie.' Sidney had conquered his surprise and was now feeling spiteful. 'I come to see *him* ... warn him off.' He jerked his head at Bill. 'He's been pestering Lucy, and she ain't interested now she's got regular work.'

'My eye she has ...'

'I was getting hitched meself for the nippers' sake, and so I can go back and fight the Hun.' He'd been deaf to Elsie's scoffing, too busy painting himself as the martyr. 'Lucy Dare ain't the best I can do, but the kids need a mother at short notice. We was all set until he started sniffing around, causing trouble.' Sidney jabbed a finger at Bill while watching his mother-in-law. She looked as shocked by his marriage plans as he'd been by hers. Sidney was still smarting from Lucy's rejection, but spreading discontent around always brightened him up. He reckoned Elsie would want some answers from lover boy.

'Ain't even going to defend meself against something as stupid as that,' said Bill. 'I am going to kick you out of here, though, Cooper.'

Elsie held Bill back as he lunged forward. She wouldn't give her son-in-law the satisfaction of driving a wedge between them. 'If you won't speak up for yourself, I'll do it for you.' She stabbed a finger against the troublemaker's shoulder. 'Bill's a decent man; not something you'd recognise cos you judge by your own standards. If you had a single decent bone in yer body, Sidney Cooper, you would have visited your wife's grave by now and taken her some flowers.' Elsie knew he hadn't as she went there every day without fail and talked to Iris, and promised to buy her a marble headstone. But somebody had been leaving flowers anonymously, and she reckoned she knew who it was, too.

'You had no right to bury me wife without me being present.' Sidney reciprocated by poking Elsie in the shoulder, but backed off as Bill made a move.

'I say different. Could've been months before wheels turned to bring you back from the front line. Iris deserved to be laid to rest as soon as possible.' All this was true, but Elsie had also wanted the whole thing presented as over and done with, to curtail Sidney's questions when he got back.

'Got no time for cemetery visits and my job's to feed me kids not waste cash buying a dead woman flowers.'

'She was your wife,' roared Elsie.

'Weren't ever my idea to marry her,' he bellowed back. 'She didn't want it neither. There was no love there; you made us get married.'

Elsie had no defence against that; it was a festering truth that had eaten away at her over many years. Though estranged from her daughter and son-in-law she had kept tabs on them from afar. She knew that throughout their married life the couple had remained apart despite sharing the same bed and the same roof.

Bill tried to draw her aside so he could throw Sidney out. But she wouldn't budge. This boil needed lancing. 'Iris deserved your respect if nothing else. You didn't even give her that for all the years she raised your kids. You've got no time and no money, so you say,' she sneered in a steely quiet voice. 'Always find enough of both to drink in the pub or knock around with yer tart, though, doncha?' There was something else to say; her daughter had made her promise not to mention this, but Iris was beyond being hurt or betrayed now. He wasn't, and she'd relish seeing him squirm. 'My daughter wouldn't need flowers on her grave, she'd still be here if you hadn't forced yourself on her when she was already in a bad way. You gave her an infection, caught off that poxy tart, I shouldn't wonder.' Elsie clenched her fists, feeling tempted to batter him and damn the consequences. 'Shame you wasn't shot in France then Iris would still be alive. You killed her, you animal.'

Bill had heard enough and seen enough. He pulled Elsie away before blows were traded, cuddling her against his shoulder. Her fury had blinded her to the suspicion on her son-in-law's face. He also looked embarrassed to have been exposed as a rapist. 'Get out of here, Cooper, or you'll leave on the end of me boot.' Bill snarled the threat through gritted teeth.

'Ain't going nowhere till I've said me piece.' Sidney no longer sounded aggressive, rather like somebody with a defence to make and a puzzle to solve. 'A man's entitled to have conjugals with his wife,' he blustered. 'And it don't give her enteritis anyhow. You said her bad bowels was what killed her.' Sidney had thought little at the time about his wife's bleeding. He'd accepted what he'd been told about her poor health. He was thinking about all of it now though. He'd had enough kids to know that a woman bled for a while after giving birth . . . and after a miscarriage. His wife had had one of those in the years between Johnny's and the twins' arrivals.

While Sidney was occupied working things out in his head, Bill decided to act. Grabbing Sidney's scruff, he propelled him out onto the front step, but the man sprang into life kicking at the door to prevent it being slammed.

Legs akimbo and fists held out in front of him, Sidney stood rigidly in the opening. His eyes darted up down and all around as his busy brain continued to whir. 'You've all been lying to me,' he announced in a holler. 'Iris was pregnant, weren't she?'

Bill slammed the door and this time Sidney reacted too late to stop him.

'I'll see the death certificate,' he bawled out. 'And the doctor wot signed it. I'll find out the truth.' This wasn't so much a threat as a whine of self-pity. 'Me wife was playing around behind me back and I can guess who with 'n' all.'

After a few moments, Elsie heard his trudging footsteps moving away. She felt as though a weight had slid off her shoulders following this showdown. She'd long wanted to tell Sidney Cooper what she thought of him. She gave a shattered-looking Bill a rueful smile. 'Welcome to the family,' she said, making him smirk and shake his head in ironic disbelief. 'And it's all right, love, I don't believe a word of his lies about you 'n' Lucy Dare.'

'She did speak to me this evening as I was coming out of the pie shop.' Bill came clean in case she heard gossip from somebody who'd spotted Lucy hanging around him.

'Can't blame her fer trying her luck,' said Elsie, resting her head against his shoulder. 'Ain't many good men like you around.' She looked up at him. 'I trust you, Bill. You've just proved me right to do so by being honest and telling me about her.' She pecked his lips, then took his hand and led him up the corridor. 'After all that excitement reckon I need a lie down. Come on, let's go back to bed.'

Chapter Nineteen

With a bit of encouragement, Sidney might have been able to love Iris, but apart from that one occasion when they'd met behind the mission house, she'd always been cold to him. She'd allowed him his dues as a husband but her heart had never been in it. Being proud, he'd never let on that he'd wished it was. She'd only herself to blame for him carrying on with Lucy after they were married.

Iris had been naive and brought up in a respectable family. Sidney had been a latchkey kid, shrewd when still in short trousers. His merchant seaman father had rarely been at home and had walked out on his mother for good when his son was nine. She, in turn, had abandoned her only child the day he turned twelve; old enough in her eyes to fend for himself. He never told anybody this; he made up stories about his dead parents even now. His father had died during a storm at sea and his mother had suffered a breakdown and gone into an asylum. This was his romantic version of his upbringing, for anybody who asked, including his girlfriend and his wife. He'd no idea if his parents were still alive and no longer gave a damn, in any case.

A handsome, well-built twelve year old, he'd managed to

scratch himself a living. He'd been earning from the age of about six, anyway, fetching and carrying for neighbours for coppers, and acting as a bookies' runner. He'd realised early on that women liked him. His mother had encouraged him to play up to the old girls and woe betide if he didn't fetch home all the tips or food that came his way. He progressed to pilfering cigarettes, or trinkets to pawn, and continued to schmooze and fleece unsuspecting women. He didn't finish his schooling but became popular with his old classmates for a while. They'd appreciated sharing his cigarettes and booze ... until they realised he wanted favours in return.

Eventually, friends drifted away and the old girls sussed he wasn't such a lovely lad. A proper job on the docks came next when scrounging and stealing netted slim pickings that rarely kept up with his aspirations. By then, he'd hooked up with Lucy Dare and realised he'd found a kindred spirit, and a source of extra income. Though he'd hit anybody who called him a ponce, including her.

He'd expected something in return from Iris after she'd shared his cigarettes and brown ale under the trees behind the mission house. She'd not mellowed, as most girls did when they'd had a drink, she'd panicked and after a couple of kisses had wanted to go home before she was missed. Sidney had resented being made a fool of, as he saw it. Knowing what he knew now, he wished he'd let her go rather than pinning her down on a bed of fallen cherry blossom. Because after that ...

His reminiscing had reached a crucial point and he stopped to lean against the wall, wallowing in his self-pity. He dug in a pocket for his tin of tobacco. There was just enough in it to scrape together a saggy roll-up. Since being widowed, he'd been on the receiving end of sympathy from people who'd no time for him before, and it often came in the shape of tankards of beer and packs of cigarettes. Generosity was wearing thin now many weeks had passed since the funeral; friends were scarce and even Lucy had turned against him. All because of his wife dying.

Without meaning to, he'd stopped close to the cemetery and his resentment for Iris started to bubble up. If he knew where to find her burial plot he'd go in there and dance on her grave and tell the cheating cow what he thought of her. What a laughing stock he would have been if she'd had another child. Everybody would've known it couldn't be his when he'd been overseas for ages. He apathetically conceded he might've given Iris an infection; he'd been burning down there since the last time he visited Sophie. He'd not admitted to anybody that he had a girl in France but Lucy was clued up and didn't need telling about Tommies and French brothels. It brightened him up to think that she might be keeping her distance from jealousy ... a solvable problem. As was him having the clap. He'd had it before and a dose of colloidal silver at the field clinic had worked a treat.

The thin roll-up had gone out. Sidney lowered his head to relight it beneath the shelter of his hat brim and started brooding on family again. His kids would have a new grandfather when Elsie Hall remarried. He wondered how Clover and Johnny would take to that news. He had other matters bugging him where Clover was concerned. The girl was in line for a clump, and so was Archie Fletcher. Sidney had heard tell, rather than knew about him, but had taken against him anyway. It didn't occur to him that hearsay painted Fletcher as a younger version of himself.

Footsteps echoing eerily in the quiet caught Sidney's

attention. He glanced up and a man he recognised passed beneath a gas lamp then headed into the cemetery with a bunch of flowers. Sidney forgot about Clover and Archie. He drew his lips back against his teeth, a weird mixture of hatred and satisfaction firing him up. He dropped the useless doofer that refused to light and crossed the road. He might not know where his wife was buried but he reckoned the bloke carrying the flowers did. And he had something to say – and do – to Bruce Randall.

Sidney stalked him over the grass, stubbing his toe on granite in the twilight and overturning a pot. Randall stopped and turned around. After some seconds had passed, Sidney bobbed his head up from behind the stone angel he'd hidden behind. His quarry was on the move again, meandering through the headstones. Soon, he'd reached his destination and Sidney waited for Randall to lay down his flowers before running and pouncing.

'That's decent of you, pal, fetching these to me wife.' He swooped on the bouquet and in a savage swing of an arm whipped Randall's shocked face with them then hurled the bunch aside. He quickly took advantage while his rival blinked and rubbed his watery eyes. A single sinewy hand was clamped on Randall's throat. 'I just found out why my wife died. She was pregnant and it didn't end well. It was you knocked her up and killed her, didn'tcha ... didn'tcha.' Sidney shook him like a terrier with a rat though he wasn't expecting an answer. The man couldn't breathe let alone speak. His bulging eyes were filled with terror and his frantic fingernails were clawing at his captor's hands in a vain attempt to prise off the stranglehold. Sidney gave him a shove that sent him tottering backwards. He'd not done with him yet but wanted to hear his wife's lover whine for forgiveness before knocking his teeth down his throat.

Randall collapsed to his knees on the crumbly earth of Iris's grave, gasping and choking. His shoulders were jumping as his asthmatic lungs fought to pump air into his body. He cast a despairing look around, but nobody was about to help him. The cemetery was deserted and only the slabs of marble and stone, limey beneath a full moon, leavened the dusk. He deliberately came here at twilight, hoping to be alone and unseen at Iris's grave.

'This'd been going on a while, had it?' Sidney didn't wait for a reply; he kicked Randall in the hip, sending him over onto his back. 'I asked you how long yer bin messing around with my wife. Even before I went off to France, was it?'

'No ... afterwards ...' The croaked answer was barely audible.

'Speak up, pal, can't hardly hear yer,' taunted Sidney, hauling the lightweight fellow to his feet by grabbing a handful of fair hair. The punch he'd given Randall over Clover's job hardly touched the sides when it came to exacting revenge. If Randall hadn't been in the background all the while, tempting her, Iris might have treated her husband better, was his maudlin view of things.

Scratch marks from the flower stems had torn thin lines on Randall's face, and bloody tear trails stretched from his eyes to his chin, making him look clown-like.

Sidney laughed and hit his rival in the face with a hefty jab that took Randall off his feet and onto his back on the adjacent grave. It was recently occupied, topped by soft earth like Iris's, but a small commemorative bronze had been stuck into it that bit into his back. Yelping in pain, he flopped over onto his belly, and expecting a kick, raised his head to shout for mercy. But he didn't. Something had caught his eye. The next grave in the row was open, awaiting a recipient, and a shovel was anchored into the mound of excavated soil. Randall started to crawl on all fours towards it, appearing to lack the energy to get to his feet. When he judged himself close enough he leapt up, yanked at the shovel, and freed it at the second attempt, showering himself in earth. The momentum took him staggering back a pace, but he found his balance and blindly charged with a fierce Geronimo cry, swinging the thing with all his might.

The scattered flowers had been gathered up and placed carefully on top of the flattened soil. Randall found the shovel he'd thrown aside and gave a final neatening scrape to the grave's edges, then he rammed the tool back in the heap of earth from whence he'd taken it. Without a glance back, he started limping towards the exit, then cursed and put on a spurt. He'd spotted the elderly caretaker swinging a lantern and ambling towards the gates. Bruce was gritting his teeth against the pain that shot through his bruised body as he slipped out into the street with seconds to spare.

'Nearly caught yer, squire.' The caretaker didn't bother much with opening and closing. Nobody was going to try to escape, after all. Tonight he had made the effort and lifted his hat with a cheery, 'Ain't a place I'd want to get stuck in all night, I can tell yer. Young feller like you could shin up 'n' over though.' He turned from fiddling with the padlock and realised he was talking to himself. The latecomer had already crossed the road and was hurrying away. He picked up his lantern, and having tested the padlock with a yank, headed for home himself.

Once he'd turned the corner, Randall collapsed back

against the flank wall of a house. He rested motionless for a second or two then stuffed a fist to his mouth to muffle a howl of relief that transformed into a fit of hysterical giggling. He could taste the gritty earth melting on his tongue and his whole body started shaking; he couldn't even keep his feet still and clods of earth peeled off his dancing shoes. He composed himself a little bit and shoved his palsied hands into his pockets, but remained overwhelmed by shock and unable to move on. He should go back; check he'd properly covered his tracks. Had the earth appeared too perfect? He couldn't remember. He could climb over and have a look ... the caretaker had said he looked able enough ...

Bruce prowled in a circle with his doubts tormenting him as he trawled back over what he'd done. Using the empty grave would've been easier, and saved him aching like the devil. But that wouldn't have worked. The gravedigger would turn up and wonder who'd ruined his job, then dig the hole again.

For a man unused to physical activity, the labour had been long and arduous. As soon as he'd heard the shovel hit the top of Iris's coffin he'd scraped enough space to roll her dead husband on top of her. In a frenzy, he'd backfilled, using the shovel and his hands and feet, until there was no sign of Sidney Cooper. Finally, Bruce had stood up, sweating and swaying in exhaustion. He'd patted and smoothed and stamped down on the mound then collected the flowers to lay on the top of the earth, repositioning stems until he felt he'd done all he could to disguise the disturbance.

Randall surfaced from his memories to the sound of footsteps. He quickly pulled a pack of Weights from his pocket to make it appear he'd stopped for a reason.

A wave of light-headed calm swirled about him as he sucked nicotine deep into his lungs. The woman had passed by without speaking to the fellow cupping a shaking hand around a struck match. He slowly started feeling better and walked back to the corner and stared across the road at the locked gates. No sign of life anywhere. He took another drag on his cigarette. A little bit more tension left his shoulders, easing them away from his neck. He set off home.

'Where in heaven's name have you been? I've been waiting ages for you to turn up. Our son's been sent home ...' Martha jerked her head at a closed door. She'd been pacing up and down in the corridor in the apartment, working herself into a ferocious temper. Her children had kept to their rooms to avoid her. Now her husband was here at last, she intended to blame him for this calamity. It *was* his fault, too. If the boy hadn't had his head filled with ideas of quitting a good school to attend a rough one, this wouldn't have happened.

'Paul's back? Why? He's only just returned to Norfolk.' Bruce had regained his wits on the way home but nevertheless it had taken him a moment to process what he'd heard. Finding his wife here had thrown him. Martha attended a women's committee meeting of some sort or the other on most evenings. He'd banked on being able to clean himself up in her absence, thus avoiding awkward questions.

'Our son has been sent home in disgrace,' she enunciated. 'He hit another pupil with a chair and broke his arm during a chemistry lesson.'

Having heard his father's voice, Paul opened his bedroom door and hovered sheepishly in the opening.

'He was sent back to London on the train, with this.'

Martha pulled a letter from her pocket and brandished it in her husband's weary face. 'It says here he's been suspended and might yet be expelled. Expelled!' She shouted in emphasis when the reaction she'd hoped for didn't materialise. 'What are you going to do about it?'

The muted light from the gas mantles on the wall did little to disguise the angry blotches mottling Martha's complexion. It also put an unattractive glisten on the spittle at the edges of her thin lips. How had he ever thought, he inwardly lamented, that this harridan and a drapery business could compensate for a life without Iris? Too late now, he damned himself. His love was gone from him forever and would spend eternity with her husband. The idea that he'd squandered his chance to change that didn't come to Bruce in a flash, it insinuated into his head and nearly started him crying. He should have excavated the plot with the plaque stuck in it, next to Iris's. The earth had been equally soft as the grave was recent.

He'd killed Sidney Cooper, with a frenzied shovel blow to the head. He'd not meant to, he'd just wanted the man to leave him alone. There had been no remorse, though, just panic. He'd set about covering up what he'd done with a maniacal speed that had prevented him seeing the best rather than the obvious solution. Bruce's pent-up breath emerged in a groan. He could have left Iris in peace though he knew, given the chance, she would have chosen to share her final resting place with their dead baby. It was too late to make that wish come true; he'd no idea what had happened to the stillborn.

Martha had been too het up to notice her husband's strange appearance when he first came in. She peered closely at him and noticed his scratched face and what looked like a bruise forming on his chin. His eyes looked suspiciously watery too and he seemed in a daze. She poked his arm to gain his attention and hurry his answer. Her fingers came away damp and gritty, and she inspected them before wiping them with her handkerchief.

'I had an accident in the dark – slipped down a ditch and bashed myself,' he reeled off, anticipating an interrogation. He started to shuffle away from her narrowed vision, trailing mud from his shoes.

'Look at the mess you've made,' she barked, pointing at the soiled rug. 'Where was the ditch? Where have you been?' She followed him along the corridor.

'Sorry, Dad,' blurted Paul, interrupting his parents and giving his father great relief.

Bruce would have laid a reassuring hand on his son's shoulder but thought better of touching him while caked in muck. 'This pupil ... was he one of the bullies tormenting you?'

The boy dropped his chin, then nodded. 'He spat in my porridge so I couldn't eat it. I've had enough ... can't take any more ...' He gulped back a sob.

Bruce's worries of transferring dirt were forgotten. He put his arm around the sad boy's shoulder and kissed his unsuspecting brow. He was getting tall and would soon outstrip his father's height, Bruce realised, as the boy sidled away, embarrassed by his father's show of affection. 'Go to bed now. We'll talk more about it in the morning,' he said.

'Is that all you have to say?' Martha spluttered in a suffocated voice of rage and bewilderment.

'It isn't, actually.' Bruce turned back. 'Well done,' he said and gave his son a fleeting smile. Then he carried on towards the kitchen, taking off his mud-encrusted overcoat and grimacing at the pain that simple task caused him.

'What on earth's wrong with you?' Martha had stomped after him and closed the door to keep their argument from the children. She paused to allow him to answer but he ignored her and started washing his filthy hands in the bowl. 'You're not drunk are you? Is that why you fell over?' She couldn't smell alcohol on him, but knew he sometimes went to a pub in the evening when she had her meetings. 'Nettie heard you snivelling last week and asked me what's wrong. It's time you pulled yourself together and stopped acting like a fool. That woman wasn't your wife. I am.'

'More's the pity.' He continued washing soil away.

'We've a shop to run,' said Martha, strident with indignation. He'd never been this direct about his feelings for Iris before. Martha would sooner he'd delivered a savage insult than sounded so indifferent. But her rival was dead and buried and sooner or later he'd forget Iris Cooper and concentrate on his son's inheritance. Bruce was a good salesman and a competent businessman. If he hadn't been they wouldn't have been able to send their boy to private school in the first place.

'Paul will go to the local grammar and you can run the business. I'm enlisting in the army in the morning.' He turned to her, drying his hands. 'And there's no use trying to stop me. If I don't make the grade to fight, I'll be an orderly or a driver or anything else they think I might be able to do. I should have found the gumption to do this before. But . . . I'm a different person now. And that's that.' He went out of the kitchen, leaving his wife open-mouthed but lost for words.

Nettie had been listening to the commotion from behind her half-closed bedroom door. When her parents shut themselves in the kitchen all she could hear was a hum of indistinct conversation so she gave up eavesdropping.

She'd been trying to pluck up the courage to speak to her mother herself about something, but before she could her brother had turned up and, of course, he took priority. She wouldn't get a look in when the blue-eyed boy was around. Like her father, though, Nettie did have a sneaking admiration for what Paul had done.

She sat down on the bed and listlessly pulled a brush through her mouse-brown curls. She didn't want to speak to her mother about this, she'd rather speak to Clover. She wished she'd made a point of doing so before to apologise for what she'd done. It worried Nettie that she might be getting as sour as her mother. Nettie regretted being mean to her friend, especially since Mrs Cooper died. Nettie guessed the family must need every friend and every penny they could lay their hands on now, and all she'd done was hinder them, not help. Archie had stirred it all up by boasting that he'd fought over Clover. But Nettie knew she was making excuses for herself. She threw the brush aside and buried her face in her hands.

In the end it was all her fault and just boiled down to her being horribly mean and jealous.

Chapter Twenty

The image of the flat iron smouldering on the table on the day her mother died had rooted in Clover's memory. Even now, when reflecting on that wretched evening, the smell of scorched wood swirled sickeningly in her nostrils. If the house had caught alight before she got home, with her unconscious mother and vulnerable little sisters still inside . . . She stopped herself from dwelling on the disaster that would have ensued. She'd no need to torment herself when the twins were thriving.

She had left Johnny with strict instructions that while she met a friend he mustn't leave the girls alone for a second. She trusted him to look after them; he'd become more concerned about his little sisters since their mother died. He was old enough to be in charge while she was out. She'd been left caring for her siblings when younger than he was. Besides, with any luck, their stop-out father might have sobered up by now and be heading home. It annoyed her that he'd not come in last night, although when he was around they all ended up on tenterhooks.

After Neil Ryan had left, she'd settled the twins down for the night and waited for her father to arrive. It had occurred to her he might be delayed gossiping to a neighbour. When there was still no sign of him after half an hour, she'd concluded somebody else had been whistling in the street. Johnny had turned in, tired out from playing football. After she'd tidied the place up, Clover had extinguished the lamps and taken herself off to bed.

There was a wintry nip in the air, unlike yesterday's mild evening for January. She hunched into her coat collar for warmth while mulling over the coming meeting with Neil. What had happened to his mother at the mission home? Had she died during his birth, or had it been a case of childbed disease, as with her own mother? She hoped he wouldn't mind her prying but she needed to know for her little brother's sake. She believed she trusted Neil Ryan enough to tell him about Gabriel.

Her baby brother's tiny pale visage occupied her mind and she wondered, as she constantly did, how he was faring. She would deliberately take diversions past the convent and loiter by the gates, hoping to spot a pram being wheeled in the grounds. She'd seen robed women, but no children at all, although she'd heard of other foundlings being left with the Sisters of Mercy.

On one occasion, the novice had been walking along the path and Clover had been ready to rush up to ask her about the baby she'd found on the step. She looked young and approachable and possibly would be more sympathetic than her superiors. The opportunity had passed when a group of nuns joined her and soon the white veiled head was lost in a crowd of black wimples. In hindsight, Clover knew she'd had a reprieve; her meddling could make matters worse, and secrets once revealed couldn't be hidden again.

She was almost at the corner and through the gloom

could see that Neil Ryan hadn't arrived yet. She carried on into the High Street and glanced about, wondering if she'd misjudged his character and been stood up.

She spotted him almost straight away, stationed outside a pub with a woman as though they'd come out of the place together and were parting company. Clover began to raise a hand to let him know she'd arrived, but hesitated and instinctively drew back out of sight. The street lantern bracketed to the wall had highlighted his companion's profile and some blonde hair trailing against her cheek.

Archie Fletcher had told her that woman's name, but it seemed Neil Ryan was also acquainted with Lucy Dare. From her place in the shadows, Clover heard bounding footsteps. He'd said his farewells then and was running to meet her. She quickly composed herself and appeared casual when he slowed down to approach her at a walk.

They'd only been together a few times, but he had kissed her and asked her to write to him when he went overseas. She reckoned that gave her a right to know why he had been with a working girl, as Archie Fletcher called Lucy Dare. He'd also said she was Sidney Cooper's tart, but Clover wasn't ready to bring that up.

'Sorry I'm late ... got held up.' He was dressed in uniform and removed his cap from his dark hair. Sensing her coolness he cocked his head. 'Something wrong?' When she didn't reply he tilted up her chin to study her expression.

She shrugged and moved away a step. He didn't badger her to enlighten him but his quiet patience was compelling. 'My father didn't come home last night, and still not seen him. So I can't stop out long.'

Neil frowned. 'Does he often stay out all night?'

'Well, it's not the first time he's done it.'

'I passed him in the street when I left you yesterday. He was almost home.'

'Are you sure it was him? What did he look like?'

'Tallish, with dark hair, dressed in a donkey jacket and flat cap.'

'That sounds like him.'

'He seemed a bit unsteady, as though he'd been drinking.'

'That definitely sounds like him,' Clover intoned ruefully.

'Perhaps he bunked down with a pal to sleep it off.'

'My thoughts exactly,' she muttered.

Neil plunged his hands into his pockets and remained quiet and thoughtful. 'If you're worried about him I can ask around ...' He glanced back the way he'd come and frowned.

'Lucy Dare might know where he is, you mean?' His small mannerism had spoken for him. Everybody knew about her father and Lucy Dare, she realised. Even his cheated-on wife had known Sidney Cooper was carrying on with a prostitute. 'Don't bother denying knowing her. I just saw the two of you together,' she blurted. 'Have you been carrying on with her as well?'

'No ...' He placed his hands on her shoulders and tightened his fingers when she tried to wriggle free. 'Listen, I wasn't going to tell you this ... I didn't want to upset you. I bumped into Lucy and bought her a drink. Being family of sorts, I couldn't just walk by after seeing the state she's in.' He let Clover go and rubbed a hand over his jaw, while deciding on the best way to phrase the rest. It couldn't be as Lucy had told it to him; she'd effed and blinded while running Sidney Cooper down. 'Lucy's got a black eye and said your father gave it to her. They had a bad argument last night and went their separate ways.

She says she's finished with him but she might know if he stopped with a pal.'

'Don't think he's got any proper friends; Jeannie's dad likes him but he's nice and likes everybody. They have a drink together sometimes. Mr Swift's back overseas though so Dad wouldn't go there looking for sympathy.' Her father had knocked his wife about so it wasn't surprising that he'd also been violent towards his mistress. Something else Neil had said had astonished Clover, though. 'Lucy Dare's one of your relatives?'

His grimace told her it wasn't something he'd boast about. 'Me 'n' her don't really get on. I like my sister-in-law. Freddie's wife Beatrice is Lucy Dare's sister, but you'd never think it. They're like chalk 'n' cheese.'

'Small world . . .' said Clover drily.

'Funny old world . . .' he said reflectively. 'Freddie and Beatrice seem like chalk and cheese as well.' He didn't explain further and simply shrugged. 'I'll go after Lucy and find out if she knows what your father's up to. If she does, I'll knock and tell you.' He understood the reason for her hesitation. 'Don't worry, I won't bother you if your dad's back.' He loosened the band in her hair and drew the ribbon from beneath an abundance of auburn waves that swept, soft as satin, over his hands. 'If he's home tie this to the railing and I'll know to go away.'

'That sounds like a tried and tested method,' she said tartly, taking back the ribbon and binding up her hair with it.

'I'm an Irish rogue's lad, Clover,' he said wryly. 'Cunning flows in my veins.'

'Too much cunning?'

'Enough to keep me alive in Flanders, I hope,' he said, turning serious.

'What's it really like over there? My dad won't speak about it when I ask him.'

'I don't blame him,' said Neil and circled a finger on her cheek. 'It's horrible ... loud and stinking.' He dropped his hand away from her. 'Can be quite a lark at times; for example, when we're billeted somebody came up with an idea to have a rat race: pick a rat each and bet on which one gets the crust chucked at them.'

She smiled though she could tell he was deliberately making light of it and neither of them found it very amusing. 'Keep safe, and come back. Promise me you'll use every bit of that cunning.'

He was relieved she'd not pressed him for more of the details of a Tommy's life. A lot of it was beyond description or comprehension. Over by Christmas they'd been promised years ago, when he gave up being a carpenter. He'd made ships' fittings in a warehouse down by the docks, but like others, had been trusting enough to enlist and fight for king and country long before he needed to. Now the most woodworking he did was as the reserve mortuary corporal when banging down coffin lids over the faces of boys. 'Promise ... I'll come back to you,' he said.

Their eyes held for a long while through the dusk. 'Thanks for trying to help,' she said eventually. 'I'd better get back.' She was on edge after learning about the trouble last night. When her father returned, he was sure to be in a bad mood and she'd sooner he take it out on her than the younger ones.

He bent to peck her cheek before she left, then kissed her slowly and tenderly when she turned her face towards him. 'Don't worry; your dad's probably been drowning his sorrows after Lucy gave him the heave-ho.'

Mrs Waverley might spot them: she was always peering out of her windows. But Clover would risk the gossip to have the tranquillity of two warm, comforting arms around her. She willingly nestled into his embrace and sought another kiss by turning her face up to his once more. She was accepting him, cunning and all, but it didn't seem wrong ... nothing about him seemed wrong.

'I've been thinking about you since yesterday ... thinking it'd be nice if we could just go for a walk ... or go to the pictures ... do something,' he said. 'It's all right, I know you can't right now. I understand you need to see to the twins.' He released her, before she asked him to, and started to walk backwards. 'Oh, and by the way. You've got a job at the factory. Just go along and introduce yourself to Freddie Ryan, Friday teatime. He's expecting you for an interview and short training session. If you make the grade you can start Monday. He'll tell you more about it all when you get there.' He gave her a wink then disappeared around the corner.

She'd forgotten his promise to speak to his brother about a job at Gudgeon's. When it sunk in that she'd got work with Jeannie, she gave a triumphant whoop. Then she remembered why she'd wanted to meet up with Neil Ryan in the first place. She charged after him, vowing to herself that she'd fetch Gabriel home and damn the consequences if he told her the nuns hadn't cared properly for his mother.

He'd already jogged across the road and carried on running. It was doubtful he'd hear her call out to him; neither would she catch him up now he was far in the distance. She started to retrace her steps, wrapped up in excitement that pushed thoughts of her father's antics aside. She was falling in love ... and fizzing with impatience to tell Jeannie her good news about her job. Playing in a football match and being able to raise funds for her grandmother's charity had come a step closer. Her mother would be proud of her. Iris Cooper's wish for her daughter to have a well-paid factory job had seen her swallow her pride and demand help from the man who'd rejected her. Bruce Randall's shrew of a wife had probably banned him from writing the reference. In the end, Clover had managed without anyway; but it was humbling to know her mother had done so much for her when very ill.

Iris Cooper had only briefly met Neil Ryan, but it had been long enough for her to form an opinion and call him nice and kind. She would approve of him becoming a part of her daughter's life. Clover's final conversation with her mother was a cherished memory she often revisited. Her greatest contentment came from having followed her instinct to reveal Gabriel's fate. Her mother had seemed at peace afterwards, knowing all her children were safe.

A faint commotion had been playing in the background, mingling with the constant hum of working factories and the noise of passing traffic. This was Silvertown, a dockside heartland that folk living in better parts of the East End took care to avoid. A disturbance of some sort was always going on. She'd been out for a while and was eager to get back and check on everything; exercising caution after a run of bad luck seemed a sensible thing to do. As the shouting got louder though curiosity won out, and she passed her turning to find its source.

Revellers weren't to blame: a man's angry voice was drowning out a woman's high-pitched pleading. A short while ago Lucy Dare had been in this neck of the woods; one thought hurtled to another and Clover pounced on the conclusion that Neil hadn't caught up with Lucy to question her, but Sidney had. Her father had bumped into his mistress on his way home and resumed their argument. Clover picked up her skirts in readiness to dash off and beat him indoors, but a shriek brought her to a halt. Her conscience wouldn't allow her to ignore a woman in distress; she set off once more towards the people taking shape in the darkness.

The street lamp was too far away from them for her to easily identify the couple. Someone her father's size was looming over a smaller cowering figure and Clover put on a spurt. She really didn't want to get dragged into this but . . .

'Stop it,' she yelled, having seen the man's open hand being raised to deliver a slap. She grabbed his forearm, making him swing around and an almighty shove on her breastbone sent her reeling before she landed on her backside. Clover was winded, but dragged herself onto her knees and gawped up at Archie Fletcher. Behind him, sobbing and leaning on the wall, was Nettie Randall.

Clover found her breath and scrambled up to comfort her friend.

'This ain't nothing to do with you.'

Archie tried to pull Clover away, but she flung him off and kicked out at him for good measure to keep him at bay. 'Don't you dare touch Nettie or me. If you do I'll scream blue murder.' She jabbed a finger at him. 'Clear off, or I'll call those blokes over to help us.'

'Don't want any more trouble,' Nettie quavered. 'Just want to go home.'

'You interferin' bitch,' snarled Archie, taking a threatening step towards Clover. But he had one eye on the two fellows on the opposite side of the road. The men had the rough garb and squat build of navvies and they had started taking an interest in what was going on. He sniffed, brushed down his uniform jacket then stepped around them with a look of distaste, as though vermin had crossed his path while he was out for an evening stroll.

'What in Gawd's name was all that about, Nettie?' Clover took her friend's head shake to mean she wouldn't say rather than was unaware of what had caused Archie to blow up.

'Did you finish with him? He doesn't like being rejected.' Clover took a guess, remembering her own experience with him.

Nettie shook her head again, but this time came clean. 'Told him he's got to marry me.' Bleary eyed, she peeked up at Clover. 'I'm in the family way, Clo, I know I am. Don't know what to do other than make him marry me. But he won't. He went mad and said to get rid of it cos he's not sticking around. He's joining up.' She covered her face with her hands and her shoulders wobbled with sobs. 'I reckon he will too, just to get away from me,' she howled.

This revelation put Clover into a momentary daze. She jerked out of it to comfort her friend, and attempt to be wise and helpful. In fact, she was as fearful for Nettie as Nettie was for herself. She didn't have a clue what to say so settled on something useless. 'Have you told your mum yet?' Of Nettie's parents, her father was more likely to be sympathetic. He had carried on an illicit affair and had an illegitimate baby so it would be a bit rich of Bruce Randall to moralise. 'How about you tell your dad instead?'

The weeping girl gurgled something that sounded negative and took the hanky Clover offered to her. 'Can't tell either of them,' Nettie finally mumbled, dabbing her eyes. 'They're arguing all the time as it is, and don't want to make things worse. Paul's got expelled from school and

Dad's had an accident falling down a ditch, and he says he's volunteering to be an orderly or something over in France.' Having rattled all that off, she gulped in enough breath to add, 'Mum's been driving herself bonkers over it all.' Nettie shook her head in despair. 'Our whole family's a bloody mess. This'll be the final straw ... know it will.'

'What will you do then, love?' Clover looked at her friend's belly. It appeared to be flat but then her mother hadn't looked pregnant at all and had managed to disguise her bump for months. 'How far gone are you, d'you reckon?'

'Missed two monthlies already,' Nettie said in a subdued voice. 'Thought it might be a false alarm but been sick in the mornings and I know this is it now. One of the girls at college got knocked up by her boyfriend and was always throwing up in the lavvie. He married her though ... lucky thing.' She scrubbed her wet face then returned Clover's hanky. 'I was coming round to speak to you tonight when I bumped into Archie and thought ... in for a penny. I told him he'd got to marry me.' She started to cry. 'He was going to hit me just now, yet a few nights ago said he loved me.'

'He's a pig,' hissed Clover, so infuriated by what she'd heard that she felt like running after Archie to set about him. 'You was always too good for him, Nettie.'

'You wouldn't say that if you knew what a cow I've been to you.' The nicer Clover was, the more anguished Nettie felt.

'Don't be daft ... All right, I'll admit I was a bit put out at first about you seeing Archie behind me back.' Clover squeezed her friend's hands in comfort. 'But we've been friends for too long to let somebody like him come between us. Couldn't care less about him now and I'm glad we both found out he's no good.'

'There's more to it than that.' Nettie looked ashamed

of herself. 'I destroyed your reference. I was feeling jealous after Archie had that fight over you.' She paused for a reaction but none came. 'Dad wrote it and told me to deliver it, but I chucked it on the fire. Shouldn't have done it ... wouldn't have if I'd known what would happen with your mum. I'm so sorry about that. I really liked your mum, y'know.' She hid her face in her hands. 'I'm just bloody rotten and mean. No wonder Archie hates me and I wouldn't blame you if you did too.'

'Well, I don't. But you're full of surprises all right, Henrietta Randall,' said Clover and turned her head to frown at the darkness. She could have snapped at her friend; it *was* a horrible thing for Nettie to have done. But jealousy was a spiteful emotion that made people behave oddly. More importantly, they shared a secret brother and that made them almost sisters. Clover wished she could tell her about Gabriel, then they could both love him. But she couldn't; she'd no idea what Nettie's reaction would be to hearing about her father's affair. Her friend was already overwrought with baby problems and Clover wouldn't add to them.

'Actually, I've done without a reference. A friend got me a job at Jeannie's factory and I'm starting next week. So, no harm done; I didn't end up working in the laundry, after all.' Clover linked arms with her friend and urged her to walk with her. 'Buck up, love; it's all in the past.' She nodded at her friend's belly. 'What will you do about it?'

'Don't know; can't believe it's true and a baby's really in there. Archie said it can't happen if you do it standing up. He said it can't be his. It is though; he's the only one I've let touch me.' She started quietly crying again.

'He'd say anything to get what he wants then get himself

off the hook.' Clover didn't waste further breath talking about him. 'I missed seeing you ... glad we're friends again.'

'Missed seeing you, too.' Nettie rested her head on Clover's shoulder. 'I think I really love Archie. I wish he loved me back.' She glanced at Clover. 'You think I'm stupid, don't you?'

'No, 'course not. You should be careful what you wish for though.' Clover stopped and turned to face Nettie. 'You'll have to make up your mind about the baby quite quickly. It'll get bigger 'fore you know it.'

'I know ...' Nettie said hoarsely. 'S'pose I'll have to get rid of it soon. Don't know how though.'

Clover didn't either; she had a sketchy knowledge of what happened during an abortion and the idea of it made her feel sick. 'If you tell your dad, perhaps he'll arrange for the welfare to have the baby adopted after it's born.'

'That happened to a girl at school,' said Nettie, momentarily distracted by somebody else's misfortune. 'Won't tell Mum; she'll throw me out once Dad's gone to war. Her precious Paul can't be dragged down by this. I'll end up in the workhouse, so they can hold their heads up.' She raised an arm to hide her weeping face behind it.

'How about we go and see Jeannie and ask her advice.' Clover embraced Nettie. 'Jeannie's older than us, and her factory pals are a right bunch, always up to mischief.' Clover gave an encouraging smile and used her thumbs to wipe the tears off Nettie's cheeks. It was a long shot, expecting Jeannie to find a miracle cure, but any ideas would be welcome.

'Jeannie hates me ...'

'No, she doesn't; she's just being Jeannie when she comes out with her hard girl stuff.' Clover struck a pose and shook a belligerent fist, making Nettie snuffle in amusement. 'That's better,' said Clover. 'We're all still friends.'

They'd set off again and reached the top of the lane where Clover lived. 'We'll have to go this way to Jeannie's. I need to pop indoors, y'see, to make sure the kids are still asleep. I've been out for a while and so's me dad.'

'Everything all right, Johnny?'

Clover had crept quietly indoors and lit a candle. She raised it to peer at her brother's face.

Johnny blinked open an eye, squinting against the wavering flame. He had a twin either side of him in his bed, both fast asleep with thumbs in mouths.

'Has Dad been back?' Clover knew he hadn't crashed out, drunk, in his bed, as she'd been in his room to check. The bedcovers were as neat as when she'd last straightened them. It wasn't yet pub closing time; but it was unlikely he'd come in and gone out again. By candlelight she'd seen that what was left of the rent money was still in the jar, and it wouldn't be if he'd been back for drinking cash.

'Ain't seen him.' Johnny yawned. 'Have you?'

'No. Got to go out again for a while.'

'Well, don't be long.' He elevated himself on an elbow. 'I had to bring these two in here cos they wouldn't settle in the cot. Keep asking for Mum, they do. Anyhow, it's your job to look after them, y'know. Don't want one of 'em peeing on me like before. Stunk of it, I did.' He grabbed her sleeve as she began to tiptoe away. 'Where is Dad, anyhow?'

'Don't know, Johnny. I'll keep an eye out for him while I'm gone. Need to speak to Jeannie.' She could see her brother was awake now and looking narked, so told him something bound to please him. 'Got a job at Jeannie's factory. Doing training tomorrow at Gudgeon's.'

'That'll please the old man … if he ever turns up,' he whispered, and sank down onto his pillow.

Clover went back to join Nettie, waiting outside, but was feeling increasingly uneasy about her father's long absence. It seemed her brother was too. Sidney Cooper was unpredictable and selfish with it. While they were fretting over him she'd bet he was nursing a sore head, and not giving his motherless children a second thought.

Chapter Twenty-One

'Is that Jeannie? I didn't know she had a boyfriend.' Nettie dug Clover in the ribs, eager for some gossip. Nettie and Jeannie had an on–off friendship but Clover, being better acquainted with the older woman, was likely to know who the man was.

Clover had been hurrying them both past a shop window display of children's toys in case the sight of them pushed her friend back into the doldrums. The dolls and toy soldiers and drooping paper chains were a relic from Christmas, yet to be cleared away.

'Certainly looks like Jeannie, but never seen him before.' Clover wasn't aware Jeannie had a boyfriend either, but she did know a certain someone put a sparkle in her eyes. If he was who Clover thought he was, there was no family resemblance between Neil and Freddie Ryan, which wasn't surprising given they didn't share blood. The footballer was shorter and stockier in build than his soldier stepbrother and his hair was lighter in colour. What surprised her was that Jeannie appeared to be more than friends with a married man.

'Cross over, shall we, and have a word.' Nettie pulled on

Clover's arm. 'She'd better not be mean to me; not feeling up to it right now.'

'Oh, Gawd, looks like Jeannie's gonna have more to do than tease you,' said Clover. 'Trouble's on its way.'

As they'd got closer it'd become clear Jeannie's beau was older than she was: more the age of the woman storming towards the lovebirds. A scandalised look widened Nettie's eyes. 'I reckon that's his wife.'

'It's not; it's his sister-in-law.' Clover had recognised Lucy Dare for the second time that evening.

The avenging angel first turned her fury on Jeannie, pushing her and sending her flying. Then Lucy attacked her brother-in-law, prodding his chest and pointing her finger in his face. Clover was too far away to hear the insults but could guess the gist of them, and was rather impressed that the slightly built blonde woman was more powerful than she looked. Whatever she'd said to him, it'd worked; Freddie made his escape, much to Jeannie's disappointment. She'd recovered her balance and rushed after him but his sister-in-law blocked her path before she'd covered two yards. Clover dashed to wedge herself between the combatants before a proper catfight started and they ended up rolling on the ground.

'Find yer own man, you trollop, and leave my sister's alone or I'll be round your house again and see to you.' Lucy's parting shot for Jeannie was blasted over a shoulder as she hurried away. She'd become agitated when Sidney Cooper's daughter materialised out of nowhere.

'You're the trollop,' Jeannie bawled after her. 'Who gave you that shiner? A punter, was it?' She forgot about Lucy Dare and ignored her friends too. 'Freddie!' He didn't respond to her call; he continued marching.

Clover would have liked an introduction to her new boss but certainly not right now. In fact, speaking to Lucy Dare took precedence. She had an opportunity to get information straight from the horse's mouth rather than wait for Neil to report back to her.

Jeannie had got over her surprise at being ambushed by friend and foe. Sulkily, she snatched a packet of cigarettes from her pocket and lit one then thrust the Woodbines at the girls. Her reluctant generosity was declined, allowing her to continue smoking furiously. 'So now you know,' she said defiantly. 'I've been seeing me boss behind his wife's back.'

'What ... *proper* seeing him? Not just for football coaching?' Clover found it hard to believe her friend would do something as rotten as that. 'Thought you only had a crush on him.'

'A crush?' scoffed Jeannie, sucking in nicotine for all she was worth. 'I'm nineteen, not a bleeding schoolkid,' she spat out with a stream of smoke.

'Sorry then ...' said Clover ironically, rolling her eyes. Jeannie could at least have had the grace to appear ashamed of herself for trying to steal another woman's husband. Thinking back, Clover realised this affair had been going on for a while. She'd never forget the sequence of events on the day Gabriel had been born early in the morning. At midday, her father had arrived home on leave and in the evening she'd gone to visit Jeannie. She'd not been the only visitor Jeannie had had. Somebody had thrown pebbles at her window to make her come outside for an argument. Knowing what she did now, Clover reckoned that woman had been Lucy Dare, championing her sister.

Jeannie's stiff shoulders drooped and so did her chin. 'He

said I was the gel with the nicest legs in football shorts. After training it was just me 'n' him went to the pub.' She paused, rubbed her finger beneath her nose. 'Lucy saw us in the Red Lion and warned me off. He told me to take no notice of her; said she wouldn't be his sister-in-law much longer. He was gonna leave Beatrice, he said, cos he didn't love her any more and they'd not slept together in ages.' Jeannie composed herself and looked up with a bitter expression. 'He just told me she's pregnant with their first baby. He's sticking by her and dropping me.' Jeannie lit a fresh cigarette from the butt dying between her fingers. 'Go on laugh ... I know I'm a bloody fool getting taken in like that.'

Clover and Nettie encircled her in their arms. She was their friend, even if she had behaved badly, and in the past Jeannie had stuck up for each of them when they'd done stupid things.

'We were just coming round to see you. Need some advice ...' Clover wasn't sure her friend was as wise as she'd thought on grown-up matters. She'd just seen a side to Jeannie that had surprised and disappointed her; the older woman had always seemed invincible. But then everybody had secrets, and flaws.

'Jeannie's got enough on her plate by the looks of it,' said Nettie.

'Advice about what?' Jeannie dried her watery eyes on the sleeve of her coat.

'I'm in trouble,' said Nettie bluntly and started gnawing her thumbnail.

'What sort of trouble?' Jeannie's air of cynicism was back. 'Bloody Archie Fletcher, I suppose. I warned you about him, can't say I didn't. You should have made him use a rubber,' she accused a bewildered-looking Nettie.

'I'll let you fill Jeannie in on all of it,' said Clover. She'd been keeping an eye on Lucy Dare, to see which way she'd headed before the darkness swallowed her up. 'I just want to have a quick word with that woman. Won't be long . . .'

'Don't need you interfering.' Jeannie grabbed Clover's arm to halt her. 'I can fight me own battles.'

'It's not about that; it's about . . . me dad.'

'Oh . . . right you are then.'

Both her friends knew about her father's philandering, although it was never discussed. Jeannie seemed to be aware of specifics. 'You could've told me,' said Clover. 'Only found out myself recently.'

'Thought you knew,' said Jeannie. 'Anyway, love, it's not something I'd want to bring up, being as that one is – ' she gave a disdainful sniff – 'what she is.'

Jeannie had wanted to avoid hurting her; Clover had the same predicament, wanting to protect Nettie by keeping quiet about them sharing a family scandal. 'Would you two wait here for me? Only be a couple of ticks.'

A renewed sense of fearful urgency came over Clover as she trotted off. Only active service kept her father absent from home for this length of time.

'Have you seen my dad?' she yelled the moment she spotted Lucy's petite shape in front of her.

The woman swung around, holding on to her hat. Having seen who was after her, she seemed in two minds whether to break into a run or let Sidney's daughter catch her up. 'Don't think I know you . . .'

Clover wasn't fooled by that act; Lucy's jitters were giving the game away. 'Look, I don't want to make trouble. I've not seen Dad since he went out yesterday and me and my brother are getting worried.' Clover could see concern on Lucy's face, and the gathering bruise drooping an eyelid made her appear to be winking. 'Neil Ryan told me you and Dad had a fight.'

Lucy shrugged in defeat. 'I told him I'm finished with him, and meant it. It sent him into a paddy. As you can see.' She angled her head for his daughter to get a proper look at his handiwork. 'My guess is he went to find Bill Lewis, if that's any use to you.' She started edging away. 'Apart from that, I've no idea where he might've skipped to. But knowing him, he'll be doing what he wants.' She paused. 'I already told Neil all of this. He likes you. He's a better man than his brother, and in a different class to Archie Fletcher, too. I saw them fighting outside the tobacconist's. You've no need to be scared of Neil though.'

'I'm not scared of him. Did he say I was?'

'No, but you look sweet . . . a good girl. Like your mum. You look very much like her, you know.' Lucy became brisk again. 'You probably think I've got no right to have an opinion on her or on any of you. You'd be right. I'll stick to speaking about my lot.' She tilted up her chin. 'Call me a hypocrite if you like, but I'll stand up for me sister. So Jeannie Swift better back off or I'll be back, and won't be so polite next time. You can tell her that from me.'

'Jeannie's a good friend,' said Clover sharply and loyally. But she felt admiration for Lucy Dare and a sort of kinship; if one of her sisters ever needed defending in that way, she'd do it.

'Your dad should be proud of you, looking out for him,' Lucy said. 'I expect you miss your mum. I was sorry to hear what happened to her. You might not believe me, but it's true.' She'd forgotten her promise not to speak of the

Coopers. She stood in diffident silence for a moment then turned and rushed across the road.

Clover retraced her steps, thinking she should have sympathised over Lucy's bruised face instead of staring at it. She felt ashamed of her father. She'd seen similar marks on her mother over the years. It was hard to like him. But he was her father and it was her duty to find out where he was. Her first conversation with Lucy Dare had been a pleasant surprise; her father's mistress had counselled her almost like a mother would about predatory men. She believed Lucy had also tried to be of help where her father was concerned. Sidney had said he intended to get his job back on the docks and it was likely he would have gone to Bill Lewis to find out what was on offer.

If her father was still absent in the morning she'd visit her grandmother. Elsie didn't come to them as often as she once had. Clover knew why that was: her dad and her nan hated one another. But Elsie and Bill Lewis were close friends; her grandmother would know if Sidney had paid a visit. If he had, she might also know where Sidney had planned on going next.

'Any luck finding him?' Neil stepped out of shadows as Clover reached her house.

She whipped around and rushed up to him. 'You didn't knock, did you?' She sounded anxious and touched the ribbon slipping loose from her hair.

'I did ... sorry. I don't think your brother was pleased to be woken up.' He added a self-mocking, 'Seems I'm not as cunning as I think I am.'

Clover slumped into her shoes. She'd left her friends walking home together and had dashed down the lane to discover if her father was finally back. Obviously he wasn't. 'Where on earth can he have got to?'

'I spoke to Lucy about him and—'

'I know,' Clover interrupted. 'I bumped into friends then into Lucy, and got delayed. She was nice to me, actually.' They drew back against the wall as the sound of traipsing footsteps and tipsy voices reached them. Two stout women had passed by before they resumed their conversation.

'I'll keep a lookout for your father and speak to Bill Lewis, if you want me to. Lucy thinks your father holds a grudge there.'

'It's all right, I'm seeing my nan tomorrow and she'll know if Dad's been over that way.' Clover frowned. 'He's got a grudge against my grandmother as well. I hope he's not been there causing trouble.'

'Try not to worry too much.' Neil slid his palms over her tense cheeks. 'You look tired. I'll let you get to bed.' He kissed her lightly but she wanted more ... comfort as well as kisses ... and put her arms about him. 'I'm frightened something might've happened to him.'

'In a way I hope it has. Without just cause keeping him away, he deserves throttling for worrying you like this.'

Clover understood what he meant. She'd tear her father off a strip if he turned up all fine and dandy, and earn herself a clout in the process, she was sure. She was weary and did want to rest but doubted she'd be able to; besides she'd sooner stay and talk to Neil.

'I saw your brother just now. He was with Jeannie; not for long though. He finished with her. You knew about them carrying on, didn't you?'

'I did. And so does Lucy know about them. The sisters don't get on, but she's loyal, I'll give Lucy that.'

'You promised to keep quiet about his affair if your brother gave me a job, didn't you?'

'Don't you approve?'

'I'm not sure ... I think I do. Freddie doesn't deserve to get away with telling Jeannie lies then turning his back on her though.'

'Jeannie's not the first and probably won't be the last of his conquests. Freddie's a weak man with a big opinion of himself. He's nothing like his father other than in looks. He married Beatrice to avoid being drafted. Family men are called up now anyway, but he's in munitions so he's got a reprieve for a while.' He sighed. 'The war's dragging on and every able-bodied man will be expected to fight before long. Women have already started replacing them in munitions factories and elsewhere.'

Clover knew that was true; posters were on every wall, encouraging women to join the workforce so the men could do their duty and enlist. 'He told Jeannie he's going to be a father. Is that a lie as well?'

'No, it's true. Beatrice told me the baby's due in the early summer.'

Talk of babies had reminded Clover that she had some-thing to ask him. 'Do you mind if we talk about your mum?' She carried on without having an answer. It was late ... time to go home ... not to pussyfoot with niceties. 'Why did you say they killed her?'

To speed his reply, she raised her head from its cosy rest-ing place on his shoulder and gazed at him.

'She jumped from the roof of the convent.' He bluntly told her the truth. 'They didn't watch her even though she'd threatened to do it. I was wrong to say they killed her; neglected her is a better way of describing it. All the babies born there were adopted, and all the girls were put to work in the laundry. She didn't want any of it; she wanted to take me with her and find my father, even though he didn't want to be found.'

'Your stepfather told you this?' Clover spoke in shock, from behind her raised hands hiding her mouth.

'No, he was gone before I was of an age to understand things like that. My gran – God rest her – didn't believe in covering things up and when I was older I never stopped asking questions about my parents. She told me about my mum and about the man who'd sired me. No boy likes to know his father is bad but the man I knew as my dad for a short while made up for it.' He smiled as memories of Donald Ryan came back to him. 'He told the Mother Superior I was his blood to bring me home. She was glad to wash her hands of the tragedy . . . disgrace, they believed it to be. My mother was a sinner in life and death in their eyes, burning in hell. In my eyes, she's an angel. She cashed in her life for mine. I believe she knew what she was doing.' His hoarse words tailed away. During the ensuing pause, Clover tightened her arms about him in comfort. 'You seem interested in the nuns,' he said. 'Have you had dealings with them?'

'Sort of . . .' Another silence followed, but how could she not tell her story after hearing his. He didn't interrupt and when she'd finished a low whistle escaped through his teeth. 'You've a family there to match mine.'

'I have. And like your family I want our baby back.'

'That won't be easy. I was lucky that Donald Ryan came to claim me.'

'I'll go there and say I'm his mother,' she stated firmly. 'They can't disprove it.'

'You'll need a man with you; husband or father.'

'I can't ask my dad,' she spluttered. 'He'd never believe I had a baby and managed to hide it, and even if he did …' She rolled her eyes to let him know that recounting such a scandal to Sidney Cooper would be more than her life was worth.

'I'll come with you.'

'You're not old enough to be my father,' she said.

'I'm old enough to be your husband.'

'Would you do that?' whispered Clover. 'Pretend … for me?'

'I would, Clover. I'd do that for you. But we don't need to pretend. I know we only met a short while ago, but I know I love you and want you as my wife. We could get married … if you want to. Will you marry me?'

Chapter Twenty-Two

'I was planning on walking over to see you lot later,' Elsie said as her granddaughter parked the pram in the parlour. 'You've saved my legs for me.'

Clover knew her nan meant she'd intended waiting until pub opening time in the hope Sidney would be out. Such precautions weren't needed; he was still missing and Clover was seriously worried.

Having been freed from the confines of the pram the toddlers dashed into their grandmother's outstretched arms. She gathered the two little girls to her sides and began taking off their bonnets and coats.

'I'm earlier than usual; I thought I might disturb you.' Clover knew that after a night shift her grandmother would get her head down for a few hours.

'Couldn't settle,' sighed Elsie. 'So I'm pleased to have company. Sit down for a little while, you look beat.' Her eldest granddaughter hadn't been sleeping well either since her mother died. Elsie was in fact sleeping better than she had now she had Bill to cuddle up to when their work shifts allowed. Better late than never, she told herself when regretting not swallowing her pride and accepting his proposal sooner. 'I've got some news for you.' Elsie sounded bright as she lifted the children one at a time onto her settee. 'It's a shame Johnny's at school or I could have told you all together.'

'Good news, is it, Nan?'

'I think so, and it should make life easier all round now your father's likely to return overseas.'

'Is that what he's up to?' Having made herself comfortable between her little sisters Clover sprang to her feet again. 'He's gone back to the army without even telling me?'

Elsie felt a stab of unease. 'Not sure I understand what you mean, Clover.'

'Dad hasn't been home for two nights. Did he come here to speak to Mr Lewis about a job on the docks?'

'He turned up a couple of evenings ago. He was in a foul mood; looking for trouble, not work,' said Elsie bluntly. Picking her words carefully, she told Clover the bones of what had happened on the night Sidney had burst in on her and Bill in bed. She omitted to mention accusing Sidney of forcing himself on his wife. Elsie didn't want to distress Clover with that, but finished by saying in disgust, 'He should be ashamed of himself, leaving his kids alone. It didn't occur to me he'd disappear to sulk; if it had I wouldn't have bothered waiting for him to calm down. I would've come straight over to see you.'

Sidney Cooper preferred being a soldier to a father, and he'd disrespect her mother by remarrying without observing a decent period of mourning. None of this came as a surprise to Clover; he hadn't settled back into home life or curbed his womanising. All the same, she was hurt; she longed for him to change yet knew in her heart he never would. To his dying day he'd be selfish and offend people.

251

'Well, Lucy Dare won't have him,' she said, being as direct as Elsie. 'They had a fight and she's not seen him since and says they're finished.'

'That explains the mood he was in when he turned up here.' Elsie began to set two cups and saucers. 'S'pose I should've realised you'd know about your father and Lucy Dare. You're a savvy young woman, which is as it should be. I can't protect you from all the bad stuff out there, much as I'd like to. But you're learning to deal with those heart-aches that men and women throw at each other.' She put the kettle on the hob grate, glancing over her shoulder at Clover. 'So, I'll tell you something else; your father's guessed the truth about your mum's illness.' Elsie crossed her arms, her expression grim when she faced her eldest granddaughter.

'He knows about the baby?' gasped Clover, sounding as though she'd not coped well with hearing that shocker.

'During the argy-bargy that went on between us all, he worked out your mum had a miscarriage,' Elsie soothed. 'Putting two and two together to come up with the man responsible for the deed won't take him long.'

'I saw Nettie yesterday. She would have told me if Dad had gone there for another showdown. They're all at sixes and sevens anyway cos her dad's enlisted.' If it had been Sidney's intention to have it out with Mr Randall he would have gone straight there, was Clover's thinking. He hadn't; so maybe he'd see the sense in letting sleeping dogs lie since his wife's death.

She sank down onto the settee, glad that her grandmother had faith in her. She would live up to it; she'd already been toughened by tragedy and would cope with whatever else came her way. It seemed hard to believe that a few months ago, finding a couple of hours to herself to visit a picture house with her friends had seemed a trouble. Every bit of her life had been thrown up into the air and some were yet to land on a future path. Her father might be battling much the same uncertainties; being the weak character he was, he would resent being forced into making decisions and changes. Brooding alone was the sort of thing he'd do. To save face he'd return pretending to be carefree.

Having pored over the pros and cons of his absence, Clover began to feel relieved by it; he couldn't interrogate her over what she knew about her mother's relationship with Bruce Randall, for a start, or ask what had happened in those last days of Iris's life. Having replayed their conversation in her mind, Clover had a question for her grandmother. 'You said "us all" when talking about the argument with Dad; was Mr Lewis with you?'

'He was, love, because we were planning something very special.' There followed a brief pause before the important announcement. 'We got married yesterday.' Elsie smiled. 'We've been friends for a long while, but it was a spur of the moment thing. We only had a quiet do at the town hall ... no fuss. But we plan to have a small celebration with you; Sidney can come as well if he's around and wants to,' she ended drily.

This astonishing news put a wondrous smile on Clover's face, lifting the strain from her features. 'Crikey, what a lovely surprise.' She rushed to give her grandmother a congratulatory hug. 'I've always liked Mr Lewis and I think you fit together just right.'

'I hoped you'd be happy about it.' A beaming Elsie disentangled herself, and handed Clover her tea. She hadn't realised how much she'd wanted her granddaughter's approval. She opened the biscuit tin and broke in half a

Rich Tea to give the twins a piece each, then settled in the armchair adjacent to her three seated girls.

Annie crawled backwards off the settee and trotted over to climb on her grandmother's lap and dip her biscuit in her tea, copying Rosie who was using Clover's cup for dunking.

'Mr Lewis is at work on the docks. He'll be sorry he missed you all today. He remembers you and Johnny from when you were both schoolkids and used to come over and play cards. But he's not had much to do with these two little 'uns.'

Clover glanced affectionately at her sisters ... good as gold now, but they could be a handful. She wiped crumbs off Rosie's chin with a hanky, and used her teaspoon to fish out a floating piece of biscuit from her cup. She spoon fed the soggy wodge to the child to stop her trying to pick it up with her fingers. She loved all her siblings but these two demanded constant attention, making her appreciate more than ever how hard her mother's daily routine had been.

With that in mind, she recalled she needed to speak to Elsie about childminding. Johnny could help out while she did her factory shifts but he was still talking about finding work himself. At twelve, her brother was too young to work full time. If their father had gone back to war, though, Johnny might not have a choice in the matter, to keep a roof over their heads.

'I've got the chance of a job at Jeannie's factory, Nan. And I had a marriage proposal.'

Choking on a mouthful of tea, Elsie rattled the cup and saucer down onto the hearth then dried her mouth with her hanky. 'Did you tell me those in order of importance to you?' she croaked.

Clover shook her head, lips compressing a smile. 'It's

just ... I definitely know what to do about the job. I've got a training session later this afternoon then if all goes well I start on Monday. Johnny's going to mind the girls as I'll only be gone a few hours. As for the rest ...' Her sigh and dreamy-eyed look weren't enough to satisfy her grandmother.

'Who is he and what did you say to him?' she demanded.

'His name's Neil Ryan and his brother works at Gudgeon's, so he pulled strings to get me a foot in the door. There's Dad to consider though.' She grimaced. 'He'll have something to say about me getting married.'

'No doubt he will,' said Elsie. 'Do you love Neil Ryan?' She sat forward to grasp her granddaughter's hands. She gave the girl a direct gaze that demanded frank answers.

'Yes, I think I do, even though I haven't known him long. He's handsome and kind and helpful and I feel ... happy and safe when he's around.' A saucy yet bashful smile tilted her lips. 'Quite excited too.'

Elsie chuckled and rested back. 'I think you want to tell him yes, don't you?' A short while ago she would have advised caution to her seventeen year old granddaughter. But these were dangerous times. Husbands and fathers were dying on foreign land; German Zeppelins were bombing this land. Nobody knew what was round the corner and even the young were conscious of their mortality. Elsie was too, especially now she'd lost her daughter. Burying a child wasn't the way it should be. She regretted not seizing the opportunity to be Bill's wife sooner. Denying herself and him the comfort of a proper bond had been wrong. And so would be dissuading her beloved granddaughter from enjoying the same sort of love and happiness.

'Your father might surprise you, Clover; he can see as well

as I can that you're grown up now. I was your age when I married for the first time ...' She'd been about to add that Iris had been younger, but it wasn't a happy example to mention. 'I'd like to meet your young man.'

'You have met him, Nan. I introduced you, but there wasn't time for conversation; you might not remember him.'

'Ah, I know who you mean: the soldier who kept an eye on the twins the night Iris passed away ...' Elsie's voiced tailed off into a hoarse cough and her hanky, screwed up in a hand, was used on her eyes. 'I do remember him.'

'He knows about Mum and Gabriel – that's the name I've given him. I trust Neil,' she quickly added, having read her grandmother's frown. 'I wanted him to know the truth about what happened that night.'

'I've something else to tell you about the baby.' Elsie stood up to deliver the most important news of all. 'A few extra fibs are about to be told where the little mite is concerned.' She noticed Clover's heightened interest and her shifting closer on the seat to hear what was said over the twins' chatter. 'Mr Lewis knows about Gabriel, as you call him. I like that name, Clover, and will keep it.' She paused. 'You've longed for your baby brother to be brought into the family, haven't you? And so have I. I couldn't say so before; it was too painful a hope, knowing it might never happen.'

Clover was holding her breath, her green eyes wide and sparkling as she waited for her grandmother to reach the crux of it.

'We're going to the convent next week to claim the boy. From now on he's my baby to anybody that asks, and my circumstances have improved, allowing me to bring him home where he belongs.' She read joyous hope in her granddaughter's face. 'It won't be plain sailing,' she warned. 'But me and your new granddad have decided we'll cross any bridges when we come to them.'

Clover jumped up and hugged her grandmother, burying her face in her shoulder.

'There ... don't cry,' said Elsie, patting Clover's back. She held the girl away from her. 'Now be prepared; your father might jump to conclusions. He knows Iris was pregnant, but he's been overseas for a long time and hasn't a clue what I've been up to. He's no proof it's not my baby, and neither has anybody else.'

Clover sobbed louder, making the twins toddle over and cling to her legs with thumbs in mouths.

'Those are happy tears, aren't they, love?' said Elsie gruffly.

Clover nodded and looked up, shining-eyed. 'I'm so glad, Nan. It's the best news ... even better than you getting married.'

Elsie smiled. 'It's one of the reasons I did get married,' she owned up. 'Mr Lewis was in agreement with it from the start. He's a good man.'

A bittersweet twinge of loss momentarily came over Clover as she sat down on the sofa again. She'd secretly believed she and Neil would rescue Gabriel and be his parents. Mr and Mrs Lewis had a far better chance, though, of swaying the nuns into handing him over than a seventeen year old girl, newly engaged and with no idea when her father might return and consent to her wedding.

She finished her tea then said, 'I'd better get moving. Be dinnertime soon and Johnny's taken to coming home for something to eat.' Clover stood up, putting the girls back into the pram and fastening their coats and hats for the journey. 'If Dad's not back to help, would you be able to have these two while I'm at work next week, Nan? Don't want to give Johnny too many excuses to bunk off school.'

"Course I will. I'm on night shift half the week, and after that, we'll work something out. Mr Lewis – Bill, or Granddad, I expect he'll like you children to call him – is doing mixed shifts as well so will be an extra pair of hands.' She paused. 'I'll be packing in work for good when Gabriel comes home.' She smiled. 'It won't be a problem having the girls at all then. They'll grow up with their brother.'

'I'm so excited about seeing him again, Nan.' Clover felt she might burst with emotion.

'I am too, love. I feel like I'm in me prime: bringing up a young family ... with a young husband.'

'You are in your prime, Nan. And I thought Mr Lewis was older than you.' Clover managed to keep a straight face.

'Get away with you ...' Elsie was chuckling as she pushed the pram to the street door. 'We've had a jam-packed half an hour, haven't we?' She pecked the twins' cheeks as the girls bounced in anticipation. The carriage was about to be bumped down the step to the pavement and they enjoyed the wobbly ride. 'I'll be over later to speak to Johnny and I'll pop into the cemetery.'

'He doesn't know about Gabriel, or any of what's gone on. I've not told him.' Clover wouldn't sully her younger brother's memory of his mother by attempting to explain the unhappiness that had dogged her life. 'Johnny's been crying and really missing Mum. Since Dad disappeared though, he's had something else to fret over.'

'Poor lad.' Elsie clucked her tongue. 'You're right to say nothing for now; hopefully having a new granddad will cheer him up. Bill likes a game of football so they've something to talk about. I've been telling Bill about your interest in the game.' Elsie added with a sigh, 'All in good time I'll tell Johnny the truth about Gabriel.' She paused. 'By the way, have you visited the cemetery recently?'

'Not since last week.' Clover waited for her grandmother to enlighten her.

'It's nothing really; I went yesterday and thought the grave looked messy, that's all. Another plot's been dug close by. I expect the gravedigger trampled where he shouldn't then hurriedly tidied up. Clumsy fool.' Something else occurred to Elsie. 'Has your father raided the kitty and left you short on rent before doing his vanishing act?'

Clover felt embarrassed and ashamed of her father. She nodded.

'Don't worry, love,' said Elsie kindly. 'I'll bring some cash over later, and some groceries.'

'Thanks, Nan.' Clover had been eking out the last of the loaf and jam to save taking from the rent jar. She kissed her grandmother's smooth cheek, wondering what she would have done after her mother died had she not had somebody as wonderful as this to lean on.

Clover pushed the pram off into the cold January air, with a backward wave. Her mind was crammed with things to pick over as she walked, but a prominent thought was that Neil might be relieved to know they could begin a life together with just the two of them. She realised she felt the same. There was a thrill in the idea of being a mother to a tiny baby, but in her heart she knew it was too soon, and a pretence. She wasn't a mother, she was a sister and she wanted to work, play football and enjoy life for a while, unencumbered by children.

Being a surrogate mother had always been her life from the time she was strong enough to bear the weight of a fretful Johnny in her arms. She'd never openly begrudged her mother that help as she grew up, but there had been many times when she'd rather have gone out with Nettie and Jeannie instead of changing nappies.

Elsie washed up the used crockery, mulling over what Clover had told her about Sidney's odd disappearance. She'd a germ of an idea in her mind and so explosive was it that she had kept it from her granddaughter. She didn't want to stir the pot until something substantial was in it. It seemed odd to Elsie that the draper with a bad chest who had no need to enlist would do so just as his love rival went missing. She'd spotted Bruce Randall in the distance yesterday and he appeared to have a mark on his face. She'd not taken a lot of notice, but her first thought had been that his old rival had given it to him. Clover seemed satisfied that there hadn't been any more trouble between the men though. Elsie needed some knitting wool so would go to the drapery and suss out the situation rather than make a fool of herself by voicing her suspicions too soon.

If Sidney had been trounced by Randall this time, he would drag himself off somewhere to lick his wounds rather than let people see him looking like a whipped cur. Elsie had told Sidney to his face that she wished him dead. She regretted saying it. He was the children's father. She hoped she was barking up the wrong tree and her fear that what she'd said had come true was unfounded. She refused to contemplate it for long; it would be unbearable if her grandchildren lost two parents in such a short space of time.

The selfish individual was probably quite hale and hearty but without Lucy Dare by his side Sidney might have decided to rejoin his platoon. Good riddance, if he'd left

260

them all in peace. Seeing him once or twice a year when he was back on leave would be enough for everybody. Meanwhile, the children were getting older, and more independent and able to stand up for themselves.

Since her marriage, Elsie was more content than she had been in a very long while; she didn't want this conundrum about Sidney spoiling her peace of mind. So she'd no option but to make some enquiries and try to solve it.

Martha had been emptying the till when the bell on the door heralded a customer. She'd been happily thinking to herself that the shop takings had picked up again, just as a reminder of why they had dwindled in the first place walked in looking elegant in her beaver coat. Iris's mother seemed younger than ever; her sallow complexion had been brightened to coral by a brisk walk in cold air, and her auburn hair, almost untouched by grey, looked youthfully abundant beneath a brimmed hat.

Surprised and vexed to find herself admiring the woman, Martha lost count of the coins and tipped them haphazardly onto the counter. 'Mrs Hall . . . what can I do for you?'

'You can address me correctly,' said Elsie mildly. 'Only teasing, Mrs Randall. You aren't to know I remarried very recently. I'm Mrs Lewis now.'

Martha snapped shut her dropped jaw. 'Bill Lewis married you?' She, like other women of her age, found that man's rough and ready looks, coupled with his good manners, most appealing.

'He did, or rather I married him . . . after much persuasion.' Elsie's infuriating smile made Martha slam the till and affect an indifferent manner. 'Are you here to buy anything?' *Or just boast*, Martha felt like adding, but didn't.

'Knitting wool. Four ply. I'm making the twins indoor jackets.'

'Colour?'

'Green, I think ... to match their eyes.'

Martha sniffed and pressed her lips into a tight line.

'I'd like to speak to your husband ... is Mr Randall in?'

'He's not. He's away on business this afternoon.' Martha stopped pulling a selection of emerald- and sage-coloured skeins from their cubbyholes to glare at Elsie. 'I'm perfectly able to help you with anything you need.'

'I believe I saw Mr Randall yesterday ... has the poor fellow had an accident?'

This wasn't the first enquiry Martha had had about her husband's appearance. 'He fell over,' she snapped.

'Few too many bevvies, eh?' said a jovial Elsie.

'Quite possibly,' said Martha sourly.

Elsie was taken aback by hearing Martha Randall, who would never lose face, hint at all not being well at home. 'I heard he'd joined up.'

'My, what interest you take in my husband, Mrs Ha— Lewis,' she corrected herself.

'Just making polite conversation, Mrs Randall ... as a person should if a family has a setback.'

Martha's cheeks became hot at an unsubtle dig that she'd not sympathised personally on the loss of Elsie's daughter. Well, thought Martha, she'd sent a card at the time to Clover and that was all the family were getting, because she knew very well Iris Cooper had been trying to steal her husband. He'd as much as admitted he'd wanted to run off with her. 'My husband has applied to be a driver with the Voluntary Aid Detachment ... he's filling in forms this afternoon.'

Both women were irritated by Bruce Randall's absence.

With her son attending the local school and her daughter at college, Martha was expected to do everything when once she'd done little other than make pretty things to hang in the window. She'd had enough of her husband swanning off to sit in West End offices and talk about himself and the new life awaiting overseas. This war was a charter for shirkers, that's how she saw it.

Disappointed that there was to be no meeting with Randall, Elsie chose her wool, paid for it, then set off in the gathering dusk. If she'd known the draper wouldn't be around she wouldn't have gone there and used up her cash. She'd given Clover almost ten shillings for rent and had felt wrathful that Sidney Cooper could put in jeopardy the roof over his children's heads. Elsie had left herself short on money and time, but intended to quickly check if the gravedigger had been back to fill in the open plot and disturbed her daughter's grave again. After that, she'd head home and change into her work clothes before setting off to Brunner Mond munitions works for her evening shift. When within a few yards of the cemetery's entrance she spotted her quarry hurrying out of it.

Bruce Randall had recognised her too and quickly ducked his head with every intention of fleeing in the opposite direction. He had been to check Iris's grave several times. To him, everything seemed normal, but then he was unaware of Iris's mother neatening her daughter's resting place because she wasn't pleased with the state of it. Elsie knew where every pebble and flower should lie.

'You've been in the wars, Mr Randall.' She thwarted his escape by striding across his path and staring at a visible bruise on his face. It could easily have been from a man's fist.

He lifted his hat and again tried to slip past. He'd pushed

his luck, as he'd feared he might, if he gave in to his anxieties and came back here.

'Just been shopping in your place.' Elsie swung the bag of wool. 'I had a talk with your wife. You're off overseas soon, then.'

He didn't utter a word, but ran a finger between his neck and his collar.

'Been visiting my daughter's grave, have you?'

He lifted his hat again in a vain hope she might get out of his path.

'My son-in-law's gone missing. Did you know that, Mr Randall?'

'It's no concern of mine what Sidney Cooper does,' he burst out then immediately regretted breaking his silence. In a panic, he barged past, forcing Elsie to step into the gutter.

'I want to speak to you,' she bawled after him, straightening her fur coat. 'Where's Sidney? I reckon you know, don't you?'

Bruce loped across the road and, once out of her sight, broke into a run.

Elsie stood still with her guts twisting into knots. She had the proof she needed that Bruce Randall was hiding something. But what? A horrible thought came into her mind. Had he disturbed the soil on her daughter's grave? Why would he? Unless . . .

Her racing mind pounced and she put a hand to her mouth, feeling sick. Don't be so stupid, she scolded herself. She was overreacting, letting her imagination run riot. Randall knew something about her son-in-law's disappearance but he wasn't capable of doing that . . . surely?

She started homeward without going into the cemetery,

hoping to find Bill back from work. She'd tell him her bizarre thoughts ... he'd laugh, give her a cuddle, and offer to find Sidney to put her at ease. Bill would know what to do; for the first time in her life, Elsie felt as though she were floundering, unequal to the task of dealing with her own family's affairs. But she had a husband now to help her comfort the children who'd lost their mother, and also their father, it seemed.

Sidney Cooper would turn up like the bad penny he was, before long. That's what Bill would say.

Chapter Twenty-Three

17 January 1917

Elsie wasn't taking her usual speedy route to Brunner Mond munitions works for her night shift; that way wound through the drab backstreets, past kids playing hopscotch in the icy darkness beneath a cat's cradle of stiff washing strung between the terraces.

Her diversion this evening would lead her through some of Bill's haunts. He hadn't been at home and she'd spent only fifteen minutes getting ready before setting off again, hoping to bump into him before reaching her destination. If they weren't planning to eat together, he routinely stopped off for a fish supper or a pie on a Friday.

A whip of wind in the air made Elsie hunch her shoulders. Her factory overalls were coarse cotton drill but the beaver coat covering them ought to have warded off the chill. For some reason it didn't tonight. She glanced up into a sky flushed with stars. The pretty sight heralded the hardest of frosts to come. Too cold to snow was a blessing; at dawn she'd be saved slip-sliding home, dog-tired, through slushy streets.

Bill hadn't been at the pie and mash shop and she was now approaching Wally Watson's place. She slowed down to stare across the road. Wally put his business before the blackout: he cooked up golden suppers with the flair of somebody who enjoyed having an audience lined up outside, mouths watering. His window blinds were rarely pulled beyond half-mast and Elsie could see Bill wasn't inside, nor was he waiting in the queue snaking along the pavement. The steam haze by the doorway and the savoury smell were beckoning her over, but she'd no time for chips and a warm-up. She'd make do with the cheese sandwich and flask of tea in her bag for her midnight meal break. She could see Wally barging about behind the counter, and smiled, wondering what had got his goat.

'You might find him at the pie shop.' Lucy Dare had also been hastening to her job, aware she'd get an ear-bashing for being late. She'd come up behind the stationary woman with an overall peeping unevenly from below the hem of her beaver coat. She'd recognised Elsie and thought she must be one of few factory hands who clocked on wearing a fur.

Elsie pivoted about to raise a nicely shaped dark eyebrow. 'Talking to me?'

'I am. I said your friend Bill likes a pie 'n' mash supper on a Friday night; if you're after him you might find him there.'

'I know what my husband likes and where to find him, thanks very much.' Elsie reckoned that would shut the cheeky cow up, and she was right.

'He married you then?' Lucy eventually said, as her dreams melted away like lard in a hot frying pan.

'Don't sound so disappointed.' Elsie felt pleased rather than annoyed to know her bridegroom was a heartthrob.

It was the second time today an envious woman had failed to conceal her fancy for Bill.

'Oh, I wouldn't be interested in somebody like him,' lied Lucy with forced brightness. 'Us ... well, we wouldn't last five minutes before I was off being me usual self. Bill Lewis is too decent for somebody like me.'

Elsie wasn't fooled and pitied Lucy at that moment. She was still a pretty girl with a good figure, but the cracks were beginning to show, and the crackle in her voice had betrayed the fact that she knew the best of her good times were over. 'Me granddaughter spoke to you about her father, I believe.' Elsie busied herself with swapping her bag from one arm to hang on the other. She'd never openly warned Lucy off her daughter's husband; it would've been a bit rich, considering Iris had had a lover of her own.

'Clover did speak to me,' said Lucy. 'She's such a dear and I wanted to help ...' Her praise tailed away. Women of her mother's age ... Elsie's age ... found unexpected compliments about family unwelcome, suspicious even. 'Anyway, not seen Sidney in days,' Lucy briskly told the stony-faced woman. 'That suits me fine, actually, since I told him to leave me alone. If I spot him, I'll let him know what I think of him. Swanning off like that with kids at home! Ain't right, but ain't a surprise either, seeing as him and responsibility never did mix ...'

'Oi! You want this job or not?' bawled Wally. From across the road he'd spotted his niece chin-wagging while he was run ragged. He had a fish slice in one hand and a frying basket in the other and shook them at her, miming they were hers to use before stomping inside to some sarcastic applause from a queue of hungry people.

'Don't feel up to this or him tonight,' muttered Lucy, stepping off the kerb. 'Wish you all the best then, Mrs Lewis. Mean it too. You deserve some luck and happiness after what happened to your daughter.' She quickly set off towards the shop, letting the cold air dry the tears in her eyes. Her castle in the air had been toppled. It had been worth trying to win him; those few times he'd stopped and spoken to her, shared his chips and a joke with her, had been the best moments she'd had in a long while.

With a final glance at the woman behind the counter, fastening her pinny, Elsie set off at a march. She recalled Sidney mentioning that his intended second wife had regular work. It seemed he'd been telling the truth. Lucy Dare was attempting to start afresh, not for Sidney's sake, but to have a life free of him, and men like him. Beneath her breath, Elsie returned the young woman those good luck wishes, pleased in an odd way that they'd had a talk. Lucy believed Sidney Cooper had abandoned his family and she knew him better than anybody else. The pair of them had grown up blighted by the other's shadow yet unable to break apart until now.

The more Elsie dwelled on it, the sillier she felt for thinking her thuggish son-in-law might have come to a sticky end at the hands of a timid linen draper. She'd been reading too many stories in *Tit-Bits* and the *News of the World*, she mocked herself. To finally put her mind at ease, though, she'd ask the council to have a quick look at what lay beneath when Iris's headstone was erected.

With the aroma of fish and chips receding, less pleasant smells took over. Elsie was closing on the River Thames and its effluence mingled with the sickly sweetness belched out by the sugar and jam factories that lined its banks. It was a nauseating concoction, but one she'd got used to clogging the back of her throat.

The din was stronger too; the clang of swinging cranes unloading ships' cargoes onto lighters was descanted by the shrill whine of saw mills. The fast patter of footsteps behind made her stop and step aside to allow a boy of about seven to whip past. He was carrying a food parcel and an enamel tea can. Such children were a regular sight darting towards the factories. They brought meals for parents doing back-to-back shifts. An air of urgency thickened the increasingly noisome atmosphere on this last stretch to Brunner Mond. Elsie was always affected by it. Her heart would beat faster at the pitiless reminder that behind the blacked-out windows of these factories a frantic effort was being made to equip a war that nobody wanted. Sewing machine treadles were rocked day and night by the feet of women making military uniforms; wood was shaped, linseed boiled for the houses and ships needed to replace those destroyed in the country's fight for peace. Munitions, most of all, were churned out and no amount of millions made were ever enough. Elsie and her colleagues filled those bombs round the clock with deadly black powder and turned themselves yellow, and to cheer themselves up they bought beaver coats from fat pay packets.

But her time as a munitionette was almost done. She was a new wife and mother; a new life was waiting just around the corner for Elsie Lewis, and soon Gabriel would come home.

'You two shirkin' again?' said Elsie good-naturedly. She'd slowed down to speak to a pair of uniformed firemen, their double rows of gilt buttons gleaming in the dusk. The brigade station was just opposite her factory and she often passed those on night duty having a crafty smoke while rewinding hoses or testing pumps on the forecourt.

'Heard you got hitched again, missus,' said the older of the two, pushing his cap back on his head and giving her a grin.

'You heard right.'

'Bleedin' taters tonight,' said the younger, letting a coil of wet rubber fall to the ground and banging his palms together.

Elsie agreed with him, but the older fellow frowned and remained quiet until he said in an awful tone, 'What in Gawd's name's happened? Look!'

Elsie and the younger fireman did look in the direction of his pointing finger, and couldn't believe their eyes weren't deceiving them either. Momentarily, they all remained mesmerised by the spear of orange flame that appeared to leap from the centre of the Brunner Mond works. It rocketed higher as though devilish bellows had been applied to it.

The older fireman regained his senses more quickly than his junior colleague. He gave the gawping fellow a shove to liven him up then turned and pelted into the fire station, bawling his warnings. Uniformed men, hastily doing up buttons and donning brass helmets, appeared to see for themselves. They stood and stared, aghast, then scrambled into action.

'Is it the danger building alight?' the young firemen gabbled at Elsie; if it was, then they would both know running was futile.

She couldn't tell in darkness any more than he where the fire had started. Brunner Mond works was comprised of various different factory blocks. But she knew the danger building; it was the place where the chemicals for high explosives were manufactured, set a little apart from her premises. She also knew that railway trucks full of the lethal stuff were waiting on the track only yards away, ready to be transported elsewhere. There was enough TNT on site to flatten London and beyond, Elsie had heard somebody say, only the other day. She'd not taken much notice; they all knew the risks ... and ignored them. What else could they do but hope their luck never ran out ...

The factory watchman bolted out of the gates, arms and legs wheeling. 'Get out, get out – the place will go up, and all of us with it,' he panted out on his flight past. Others ran behind, weeping, screaming, faces distorted in fear as they tried in vain to find a place of safety.

Elsie stood where she was as the alarms in the station clattered and the firemen milled, yanking at pumps and equipment. Pandemonium was all around. Some people fell flat to the pavement or hugged against walls in desperation for something, anything, to cling to. Finally, Elsie's sense of survival subdued her shock and she barged backwards through the throng before turning to run. In the melee, the lad who'd skipped past with his mother's meal stumbled to the pavement in front of her.

She remembered him and yanked him up. 'Fast as you can now ...' She pushed at his back to hurry him away from the factory. His young legs could, God willing, carry him far enough.

'Mum ...' he said, gulping and sobbing, and pointed to the inferno, the place where his mother was.

'She wants you gone,' cried Elsie, shoving him away, but he was petrified with fear and rushed back to cling to her hip, hindering her movements as she tried to save herself.

Elsie's arms cocooned him; accepting they were in their

final moments despite a spirit of defiance demanding a last second reprieve. She shouted and swore; she rattled off a prayer for him and for those she loved. Then for herself.

She'd had a life of snakes and ladders, as most people did. A workhouse kid sent to adoptive parents who'd hardly treated her better than the master. Her marriage to a good man and a family to make her proud had obliterated those early years, then her daughter had Clover and talk of orphanages was back. She'd mourned the loss of her son to a woman overseas, and her daughter to Sidney Cooper. But they'd all risen again. Her boy had his own business in America and her daughter had given her grandchildren to adore before dying and ripping out Elsie's heart. Bill had put it back. Bill ... her friend and lover, the sturdy ladder that bore her right to the top. Happiness like that couldn't last. It never did. She should have known it would end like this ...

The blinding flash came and she closed her eyes, shielding the boy beneath her coat. There was nothing else she could do.

Clover had steeled herself to expect the noise; Jeannie had warned her about that. The smell of the place was also overpowering: a sharp coppery smell, like blood. She'd already spent an hour in Gudgeon's, being shown the ropes, but there was still more to see and do. She'd cope with working here, though making metal parts for munitions was more complicated and dangerous than she'd expected. Certainly not the pleasant work she'd been used to. Clover wasn't precious about what she did and the pay was generous enough to allow a person to overlook drawbacks. Nevertheless, she was hoping she'd be able to go home soon. She had a headache from the repetitive thump of pedals pushed, and levers pulled to spit out whooshes of copper discs. She'd stuff her ears with cotton wool, she'd said to Jeannie, who'd told her she couldn't. Employees must see and hear everything in case accidents happened. Fingers got trapped in cogs, and once a lathe had fallen off the bench and crushed a woman's leg.

She followed Jeannie from place to place, looking at equipment and testing her skill on it, but her mind was still at home. Johnny had been in a funny mood when she left him in charge. Clover imagined he was brooding on the changes in the family; his father had gone and a new man had appeared, not to take his place, but perhaps that was how her brother, battered by loss, saw Bill Lewis's presence in their lives. She fretted Johnny might get restless and leave the twins asleep in their cot, and go outside with his pals. He'd only be in the lane, so where was the harm in it, he'd argue, as he always did. He was becoming increasingly bolshy.

'Here . . . keep that under there.' Jeannie tucked a lock of Clover's thick auburn hair beneath the drab mob cap she wore. 'If the old dragon sees she'll come down after you.'

Clover glanced at the middle-aged woman seated in an office on stilts. It was situated centrally on the factory floor and had windows on four sides that provided the management with an encompassing view of row upon row of wooden workbenches. Either side of these were gowned munitionettes, heads bent, fingers flying over wheels and pulleys. Some of those women would no doubt be footballers in the firm's ladies' team, and become her new friends.

Freddie Ryan was up in the office too, doing his best to avoid Jeannie's eye. His jilted girlfriend did often look up at him, but he remained for the most part with his back to her, barking orders at men loading barrows that were then wheeled into a warehouse ready for a lorry to collect the crates.

Clover had spoken only briefly to Freddie on arrival. He had seemed eager to pass his brother's new girlfriend over to his female colleague for dockets to be filled in, and then on to Jeannie to train her. Clover had gained the impression he was uneasy in her company, perhaps having guessed she'd learned things about his complicated personal life. He'd been pleasant enough, though, and in time she'd form her own opinion of him.

'This pressing machine will make your arm ache at first, in fact it might feel like it's been ripped out of its socket, but you'll get used to it.' Jeannie demonstrated yanking rhythmically on a handle then stamped on a pedal and, lo and behold, shiny metal clattered into a box on the floor. 'Right, your turn,' she said. 'I reckon you've seen and done enough then, and can call it a night.' She patted her friend's back. 'Quite an experience when you ain't used to it, eh, Clo?'

Clover had been crouching down to examine the fruits of the machine. Luckily, she'd turned her head to smile at Jeannie for promising her she could soon head home. Had she not, she would have caught the full force of the box's metal contents in her face. Her mob cap padded with thick hair cushioned the worst of the impact of the pellets that were shot up into the air in an orange shower. The force of the explosion had sent Clover onto her back and Jeannie, knocked off her feet, collapsed on top of her.

They were among the first to scramble up as the shattering of glass preceded the perched office's disintegration. Silence followed then screams as a girl realised their supervisor had fallen fifteen feet and was lying on a bed of shards behind her.

Clover and Jeannie blinked at one another in shock, then surveyed the destruction in the factory. Their colleagues were staggering to their feet and from different corners of the building came groans, not only human but structural. Suddenly, a section of ceiling came down, showering cement and debris on the cowering workers beneath. Miraculously, nobody appeared to be seriously injured, apart from the supervisor. There were plenty of people nursing painful arms and legs and cuffing blood from cuts and grazes though.

Jeannie started clambering over obstacles to find Freddie. The last time she'd glanced his way he'd been in the office. But by some good fortune he had descended the stairs just seconds before to break up an argument between two transport workers. He was soon pushing his way through the crowd to bend over the unconscious supervisor.

'The Germans are bombing us,' screeched a woman with a gash across her forehead. She'd jumped to the most obvious conclusion for the chaos.

'Gawd help us! Must be a Zeppelin overhead,' shouted another voice, which sent a couple of intrepid souls towards the exit, intending to take a look.

'Don't do that! Find shelter! They might drop another bomb,' yelled one of the men with a barrow. Several women promptly fell to their knees and crawled beneath the workbench, with others following.

Clover exchanged a look with Jeannie. Getting under cover seemed a sensible thing to do and they were about to drop down when a young fellow of about twenty burst into the factory.

'There's been an explosion! Brunner Mond's gone up!' he shouted. He'd been driving to pick up Gudgeon's merchandise when his ears were deafened and his lorry hit by a blast of flying masonry. Once he'd brought the vehicle under control he'd jumped out of his cab to see – as could everyone else in the vicinity – the gargantuan fire burning close to the river. 'It's just a pile of rubble over there. People screaming 'n' crying. I'm going to help – anybody else volunteering to give a hand finding survivors?'

A collective sigh of thankfulness that they weren't under enemy attack petered out into stunned silence. People began clambering over debris to question the messenger. Everybody had family, or knew somebody, who worked at Brunner Mond. Including Clover.

'Have the Germans done it? Have those damned Hun bombed Brunner Mond then?' were shouts from the back.

'Ain't sure. Could be. There's talk of a fire took the place up.' The lorry driver whipped off his cap and raked his fingers through his hair. He shook his head to indicate he knew little more than they did about the cause of the disaster.

'I'll come . . . my nan's there.' Clover pushed herself to the front on trembling legs.

'I will too,' said Jeannie.

'I'll help.' Freddie brushed down his spattered suit with his hands. 'As soon as I've arranged an ambulance for those injured, we'll form an aid group. Make yourself known if you're badly hurt,' he called out to his assembled workforce. 'Cuts and scrapes, go to the first aid room and help one another. The hospitals will soon be overflowing.'

Some hands wobbled into the air, but thankfully only a few women deemed themselves in need of an ambulance. If they had found no broken bones and could walk, they were fit enough, the stoic lot said.

'What about the houses?' Clover yanked on the driver's sleeve to get his attention. He was being questioned from all sides. 'Is there bad damage in the surrounding streets?' Clover realised she'd volunteered too soon. The children had to be her priority.

'A copper outside told me Fort Street's wrecked,' he said. 'But won't know the worst of it till morning when the light's better and dust has settled.'

They all knew Fort Street was only yards from the explosion site and situated along it were terraces of houses for factory workers. The Coopers lived about an equal distance from Brunner Mond as was Gudgeon's building. This place had been damaged and there were casualties. 'I can't come straight away.' She shook Jeannie's arm in emphasis. 'I have to go and see how the children are first.'

Now initial shock was collectively receding, she wasn't the only one who had turned her thoughts to home and children. From all corners of the factory floor, local women, with wild determination etched on their faces, began heading for the exit. Clover received a croaky 'good luck' from Jeannie but didn't hear it. She had already started dodging through the crowd. Once outside, she started to run.

A coral coloured smog lit her way as she hurdled rubble, or swerved around larger obstacles. The clatter of bells was all around as ambulances and fire engines headed towards the explosion site. She also heard people howling in pain and terror, but couldn't stop to comfort them. Some houses had sections blown from roofs, and within the ruins, dim candlelight could be seen through shattered windows. Here and there appeared a ghostly pale face staring out of ripped open doorways. She sped along the towpath that gave her a view of the Thames, ruddy with the reflection of the conflagration. It seemed to Clover at that moment as though the whole world was on fire and she forced her legs to pump faster until they burned too.

Chapter Twenty-Four

'What's going on, Clo?'

Johnny had been sitting on the settee, but the moment he heard his sister pounding down the passage he jumped up and collided with her as she burst into the room. She gave him a lengthy hug, her chest heaving from having run almost a mile without stopping to get home.

Charlie Pincher had remained seated on the settee with a twin on either side of him, but he sprung up now hoping to hear what had caused the catastrophe. The boys had been in the street playing football when the massive bang and glass and roof slates raining down had sent them hurtling indoors so fast that Johnny had left behind his prized possession: the leather football his father had bought him.

'Is it the Germans?' asked Johnny anxiously. 'Have they come up the Thames and landed?' While huddling together, they had created their own version of what had occurred to scare them witless and put a hellish fire in the sky. The enemy soldiers were bombing and ransacking and would soon be outside, bayonets drawn, they'd whispered.

'No ... nothing like that. There's been an explosion, at Brunner Mond munitions factory,' Clover breathlessly said over a shoulder, as she hurried past to drop to her knees in front of the little ones. The girls were quiet, no doubt having picked up on a strange, fearful atmosphere. Clover enclosed their delicate hands in her trembling fingers, murmuring a prayer of thanks that her brother and sisters were safe.

'Bobby's gone to find me mum,' Charlie piped up. 'She was after a job making uniforms. They give you a sewing machine to do work at home.' He started to cry quietly. 'She's not come back. Is me mum dead, d'you think?'

Clover knew the clothing factory was situated close to Brunner Mond, and so did Johnny who clumsily tried to give his pal a hug.

'There's chaos everywhere; lots of police and firemen about. Your mum's probably held up, that's all,' reassured Clover.

'Has Nan gone to work this evening?' Johnny was only slowly digesting what his sister had said, and the significance of it for their family was dawning on him.

'Don't know,' said Clover, keeping her face averted. She did know Elsie's shifts, but didn't want him to fret unnecessarily over their grandmother. He'd trouble enough coping with the loss of their mum and with their father's unexplained disappearance. Elsie could have swapped shifts at the last minute; she'd done it before. Luck must surely be on their side for once ...

'That's me mum.' Charlie cuffed his running nose and broke into a grin as a woman's voice was heard yelling his name from the street. 'Bobby must've found her and she's come looking for me. 'Bye.' He vaulted over an upturned chair on his dash to go to her.

Welcome news for the Pinchers seemed like a good omen for them all. Clover bucked herself up and, taking the oil lamp with her, went to inspect their rooms for damage. Pelting down the lane, she'd given thanks that these houses hadn't suffered as much as those closer to the explosion site. But almost every neighbour had been outside sweeping up window glass or milling about in groups seeking information from one another. Doris Waverley had called to her, but Clover hadn't stopped to report what she knew. Her only focus had been reaching her home and family.

She'd passed her old place of work and had been sorry to see how badly Randall's had been affected. Merchandise, and a child-size display dummy kitted out in knitted garments, had been blown out of the drapery's windows. Looters had been pouncing like carrion on the jumble of linens scattered in among the glass. Martha had poked her head out of a gaping upstairs window and screamed at them, and they'd scattered. Nettie and her brother Paul – doubtless on their mother's instruction – had dashed from the shop to salvage what they could. Nettie had spotted Clover on the opposite pavement, but the dazed and furiously busy friends didn't have the time or energy to acknowledge one another and carried on about their own business.

'Your face is bleeding,' said Johnny, following his big sister into the bedroom. The wardrobe had tipped forward on its front, resting on Johnny's bed and scattering their clothes all over the place. Had he been asleep in it, with the girls, they all might have been crushed.

Clover rubbed her face and felt stickiness on her fingers. She'd not completely escaped being hurt at Gudgeon's then; copper pellets had grazed her cheek though she'd not felt it at the time. They trudged out into the corridor and into the big back bedroom which appeared to be in the worst state of all. A chill breeze made them shiver as it flapped one side of the curtain, the other being caught on a jagged edge of broken glass.

Johnny's soft snuffling sobs made Clover steer him out of there, a comforting arm about his shoulders. 'Hush ... we can clean everything up between us.' She shut the door on the room that held memories of their absent parents. 'We can put newspaper over the windows until we get them boarded up. And the cut on my face doesn't even hurt.'

"S'not that ...' He sank down onto the sofa and Rosie, seeing he was upset, leaned against him to put her arms about his neck. Her sweetness made him howl louder, but he settled her on his lap and hid his face in his little sister's soft brown hair. 'I didn't want to go to bed early again,' he hiccoughed. 'I was fed up of these two getting on me nerves. So I went out with Bobby and Charlie. I left the twins and played football,' he owned up. 'Put 'em in the cot and left 'em. They could've been hurt by the glass flying about. They was so frightened by the noise. When I got back, they was yelling fit to burst.'

Clover sank down to sit on the floor in front of him, feeling disappointed in his selfishness yet thankful for it too. 'You shouldn't have left them, Johnny. But if you'd all been in your bed together then ... things would've been worse.' She refused to think of the injuries the heavy mahogany wardrobe would have inflicted on these three beloved people. 'Reckon Mum's looking down on us, keeping us all safe.' She stood up, praying that her mum was watching over Elsie too on this terrible, terrible night.

'You and the girls will have to bed down on the settee this evening.' She looked around at the disarray; her brother didn't appear to have made much effort to straighten things up. She set the fallen chair upright but the rest would have to wait. 'I'm going out again,' she told him. 'Gudgeon's is taking an aid party to help the survivors. I said I'd go with them.' She knew there was no point looking for her grandmother at home; if Elsie was safe, she would be here by now, making sure they were too.

Johnny nodded and drew his sisters to his sides, placing a kiss on their foreheads. 'I'll treat them to some biscuits.'

'If you can find the tin.' Clover glanced ruefully at the jumble of crockery and pots and pans that had been shaken off shelves. 'Give them a drink of milk each.' She'd spotted the bottle, somehow still intact. 'Then put them on the potty and try to settle them down. I'll be back by morning.'

She hadn't yet recovered from her sprint home, or from her immense relief at finding the children well. Fear of the unknown was also sapping her energy, yet the sooner she reached the explosion site, the sooner her fears might be allayed over her grandmother's safety, she told herself, setting off at a brisk walk.

Nettie and Paul were gone from outside the drapery. Their father was on his own, sweeping up debris in the throat-clogging atmosphere that made her lungs feel tight. He saw her and propped the broom against the wall.

'Have you suffered any damage at home?' Bruce Randall asked, striding towards her. He owed this girl and her siblings more than he could ever repay. He was responsible for their mother's, and their father's deaths. It had been unintentional; but it had happened all the same and his guts twisted in torment when he thought about having orphaned the Cooper children.

'We're all fine, thankfully – only some mess and broken windows to deal with. We're far luckier than some.'

'That's a relief,' he said with conviction. 'I'll have the glass replaced for you.'

'Thank you,' she said, somewhat surprised by his generosity. She had always liked Mr Randall; he had been a fair employer, never nasty like his wife. She could understand why her mother had fallen for a fellow so different from her violent, womanising husband.

His quietly miserable expression told her he was thinking of Iris and feeling guilty. In making her pregnant he'd been indirectly responsible for her death, and he knew it. He didn't know his son had survived though. And Clover didn't know if she would ever tell him. Her grandmother had said she'd claim Gabriel as her own, but that had been this morning ... and everything had changed now. Clover knew it had. 'I'm in a rush so I'll say goodbye.'

'Are you going to work this evening?' Bruce had followed her along the littered pavement to continue their conversation. He recognised her cap and tunic as that of a factory hand.

'No, I've just finished a shift.' Clover had forgotten she was still wearing Gudgeon's ugly uniform; she removed the dusty mobcap and stuffed it in her pocket. 'My grandmother works at Brunner Mond and I have to find her and make sure she's all right.' She wouldn't allow herself to believe that Elsie – the person who battled problems and always seemed stronger for the ordeal – had fallen victim to a random disaster. And mentioning her destination had given her the boost she'd needed to make a dash for it.

'Oh ... of course, you must go. I won't hold you up ... good luck to you all.' Bruce patted her arm in a paternal way before she ran off.

'I thought you'd finished out here.' Martha had heard her husband talking to somebody and had come to investigate, and to hurry Bruce up. 'There's still a lot to do before we'll be able to settle down for the night. We can pin the curtains over the broken windows until morning to stop the worst of the draught,' she told him. 'Then early tomorrow we must make an appointment with the glaziers; they're bound to be run off their feet. First, everything salvageable needs locking away; those scavengers will be back.' She nodded in the direction that Clover had taken. 'And what was all that about with her?'

'I'd forgotten Clover's grandmother works at Brunner Mond. She's gone to search for her ...' He raised his eyebrows and gave a sorrowful sigh.

'Oh, of course; it slipped my mind as well. Elsie's just remarried, too.' Martha was aware of her husband's surprise on hearing that. 'She bought wool earlier and mentioned she's now Mrs Bill Lewis.'

Elsie Lewis was one of several of Randall's customers who worked at Brunner Mond; local families would inevitably be badly affected. Martha had cause to dislike the Coopers but she wouldn't wish this sort of tragedy on anybody.

Nevertheless, Martha's business brain had begun to whir; from a personal point of view she'd spotted a silver lining to this cloud. The insurance company would become involved in the reinstatement of their premises. Much needed improvements to the shop and flat could be incorporated in the claim for damages. She started to tell Bruce her ideas but could see he wasn't listening to her; he was still gazing after Clover Cooper, looking thoughtful.

Bruce had no intention of telling his wife about his hostile meeting with Elsie outside the cemetery. But he did say, 'I think I should go and offer to help the rescuers. It's our duty to do what we can.'

Martha sighed in irritation. But he had a point. 'I suppose it won't hurt our reputations to be seen to be generous at a time like this. Paul and Henrietta will have to help me clear this place up while you're gone. Take a box of blankets with you to donate to the victims: those seconds we were going to return to the wholesaler, not the good ones.' She paused. 'I'll speak to the committee about getting up a collection for the affected families. There are sure to be bereavements, and children orphaned.'

Nettie had been upstairs in the flat, wrapping a strip of rag around her gashed finger, when she recognised her friend's voice. She'd squinted out of the shattered casement into the dark and, seeing Clover below, had been about to go down to speak to her. But in no time at all her friend had gone.

'You'd better give me a hand with this,' Nettie told her brother, who'd been pacing about like a caged lion.

'I didn't know London would be dangerous. It's full of louts and stinks. I wish I'd stayed in Norfolk at school,' he moaned.

'For what bloody use you are, Paul, I wish you had, too,' muttered Nettie, sitting down at the table in the parlour. Its top was piled with woollen garments from the destroyed window display. The gas mantles were still on but the pressure was wavering in the draught whistling through the broken panes. In the dim light, splinters could be detected winking in the yarn. 'Don't just stand there; Mum said to salvage what we can.' She pushed an empty carton towards him on the floor, using a foot. 'Put the pieces of glass in there. And be careful; I've just cut my hand. Don't get blood on the stuff or we can't sell it, then that'll start her off.'

'Are we going to be poor now, like everyone else round

here?' Paul had been at public school since he was eight and had become disdainful of people he saw as beneath him. Like his sister.

Nettie was aware her younger brother was turning into an awful snob and delighted in acting vulgar to wind him up. 'Get stuck into this then, if you don't want to be eatin' bread 'n' dripping fer evermore.' She threw a cardigan at him to pick over. Her brother was his mother's son, and she was like her father. She was also like the girl she'd gone to school with and had been friends with since they were six years old.

If things had been different, Nettie would have taken Clover Cooper's advice to speak to her father about the baby she was expecting. But he never seemed to be around much any more, and when he was, her mother commandeered his time and made it impossible for a private conversation. If she asked for money before he went overseas, her mother, especially, would be suspicious about why she wanted it. She had friends to turn to, but Clover always had problems of her own. Her father had gone off gallivanting, she'd overheard her parents say when discussing Sidney Cooper's disappearance. Nettie knew Clover's grandmother was a Brunner Mond munitionette and her friend would be frantically worried about her. Nettie realised her own troubles paled into insignificance when compared to what Clover must be going through.

Jeannie hadn't come up with any suggestions Nettie hadn't already known about. She'd been to Poplar baths with a bottle of gin from the drinks' cabinet stuffed in a pocket of her coat. She'd soaked in boiling water until she looked cooked. Nothing had happened. An abortion might prevent a scandal . . . so might a wedding ring. But Archie hadn't been bluffing: he'd been to the recruiting office. He was bound to deny everything and if her father went after him, he'd make out she was a slag who slept around. Her dad had come off worst in the scrap with Sidney Cooper, a man his own age, and he was still bruised from falling in a ditch. She didn't want him getting seriously hurt fighting with a much younger man.

Nettie knew this was something she had to deal with alone, like other girls did. They pretended they weren't in the family way, and when the bump grew big, hid in a women's refuge to give birth then had the baby adopted. She'd decided that's what she'd do.

'Make yourself useful and take these downstairs, Paul.' She winced and sucked her finger as she pricked it again on a glass sliver. 'Tell Mum I've done what I can with them.' She tapped a pile of folded woollens and kicked her brother's shin beneath the table to stop him chewing his nails and feeling sorry for himself.

A lot of the shop's stock had been shaken from display cases and drawers onto the floor. While his wife was retrieving items and putting them onto the counter, Bruce found the carton of blankets, still intact. He set off along the street, carrying it. He knew there was no point driving: the roads would be jammed with the rescue vehicles he could hear clamouring in the distance.

He began brooding on his meeting with Iris's mother. He knew her for a canny individual but hadn't expected Elsie to work out his involvement in Sidney's disappearance. Most people believed Bruce Randall to be incapable of saying boo to a goose.

He held no grudge against her and felt wicked for wishing the newly married woman ill; but his survival instinct

overrode his conscience. He truly believed he'd been fighting for his own life when he had killed Sidney. He couldn't
risk owning up and pleading self-defence; the verdict might
not go in his favour and he'd hang. He realised he wasn't
too bothered about that for himself; he'd be reunited with
Iris and their baby, for one thing. But he'd blight his living
children's futures with the scandal.

A seed of an idea was taking root about how speculation
over Sidney's disappearance could be laid to rest with Elsie
Lewis . . . if she was dead.

He put on a spurt, adjusting the weighty box in his grip.
Before he could act he had to discover if she was a victim
or a survivor of the Brunner Mond explosion.

Chapter Twenty-Five

The glass that had been broken by Archie Fletcher was shattered again, and so was every other mullion in the tobacconist's window. As Clover approached at a run she saw her old boss surveying the wreckage of his business by the glow of a hurricane lamp. He'd always appeared puny but this disaster seemed to have shrivelled him to a gnome stranded in a puddle of yellow light. She was tempted to divert to assist him. But she daren't stop. Instead she called out, 'I'll be back tomorrow to help you clear up, Mr Bailey.' And she would be. She had got on well with that dear fellow until Archie Fletcher had caused trouble.

'Thank you, Miss Cooper.' The forlorn man gave a feeble wave, acknowledging her offer, but all he caught sight of was her long flag of hair, and a pair of flying heels. While he'd been distracted, a youth who'd been loitering in the shadows leapt forward to push him aside and raid the display of tobacco, open to the world. Mr Bailey simply turned away in defeat and went inside, letting the thief help himself.

Clover was soon close enough to the hellish inferno to feel its lethal heat. She slowed down; she'd no idea where to start looking for her grandmother or the Gudgeon's work's party, but saw somebody else she knew and rushed up to him, rasping for breath.

Sooty-faced and with glistening red-rimmed eyes, Bill Lewis turned around to see Clover Cooper accosting him. They stared at one another in silence, momentarily deaf and blind to the surrounding mayhem. Slowly, Clover's hands were raised to her face and she backed away.

Not true ... not Elsie, not like this, with no warning. Her mother's death had been a shock but not wholly unexpected; there had been signs of her weakness and disease. Elsie was strong, brave, a warrior. Going to work couldn't snuff out her life just like that.

Bill followed and enclosed her in his arms, steady as a rock as she howled and attempted to break free in a need to caper about in agony and disbelief.

When she was calm enough for him to lead her away from the noise and smoke to talk to her, he said, 'Your grandmother's been found, Clover.'

'Has she been taken to hospital?' Clover asked in hope, though she knew there was none.

'To the mortuary,' he said and blinked his bloodshot eyes.

He had believed he'd dress it up in less stark terms when he broke the news to his wife's grandchildren ... his grandchildren. But when it came to it what else was there but the plain truth? Elsie had adored this girl; *bright as a button and not a cowardly bone in her body*, she'd described Clover. Bill wouldn't insult his wife's memory by treating Elsie's eldest granddaughter with kid gloves. He was going to need this young woman's strength to get through the next days, as much as she would want his.

Clover saw the tears in his melancholic eyes drip to his

cheeks and plunged her arms around him as though it were the most natural thing to give and to demand comfort from this man she hardly knew. Her nan had known him, and had loved him. For Clover that was enough.

'You should feel mightily proud of your nan.' Bill moved Clover's tangled hair back to stroke her anguished face and quieten her sobs. 'She shielded a boy from the worst of it. Saved his life.'

'Is he here?' Clover hiccoughed and rubbed her wet cheeks, smearing the smuts. She was desperate to talk to somebody about her nan's last moments.

'He's gone in the ambulance. Broken leg and some other minor scrapes. The explosion took them off the ground and some distance away. One of the firemen was found over there . . .' Bill swung an arm to indicate ground beyond the devastated fire station. 'His colleague survived; said they were talking to Elsie. He remembered they spoke about us getting married . . .' Bill's smile disintegrated to ashes. He hung his head, covering his face with his fingers.

'I've been looking for you.' Neil had shouldered a path towards Clover through the rescue teams digging in masonry, and the people wandering about, howling out names of missing family members. The ring of dozens of busy shovels was backed by the unremitting roar of the fire as it swallowed up what remained of the Brunner Mond plant and nearby factories. In the adjacent streets, house roofs had been set ablaze by embers, and burning grains from the smashed flour mill eddied in the air like fireflies.

'I went to your home. Johnny told me I'd find you here.' Neil crushed her against him in thankfulness that she seemed unhurt. He held her away, cradling her face between his palms to gaze into her eyes.

'This is Bill Lewis, my nan's new husband,' she said, noticing his curious glance. 'It's not fair!' she choked out. 'They were only married a few days ago.'

Their raw grief was plain to see and gave Neil the answer to a question he'd dreaded having to ask. Johnny had told him their grandmother worked at the plant and his sister had gone to find out what had happened to her. 'Do you want to go home now, Clover?' Neil drew her again into a fiercely tender embrace. 'I'll come with you ... tell Johnny what's happened ...'

'Don't know how to tell him,' she said flatly. 'He's already upset but at least he and the girls are safe.' She pulled away to gaze around at a fiery alien landscape. 'How d'you explain this? Don't understand it meself ... feels like I didn't watch me step and fell into the abyss.' She shook her head in despair. 'What's happened to us all? We thought the war wasn't really about us over here. We thought we were doing our bit but were spared the worst of it. We were bloody wrong about that.'

Neil wished he had something clever to say to make her anger and pain go away. But she was right: there was no wholesome way to build bombs or to win this war. He trained boys in using rifles and bayonets; she would soon shape metals to make those weapons. They'd carry on because nobody knew any more how to retreat from the edge. There was nothing for it but to sprout wings or tumble over.

'Jeannie's over there with Freddie,' he said. 'They're ferrying the walking wounded from here to the Methodist church hall.' Neil took one of her hands, smoothed a thumb over it then kissed the back of it. 'There's going to be a lot of people needing a meal and a bed for the night.'

They gazed about at the rows of houses that had been virtually demolished; some had walls but no upper floor or roof and were open to the mercy of the elements.

'Shelters are being set up for the homeless. Lots of volunteers will be needed to deal with them,' he said. 'Could be hundreds of people affected.' He hadn't exaggerated. Some cottages housed more than one family with people crammed cheek by jowl in the rooms.

'Here's an extra pair of hands.' She raised them, grimy and aquiver, to rest on his shoulders and stared at him without a hint of bashfulness. She'd no more time for that. No more enjoying the thrill of wondering if this was sweet romance or the real thing. Happiness was to be grabbed before fate snatched it away. 'I love you, Neil,' she said and put her lips to his bristly, salty-tasting cheek.

'And I love you, Clover.' He returned her a kiss that caressed her lips.

Jeannie had spotted the couple standing, eyes and hands locked together. She left her Gudgeon's colleagues and bounded athletically over hillocks of masonry to reach them. 'Your nan?' was all she burst out with, staring wide eyed at Clover.

Clover dropped her chin until it almost touched her chest then shook her head.

Jeannie hugged her for a full minute then broke away. 'She's still here watching you, Clo. Ain't left yet ... not Elsie.'

Clover grunted wryly in agreement. 'That's my nan; stick it out to the bitter end.' She threw back her head to punch a defiant fist at the night. 'I'll do you proud, Nan. So will Johnny and the twins. And ...' She lowered her hand and her voice to say, 'Gabriel.'

Jeannie hadn't heard the whisper; she'd remembered

she had more to say herself. 'A policeman over there told us St Barnabas parish hall's badly damaged. Some Band of Hope kids were inside, having a party when the roof caved in. Could be as many as seventy of them. Me 'n' Freddie and the others are going there to lend a hand.' She paused. 'Might not be a pretty sight.'

'Neither's this,' said Clover, watching a heavily pregnant mother and two boys: infant school age, she guessed they were. The family was clambering over the ruins, trying to salvage what they could. The mother was burning her fingers, sucking at the pain, then dipping in and out of smouldering timbers again. She handed the precious bits and pieces to the children to put into a pram so they could take away something from the wreckage of their home.

'Coming along to the Mission Hall then?'

Clover sniffed and knuckled her eyes. "Course I'll come.'

While Clover had been busy with her friends, Bill had taken notice of an urgent shout for assistance, coming from the rescuers. 'Firemen have located somebody trapped ... they're trying to lift a fallen timber over there.' He turned to the man he'd just learned was Clover's sweetheart. 'How about you? Feeling fit?' He spoke over a shoulder, already on the move himself. He needed to do something useful and exhausting to keep the pain at bay. The long weeks and months ahead would be there for grieving for Elsie.

'I'll come and find you later,' Neil said to Clover. He tenderly stroked her cheek before following Bill. They jumped over rubble towards the fire station, beyond which was sited accommodation for some brigade families.

At St Barnabas Mission Hall, the Band of Hope youngsters had miraculously escaped serious injury although some were hysterical. And little wonder at it; the collapsing roof would have crushed them all had a brave few not risked propping it up, allowing others to escape first, before making a dash for it themselves. Parents had already begun searching for their sons and daughters and tearful reunions took place outside the damaged building before they were hurried away to safety.

Once everybody had been accounted for at St Barnabas, the Gudgeon's team disbanded. The other munitionettes were mainly unmarried women of about Jeannie's age and they headed home to assist their parents with domestic cleaning up operations. Freddie said he was off as well, as his wife would be worried and waiting for him. That earned him a frosty look from Jeannie, but they maintained a civil front and goodbyes were nicely said as the group parted company.

Clover and Jeannie continued on their own to the Methodist hall, a short walk away, Jeannie keeping up a constant chatter about this and that to prevent Clover falling into despair over her grandmother. Jeannie admired her friend's fortitude in coping with her mother's passing and her father's neglect; this on top though was enough to try a saint to the limit.

The Methodist hall was crammed with distraught people milling about beneath oil lamps strung up along beams. Every mother was trying to find a free nook to settle down into with her children. The girls' offer of help was gratefully received by a harassed-looking fellow with a clipboard. While he listed down names of the dispossessed, they made themselves useful to his wife. Soon they were occupied making tea and slicing bread. They loaded the filled plates and teapots onto a trestle table, spread with an array of hastily assembled sandwiches and cakes and strategically placed burning candle stumps. A hungry crowd had already gathered and no sooner had a plate of food touched the table than grimy hands descended upon it.

'Would you be able to spare some of that boiled water? I've a wound to wash and dress.'

Clover had just taken the steaming kettle off the range when a polite voice spoke to her. On turning around, she nearly dropped the teapot she'd been filling. A slender figure dressed in white was holding out a bowl.

'Sorry, didn't mean to startle you.' The young nun smiled as Clover continued to gawp at her. 'I'm Sister Louise from the local convent.' A nod indicated a couple of fellow nuns. Clover hadn't noticed the women in their dark habits, blending with the shadows while moving among the crowds. 'We're treating the cuts and bruises of those who don't need to go to hospital. We're nurses, you see.' She winked. 'Actually, I'm a probationer, so they give me the easy jobs.'

'I know you're nurses.' Clover had conquered her surprise at being confronted by a person who had constantly occupied her mind since the day Gabriel was born. The kettle was clattered against china as her shaking hand tipped water into the bowl.

'Wouldn't mind a cuppa myself when I've got a spare minute to drink it ...' Sister Louise rolled her eyes at the set cups and saucers.

'Righto,' said Clover, relaxing a little bit. The sister seemed the warm friendly character she'd hoped she'd be. Clover automatically resumed filling the teapot. She glanced frequently at the dainty young woman, picking a careful path through the crowd while holding her bowl of washing water. Too impatient to wait for the tea to brew,

Clover poured out a single cup. 'Won't be a second. I'm just going to have a word with somebody,' she told Jeannie, making jam sandwiches beside her.

'Sorry to bother you so soon,' blurted Clover, holding a rattling cup and saucer in her hand. Sister Louise was crouching beside a boy of about eight who was seated cross-legged on a pallet mattress on the floor. She continued dabbing at his gashed arm but slanted up a smile at Clover.

'Is that my tea?'

'It is . . . I brought it while it's nice and hot. I'd like to speak to you as well, please, when you've a quiet moment.'

'Might not be for a while then,' said Sister Louise ruefully, glancing around at the chaotic scene.

Able-bodied men were mostly absent, needed in the rescue effort. Women and children made up the majority occupying the hall. The elderly of both sexes were in evidence, wearing a common look of bewilderment to this disruption to their routine. Overexcited youngsters were running around; harassed mothers were putting fretful infants to the breast while calling out scolds. And huddled in a corner were the pet owners. A couple of terriers, several cats and even a ferret in a cage were being guarded. The animals at least were subdued, curled protectively, having doubtless sensed that with Silvertown burning, this was the safest territory for now.

Sister Louise finished tying a bandage around the lad's wound then patted his cheek. She rose to her feet, carefully holding the bowl of bloodied water in one hand, and her medical bag in the other. She gave Clover an expectant look.

'Would you mind if we just moved over there to talk? It's a bit quieter.' Clover started to head off, hoping the nun would follow. People had avoided taking root close to the draughty doorway so she halted there. She had no prepared speech ready and must present Gabriel's tale off the cuff while protecting her family's secret.

'Are you hurt, dear?' asked Sister Louise, having noticed the young woman's nervousness. 'If you'd rather undress somewhere private and show me ...'

'I'm not hurt ... thank you.' Clover was determined to see this through. Her grandmother was watching over her and had brought about this opportunity. Clover could almost hear ... almost feel ... Elsie prodding her. *Come on,* she'd be saying. *Don't waste it ... no time like the present ...*

'You might think it's wrong to bring this up now, but it is very important to me. You see, I've been hoping to bump into you for quite a while.' Clover paused to make a final decision. Close up she could see Sister Louise had grey eyes and fair brows, an indication that blonde hair was tucked beneath her wimple. She looked slightly older than Clover had first thought; perhaps twenty-three or four. But her kindly expression persuaded Clover to trust her and to believe she'd be sympathetic. 'I wanted to ask you about the baby,' she rattled off.

'The baby?' Sister Louise glanced about, believing one of the children at the mission was being referred to.

If she wasn't quick the chance would be lost. Jeannie or one of Sister Louise's colleagues might come over and interrupt them. 'The baby on the doorstep,' Clover burst out. 'I only want to speak to you about him.' She noticed the increased spark of interest in Sister Louise's eyes. 'I put him there and watched you carry him inside.'

'Ah ... so you're the wee one's mother, are you?' Sister Louise's features relaxed; she almost smiled. 'We wondered who she was; didn't expect her to be as young as you.'

The sister had remembered him straight away and Clover took this as a good sign. 'Is he well? I want him, you see. I can take him home now.' Her optimism faded. She'd read dismay in the sister's face. 'What is it?' A dread of knowing the answer was twisting her insides but she met the fear head on. 'Didn't he survive?'

'He did,' Sister Louise softly said, laying a comforting hand on Clover's arm.

Clover exhaled in relief. 'Me and my fiancé are in agreement; we want to bring Gabriel back home with us.'

'Is that what you called the little love?'

'He looked like an angel,' said Clover, emotion bobbing her chest. In her mind's eye she could clearly see his tiny face.

'He is indeed a beautiful child and our Lord bestowed on him a fighting spirit. Being very premature we didn't expect him to live. I'm glad he did and pray he continues to thrive.'

'Our family are fighters; and I'll keep on fighting until I've got him back. My fiancé is a soldier but we're getting married soon. I can cope with a child now. Please let me have him.'

Sister Louise flicked a vigilant glance over Clover's shoulder as though she would also keep this conversation private. 'If it were within my power I would give him back to you.' She sighed. 'It's too late, though. After a while when he was suckling well and putting on weight your little Gabriel left the convent. He's been taken elsewhere.'

'Left? Taken where?' Clover's tone combined anger and disbelief.

'War babies are sent to orphanages or foster carers. From those places, some of the lucky ones are adopted. He is such a sweet child that I expect he will attract a nice home.'

'He's not a war baby ... he wasn't abandoned ... I just left him with you for safety until I could come and get him. Where is he? I'll collect him myself,' Clover said forcefully.

'Please, don't upset yourself, my dear,' said Sister Louise. 'The Municipal Welfare Department deals with the children's placement, we at the convent are just first port of call for desperate girls such as yourself.' She rested a hand on the crown of Clover's dishevelled auburn hair. 'I do know homes in the countryside are favoured by city authorities, to help the children bloom. Your little boy might be settled in a place with fresh air and peace and quiet.' She paused. 'Silvertown ... even before this tragedy ...' She shook her head. 'Life here is difficult for the little ones, for everybody, and made worse by the war dragging on and by the factories chugging away night and day.'

There was nothing in that speech that Clover could disagree with. Smoke, stench and constant grind were the background to her life and always had been. Nevertheless she said stubbornly, 'He's my family, and I want him.'

'You're young and God willing, will in time have more children with your husband—' Sister Louise broke off to suddenly say, 'Mother Superior is coming over; she is probably wondering why I appear to be chatting when there is so much to do.'

'I'm sorry, I didn't mean to keep you so long.' Clover took a wary peek at the stout dark figure approaching. 'You won't tell her ... please ...'

'I won't betray you, I promise.' Sister Louise patted her arm. 'Here, give me that.' She put the bowl of washing water on a window ledge and took the cup and saucer from Clover. 'This kind young lady has brought me a cup of tea. She might spare one for you, Mother Superior, once the kettle's been re-boiled.' Sister Louise picked up the cup from its saucer and sipped the lukewarm drink. 'You volunteers do a fine job but you look exhausted, young lady, and perhaps need to go home to rest.' She handed back the crockery with a significant look in her calm grey gaze.

It hadn't occurred to Clover before that she was flagging, physically and mentally. The hectic dashing from place to place earlier had caught up with her. This meeting had brought mixed blessings and further drained her emotionally. Her baby brother was alive and healthy but she was bereft to learn he'd been spirited off to an unknown destination.

Sister Louise picked up her bowl of dirty washing water and the two nuns moved off. They stopped by an elderly fellow holding a piece of blood-stained cloth to his head. The women appeared to be discussing his treatment. Sister Louise glanced over her shoulder. *Think about what I've said, and gain comfort from it,* Clover read from that expressive look.

Now she'd acknowledged her fatigue she stopped ignoring something else as well; it was time to return home not only to rest but to see her family. It wasn't fair to leave her brother fretting. He would be waiting for her to report back to him. Once she did she would have his grief to cope with as well as her own. She'd told Sister Louise they were a tough lot. And she'd live up to that boast and see them all through this. Her little sisters were thankfully young enough to be spared the anguish of the mounting loss of family members. Their father's absence had helped the girls rather than hindered them. Clover knew they were all happier without him, even Johnny, his father's favourite, was more relaxed when unpredictable Sidney Cooper wasn't around. They'd got used to not seeing him after he joined up. Yet he was their father and the uncertainty of what had happened to him was a constant niggle at the back of her mind.

Here at the shelter it was easier to cope with her raging feelings; she was among people who were also grieving and many were in a horrible limbo of not knowing how many loved ones had been lost. She had the meagre comfort of knowing her grandmother's fate.

The devastation, still unfinished, outside these rickety walls would be so far reaching and absolute that Clover knew it would be days, maybe weeks, before the full extent of the calamity at Brunner Mond was established and its cause found.

Chapter Twenty-Six

'Would you help me share these out, please?'

Clover was washing up the used crockery when Nettie's father stopped to talk to her. He put an open box down on the floor and she glimpsed blankets stacked to the top inside.

'I didn't see you come into the hall, Mr Randall.' She gave him a surprised look while drying her hands.

'I've only just arrived. Those fellows were unloading mattresses outside and sent me in. I've bedding to donate.'

The fellows he'd referred to were off-duty policemen. They had volunteered to chivvy local businessman to gift equipment for the emergency shelters springing up on the outskirts of Silvertown. Most merchants were willing; they felt compelled to help even if they'd suffered losses themselves.

The horsehair mattresses, got from a furnishings warehouse on Royal Albert Dock, were being dropped wherever sufficient space on the floor was available to unroll them. Immediately, women began to mark their territory by planting a toddler or a bag of belongings on a precious place to sleep.

'Mrs Randall and I wanted to do our bit.' Bruce shook his

head and said hoarsely, 'I didn't expect this. What I've seen out there defies description.' He rummaged inside the box while composing himself.

Self-serving motives had spurred him into coming to the explosion site. He had been staggered and terrified by the scenes. The selflessness of the haggard-faced firemen, exhausted yet returning to the fray time and again to direct a hose or employ a shovel to shift timbers that were feeding a fire, was humbling to behold. As was the courage of those watching and waiting. A shout would go up and local men would plunge forward into the dark bowels of a collapsing building to save somebody trapped. His boxes of blankets were paltry offerings in comparison. The first lot had been wrapped around hysterical or unconscious victims found close to Brunner Mond. The box had been empty in seconds and he had rushed home to fetch more. These were the best ones his wife had wanted to keep. He'd told her he was taking them and unusually she had let him, without argument.

He handed nearly half of the box's contents to Clover to carry and the rest he wedged beneath his arm.

'I'll start that end then.' Clover started off to the left of the room. Her arms were aching with the weight of the wool but the supply had gone before all the begging hands had been filled. She met up with Mr Randall close to the centre of the hall.

He steered her to the edge of the room to talk to her. 'I'll come back tomorrow with more and some clothing as well.' He looked around at bedraggled mothers doing their best to spit and polish grubby faces before settling children beneath his blankets. He wished he'd ten times as many to give.

Clover scraped her fingers through her hair, attempting to neaten locks that felt gritty with soot. 'I was sorry to see your shop damaged, Mr Randall.'

He dismissed the loss with a hand movement. 'It's nothing compared to this. We're all safe.'

'Our end of Silvertown escaped the worst of it,' said Clover, thinking of her brother and sisters. 'I'm off home now, to see to the younger ones.'

Bruce had noticed her eyes brighten as she caught sight of the dark-haired soldier who had just entered the hall. The gaze that passed between the couple made it plain to any observer that they were sweethearts.

She wasn't battling alone to rear her siblings then; she had somebody to support her in the future. That pleased Bruce, and emboldened him to say, 'Did you ... that is, earlier you said you were hoping for news of your grandmother.' He noticed her eyes gathering tears and felt ashamed of himself for bringing this up so soon. But he was obsessed with discovering Elsie's fate, and private times to talk to Clover would be few and far between.

'She has been found ...' Clover couldn't say the word and simply shook her head.

Bruce put an arm around her. 'You're such a brave young woman and I'm sorry to have upset you,' he croaked in genuine remorse. 'I shouldn't have asked.' He let her go and exhaled slowly as relief settled on him. Elsie couldn't challenge his concocted version of events. The spinning of his rotten plot had begun and he would sooner get it finished before it unravelled.

'You've had more than your fair share of sorrow, haven't you?' he said. 'My daughter mentioned you've not seen your father for a while.' His voice quavered but she didn't appear

to notice his nervousness. 'I bumped into him earlier ...
close to the cemetery; he seemed angry and said he wanted
to speak to your grandmother. He thought he might find
her there.' Bruce was aware he had gained her undivided
attention and that her boyfriend was approaching through
the crowd. He rattled off quickly, 'Your father went on his
way saying he'd catch Elsie by the factory gate as nobody
was at her home.'

It was done. No going back. Bruce hung his head, disgusted with himself.

'You saw my dad *today*.' Clover finally found her voice
after that shock.

Bruce nodded but avoided her eyes. 'Unfortunately,
after we parted he was on his way to Brunner Mond ...'
He couldn't continue with the deceit. He dashed the wet
from his eyes: tears of shame and sorrow for her and her
orphaned siblings. He hoped that they could all lay the
ghost of Sidney Cooper to rest after this. 'I'm so sorry,
Clover. So sorry for everything that's happened.' Heartfelt
emotion vibrated in his voice. 'I'll say good night now ... I
can see you have company.' He hurried away and made his
exit through the back door of the hall.

'Who was that?' asked Neil, having arrived at her side a
moment after Bruce departed.

'My old boss from Randall's drapery; his daughter Nettie
is a friend of mine.' She paused, frowning in confusion. 'He
told me he saw my father earlier today. He said Dad was in
a bad mood, looking for Elsie at the cemetery. He knew her
routine of going there daily.'

Neil's smile disappeared as he comprehended this wasn't
being taken as good news. 'Aren't you pleased he's been
seen at last, love?'

'Nan wasn't at the cemetery. He told Mr Randall he'd wait outside the factory to speak to her instead.'

There was a long pause before Neil said quietly, 'He might have changed his mind, Clover.' He put an arm around her. 'He might be at home with the children. Let's go and see.'

Clover nodded. 'I'll speak to Jeannie – see if she wants to walk back with us.'

Jeannie had decided to stay and help the Methodist minister and his wife for a while longer, but she had encouraged Clover to leave and check on her younger siblings.
Outside, people had already begun evacuating the area, leaving behind the rubble of their homes and a pall of choking air shrouding the streets of Silvertown.

Clover and Neil joined the column, walking behind a woman pushing a wheelbarrow. The refugees seemed disinclined to talk to one another. Exhausted but with grim determination on their faces, the adults tramped silently, one behind the other. But the babies cried, and small children stumbled along behind their mothers, wailing to be picked up and comforted.

Clover spared the legs of one little girl, and Neil picked up her bigger brother. Their mother acknowledged them with a nod; it was all the thanks she could manage as she pushed the wheelbarrow loaded with detritus and a pretty pottery vase that had somehow escaped being smashed into smithereens.

Clover looked about at the traumatised but unbroken East Enders, carrying washing baskets and sacks stuffed with remnants of their lives; displaced, maybe, but they had grabbed as many reminders of better times as possible.

The enemy couldn't defeat these stoics and neither could a home-grown disaster.

'They'd had an argument,' Clover suddenly said to Neil. While walking she had been mulling over what Mr Randall had recounted about her father. She'd collected together the bits of information she could relate to the Sidney Cooper she knew. She shifted the toddler in her arms to look at him for his reaction. 'When I spoke to my nan earlier she said Dad had been round to cause trouble. If the argument didn't finish the way he wanted, he'd have it out with her again. That was his way ...' She bit her lip having realised she'd referred to him in the past tense.

Neil was holding the boy easily in one arm. He put the other about her shoulders, urging her closer. 'You're almost home,' was all he soothingly said.

'Thanks for helping; I'm off this way,' said the woman in front. She had halted to take back her children. The little girl was wedged on the edge of the wheelbarrow and the boy was put on his feet, to walk. 'Me aunt lives up here. She'll shelter us until morning. Then see what tomorrow brings.'

'Good luck,' shouted Clover as the woman trudged away into a side street, though on reflection, it was a bit late for that.

About to rejoin the queue, Clover glanced across the road and saw men scuffling outside the tobacconist shop. Mr Bailey seemed to have changed his mind about tolerating thieves. Youths were shoving him while taking it in turns to snake their hands between jagged edges of glass to snatch the expensive cigars at the back of the display.

'The rotten swine, doing that to an old man. I'll give them what for.' Clover stepped off the kerb about to rush to his assistance.

Neil fastened an arm around her waist and drew her back against him. 'No you won't. I'll go; I'll catch you up later.' He knew that looting would be rife as desperate folk tried to claw themselves something from those they saw as better off.

Clover continued being swept along by the flow of people. She had a home still and felt herself fortunate. She knew her father wouldn't be there. Deep in her heart she knew, alive or not, he wouldn't come back. He'd been a misfit, caged by a life he didn't want. His disagreements with Lucy Dare and his mother-in-law had given him the excuses he'd been looking for to go away.

In the space of a few hours Clover had got used to the differing sounds of people's misery and suffering. Apart from a kind word she'd nothing to offer to help. The first groan issuing from behind thus went virtually unnoticed by her.

The second was different though. The woman sounded in pain as well as in despair. She halted and turned around. The pregnant woman she had watched salvaging with her boys in Fort Street was leaning on the handle of her pram. Her sons stood one on either side of her, staring-eyed. Her knees began to buckle and it seemed she might overset her support. The youngest lad started to cry, and the elder boy cuddled him.

'Me waters have broken,' the woman gasped out to Clover, who'd rushed to help her. 'Please Gawd ... not now ...' she cried in frustration at the smoggy sky.

Wildly, Clover swung a glance about, hoping somebody else might give assistance. People doggedly traipsed past, keeping their heads down. They had children, they had miles to go to a relative who might or might not be welcoming; they had enough troubles of their own to contend with. 'Where's your husband?' Clover asked.

'Ypres ... maybe Passchendaele. He's never where he's bleedin' needed, that's all I know,' she bitterly said.

'Hush ... you'll be all right.' Clover knew the woman was starting to panic. And so was she, although she did her best to hide it. She glanced across the road but Neil had seen off the thieves and disappeared inside the building with Mr Bailey. A faint light came on in there and she guessed he would stay to pacify the elderly fellow and board the window.

Clover stepped in the path of a youngish man on his own. Over his shoulder, he carried a hessian potato sack, knobbly with belongings. 'You have to help me,' she said. He tried to avoid her but she again blocked his path. 'My home's not far. You only have to push the pram for a few minutes while I hold her up.'

Reluctantly, he did so and the two boys, wary of this grizzled stranger, nevertheless held the pram handle and trotted either side of him as he yanked them along.

When they got to the house he made himself scarce and slung a look over his shoulder on rejoining the procession.

Clover left the woman propped against the open doorway and scooted inside, shouting for Johnny. Her brother had been asleep on the settee with his sisters, but he stumbled to his feet. Bleary eyed, he stood with his hair on end, blinking at her by the light of the candle stump, left burning to light her home.

'Is Dad in there?' She burst out, jabbing a nod at the bedroom door. He continued gawping in a daze and she rushed to open it and find out for herself. The room was as she'd left it earlier; an icy draught still mournfully moving the curtain. But the bed was made; and it was empty. It was somewhere to lie and all she had to offer.

A speechless Johnny assisted her getting the woman and the children inside. Clover helped her onto the bed while Johnny did as he was told and corralled the boys towards the settee.

'Go and get Mrs Waverley for me, Johnny. Bang on the door till she wakes up and say it's an emergency.' She gave him the once-over, relieved to see he'd slept in his clothes and just needed to put on his shoes.

He gave her the once-over and she could tell he thought she'd gone mad. But she'd no time for explanations. 'Go on! Say a woman's in labour at our house. Hurry!'

He jammed his feet in his boots and scampered outside and the woman's two boys, not knowing what else to do but recognising a kindred confused spirit, jumped up off the settee and ran up the road with him.

'Where's me kids?' the woman cried.

'They're fine,' said Clover, glad to see the breathless boys soon back with Johnny. She took their hands, gave them reassuring smiles, then led them into the bedroom to see their mother.

'You be good for the lady,' she panted. 'Don't even know yer name,' she said to her Good Samaritan.

'Clover Cooper. What's yours?'

'Polly Jones.' She groaned, and pulled up her knees as a contraction rolled over her abdomen. 'Someone coming to help me, are they?' she said pleadingly.

'That'll be me,' announced Doris Waverley, who'd entered the Coopers' lodging and been pointed in the right direction by Johnny. 'Got any more of these?' She held up the single candle. 'Thought it must be you, Clover, but then I thought, no, can't be; that gel's not got a belly on her—'

Clover interrupted Mrs Waverley's ponderings. 'Might

313

have another couple of candles and can fetch the oil lamp.' She jerked her head at Johnny, standing at the door with the two boys. He disappeared to get the lights and the lads followed him like lost puppies.

'You certainly know how to pick yer moments, doncha, Mrs . . .'

'Jones.' Clover supplied the patient's name to the midwife.

Doris Waverley patted the grimacing woman's arm. 'Well on yer way, I'd say you are, Mrs Jones. Clean meself up, then I'll take a look at you.'

'Shall I boil some water?' Clover remembered being asked to do that when the twins were born.

'Be a good idea,' said Mrs Waverley, taking the lit oil lamp from Johnny and positioning it on the floor.

'Anything else?' Clover asked, feeling relieved and calmer now she'd got somebody capable taking charge.

'Yeah, ask that big 'andsome chap of yourn to fix this curtain over the window, stop the draught freezing me half to death. And if you've got some old newspapers and rags, that'd help 'n' all.'

'Got a hammer and a few nails?' Neil asked. He'd arrived to find a drama playing out, but then this was Clover Cooper and he'd expect nothing less. He winked at her to let her know she only had to ask and he'd do it.

'Johnny . . .' It was enough to send her brother on another errand, this time to find their father's few tools. She smiled at Neil, wry apology and a promise of an explanation at some time.

He shrugged, pulling a face.

Once the curtain was being fixed and Mrs Waverley was spreading newspaper around, Clover went to check on the children.

The twins had woken up; they were intrigued by the new faces and had made room for the Jones boys to sit down.

'Put the kettle on, Johnny,' Clover said.

'Ain't got enough cups for this lot,' he spluttered, finally having found his voice and his mood.

'It's not for tea, love,' she said. 'You'll have to wait for that.' She started to giggle hysterically.

Chapter Twenty-Seven

The dawn was dusty as rose petals. Clover hadn't been to bed but she no longer felt tired or able to cry, although everything was catching up with her now. The sting and prickle was dammed at the back of her eyes, waiting to be released. She knew once it started a torrent would be unleashed. But there were still things to do.

The children were all asleep. Even the new one. And so was her exhausted mother. Doris Waverley had gone home a couple of hours ago, refusing Clover's offer to settle up later for her services. At times like this, nothing was needed, her neighbour had gruffly said.

Neil had righted the wardrobe in the smaller bedroom and the children, Johnny, Rosie, Annie, and Ricky and Danny Jones, were all asleep, crammed top to toe in the two small beds.

'I had something to tell you yesterday, before all this started,' said Neil, and took a gulp of tea.

Clover stirred from where she had been resting back against the railings in front of the house. They'd come outside, though it was another icy January morning; it had seemed worth bearing the cold to have some time and space to themselves. And to see what a new day had done to Silvertown.

She finished her tea and returned the cup to its saucer. 'You're going back over there, that's what you wanted to tell me.'

He smiled wryly. 'How did you guess?'

She gazed over towards the deepest dustiest rose in the sky – the place where the fire still burned, branding the heavens. 'Because I've lost everybody and now you're going away and ...'

'Hey, no more of that.' He put their crockery down on the step and put his arms around her. 'You're not losing me. We've got a life to live ... memories to make ... babies to make.' He nuzzled her cheek. 'I know you've been through the mill. You're the bravest girl I know – a real fighter. You'll keep fighting ... for me ...won't you?'

'Got no choice in the matter really, have I?' She found him a smile. 'Moaning Minnie, aren't I? Just tired and feeling sorry for myself, that's all.' He rocked her in comfort and she closed her eyes, wishing they could just stay like this and sway into sleep.

'You know, I fell for you from the first moment I saw you sitting with Jeannie in the caff,' he said. 'Was gonna come in and introduce meself.' He rested his chin on a cushion of auburn tangles, smiling at the memory. 'Then I thought, nah, play it cool.' He chuckled in self-mockery. 'So I waited a bit and then found out you worked at the tobacconist. Wasn't just by chance I turned up to buy fags that day. I came because I knew you'd be there. I wanted to see you. Felt like a punch in the guts when I saw you with Fletcher. I was going to turn around, not bother you, then I saw him manhandling you.'

'Glad you waited and stuck by me.'

He tilted up her chin. 'I love you, Clover. I'd do anything for you. I know I can't take away all the hurt you're feeling or make up for the people you've lost. But I'll make you happy. We'll be all right ...' He nodded to the house to include her brother and sisters in his promise. 'All of us ... we'll be all right. I know we will.'

She lifted her weighty eyelids and felt warmed by the glow of love in his eyes. 'We will. We're still here, the lucky ones.'

'Your new granddad seems nice.'

'Yes, he is.' She knew they were putting off bringing up their long parting. But she was brave ... everybody told her so, so she asked calmly, 'When are you leaving?'

'End of next week.'

Her heart jerked painfully beneath her ribs but she said, 'I'll write to you.'

'You'd better. We can still find out about your little brother Gabriel before I go.'

There had been no time to tell him about her talk with Sister Louise. She did so now and waited for his reaction.

'We'll ask the council to check their records. Somebody will have a note of what happened to him.'

'I'm not sure what to do. I want to think carefully ...' In fact, she had been thinking about what Sister Louise had said about fresh air helping children thrive. And she had been thinking about her mum. What would she want for that precious son, believed lost? She'd passed away peacefully knowing Gabriel was still battling for life. Would Iris Cooper choose Silvertown smoke and siblings, or green fields and good health for Gabriel? Clover hadn't lied to Sister Louise; the nun had assumed her to be his mother without her confirming or denying it was so. But she wasn't Gabriel's mother, Iris was, and Clover must honour her wishes. She knew the answer to the question she'd set herself. She loved her little brother and wanted him in the family, but bringing him home would be selfish; and it would raise eyebrows and impertinent questions that would reflect on the other children. And if their father ever returned . . .

'It's a big decision.' Neil kissed her brow. 'You're right not to rush it.'

'We got any nappies?' Johnny was shivering on the door-step in his underclothes. 'Annie's wet and there's none in the drawer. Gave those clean ones to the new nipper . . .'

'I'd better be off now, anyhow,' Neil said. 'Be locked out of barracks; they'll think I've gone AWOL. I'll be back later though.'

'You'd better be.' She kissed him swiftly before letting him go, but continued watching him until the morning mist closed over him.

Inside, the children were all straggling out of the bed-room, rubbing their sleepy eyes.

'Who's hungry then?' said Clover brightly. All hands went up. She was thankful her Nan had brought in the gro-ceries. A last loving gift to them all. There was a loaf and margarine, and a pot of blackberry jam. She was thankful too that with everything going on, Johnny hadn't yet asked about Elsie. But he would . . .

'Let's get the kettle on and some toast made, Johnny,' she said. All the children looked grubby, the Jones boys in particular were still carrying the dirt of their ordeal. 'First though, hands and faces need a wash.'

After breakfast, Clover became aware that all was still

and quiet in the maternity room. A chill came over her and she swiftly went to the door and stepped inside.

Mother and baby were fast asleep; Polly had protectively curved about her child with the infant's mop of dark hair resting against her cheek.

'Sorry, didn't mean to disturb you,' said Clover as Polly opened an eye. 'Thought you might like some tea.' She daren't say what reason had really brought her in.

'Thanks,' croaked Polly and elbowed herself up in the bed, wincing in discomfort.

Her boys had heard their mother's voice and crept into the room. Polly beckoned them closer. 'Here's your new sister,' she said, matter of fact. 'And I expect you two to look after her.'

They nodded solemnly then sidled up to touch the baby's tiny hands.

'Her name's Lizzie, after yer granny, and Clover after this lady wots been so kind to us. Elizabeth Clover Jones.'

Again the boys nodded and they perched on the bed either side of their mother and their infant sister.

'Can't never repay you for helping us ...'

'Don't need to,' said Clover gruffly, rather choked up to know the baby was named after her.

'Won't be in the way fer long,' said Polly, sniffing back tears. 'Was only laid up a couple of days last time with Danny. I was on me way to Walthamstow, to me sister's place. She's like you ... good as gold. She'll put us up.'

'You're not in the way,' Clover said. 'The room was empty anyway.' She continued to gaze at the bed, seeing no happy scene but Gabriel shrouded next to her heartbroken mother. Then, the image had gone, and with it the melancholy that had filled this space for so long. There was purpose in her heart and in her step as she went out of there to make Polly her tea.

She could feel her mum and her nan here with her, as she rattled cups onto saucers and filled the teapot with steaming water. Their embraces were as warm and light as a butterfly's cocoon; their voices silent but reassuring her that it was all right to let them and Gabriel go.

Epilogue

January 1917

The ground underfoot was as unyielding as iron, making the stiff studded boots feel like weights. Clover hadn't worn a football kit since she and Jeannie had trained in the park. So much had happened since then that the particular afternoon seemed years, not months ago. The breeze on her bare knees had taken some getting used to, but now she was warm from exertion, the chilly air had become refreshing.

She'd no match experience, but had agreed to come on as a substitute, if needed. Her summons had arrived startlingly swiftly when a defender suffered a bad tackle and was retired to the bench. It had been a baptism of fire, but Clover was modestly pleased with her performance so far.

In the aftermath of the Silvertown explosion, public collections and charity events had been arranged to raise money for the bereaved families. A fixture had been set up between the Gudgeon's ladies' team, or Beckton Belles, as Jeannie had glamorously named them, and a side from a munitions factory in north London.

'That Islington mob need to back off a bit,' moaned the goalkeeper, who was feeling hard done by having let one in and put the Beckton Belles behind. 'They know it's for a good cause.'

'We don't need no favours off them. We can win this fair 'n' square,' announced Jeannie to mutters of approval. 'We're playing to win and so are they.' She took her football seriously and got annoyed when people underestimated the women's game. 'I'll take on that bruiser at the back,' she added belligerently. 'She's the one nobbled our girl.'

'Want you up front, scoring goals,' said Freddie. 'We're only one behind; there's time to turn it around.' He tapped his forehead beneath a fringe of floppy fawn hair. 'I want you all to keep up here what's at stake. Our governors have pledged a bonus of twenty pounds if we come away with the cup. The Sally Army will get that and the entrance money for their new homeless shelter.'

Presently, the two teams were in a huddle at their respective goal mouths. Oranges had been quartered and were being greedily sucked while the players listened to their coach's advice.

'The defence needs to tighten up,' said Freddie. 'Clara and Maria, don't leave yourselves open by marking the same man ... woman ...' he corrected himself, to some smirks. 'For a first proper run-out you've done all right,' he told Clover. 'Be a bit more forceful though.' Freddie punched a fist into a palm. 'Football's not a dainty game.'

Clover nodded and pulled her woollen cap down to cover some auburn curls that had frizzed prettily around her perspiring face. She thought she'd feel self-conscious in knickerbockers and jersey in front of an audience, but apart from a few youths' whistles, nobody was taking much notice of female knees being on display. For the first ten minutes she'd been like a headless chicken then, heeding the more experienced players and Freddie's bawled instructions, her passes had become more accurate.

'Clo!' She turned to see her brother Johnny giving her the thumbs up as the teams took up position for the second half. The spectators were ranged either side of the pitch, two or three deep. Despite the bitter January weather, locals had turned out in force to support this fundraiser and had paid their tuppences at the park gate.

Bill Lewis was here to cheer them on. He had Rosie in one arm and Annie in the other to prevent them running onto the pitch to be with their big sister. Clover gave him a wave but with no free hand to wave back, he jerked his head at the opponents' goal, encouraging her to put one in the back of the net.

Somebody else in the crowd had noticed Bill Lewis. She worked her way along the back edge of spectators until she was close enough to touch him. She didn't dare though; she waited, unseen, gathering the courage to talk to him. 'Hello, Bill. Got your hands full, I see.'

Annie was struggling to get down and he put her onto her feet, and retied her bonnet to ward off the chill, before turning around. 'How are you, Lucy?'

He hadn't ignored her so that was a good start, she thought. His heart was broken yet still he was polite. He was a lovely man . . . one of the best. She cleared her throat. 'I was so sorry to hear about Elsie . . .'

'I know . . . thanks,' he said and twisted a smile.

'Bet you miss her dreadfully.' Lucy pressed her lips together and shook her head in apology. 'When I said that day about Elsie dying, I wish I could take it back. It was only a joke, but I'm a stupid fool with a big mouth and I want you to know I could cut me tongue out—'

'It's forgotten,' he interrupted her. 'I know you were joking.'

'Sorry, talking too much and don't want you to think me impertinent coming over like this when you probably wish I'd leave you alone.'

'It's all right; you're not being impertinent.'

Lucy gave a hesitant smile and settled in beside him to watch the rest of the match. After a few minutes, she raised her hand to acknowledge somebody in the crowd and received a quizzical look from Bill.

'Me sister Beatrice is over there watching the game. Her husband's the one coaching our team,' explained Lucy. 'She's cold-shouldered me for years, but since Uncle Wal told her I'm respectable she's been giving me the time of day again.'

Bill gave her a rueful smile then turned his attention to the pitch.

The whistle blew and within the first minute of the second half a groan went up from the spectators; the Beckton Belles had given away a corner that looked dangerously likely to end in another goal being scored against them. Having watched the exciting bit that turned out to be a false alarm, Bill turned his attention back to Lucy. 'Are you still working at Wally's place? I heard it got a bit smashed up.'

'Oh, all the broken windows were fixed straight away and we opened up again in no time. Those fryers didn't get no rest and nor did I.' She rolled her eyes. 'The old tight-fist wouldn't let a German spy rob him of his profit.' Her smile withered. 'Sorry ... done it again, ain't I, bringing that reminder up.'

'I don't reckon it was an inside job, anyhow,' he said to

reassure her. 'The German scientist fellow who worked at Brunner Mond died trying to put out the fire.' He paused to allow the simmering rage inside to subside. 'That place was a powder keg, an accident waiting to happen.'

'Probably never know the whole truth of it.' Lucy could see muscles in his jaw jumping and changed the subject. 'Sweet gels, ain't they? Can see they've taken to you, Bill.'

He smiled ruefully. 'Kids are hard work when you ain't used to it. I take me hat off to you women doing this job.' It was his turn to feel awkward. Lucy was childless and she wore a poignant expression that spoke of her regrets about that.

'I can amuse them – if you want me to, that is – so you can watch the football.' Lucy sounded diffident. Given what had gone on in the past, offering to care for the Cooper kids might be seen as a sauce. But then nobody would be surprised about Lucy Dare acting in that way.

Annie decided for herself. She stopped tugging on her new grandfather's hand and grabbed his friend's fingers instead.

Lucy crouched down to talk to the little girl. 'You want to chase, do you? Come on then, I can run faster, though,' she teased and set off at a trot with Annie toddling after her. Soon Rosie was keen to join in the game and was struggling to get down. The children ran up to their brother, standing with his friend, and Lucy chased them in a circle around the boys before they were off to open green space behind the throng, the twins squealing in delight.

'D'you get on with Mr Lewis?' Charlie Pincher was watching Bill joining in playing with Johnny's little sisters.

'Yeah, he's a diamond. He looks after those two a few times a week so Clover can do her shifts at Gudgeon's.'

'You could pack in your errand boy caper and watch 'em instead,' ribbed Charlie.

'No fear,' snorted Johnny, who'd unofficially left school. He liked his job working for the grocer, and he liked his free bike and pay packet even more. Apart from that he was glad a new family member sat in the Coopers' parlour from time to time because Johnny found seeing the empty chairs hard to bear.

Clover had moved into the big bedroom when Polly Jones left for Walthamstow a few days after having her baby. Johnny had felt able to sob his heart out at night about the loss of his mum and dad and his grandmother, without disturbing anybody. But he'd calmed down now even though he knew his sister wouldn't be using the big bedroom if she thought there was a chance their father might come home.

Johnny felt luckier than Charlie; he'd lost his elder brother and now only had his mother left. And she wasn't very nice. Bobby Pincher had been killed when a wall collapsed on him in Fort Street; his mum had been safely on her way home when he set off to search for her.

Johnny had rescued his leather football from beneath the mess left in the street by the explosion. He always thought of his dad when he played with it; he hoped Sidney would be pleased about that. 'Reckon our lot has lost.' He bounced the football while throwing a disgusted look at the pitch. The action was slow and the Beckton Belles were unfortunately doing most of the defending. 'Let's have a kick about with Mr Lewis and the twins. Might make a footballer out of one of them instead,' he said, making his pal guffaw as they loped towards the toddlers.

With five minutes left to play the score was one all, their centre forward having sneaked one past the opposition's keeper while she was flaked out on the ground. She'd missed a save and the ball rebounded off the post and was tapped in easily by Clara.

'D'you reckon our governors will pay out on a draw?' panted Jeannie. She was red faced from having run herself ragged in these last minutes of the game.

'No, I don't,' said Clover, lungs heaving out clouds of steamy breath into the cold air. She was as determined as Jeannie not to be beaten and to have the money for the Silvertown charities.

'Last push then,' shouted Jeannie to her team members. 'Twenty quid bonus in it. And we're doing this for Clover's nan and all the others who didn't make it.'

Clover found her second wind; she intercepted a stray ball and ran like mad with it, watching Jeannie from the corner of her eye. She passed with her left foot, making Jeannie swing around to find the ball behind her. But it helped in a way, throwing her off balance, as her opponent went the wrong way too.

Jeannie shot at goal wildly but it hit the target and an almighty roar of victory went up from the Silvertown crowd that echoed about the park and drowned out the sound of the final whistle.

Nettie had been watching the game with her father; she hared onto the pitch to give congratulatory hugs to her friends. 'Never thought you'd actually do it,' she gasped.

'Thanks fer the vote of confidence,' said a grinning Jeannie. 'Is he with you?' She jabbed a nod at Archie Fletcher, smartly dressed in khaki, standing on the edge of the spectators.

Nettie glanced over her shoulder then tossed her head. 'He's not said a word to me. Didn't want him to, anyway,

329

with me dad around.' She peeked at him again. 'Perhaps he'll come over now I'm with you.' There was a yearning in her voice that wasn't lost on her friends. But Archie was already on his way towards the exit.

'You should get your dad to punch his lights out,' said Jeannie. 'If he won't, I will.'

'What are you going to do about the baby, Nettie?' Clover quickly defused things, asking her question in a voice only the three of them could hear.

'Dad's shipping out in a few days. Mum's in a tizz over getting the shop straight without him. I've got to give up college and help in the drapery. When it's time, I'll clear off to a women's shelter then have it adopted.' She swiftly shifted the focus from herself. Her intention to go it alone had shocked them. But she didn't want their advice now she'd settled the matter in her own mind. 'How about you, Jeannie?' They'd all seen Freddie Ryan walking off the pitch arm in arm with his wife.

Jeannie didn't turn around to look at the couple. 'He's off limits,' she said, affecting to sound blasé. 'We're still friends of sorts. It was me own fault; I should've known what I was getting into chasing after a married man. Anyway, he's joined up. After what's happened, he said he might as well go over there as stay here and get blown to bits in the street.' Jeannie too was keen to duck the spotlight and change the subject. Not least because they all knew being blown to bits in the street was the likely fate of Clover's dad. Jeannie wished she'd kept her mouth shut. 'Will you and Neil get hitched when he gets leave, Clo?'

'I'm not making any plans yet. Just hope when he comes back it'll be for good.' Clover put her arms around her friends and hugged them. They were all feeling battered and bruised. One way or another they'd all lost people they loved. 'This bloody war's gone on for so long I wonder if it'll ever end . . .'

Somebody else had similar thoughts . . . though he had mixed feelings about the war dragging on. While it did, he had a place to hide, though he'd no intention of returning there to fight. But a Tommy learned useful lessons in survival on a battlefield. Clawing your way out of a blanket of exploded clay that filled a shell hole was nothing new to Sidney Cooper. Being clobbered unconscious with a shovel first, was though. He thanked his lucky stars that army training had made him instinctively turn his head to find an air pocket as earth hit him, bringing him to. The reminder of almost being buried alive made the scab on his head throb and he touched it gingerly.

The park was beginning to empty of people; some of them he watched with narrow-eyed intensity while skulking beneath the bare branches of the lime trees around the perimeter of the grounds.

Lucy Dare, Bill Lewis, Bruce Randall, especially him . . . they all put a scowl on his face as he watched them. In his opinion, those people had no right to happiness, or to his family, no matter that he wasn't keen on having the kids himself.

Bill and Lucy had hold of the twins' hands between them and seemed very cosy together as they walked towards the gates. But it was the fair-haired fellow who looked for all the world as though butter wouldn't melt in his mouth that drew Sidney Cooper's attention for the longest time, even longer than the sight of his children.

The twins he'd never really known, and Clover had always been a mummy's girl. Johnny had been his favourite, but even his son seemed happy without him, laughing and joking and bouncing that expensive ball he'd bought the kid. He'd like to have that cash back in his pocket. Well, he could do without any of them; in fact he was better off without them.

His vicious gaze returned to the man walking on his own. Bruce Randall had been a thorn in his side for decades; he'd stolen his wife and it was his fault Iris got sick and died. Then he'd tried to kill him. But no luck, there, he smirked.

Revenge was a dish best served cold, so they said; Sidney Cooper felt as though he'd emerged from hell's fires just minutes ago. He could wait. He'd go back to France to his platoon then abscond to Sophie. After what he'd been through, being a deserter held no fears. He'd keep his head down and come back here when the time was right; for judgement day.

He noticed his daughter was looking around, laughing with her friends, and then Clover's eyes travelled back and became steady and she frowned. Sidney pulled down his hat, pulled up his collar, and having lost a lot of weight, managed to easily slip between the buckled railings and exit the park straight onto the highway. In seconds, his hunched figure was lost to sight.

'What is it, Clo?'

Jeannie and Clover were on their own now; Nettie had caught her father up to walk home with him.

'Nothing ... just thought ... oh, it doesn't matter. It's getting dark ... come on, time to go home.' She linked arms with Jeannie and they strolled to say goodbye to their team-mates as the January afternoon light faded and the breeze sharpened and whipped their faces.

Stop wishing and hoping. Concentrate on the living, not the dead, her nan and her mum would tell her.

Be thankful for what you've got, she told herself. Still she glanced over a shoulder. But the fellow she'd seen squeezing through the park railings had gone. The park, but for a few stragglers, was deserted.

June 1917

With a gasp of dismay Sister Louise swooped on the bundle that had been left on the step and rose with the foundling secured in her arms.

Since the explosion months ago that had rendered the Silvertown poor even poorer, they had found several children abandoned outside. A girl of about two had been tied to the door knocker by the wrist with a piece of string to prevent her following her mother. Yet the woman had loved the child; a heartrending note had been pinned to the crying tot's coat, begging the sisters to care for her as her mother couldn't.

The infant in her arms was heavily swaddled despite the heat. From its light weight she guessed the baby was premature. But not as premature as the one that she would never forget. Gabriel was imprinted on her heart and her mind because she had nurtured him and she had met his mother.

Though the evening was drawing in, the daytime warmth lingered and it felt humid. Sister Louise closed the door quickly, and in the dim coolness of the flagged hall, began to uncover the little mite. Her hand stilled on the pristine blanket that looked as though it had come straight from a drapery. She gazed at a child that though larger could have been the twin of tiny Gabriel, found all those months ago. This boy was pink in the face from being in his cosy nest, not deathly pale as Gabriel had been. But the small neat features were very similar. They couldn't be brothers; Sister Louise had seen Gabriel's mother a few months ago, at a charity football match, and she'd looked athletic and slender as a reed. They'd not spoken, but their eyes had held for a moment and perhaps a fleeting smile had passed between them. Sister Louise had felt content that Gabriel's mother held no resentment over that talk they'd had.

'What is it? Oh, for mercy's sake! Not another one,' said Mother Superior, hurrying up and taking the bundle from her colleague. She stared at the child. 'Heavens above. I've seen that face before. Do you see the likeness?' She received a nod and carried on. 'The same family I'd say. Perhaps the children are cousins.'

'Where will this one end up?'

'Who knows?' sighed the Mother Superior, putting the baby to her shoulder and massaging his back as he mewled.

'It would be nice to keep them together,' said Sister Louise. 'In case they are kin of some sort.' She very much liked the idea of the boys growing up as company for one another.

'It would indeed,' Mother Superior said and smoothed the fair hair of the peaceful infant. 'When he's collected by the Welfare people I'll ask if it might be arranged.' She sighed. 'I don't hold out much hope. These pen-pushers are more concerned with their quotas and statistics than with the babies themselves.' She handed the child back. 'Settle him in a cot and I'll arrange for a wet nurse.'

Sister Louise looked at the baby with a smile. She felt none of the dread she'd had when holding Gabriel and willing him to live. This boy was hale and hearty in comparison, yet not quite so beautiful. 'I hope you and Gabriel find one another, whether kin or not,' she told him. 'I hope you'll be loved and live in a happy home as brothers. I won't forget either of you ... or ever stop hoping that life's being kind to you both.' She added wistfully, for herself, 'How wonderful it would be if one day you should come back to Silvertown, for I might then find out ...'

Author Note

The Silvertown Explosion, 19 January 1917

Over seventy men, women and children were killed and hundreds injured as a result of the wartime explosion at the Brunner Mond plant in Silvertown. Considering that high explosive was being manufactured and stored at the factory, it is a miracle that the outcome was not far worse. It was, and remains, the city's worst explosion. In addition to the loss of life and the injuries sustained, whole streets of houses were destroyed, and hundreds of people made homeless. Windows throughout London were shattered and the blast was heard up to a hundred miles away.

The cause of the fire that sparked the explosion has been the subject of speculation. Enemy sabotage was one theory, but the German scientist who worked in the 'danger building' was also hailed as a hero. He died during his attempts to combat the fire.

The constant demand for increased production of TNT in a highly built-up area housing other factories manufacturing combustible products, such as paint and varnish, combined to create an accident waiting to happen.

Brunner Mond was destroyed and never reopened, but other munitions factories, staffed in the main by female workers, continued producing bombs and munitions in the East End, and throughout the land, until the end of the war.

The Rise of Women's Football
During the First World War

With the war dragging on, and men being drafted to fight in 1916, the professional football clubs were under pressure to close up, to encourage the players to enlist. More and more women began working in factories to fill the vacancies. Female munition workers started forming football teams, mainly based in the north of England. But the trend for ladies' football gained popularity nationwide.

My fictional East End team, the Beckton Belles, is loosely inspired by the AEC munitionettes. Fixtures were arranged between teams to generate money for wartime charities, and initially these were treated as novelties with squads playing in fancy dress or with their legs tied together to make them seem of little threat to the men's game.

The most successful ladies' football team of the time was Dick, Kerr Ladies of Preston. They raised over a million pounds for various charities during their playing years, and their attendances ran to tens of thousands of spectators.

After the war, with the men home, the Football Association decided the popularity of the women's game was to be discouraged. In December 1921, women's football was banned from professional grounds. The teams carried on playing on parklands, but constant pressure from the FA resulted in many of the teams giving up.

In 1971, the ban was lifted and women's football began to rise again. In recent times, spectacularly.

Exclusive Sneak Peek

Keep reading for an exclusive early peek from the next book in the series . . .

Prologue

1923, Mayfair, London

She'd never loved him as her husband had. In her opinion the boy was rather too clever for a seven year old orphan gifted advantages in life. By birth he would have had nothing but his angelic looks to recommend him. As a baby he had charmed her with his pale hair and brown eyes that had shaded into green. His colouring mirrored hers ... a good omen she'd thought when bringing him home. But from his developing character she knew they would never have anything else in common. Praise from kith and kin for her handsome son were scant compensation for the challenge he'd present as he grew. She was unwilling to rear the mischievous brat. Others would judge her though so she kept this to herself. Everybody understood a mother on her own faced problems. Educating one child was costly, two were beyond her means if she were to keep this house. She'd made her choices and one of the adopted East End waifs had to go. She knew which one.

'Is it wise to tell the boy the truth, Mrs Harding?'

'Wiser than it is to lie to him I think, Sergeant Drover,'

she responded tartly. Having poured the tea she handed a cup to the policeman. 'Jake is sharp and has been taught to be honest. I would be a hypocrite if I didn't practice what I preach.' She glanced dispassionately at the child standing silently by the door. 'I hope his new guardians will continue to discipline him so our efforts with him are not wasted.'

The sergeant turned ruddy at the set down. His top lip took on a faint curl. Madam High and Mighty pointed out the boy's talents but didn't want him. Such was the way of people determined to be posh. They believed themselves superior but could be incapable of showing kindness. Not that Sergeant Drover didn't pity her for being widowed in such a wicked way.

'Has there been any progress on finding the villain who robbed and murdered my husband?' She had read the turn of his thoughts.

The sergeant took a gulp of his tea then put down his cup and saucer. He swivelled his eyes to the child. He hadn't reacted but still Drover didn't think it was right to talk about this in front of him. He appeared a stoic little chap – no wobbly lips in evidence – even so it seemed unfeeling to imagine he wasn't moved by recent events. He'd lost his father and soon would lose his mother to cruelty rather than crime. 'I'm afraid our enquiries haven't turned up any new leads, Mrs Harding. But of course we haven't concluded our investigations.'

'Oh, investigations!' She gestured dismissively. 'Admit it; there's little prospect of recovering what was stolen.' The loss of ten pounds and a gold timepiece wasn't the crux of Violet Harding's problems, though she could do with the cash and with pawning the watch to raise funds. Without her husband's regular salary from his position in Whitehall, she found herself reduced to living on his pension. At the reading of Rupert's will she'd discovered that was not the crux of it either.

The ignominy of being told by a stranger that her husband's mistress had given him a child of his own had topped everything; unbelievably, worse was in store. Rupert had left instructions that his assets must be divided. The only respect he'd shown his legal wife was allowing her the marital home and banning his paramour from the will reading. Weeks on, Violet's guts continued to squirm at the idea that she might have found herself sitting a yard away from Molly Deane while the smirking solicitor acted as their referee.

On the cab ride home from the galling episode Violet had understood something else, equally hurtful: she was barren. She'd believed her husband to be at fault when she'd not conceived in eighteen years of marriage. Both her sisters had children but no, he had a natural daughter, named Emily. By her calculations the child had already been born when they adopted their babies from the orphanage.

Had Rupert not been set upon when leaving his club on a stormy evening a month ago she'd still be ignorant of any of this. In a way, she was glad about that. She might have stabbed him herself, had she known.

Violet had little recourse to revenge now he'd gone, though she dearly wanted to hurt him back. But Rupert had had a favourite son even if the boy wasn't his flesh and blood. Cutting ties with Jake would be little hardship for her but her dead husband would be grinding his teeth to dust in his grave. The child she had come to adore would miss his brother, but Toby would be occupied with a good education and forget Jake in time.

'You should go to Lambeth and ask the lady who lives there about my father. She might know what happened to him.'

Violet swung around to stare at Jake who'd unexpectedly reminded her of his presence with his shocking outburst. 'Be quiet and speak when you're spoken to,' she hissed. After the sergeant had gone she'd interrogate him about how he knew where Molly Deane lived. She felt enraged that Rupert might have taken Jake with him when visiting his paramour.

'What lady might that be, Master Jake?' Basil Drover bent his knees, lowering himself to gaze into a small face that was earnest and undeniably handsome.

'I saw them walking together in Andover Street,' explained Jake. 'There was a girl with them as well ... smaller than I. She had brown hair like the lady.' He was sure he was being helpful but though the policeman seemed interested, his mother was angry.

'Stop that nonsense,' she snapped. 'Go to your room, Jake.'

'Let the lad have his say.' The sergeant sounded blithe but there was a curious gleam in his eyes.

'I told you he is a clever boy,' said Violet. 'It doesn't do to encourage him, Sergeant. He likes being the centre of attention.'

'I'll hear him out. He might have a point ... about the lady ...'

'I doubt he saw anything. He has a vivid imagination,' Violet fumed. 'He entertains his brother with his made up tales. Don't you?'

Jake nodded.

'A Charles Dickens reader, eh?' chortled Drover.

'Certainly not,' she snorted. 'The boys are instructed in the classics.'

She jabbed her head and Jake obediently left the room although he knew the policeman wanted him to stay. Outside he hesitated to listen to what happened next but he saw Dora Knox hovering some yards away. Being the clever child he was, Jake realised the maid had brought in the tea tray then loitered to find out what the policeman wanted. His mother had sent her outside, saying she'd pour herself.

They stared at one another and the girl gave him a sympathetic smile before disappearing downstairs to the servants' quarters. She was the only one left now. The proper cook had left soon after the day of the funeral. Now Dora did everything and the meals were horrible because she was only sixteen and untrained. Jake could hear a muffled conversation through the door panels but gave up trying to make out what was being said. He guessed it was about him misbehaving. He heard a scuffling noise and saw his younger brother peeping from between the banisters. Jake bounded up the treads to sit beside him.

'You're not really going away are you?' asked a mournful Toby.

'I am, but you won't have to go,' Jake said and put a reassuring arm about his shoulders.

'Don't want to be here on my own without you.'

'You'll be alright; Mother likes you.'

'You'll come back though, won't you, when you've learned to be good?'

Jake nodded although he knew he wouldn't. His mother didn't want him anymore. He felt upset but also invigorated at the idea of a new beginning and another place to explore. He'd liked his father but he was gone, and now it was his turn to be released from a home he'd never fitted

347

into. Jake wondered if his late father had felt uncomfortable too and that's why he'd stayed out a lot and become friends with another lady. He'd miss his brother, although he truly believed Toby would be alright without him. Their mother was different with Toby. She called him her poppet whereas he himself was referred to as the boy or the orphan.

The brothers understood they were adopted children: their father had sat them down and told them that the Great War had made it impossible for their real mothers to keep them. He'd said that even though they looked alike, they weren't brothers but would be now and no longer orphans. They had a new home and would be loved and cared for. Their father had lived up to his promise but their mother had stopped halfway.

'Come on, let's go and play in the bedroom with the train set.' Jake grabbed his brother's elbow and urged him to run up the stairs.

'Where is the school you're going to?' Toby looked up from removing items from the Hornby box.

Jake shrugged and leaned forward on his knees to put a locomotive down on a length of track. 'Somewhere in London I think. Sergeant Drover's coming back later in the week to take me there. Mother doesn't want to go with me.'

'London ... so it's not far then,' Toby sounded relieved. 'You'll come back at the weekends I expect.'

'Perhaps ...' Jake doubted he'd be allowed back and knew he'd miss Toby. 'I heard them say it's Dr Barnardo's home so I suppose he's the headmaster.'

'Doctors are nice,' said Toby, remembering when he'd had chicken pox and a kindly old gentleman had given him medicine to soothe his skin. 'I bet you'll have lots of friends,' he said wistfully. 'You won't forget me, will you?'

'Never ...' Jake solemnly promised and sat back on his heels to gaze at his younger brother.

In the parlour Sergeant Drover sucked his teeth in sympathy while being regaled with the shocking costs of funerals these days and school fees shooting ever upwards. Inwardly he was wondering why Mrs Harding didn't move to a less fashionable address to keep the family together. She couldn't really prefer her big house to her little son, could she? He allowed her the benefit of the doubt; the woman would still be in shock over her husband's murder and in a panic over the prospect of coping without him. She might right the wrong she'd done young Master Jake by fetching him home in the New Year when she was more herself. Whatever excuses he found for her it seemed a mean thing to do to any child just a month before Christmas. He was a bright kid, no doubt about it. Thanks to him there was another lead to follow in this murder case.

The upstanding husband had been walking with a dark haired woman in Lambeth's Andover Street. No prizes for guessing the nature of that relationship. Parts of Lambeth were renowned as popular with rich gentlemen who wanted to house a mistress. Not flash enough to draw attention, but not too shabby either. An ambitious young woman, living on her looks, would find the area most acceptable.

'Does your late husband have kith or kin Lambeth way?'

'I told you the boy was fantasising, Sergeant Drover.'

'So ... nobody for Mr Harding to have visited over there that you are aware of? Female cousins or nieces of any sort?'

Violet resisted calling him insolent. Later in the week he was to do her a great favour; she wouldn't antagonise him. 'I know my husband's family, Sergeant. We were together almost twenty years and married for eighteen of them.'

'Yes ... of course.' He put away his notebook and pencil. 'Well, I'll be off for now then.'

'You won't forget to come back, will you?' She picked up a letter from the Barnardo's home in Stepney. 'They have confirmed arrangements and expect Jake at ten o'clock on Friday.' She should thank him for having offered earlier to escort the boy for her when she said she was loath to ask the solicitor to do it for an exorbitant fee.

'I will, unless you change your mind and wish to accompany him yourself.' He hesitated in taking the letter.

'It would be too upsetting for me to go there.' And indeed it would be, she thought. Offloading a child at an orphanage was what the lower orders did. 'Thank you for assisting in this, Sergeant.' Drover was treated to the first smile of his visit. 'I appreciate your help. I won't change my mind, you see.'

After he'd gone she went upstairs and called Jake from the bedroom where he and Toby were mimicking the sounds of steam trains. He closed the door obediently behind him and she gave him a stern look. He held her gaze steadily without flinching. She found him far too sure of himself and those green eyes of his were quite unsettling at times. 'This woman you spoke of,' she said. 'When did you see her with your father, Jake?'

'Last Christmas. Carol singers were in the street ...'

'Last Christmas?' she interrupted, in surprise. She had imagined it had been a recent sighting, not almost a year ago. 'Were you with your father?'

'No ... with Mr Nash. He was taking me to a Christmas concert in Lambeth. Toby didn't come. He was in bed with a cold.'

So not only did Jake know about this woman and Rupert;

the boys' tutor did as well. Nash would be dispensed with soon in any case. Arranging a boarding school for Toby was next on her list of things to do. She'd miss his company but if he were to fly high, a good education was essential.

'I think you are mistaken; it was a long time ago and you might have forgotten exactly what you saw. No more of it, to me or to Sergeant Drover. Do you understand?'

He nodded solemnly. As his mother turned away he said, 'I remember it, though. I don't forget anything.'

Well, the deceased Lothario had a wide ranging taste in women thought Basil Drover as he entered the house in Andover Street and followed Mrs Deane along the hallway. Harding's widow was a slender blonde, in her late thirties; his mistress had a buxom figure and dark hair and was easily ten years younger.

Once in the back parlour he glanced around but there was no sign of the child Master Jake had spoken about. He knew there was one; when making enquiries in the street to discover at which house he might find a dark haired woman with a young daughter, the neighbour had confirmed with a sniff that he was looking for Mrs Deane who lived at number two.

'So what can I do for you, Constable?' asked Molly Deane with admirable insouciance considering her fists were clenched behind her back. She feared she knew what he wanted, and after a night of carousing had left her with a thumping head, she could do without this trouble.

'Well, as I said, Madam, I'm investigating a crime and I believe you might have known the unfortunate victim.'

'A crime?'

'A murder.'

'Oh, Mr Harding, you mean.' She'd been mistaken in what had brought him here and had allowed a note of relief to creep into her voice. Rupert Harding's comings and goings had been regular and over time neighbours had cottoned on to their relationship. His murder and his photograph had been in the newspaper as he was a bigwig in the City. She imagined somebody had ratted on her and brought the coppers sniffing around.

'Did you think I'd another crime in mind?' Drover's ears had pricked up at the inflexion in her tone.

'No ... although I have to say the area is going downhill. Three times this week I've been tormented by little blighters playing knock down ginger. If it happens again, I'll summon you myself.'

'I see ... well, as to Mr Harding, you did know him then. Might I ask the nature of your relationship?'

'You might, though I imagine you are able to guess at it. We are both adults, Sergeant Drover, so no need for either of us to act coy.' She gave him a cheeky smile. He wasn't bad looking and probably only a few years older than she was. Having the name of the local rozzer in her little black book could be a smart move.

His sardonic smile let her know he'd regretfully decline. 'You have a daughter, I believe, Mrs Deane. Is she Harding's child?'

'Who told yer that?' Molly barked, forgetting to act refined.

'I can't disclose my sources. Is she his offspring?' Drover sensed he'd touched a nerve.

'Yes,' she said and turned away. 'Out of respect for all concerned I'd like that to remain between us.'

Basil nodded his agreement although it seemed bit late to

consider the feelings of the betrayed wife. He began to sympathise with Violet Harding and to understand why she was a sourpuss. Maybe she'd known about her husband's mistress and had been protecting her pride by keeping schtum about her rival.

'Where is your daughter?'

'Staying with a friend. Now if that is all ...'

'Had you seen Mr Harding on the night he was murdered?'

'I was expecting him to call but he didn't turn up. I assumed he'd gone straight home. He did that sometimes if he came out of his club the worse for wear.'

Drover knew from the coroner's report that the deceased had been intoxicated on the night in question. 'Will you be leaving here now your circumstances have changed?'

'What concern is that of yours?' she asked spikily.

'I might need to speak to you again and wouldn't want to find you gone.'

'I'll be here; Mr Harding wasn't my only gentleman friend. I don't think I need to say more than that. Now, if you'll excuse me ...'

He allowed her to lead him back along the hall and once outside set off into the early dusk of the November afternoon. He put away his notebook and buttoned the pocket flap over it. There was no point in stirring up a hornets' nest because the dead man couldn't keep his trousers buttoned. Sergeant Drover decided to close his line of enquiry with Mrs Deane. Pursuing it unnecessarily would only unearth sordid details to upset his family and spoil the children's memory of their father when they were older.

From behind a screen of curtain Molly Deane watched his back until he was out of sight around the corner. Before she dropped the net into place she spotted someone along the street, emerging from the shadows. He was holding the hand of a young girl and hurrying the child in the direction of the house. When she stumbled he picked her up and carried her.

'What was that all about?' George Payne had burst out with a question before the door was shut. He put the little girl down and the bag containing the bottles of brandy and port was carried into the kitchen and dumped on the table.

'Nothing I can't deal with,' Molly retorted. 'What did the doctor say about Emily?' She bent to soothe the child, who'd trudged up to her mother and started to grizzle.

'Tonsillitis, he reckons.' A medicine bottle appeared from a pocket. 'He said to dose her with this twice a day.'

Molly lifted Emily and kissed her pale cheek. 'Let's get you into bed then I'll bring you up some warm milk.'

She nodded her dark head.

George followed mother and daughter up the stairs. 'I've got a delivery turning up later; I don't need coppers sniffing around. I recognised him and he would've known me if he'd caught a look at me. Drover's his name and he's a bloodhound from the other side of the water. Must be my lucky day: clocking him first and getting under cover.'

Molly soon had her daughter tucked up in bed in her nightclothes. Then she turned to answer George. 'It was Sergeant Drover. He's investigating Rupert's murder. I suppose I should've guessed I'd get a visit about that.' Molly sat down on the edge of the bed and smoothed the child's hair until she put her thumb in her mouth and started to doze.

The couple tiptoed outside the room and shut the door then Molly lit two cigarettes and handed one to him. 'No need to fret, Georgie.' She patted his cheek. 'Your pals can come with the stuff this evening. Now I think about it, I reckon his wife's got a bee in her bonnet after the will reading. The cow sent Drover here.' She smirked. 'Can't blame her I suppose. The copper's not a fool though; he knows she's a jealous woman with her claws out. Drover won't be back.' She blew smoke from the corner of her mouth. 'So, it's business as usual.'

Acknowledgements

My grateful thanks to Juliet Burton for almost forty years of encouragement and support as my literary agent. Happy retirement!

Also, thanks to the Piatkus editorial team: Anna Boatman, Kate Byrne, Rebekah West and Christopher Sturtivant.